Carry Me Home

Raised in the Deep South, for the last twenty years Terri
Wiltshire has lived and worked in the UK, where she runs
a corporate role-play company. A former journalist and
NBC News presenter, she is also an actor and director.
She lives in Newport, South Wales.

Carry Me Home

Terri Wiltshire

PAN BOOKS

First published 2009 by Macmillan New Writing

This edition published 2010 by Pan Books
an imprint of Pan Macmillan, a division of Macmillan Publishers Limited
Pan Macmillan, 20 New Wharf Road, London N1 9RR
Basingstoke and Oxford
Associated companies throughout the world
www.panmacmillan.com

ISBN 978-0-230-74339-7

1 3 5 7 9 8 6 4 2

A CIP catalogue record for this book is available from
the British Library.

Typeset by Intype Libra Ltd, London
Printed in the UK by CPI Mackays, Chatham ME5 8TD

Visit **www.panmacmillan.com** to read more about all our books
and to buy them. You will also find features, author interviews and
news of any author events, and you can sign up for e-newsletters
so that you're always first to hear about our new releases.

To my friends and family in Alabama.
No matter where I live in this world you
will always be home.

Acknowledgements

I'd like to thank the amazing friends I have in Wales who have supported and encouraged me through this twelve-year journey, especially those of you who read every version of the manuscript with patience and enthusiasm.

Thanks also to the members of the Cardiff Writers' Circle who were so generous and kind in helping to shape and sharpen my writing skills; to the 'Barnies', the best girlfriends and cheerleaders a woman could have; to my family who loved me and let me know they were proud of me; to Mary Chamberlain who 'discovered' me and guided me gently through many minefields; to my editor, Will Atkins, who made the process far more enjoyable than I ever imagined.

And a special thank you to Derek Rowe who believed in me and said, 'Just give it one more go,' after I'd packed everything away and given up.

Luke: The Beginning

October 1904

Nobody ever stayed in Lander, Alabama. Not if they'd been there before. It was the last stop before crossing into Georgia and if a man was looking for work he could cover three states in one night before hopping an L&N all the way to Norfolk, Virginia. Most of those coming in on the eleven o'clock from Chattanooga just hunkered down in the shadow of the box-car and kept going. Those who did stop were usually new to the line. Or desperate. They would have heard there was a cotton mill in town and figured they could smooth-talk their way into a few weeks' work. But they'd soon learn. The foreman at the mill never hired casual help. Not when his own people worked overtime without pay and wouldn't dream of complaining. They lived in houses owned by the mill, built on a few acres of wasteland and rented out to the workers, cheap. Just thirty-five lucky families who'd rather work a few hours without pay than risk losing a roof over their heads. The houses in the mill village had been built with warped timber and the inner walls were made from reinforced card-board. Moss grew in the cracks of the floorboards because the roof leaked every time it rained. But it was better than picking fruit and sleeping in an open field.

Most of the hobos who traveled the Chattanooga line

knew about Lander, but there were always some who hadn't heard. A Yankee who'd left the slaughterhouses of Chicago in search of green open spaces. Or a new kid who'd just joined the rails, full of romantic notions and still living off the biscuits his momma had made a few days before. Then there were others who'd been riding the line so long they'd stopped looking for reasons to go anywhere in particular. They were just along for the ride and Lander was as good a place as any to snatch a bit of conversation and dip a tin cup into a pot of watered-down soup. So in spite of Lander's reputation, there were always a dozen or more vagrants loitering around the railroad yard late at night, pulling out their best traveling stories, waiting for morning and their chance at the cotton mill.

When the eleven o'clock rolled in the men who'd come in on the Memphis line had already claimed their spots for the night. It was mild for October and the air was filled with the sound of distant farm dogs, a few contented snores and the low conversations of the men gathered around a small fire and a pot of hobo stew. As the train slowed to a crawl, the doors of the boxcars were pushed open and men with dirty, vacant faces appeared from the shadows, each swinging himself to the ground with one arm. A few hurried to grab whatever corners were left for sleeping. Others joined the group around the fire. A kid, no more than fifteen, ambled towards them but stopped, calling over his shoulder.

'Hey . . . Cornell! Corny? You need help gettin' down?'

An elderly black man, crippled with rheumatism, shuffled into the light at the edge of a boxcar and smiled apologetically.

'Yes, sir, I reckon I do.'

The boy helped him down and held his arm a few paces until the old man regained his balance. Corny reached into his pocket and pulled out a small onion. He handed it to the kid and winked.

'Carried that all the way from Johnson City. Add it to the pot fer me.'

The young man tossed it into the air.

'Ain't you comin' over? There ain't likely to be much left by the time them greedy bastards get to it.'

The old man shook his head.

'Naw. I got a bellyache been givin' me trouble since I left Kentucky.'

He patted the bottle of whiskey in his top pocket and smiled.

'Been takin' my remedy, but it ain't doin' much good. I'm gonna get me some shut-eye.'

The kid gave his shoulder an affectionate pat.

'I'll save you a cup for later.'

The old man nodded as he headed towards the rusted hulk of a derailed boxcar. The kid joined the men around the fire and settled down for a few hours of tall tales and one-upmanship.

They heard the wagons first. More than one, traveling lickety-split down the old Mill Road. Then they heard the agitated whine of dogs; a couple of packs it sounded like, and the low rumble of men with a grudge. It was almost midnight and could mean only one thing. The hobos scattered across the yard, quietly rousing those who were sleeping before running into the woods and heading for the river. The kid followed blindly along, terrified by the fear he'd seen on the other men's faces; men who were hardened veterans. He was wading waist deep in river water before he remembered Corny.

In the woods nearby David-Wayne Calhoun scrambled frantically through the labyrinth of pine trees. The branches obscured the sky, but sporadic pinpoints of moonlight guided him. The carpeted layers of pine needles cushioned the woods of sound and amplified his breathing. He yelped as a stray pine cone wedged between the soft flesh of his toes. He limped for a few feet but the angry yelps of the dogs grew louder, urging him on.

Cornell was asleep and dreaming of lavender. Lavender water dabbed lightly behind her ears. He hadn't smelled it in almost forty years, but in his dreams it was as strong and as sweet as ever. He'd heard the shouting but paid no attention. Nothing but drunks gettin' too rowdy on moonshine. Cornell had learned to sleep anywhere – in any conditions. The only thing that could rouse him into action was some good-fer-nothin' son-of-a-bitch trying to steal his shoes. They might think he was old and feeble but they'd have a time getting his shoes off him. He'd fought too hard for them. They'd belonged to Clarkie Potts before him; fine leather, with double stitching across the toe. Better than anything else he'd seen on the line. When Clarkie Potts died of fever, he figured they rightly belonged to him, but they hadn't come easy, not without a good fight; and he knew he'd spend the rest of his life fighting to keep them.

A beefy hand grabbed his foot and he reacted quickly, but there were more hands, reaching and pulling. His ankles. His crotch. He grunted in surprise as he was dragged from beneath the boxcar but he raised his fists, ready to take on any man who dared steal what rightly belonged to him. Too confused to be frightened he stared into a circle of lanterns, trying to make out the shadowy images behind them.

'You tryin' to hide, nigger?'

The man with the beefy hands kicked the old man in the thigh. Corny lowered his fists, relieved. He wouldn't have to fight some young upstart for his shoes after all. He'd been run out of town enough times to know what this was about. They'd rough him up a little, drive him out past the county line, and warn him about ever coming back, but they wouldn't take his shoes. He smiled up at the man.

'Naw-sir . . . I thought you was—'

Someone stepped from the circle of shadows and slapped him, hard, with the back of his hand.

'Cain't hide from the law, boy.'

The leader raised his gun into the air and fired three times. Another shadow lunged forward, smashing the old man's face with the butt of his rifle and the leader squatted in the dirt, holding the lantern over Corny's head.

'You like little girls, nigger?'

The old man's eye was swelling to a close and thick black blood oozed down the side of his face. His expression had changed from confusion to fearful realization. He tried to squirm out of reach, under the boxcar, but they grabbed his legs and dragged him back.

'You been playin' with white girls, ain't you, boy?'

He struggled to stand . . . groping up the side of the boxcar.

'Naw-sir. I ain't never. I been sleepin'. That's all I was doin'.'

Someone slammed a rifle into the small of his back and he slid back down into a heap. He began to whimper, rocking back and forth, his head buried in his arms.

'I ain't never. I never did. I been sleepin'. That's all I been doin'.'

His shoulder was wrenched back and he felt the coarse rope yanked over his head. His bladder emptied and he began to cry.

In the woods nearby, David-Wayne kept running.

Canaan

August 2002

It was the mailbox she saw first, leaning to the left – an abandoned flag of discovery on a plot of land that no one wanted. The door was hanging by a hinge and rust had nibbled away most of the hand-painted letters on the side, but it was still there, feeble and defiant, marking the long dusty road that led to the Old Stewart Place. People still called it that even though her grandmother had been a Phillips for almost sixty years. To a stranger, it sounded like a grand plantation instead of a timber farmhouse with a couple of sheds tacked onto the back, pretending to be bedrooms.

Canaan Phillips twisted her wedding band around her finger with her thumb. The mailbox had never held any significance before but suddenly there it was – and just the sight of it made her feel queasy.

The bus pulled onto the dirt shoulder and hissed to a stop. There was no one there to meet her. And no one on the road. The house looked further away than she remembered. And much smaller. The sun was just rising above White's Gap Mountain, and its pink rays turned the Alabama clay road the color of dried blood. She thought her grandmother might have walked down when she heard the bus make the hairpin turn at the Wilson Farm. Sound carried across the cornfields when the wind had a lift to it and this gift of nature had always served her grandmother well. Visitors had never been able to take her by surprise. *Maybe she didn't hear. She's a lot older now. Probably not as able-bodied as she used to be.*

Canaan watched the bus leave. Watched it travel down the long stretch of Highway 16. Waited just in case she decided to run after it – leave her worldly belongings to die a quiet death along with the mailbox and hightail it across the fields, cut it off before it reached the bend and crossed over the Chickasaw County line. A thin heat-haze was already hovering a few inches above the tarmac and she could feel the first dribble of sweat down her back. She'd forgotten how hot August could be down South. *Welcome home, missy.* She'd probably pass out before she reached the bus, collapse below Mr Wilson's soybean plants and no one would find her until September. The bus disappeared behind a clump of scrubby crab-apple trees that her grandmother insisted on calling Harper's Wood. Her chance had passed. She looked towards the house. Her grandmother had come out onto the porch, wiping her hands on a dishtowel and squinting down the road. Canaan waved. Her grandmother turned and retreated behind the dark screen door, so she picked up her suitcases and started her last trek home.

Some glad mornin' when this life is o'er . . . I'll fly away . . . to a land beyond celestial shores . . . I'll fly away – Canaan rolled over and faced the clock radio as the Jubilee Gospel Singers continued to rock for Jesus. She pressed the snooze button then slowly eased her legs over the side of the bed. They were still in good shape. Not bad for thirty-six, she thought, if you ignored the rest of her.

The early-afternoon sun cast low shadows at her feet as the arthritic blades of the window fan tried, in vain, to fluff up the soggy summer air. It was too hot to get dressed, but her grandmother didn't approve of her wandering the house in her underwear. Her hair was still damp from the shower. Good to wash the diesel fumes out – even better to crawl into her old bed after all these years. But those safe, contented feelings had already faded. She hunched forward, allowing herself a deep, self-pitying moan. The medication was wearing off. She was beginning to ache again. She inched her fingers down her spine towards the deep purple bruise on the small of her back. More bruises crept up her ribcage, in angry contrast to her pale New York skin. Still groggy, she rummaged through the suitcases that lay open on the floor and the bed. They spilled over with clothes dumped hastily from drawers and torn from hangers: dried flowers, crushed and broken; a few crippled baskets; a toaster. The pitiful remains of her life in New York. Wrapped inside a sweater was the espresso machine Jonathon had given her the Christmas they couldn't even afford wrapping paper. She didn't drink espresso. Hated it, in fact, but Jonathon loved it and that was reason enough to take it with her when she left.

She kicked one of the suitcases and nearly lost her balance. *I know I packed them.* Her head was pounding. She opened the dresser drawer, digging through her junior-high knee socks and the flannel nightgowns that her grandmother had bought her every single birthday from the Sears catalog. Her childhood bedroom had not changed in eighteen years. Not since the morning she'd stuffed a small duffel bag with blue jeans and halter-tops and traveled North in search of a more adventurous life than Lander could offer. Not once, in all the years she'd been gone, had she thought of her old room with any shred of nostalgia or homesickness. But that morning when she opened the door, there was something comforting about the earthy smell of old quilts and the reassuring permanence of the four-poster bed. The bed had belonged to her great-grandmother, Emma Stewart, and according to family folklore, had been built inside the room as a wedding present and had never ventured beyond the bedroom door. It had weathered generations of ill-treatment by overcrowded siblings and sullen, daydreaming teenagers. It had survived the peace stickers of the sixties and the psychedelic paint tricks of the seventies, remaining untouched and unchanged except for a few superficial nicks and dents. *My momma had ever' one of her babies in that bed.* Canaan's grandmother, Lou Venie, dragged this scrap of ancestral history out as often as possible as if this fact alone endowed it with some special privilege or respect. That morning, travel-weary and emotionally drained, Canaan had enjoyed the firm support of the feather-tick pillows under her neck. She'd run her hand over the back of the headboard, relieved to find the petrified remains of chewing gum that her mother, as a teenager, had deposited just before going to sleep. Lou Venie had threatened to scrape them off for years, but Canaan had fought to keep them. They were tangible proof that her mother had existed. Each night as a child, before closing her eyes, Canaan had touched them for luck, assured that she would be kept safe until morning. But not anymore. She'd discovered a new magic.

She slammed the last drawer of the bureau and looked around, trying to remember where she'd hidden them. Slumping at the dressing table, she stared into the mirror. The edges of her black eye had already turned a plummy yellow but the bruise around her lip was still a deep navy blue. She leaned closer and studied her bloodshot eyes, her reflection framed with souvenirs of an earlier life, relics of hope and expectation. The corsage from her senior prom clung to faded ribbon and her graduation tassel dangled below it, partially obscuring a small snapshot of Canaan in a cap and gown, standing beside her grandmother. At the top of the mirror, tucked inside a cardboard frame, was a photograph of Canaan at the Homecoming dance in 1984. She was standing on a Japanese bridge, with a pimply-faced date she vaguely remembered was named Dougie or Petie. She had planned a better homecoming than this; dripping with success, not stumbling down the steps of a Greyhound with a few battered suitcases. Not dressed in a shabby pair of Jonathon's blue jeans and an old football jersey from a quarterback she'd dated for two weeks in high school. *Not feeling so old*.

Her hair, dead and lifeless, fell below her shoulders, a tired version of the style she'd worn in her teens. Her hair had been a luxurious thick swirl of chestnut and, although she'd never been a beauty, there had been a spark in her eyes that made people notice her. But now, unloved and untouched by fashion or style, her hair was brittle and shapeless and the sunken hollows below her eyes had deepened like the bruised flesh of a peach. Her soulful eyes and delicate lips had rarely touched make-up, but what as a teenager made her look wholesome and freshly scrubbed, now just made her look exhausted.

She picked up an old handbag, streaked with city grime, and heard the pills rattle reassuringly inside. She remembered now. Her grandmother had come in to coax a sausage and biscuit down her malnourished throat and she'd shoved the pills into the first thing she could find. There were only a few left, but she was a pro at getting pills when she needed them. Once the bruises had healed, she'd choose one of the anonymous doctors at the new clinic, someone who'd come from somewhere beyond Lander; a stranger who didn't know her. She'd say something like, *It's the damn crickets. Just can't get used to them. I miss the city, you know . . . traffic and sirens*. They would share a good-natured laugh about living in the country and then she'd tell him, with the slightest hint of humility, *I don't usually take pills*. He'd smile as he handed her the prescription, maybe pat her hand, the way Southerners do: *Everybody needs help once in a while*.

The doctor in New York had said the same thing, and she'd believed him, convinced her troubles with Jonathon would smooth over after a while. The pills had been a temporary solution to help shorten the nights when her husband had been huddled over his piano in some jazz club on the West side of town. She'd never been there and he'd made it clear she wasn't invited. The pills had helped muddle up the mornings-after and had mercifully broken her of certain habits. Like sniffing his shirts . . . searching obsessively for the perfume she didn't wear.

She tossed the pill to the back of her throat and took a swig of flat cola.

'Canaan? You up?'

She hid the bottle in the back of her sock drawer and grabbed a robe.

'Just a minute.'

As usual Lou Venie ignored her. Shoving the door open, she glanced suspiciously around the room. Thirty-six years old and her grandmother still tried to catch her smoking or reading what she called trash. Lou Venie Phillips had a well-seasoned face but, in spite of her years, she had a strong handshake, a confident walk, and a tart tongue. Her complete lack of vanity, an eccentricity that had embarrassed Canaan in her teenage years, was still apparent in the cast-off clothing she wore: plain cotton trousers, raggedly cut off below the knee, and canvas tennis shoes that were missing their laces. Her sleeveless blouse exposed arms that sagged with spare, suntanned flesh, but revealed the lingering evidence of the powerful muscles she'd developed as a farm wife. Her slate-gray hair was pulled back with a turquoise elastic band and a pair of cheap drugstore reading glasses dangled around her neck from one of her missing shoe strings.

Canaan tied the robe around her and sat at the dressing table trying to work out the damp tangles of her hair. Her grandmother snatched a towel from the bedpost.

'Canaan, how many times I told you not to hang wet

things on the bed? My momma had ever' one of her babies in that bed. You oughta show more respect.'

She spread the towel over the windowsill and stooped to collect a pile of Canaan's clothes from the floor.

'I take it these are meant for the wash.'

'No, some are clean. I'll sort them later.'

Lou Venie sighed as if she knew better and dropped them on a chair. She slid the suitcase from the end of the bed to the floor before tugging and straightening the sheets.

'I left you a plate lunch in the oven.'

'I'm not hungry.'

'You hardly touched breakfast.'

'I had a candy bar on the bus.'

Her grandmother frowned and grabbing two corners of the quilt, she snapped it sharply in the air before smoothing it into place.

'In my house you eat regular meals. Don't care what bad habits you got into up North.'

She punched a pillow and slammed it into position. Canaan closed her eyes and swallowed.

'Lou Venie – I'll do that.'

'Don't take a minute.'

Canaan gritted her teeth, digging through the pile of clothes for something to wear.

'Did you set my alarm?'

'It ain't good for you to sleep so much in the day.'

Lou Venie tossed Canaan's gaudy collection of carnival-prize teddy bears on top of the pillows.

'I called up Kyle Bernard this mornin'. You remember Kyle. Year or two below you. He's assistant manager at Piggly Wiggly now. Says he can give you a job at the deli counter.'

Canaan could feel the heat rise in her face. She swallowed.

'You talked to him about me?'

'Now don't get all uppity. I didn't give no particulars.'

Her grandmother pulled the citrus-yellow bear out of the line-up and shoved him next to the pink one.

'I don't need you to find me a job, Lou Venie. And if I did it sure wouldn't be Piggly Wiggly.'

'You think you're too good for that kind of work?'

Canaan sighed and tried to sound sure.

'No. Of course not.'

'Well, that's what it sounds like to me.'

Canaan dropped the robe to get dressed and in the mirror she saw, with guilty satisfaction, the shock on her grandmother's face. Lou Venie looked away.

'Well, you gotta work somewhere.'

'I'm not planning to stay that long.'

Lou Venie snorted.

'Ain't been here two minutes and already lookin' for a way out.'

'There's nothing for me in Lander. Never was.'

There was a flicker of hurt in the old woman's eyes, but before Canaan could apologize, it was gone and her grandmother had moved on to other things. As Canaan pulled on a pair of shorts, Lou Venie picked up the suitcase and returned it to the end of the bed.

'Anyway . . . I told Kyle you'd come by and talk to him about it.'

'I can't see anybody looking like this.'

'I said you'd be around in a few weeks. Once you was settled. You'll be healed up by then.'

Lou Venie opened a bureau drawer and started unpacking Canaan's suitcase.

'Please don't do that. I'll get to it later.'

'If I left it to you, it'd be here come Judgement Day.'

Canaan gave up. It was a battle she'd never won and her weapons were rusty. She pulled the T-shirt over her head and wandered over to the window. Gazing out over the cornfields she could just see the glimmer of a tin roof and the glint of a metal stovepipe.

'Does Luke know I'm back?'

'Came up here while you was sleepin'. Didn't want me to bother you.'

'How is he?'

'Gettin' more peculiar every day. People up town are complainin'. But I cain't exactly tie him to his bed.'

'Damn rednecks.'

The suitcase empty, Lou Venie checked the side pockets.

'Well, your aunt Peggy thinks I oughta put him in a home. Says if it was her—'

Lou Venie lifted a small black-and-white photograph from behind the elastic pocket. It was a picture of Canaan's mother Ruthie, a young woman, barely seventeen, leaning towards the camera like a Hollywood siren. Her cheek was cradled in the cup of one delicate hand. Her fingernails were short and painted and around her slender wrist was a heavy gold charm bracelet. Lou Venie's face was rigid with anger as she moved accusingly towards her granddaughter.

'Where did you get this?'

Canaan glanced at the picture.

Stupid. So stupid. Should've known she'd find it.

'I said . . . where did you get this?'

Canaan tried to be dismissive.

'I had it in college.'

Lou Venie was shaking now, a pink rash rising from her collar.

'You stole it.'

'I found it.'

'You *STOLE* it! You got no right to have this!'

She began to tear it into tiny pieces and Canaan lunged forward.

'Give it back!'

'Takin' a person's private things. You got no right!'

14

As Lou Venie continued to rip and tear, Canaan scrambled for the pieces.

'You didn't want it! You didn't want anything of hers. Not her pictures, not her things, not me!'

Lou Venie stepped back, releasing her grip, and Canaan retrieved the pieces from between her fingers. Her grandmother's face slackened and she said it again but with less conviction.

'You've got no right.'

Canaan snatched the last few pieces that had fallen to the floor.

'She was my mother. You can't change that, Lou Venie.'

She stormed out, clenching the pieces in her fists. As she stepped off the back porch and headed towards the cornfield she heard her grandmother at the back door.

'This is still my house!'

She walked faster as Lou Venie continued to shout.

'Come back here! Canaan? You hear me? Always runnin'! Just like your momma!'

Canaan stopped running when all she could hear was the rustle of corn. It was the same place, the same sound she'd run to as a child. Sitting in the dirt, trying to piece the fragments of her mother's picture together, she suddenly felt like an idiot. A grown woman hiding in the cornfield. Scrapping with her grandmother like a playground delinquent. She'd been crazy to think that time might have unraveled the old patterns.

Throughout her childhood, the subject of Canaan's mother had been buried as deeply as the unadorned grave in the White's Gap Baptist churchyard. She had grown up hiding the handful of photographs she'd found in the old shoebox and sneaking out to the safety of the cornfield to look them over again and again. As far as her grandmother was concerned, Canaan's history began the day she arrived at the Old Stewart Place. Nothing before was allowed to exist.

Luke

March 1905

The groom was late and for a wild moment, Myra thought there might still be a chance. If Thom backed out she was sure she could talk Travis into sending Emma away until after the baby was born. Put it up for adoption. Let it grow up with its own kind. They could start over in another town. No one would know.

The night Emma had come home beaten and raped, Myra's first concern had been to keep it secret. No need to let misfortune ruin her daughter's chances at a decent marriage. But the lynching had ended all hope of that. Myra would have preferred to pretend it never happened but Travis had insisted on justice for his little girl. Later, when it was obvious that a baby was on the way, they had decided the best option was to marry her off quickly.

Now, as the three of them waited in the front pew of the White's Gap Baptist church, listening to the preacher sucking his teeth and tapping his New Testament with his middle finger, she wasn't so sure. More than anyone, she knew how difficult it was to overcome a bad marriage. According to her own family, Myra had married beneath her and over the years she'd been forced to admit they were right. Travis was a kind husband, generous and easy to manipulate, but he would never be able to give his wife the things she desperately wanted. As the owner of the town's one and only barbershop, Travis had kept her in decent dresses but they'd certainly never reached the pinnacles of respectability that she desired. Travis was a well-loved character in town. A congenial storyteller who was quick to laugh and even quicker with free haircuts when he deemed it a special occasion. *Tillson boy got his first job in Garland, Myra. Couldn't send him off shaggy-headed. He don't have much money. Ain't started his job yet. After he gets settled in, you just watch, he'll be back to pay up.* Of course the Tillson boy never did come back. Nor did anyone else. Not to cheat Travis. They simply forgot, or took him at his word when he repeatedly waved his hand at them dismissively. *Don't you worry about it. You got a new baby to feed.* It was obvious to Myra from early in the marriage that if there was any respect to be gained, besides the lovable buffoonery her husband had cultivated, it was up to her. She'd imagined herself the proud matriarch of half a dozen children. Boys who'd go on to become doctors or bankers and daughters who'd marry wealthy businessmen. But those visions had shriveled away when Emma was born and Doc Caldwell had told her that was it – the well was dry. From that day forward Emma was expected to provide redemption for her mother's bad choices. For years, Myra forced her way into distant friendships, grasping at the tiniest threads of acquaintance, hoping to plant her daughter's dainty feet firmly within the borders of higher society. Emma's wedding day was to have been her reward for all the sacrifices she'd made. An affirmation of her rightful place. But it had not turned out that way. There would be no cake, no guests and no flowers except for the pitiful handful of black-eyed Susans that Travis had insisted on picking. She'd caught him that morning sneaking up to Emma's room, the roots still clinging to the soil they'd been forced from. *A girl oughta have flowers on her weddin' day, Myra. It ain't her fault.*

But Myra couldn't help feeling that it was.

Travis reached over and took his daughter's hand, giving it a gentle squeeze and Myra felt a pang of jealousy. He'd always doted on Emma, but he had been overly protective since the night of the rape, determined to make everything all right. For the first time in their married life, Travis had decided to take a stand, to make decisions without consulting his wife and she didn't like it one bit. Not that there had been much choice to begin with. She had to admit that Thom Stewart had been their one and only prospect, but she would have liked to have had her say. Thom was a shy, reclusive bachelor, over twenty years older than his fourteen-year-old bride. His mother had died when he was born, and his father when he was seventeen. As word had spread of his father's death, women of varying ages had mentally rubbed their hands together in anticipation of a vulnerable new recruit to the marriage stable; one who now owned his own farm. For weeks after the funeral, a steady stream of women dressed in their best finery from ruffles and flounces to silk widow's weeds had pushed and shoved their pot roasts and buttermilk biscuits in the poor boy's face. When he'd made it clear that he wasn't in the market for a good woman, female visits and hot meals had dwindled until at last he had been left to his own company, forgotten and ignored. But it didn't stop the women of Lander from speculating on the oddity and downright selfishness of a man of thirty-seven living alone.

Myra was working out her 'moving away and starting over' speech for Travis when Thom appeared at the back door of the church, shaking and terrified, in a pair of lifeless denim overalls and a new shirt. During the vows his eyes had remained fastened to the floor and his calloused hands had taken hold of Emma's only at the insistence of Reverend Miles. Afterwards, as Myra stood on the church steps with

Travis and the preacher, she'd watched Thom help his child bride into the rickety buggy and motioned for Travis to put the wedding present in the back. Myra's mother had always said, *Can't start a marriage without a good washtub.* Thom had tipped his hat in thanks and Myra, determined not to let the preacher see her cry, had stared after them, watching her dreams disappear around the bend of the dirt road.

Canaan

As a frightened four-year-old, Canaan had begun her life in Lander clinging to a pink vinyl suitcase with a black plastic handle and decorated with a French poodle in a beret standing at the base of the Eiffel Tower. It was the small, useless details – like the suitcase – that she remembered. Nothing useful. She'd arrived on a bus and her grandmother had met her at the mailbox. She didn't remember the bus trip or the chaos that must have surrounded her departure from the dreary apartment she'd shared with her mother. She remembered nothing of the seven days she'd survived on corn flakes, the only thing her mother had taught her to fix by herself. Nothing of the many times she must have peeked through the bedroom door, tiptoeing back to her camp cot because her mother didn't like to be disturbed when she was taking a nap. Nothing of the smell of vomit that must have filled the airtight apartment. Nothing of the empty pill bottles on the side table and nothing of the neighbor who found her and helped her pack her little pink suitcase. Most of the facts had been filled in by her aunt Peggy: family gossip, whispered behind Lou Venie's back. But there was one image that Canaan knew must have come from her own inner scrapbook. Sometimes just before she fell asleep or in that early-morning dream state she would see it – her mother's hand hanging over the side of the bed, her slender wrist weighed down by a gold charm bracelet. Canaan knew there were other scenes swimming around inside her head, like piranha waiting to nibble away at any happy memories she had managed to collect. She couldn't remember them but she knew they were there, because the smell of bus diesel still made her chest ache with panic, and corn flakes tasted bitter in her mouth.

Canaan arranged the last piece of the torn photograph. All pieces were accounted for. Very carefully, she tucked each one into the pocket on her T-shirt. Why had she thought things would be different? And why the hell had she believed, when she'd left Lander all those years ago, that her life would be different? She'd been away for less than a year when she'd met Jonathon and their marriage was proof that she would always be a spineless shadow in someone else's life.

Where do you think you'll go, Canaan? Home? To Alabama? She could still hear the sneer in his voice. He'd known all along. Known she'd put up with just about anything before she'd go back. And he'd used it to his advantage. He wouldn't be coming after her, though. She was certain of that. He'd never been the possessive type. Just an opportunist. And it wouldn't take him long to find someone to alternately fuck and bully. He'd always been surrounded by cults of devoted women who were drawn to the dark and dangerous side of talent. It was certainly what had first attracted Canaan, had led her to make excuses for his behavior and made her believe she was lucky that he'd chosen her above all the others. She couldn't survive without him, he'd said. She was too weak, too naive. She couldn't even choose an entrée from a menu or decide what brand of toothpaste to buy without him. She'd never dared buy a pair of earrings or a dress without his approval and she'd never offered her own opinion without being asked. If she'd had any friends they might have warned her, but left on her own so much, she'd convinced herself that things weren't all that bad. Not compared to what she'd read in women's magazines. He wasn't a wife-beater, for God's sake. Just a man with an artistic temperament who slapped her around a little when she embarrassed him. He'd never punched or kicked her.

Not until she told him she wanted a divorce.

The decision to leave him had shocked her. It had come in a flash one morning when she'd awakened on the bathroom floor, lying on the cold tiles, among the spilled contents of the medicine cabinet. She'd remained there throughout the morning, curled in a fetal position and listening for his key in the front door, piecing together the jigsaw of her neighbors' lives, envious of their purpose, measuring the weight of their footsteps and the length of their showers. By the time the last of them had scurried out into the world, she'd decided. *I could leave him. Get my own place. Get a job.*

On the night she'd told him – was it only thirty-eight hours ago? – she'd been for a walk. To gather her courage. She'd started talking as soon as she opened the front door, afraid she'd lose her nerve if she saw him first. The apartment was dark except for the dim light of a reading lamp. Jonathon was sitting in the corner, in a crumbly leather armchair – *his* chair – too far away for her to smell the putrid sweetness of old whiskey. She continued, bolstered by his silence, determined to get it said. It wasn't until she saw the flash of the bottle as he lifted it to his lips that she knew she'd lost.

'Where do you think you'll go? Home? To Alabama?'

She wanted to sound defiant, but panic had turned her words to squeaks.

'No . . . I . . . I don't know.'

She didn't see him move. Didn't hear the bottle drop to the floor. One minute he was in his chair, the next it was empty and the next she was flying across the back of the sofa.

'You know how lucky you are?'

She couldn't tell where he was. The darkness and the shock of the attack disoriented her. She decided to lie still and speak quietly.

'Please, Jonathon . . .'

The first kick took her breath. With the next one she bit her tongue and her mouth filled with blood.

'You think it's easy coming home to a sniveling little piece of trailer trash every night?'

'Please . . .'

He pulled her to her feet, then punched her so hard that she vomited as she fell to her knees. She wiped her mouth on her sleeve, and bowed her head hoping he had finished, but he grabbed her by the hair. As she struggled to stand, he jerked her head lower to the floor, dragging her by the hair down the hall. She fought to remain standing, kicking and scrambling for the walls, trying to find anything to hold onto.

'Who do you think's gonna want you? Huh?'

In the bedroom he threw her onto the bed, forcing her to a kneeling position with her arms wrenched behind her. With one hand he reached under her summer skirt and grabbed her panties, yanking and tearing them from her body. His angry grunts grew louder and more intense. Each thrust smashed her head against the wall, her cries smothered in the pillow. She tried to lift her head so that she could breathe, and as the dizzying thumps to her head continued, she fought to keep from passing out.

Afterwards he'd snuggled up to her as if they'd just shared an intimate moment and draping his arm and leg over her body had mumbled in her ear.

'You weren't really going to leave me.'

She had stared at the ceiling, swallowing the tears and fighting to keep her voice controlled.

'No.'

'That's my girl.'

He'd fallen into a drunken sleep and she'd slipped from

beneath his dead weight and huddled on the floor beside the bed, trying to stifle the explosive sobs that were building inside. She couldn't remember whether she'd had the idea first, then seen the bat; or seen the bat and had the idea, but suddenly she was standing over his sleeping body, bat raised high over her head. The strength that had deserted her before had returned and she took several deep breaths. She wanted to hurt him. To smash his slender piano-fingers, destroy his sensitive good looks. She wanted to kill him and the fierceness of the feelings terrified her.

She dropped the bat and stumbled in the dark towards the bathroom, where she vomited into the bathtub. For over an hour, she sat on the side of the tub crying into a towel, letting it soak up the mess she'd made of her life. When she was calm, she emptied a bottle of sleeping pills into her hand and filled the glass with water as she stared into the mirror.

Momma? Momma, you still sleepin'?

Her shoulders began to shake and some of the pills toppled over the side of her cupped hand and scampered down the drain. In the other room Jonathon rolled over.

'Canaan! You up? Bring me a glass of water.'

He's left you no choice.

She popped open two of the capsules and poured the powder into the glass of water, stirring it with the end of her toothbrush. She watched him drink it, then lay beside him until she heard deep, sedated snores. Creeping quietly around the house she packed what she could, realizing that few of their possessions actually belonged to her. She scooped up the wad of dollar bills from his tip-kitty and rifled through his blue jeans for the larger bills that he called his fun money. She'd left the front door standing open and had walked the entire sixteen blocks to the bus station, her way of saying goodbye to New York and all the promises she'd made to herself when she was a teenager.

As the bus had pulled out of the depot and the smell of

diesel had drifted up from under the seats, she had begun to sob and had continued to do so, off and on, for the entire twenty-eight-hour journey. A large black woman with kind eyes had smiled and patted her shoulder as she passed by, but the other passengers had left her to her grief. Her body had shut down to all physical needs and her emotions had rocked back and forth between fear and relief, regret and hopelessness. In the midst of all the confusion, however, one thing had become clear. She'd come to realize that the strongest motivation for leaving had not come from a hope of something better, but in knowing that she didn't want to die so far away from home.

Luke

Just a minute or two. That's all it would take.

It was only a passing thought. A snippet of a half-whispered prayer. *No one would know.* Myra Scott held tightly to the newborn's arm as she cleaned his mother's blood from his neck. She worked quickly, her elbows knocking steadily at the side of the washtub. The baby's shoulders fit snuggly into the palm of her hand. *Just a few inches lower and his head would be . . .*

She held him still, tiny and helpless in the blood-brown water. Testing her willpower. Tempting her deepest secrets.

No.

She snatched him from the tub and away from her murderous daydreams. *It don't matter that he's what he is.* She wiped him down with a strip of toweling and raised apologetic eyes to the ceiling. She was still a Christian woman even if God had seen fit to inflict her family with such a hardship.

Beads of sweat were gathering at her hairline and she swiped at them with her sleeve.

'Could've at least offered somethin' cool to drink.'

Her voice sounded hollow in the sparse kitchen. No one had cooked in the room for years. There were no pans or utensils. Shelves lay empty. The cast-iron stove was cold, its ashes from past meals long disintegrated. A single clothesline stretched across the rafters, draped with neatly shredded squares of wet sheeting. Dark wet patches dotted the wooden floor.

She wrapped the baby in a clean sheet and carried him to a basket that was wedged between the wall and the old stove. When she placed him inside, he let out a mewling cry and shoved his fists defensively into the air before settling into his new position. Myra arched her back in relief as she stood. The air was stagnant with a damp, clinging heat and another droplet of sweat broke free from her scalp, finding its way to her eyes. She snapped a cloth from the line above her and held it under the cool water from the pump, wiping her face and plunging it between her breasts. As she mopped up the dampness at the base of her neck, she opened the screen door, leaning against it.

'It's done.'

Her husband answered without looking up from the rocking chair where he'd been posted on the front porch throughout the morning's ordeal.

'Thought as much.'

Travis Scott was a round man with plump, swollen hands that dimpled above each knuckle. His pudgy lips sucked thoughtfully on a pipe.

'What is it?'

'Boy. Looks all right.'

Travis rocked silently, letting the question build between them.

'What color?'

'White.'

He nodded, letting the smoke snake slowly and evenly from the corners of his mouth.

'Reckon I oughta go get Thom?'

He looked eagerly at his wife, searching . . . hoping for permission to head for Duke's. Have a drink with the boys.

A celebration. After all, good or bad, he was still a new granddaddy. Myra frowned.

'No need to. He'll be along directly.'

His face slumped in disappointment.

'He may be a while. Probably havin' a few drinks at Duke's.'

She nodded and crossed her arms.

'I don't take to folks drinkin', but cain't say I blame him. Cain't be easy havin' a son that ain't yours. 'Specially not when ever'body knows it.'

She felt a sudden catch in her throat and Travis smiled gently.

'He's a good man, Myra.'

'I know. You made the right choice.'

She leaned over, squeezing his shoulder with a discarded tenderness.

'I'd best go check on Emma.'

Myra liked being in charge. And she couldn't recall a single time when that hadn't been the case. Travis had always let her have her way and even her daughter Emma, as strong-willed and stubborn as she was, could usually be managed. But things were different now and Myra hadn't had time to adjust to her new role. She was a visitor in someone else's house and Emma was no longer her little girl, easy to control with a well-aimed slap of sense.

She knocked timidly and eased open the door.

'Emma? Honey?'

Her daughter had kicked the quilt to the floor and lay on her back, stretching her cotton nightgown, transparent with perspiration, tightly across her body. The youthful fifteen-year-old figure had all but vanished and Myra watched as Emma studied the unfamiliar breasts and saggy middle. She was a pretty girl, with tiny wrists and hands and delicate features, but her face was drawn and pale from the labor. Her wheat-colored hair had dampened to a muddy brown and it sagged across her shoulders in exhausted strands.

'Thought we better get that gown off.'

Emma didn't move but closed her eyes as her mother moved lightly across the room and dropped a freshly pressed gown, a ribbon and hairbrush on the nightstand.

'Don't want yer husband seein' you like this. Might change his mind.'

Her voice simmered with a strained sweetness as she pulled Emma to a sitting position, ignoring the girl's darkly brewing scowl.

'Probably ain't comin' back.'

'Course he is. He's just lettin' you have your privacy.'

Myra lifted the damp gown over Emma's head and tossed it to the floor, nudging her until she grudgingly raised her arms to the fresh nightgown.

'He ain't said hardly two words since I moved in.'

Myra busied herself with brushing Emma's hair.

'He just ain't got used to bein' a husband is all. He'll come 'round.'

Emma flipped her mother's hand away.

'Maybe I don't want him to come around.'

'Now you listen here, missy. You're lucky he's agreed to all this.'

'I didn't ask him to marry me.'

'No, but your pa had to ask him. Hardest thing he ever done, but he done it, and you better start actin' grateful.'

Emma's chin trembled as she tried to speak.

'But Momma, he's an old man.'

Myra squeezed her daughter's fragile jawbone tightly between her fingers and forced her to look at her.

'You think there's any young bucks out there's gonna take you on? With *that* baby? No, ma'am. Not a one, I can tell you.'

Emma pulled away from her mother's grasp and Myra parroted her husband's earlier reassurances.

'He's a good man, Emma. He's the best you're gonna do.'

Emma fell back against the pillows, fighting to collect her composure, but her eyes brimmed with tears. She brushed them aside defiantly and turned towards the window.

'I wanted a nice weddin' with a new dress and parties. That's what you always said.'

Myra picked up the washbasin from the side and stooped to collect the toweling that scattered the floor.

'Well, you shoulda thought of that 'fore you went wanderin' where you ain't got no business.'

She knew she should feel more sympathy for her daughter but she couldn't help feeling that Emma had ruined everything. Travis had been sympathetic enough for both of them. Fussing over the girl like she'd break in two if anybody so much as frowned at her. *She ain't the villain in this piece, Myra.* Other people had said the same. But she couldn't help it. She felt cheated and lately it was bitter words, not sweet, that filled her mouth first.

Myra picked up Emma's soiled nightgown and added it to the pile of toweling as Emma rolled over, turning her back to her mother.

'I'm tired. I wanna sleep now.'

Myra's eyes narrowed and her lips shriveled to a distrustful pucker.

'Mind you talk nice to him when he gets here.'

She spent the afternoon scrubbing the reminders of that morning's labor from the sheets and surfaces of the house, trying to cleanse the air of the heavy iron smell of blood that clung stubbornly to the heat. She'd brought a stick of cinnamon from home and after much effort she coaxed the old stove back to life, filling the house with the woody fragrance of boiling spices. The Old Stewart Place was a typical farmhouse, cavernous and dark and thick with the dust of plowed fields. The only clue of inhabitance was a small fireplace in the front room where Thom fixed his evening stews, content with one battered pot for cooking all his meals. *Backward. Just plain backward for a man to resort to such primitive habits when there's a perfectly good stove in the kitchen.*

By dusk, Thom had not returned and Myra was nervous.

'Been livin' out here too long by himself if you ask me. Ain't used to thinkin' about other people's feelin's. Don't you think he oughta be here by now?'

She waited for a response before shoving the screen door open. She expected to see her husband sleeping with his mouth drooping to one side and was perturbed to see him peeling an apple.

'You listenin' to me?'

'Course I am. Don't rightly know what we can do about it now. It's gettin' dark. I offered to fetch him.'

'You don't reckon he's gone off, do you?'

Her look of irritation suddenly changed to genuine concern.

'What on earth'll we do if he don't come back, Travis?'

She'd never been sure about this arrangement, but now that things were settled legally, she didn't like to think about taking Emma and that baby back home with them.

'Myra, for cryin' out loud. He's lived here all his life. This is his home. Why the blue blazes would he off and go?'

She shrugged, only slightly reassured. Thom Stewart was a nice enough man, she reckoned, but she thought he leaned more on the peculiar side of humanity. He didn't tip his hat or look people in the eye when he passed them in the street. *Wasn't honest not looking people in the eye.* Travis always took the man's side of things, or anybody's side, she figured, if it was different from hers. *He's shy, Myra. Poor man's been on his own for twenty years.*

Peculiar or not, however, Myra had to admit that his

addition to the family was better than the alternative and her fears were at last soothed when she heard the sluggish swagger of the carthorse and the creaking sway of the buggy over the brow of the hill.

'That him?'

She squinted towards the sound, trying to make out the shape. Travis grunted what she took to be a yes and she made a silently grateful promise to put a little extra in the collection plate on Sunday. Travis walked to the edge of the porch as Thom climbed down from the buggy.

''Bout given you up, Thom.'

He winked good-naturedly and gave his wife a nod to encourage a friendly welcome. She joined him, gushing with enthusiasm.

'Ever'thing turned out fine, just fine. Emma's restin' but I know she'll want to see you.'

They hovered around him, blocking his way until Myra stepped aside and Thom reached for the door with a timid urgency.

'It's a boy, Mr Stewart. And he's white.'

Thom stopped, the back of his neck rigid. The door slammed behind him but she followed, bustling eagerly into the kitchen.

'She's a tough one, our Lou Emma. Had that baby like there was nothin' to it.'

As she spoke, she cleared the bucket and brush from the floor where she'd been scrubbing. She thought the least he could do was to mention her hard work. Maybe thank her. But instead he leaned against the table and stared at some unseen blemish on the floor. Myra hesitated then scuttled down the hall towards Emma's room.

'I'll just go make sure she's awake.'

Emma's face was creased with the remnants of deep sleep and she rolled her head back, wrinkling her brow and moaning as Myra shook her by the shoulders.

'Come on, Emma. Mr Stewart's here. You got to look presentable.'

She fluffed and fussed over her daughter until she was satisfied that Emma wouldn't curl up under the quilt as soon as her back was turned. When she brought Travis and Thom in a few minutes later, Emma was the picture of glowing motherhood.

'Don't she look purty, Mr Stewart? You'd never know what she'd been through this mornin', would you?'

There was a pause as Myra waited for a response. Travis cleared his throat, throwing his wife a look of uncertainty. Thom shifted his weight from one foot to another.

'She looks real nice.'

'Yep and tough as a nut. She's gonna have this farm lookin' good in no time.' She hurried on. 'Not that it don't look good now, of course. It could just do with a woman's touch, is all.'

She moved a chair to the side of Emma's bed.

'Here you go, Mr Stewart. Have a seat.'

'You can call me Thom.'

Myra beamed and pushed the chair towards him. He hesitated then slid into the seat. Emma deliberately turned her head towards the wall and Myra tried to hide her embarrassment.

'I was just tellin' Travis what a fine job you did with this bed. It's one of the finest beds we seen. Ain't that right, Travis?'

Travis nodded. It was true they had admired his carpentry and carving skills. And they'd agreed that the sagging, lopsided single bed it had replaced had not been suitable for a newly married couple. But they'd also doubted the common sense of a man who would build a four-poster bed of such huge proportions. Thom had spent the last few months locked up in the room which he and Emma were meant to share, secretly building and carving this most personal of wedding gifts for his new bride. Its construction was sturdy, its decoration elaborate, but as Myra pointed out, he hadn't considered the size of the door, condemning the bed for ever to the same room.

Thom blushed at the compliment and shyly pointed to the ornately carved border of wild roses on the headboard.

'I carved Emma's name in that rose there.'

Myra leaned over for closer inspection.

'Why, look at that. Ain't that nice, Emma?'

She nudged her daughter roughly and Emma scowled.

'It's nice I reckon. Bed's too big though. I'd rather have my little bed from home.'

'Don't be rude, Emma. Mr Stewart's been more'n patient lettin' you have your own room all to yourself while you were in your condition and all, but he cain't keep sleepin' in the front room.'

Thom's ears deepened to a dark crimson.

'I don't mind . . .'

He tried to rise but Myra placed her hand firmly on his shoulder.

'No-sir. Now don't you mind her. She just ain't thought this through.'

She turned to Emma.

'You're a married woman now. You're meant to share your bed with your husband.'

Thom rose from his chair.

'I don't need to . . . I mean, she can have this room to herself . . . all to herself . . . for as long as she likes. I don't mind sleepin' in the front room.'

Myra patted his shoulder, her voice soothing.

'Course, you do what you want. Sit yourself down and I'll be right back.'

He looked unsure but allowed her to guide him back to the chair. She returned moments later with the baby, sweeping grandly into the room. With a flourish she placed him in Emma's lap.

'Here he is. Healthy and strong. Gonna be a big help on the farm, this'n.'

Emma's arms stiffened at her side and her legs became rigid under the covers.

'Get it off me.'

They stood transfixed as she kicked and screamed, her face ugly and distorted.

'Now! You hear me? Get it off.'

Myra scooped up the baby and glanced nervously at the others. Travis nodded towards the door and they filed out quietly as Emma coiled tightly in the bed, sobbing.

The baby's bleating cries finally subsided as Myra paced the kitchen, holding a small stick of sugar cane for him to suck on. Travis worked diligently to fill his pipe while Thom rocked gently by the stove. Myra shifted the baby to her left shoulder.

'I just don't understand it. Emma was always so good with babies. Used to take care of the Loller kids, when Cora was poorly. She said Emma was a natural little mother hen. Ain't that right, Travis?'

Travis nodded solemnly, and sucked on his pipe, welcoming the first deep taste of tobacco. The smoke rolled from between his teeth as he spoke.

'Course, she's been through an awful lot these past few months.'

'That's right. She's only fifteen. Poor thing's probably scared half to death. And new mothers are skittish sometimes, takes 'em a few days to get used to the idea.'

Myra kicked the basket from beside the stove, and leaned over to deposit the baby. She stopped when Thom held out his arms and she handed him the bundle, moving to Travis and nudging him in delighted triumph. Thom studied the exhausted creature, whose face still bore the angry red blotches of temper, and held the soggy sugar cane to the baby's hungry little mouth.

'You got a name you want to give him, Mr Stewart?'

Thom continued to rock, without looking up.

'Luke.'

'Oh, that's nice. Ain't it, Travis?'

Myra nudged her husband again and he mimicked her automatically.

'Nice. Real nice.'

'Family name?'

Myra thought she saw a slight nod, but she couldn't be sure.

'My dog, when I was a boy.'

She struggled with her response.

'Well, I reckon that's practically family.'

Canaan

Lou Venie let the phone ring eleven times before she answered. She knew who it was and she wanted time to prepare for the interrogation.

'Momma?'

'Uh-huh.'

'She get back OK?'

'Yes, Peggy.'

'I was about to hang up. Where were you – out back? Did you show her the new bird bath me and Mert put in for you?'

For someone who'd had to line her school shoes with newspapers every September to get one more year out of them, Peggy had taken to middle-class life like a whore to silk sheets. Her husband Mert had never been a bundle of personality but he'd inherited a Farm Life Insurance business from his father, allowing Peggy to slip quietly from daughter of a failed dirt farmer to member of the Etowah County Country Club, officer of the Lander Ladies Circle and Respected Resident of Mimosa Ridge.

Caught between Christian duty and family shame, Peggy continually tried to drag her mother from the bowels of poverty. The bird bath had been her most recent and, in Lou Venie's opinion, most ridiculous attempt to camouflage the

Old Stewart Place with trinkets of suburbia. Peggy had hauled it back from a weekend trip to Gatlinburg and had insisted that poor Mert lay a six-foot-square concrete slab for it to rest on. Lou Venie had tried to tell her that no self-respecting country bird was going to use such a thing when there was a perfectly good creek a few yards away.

'We didn't get around to it, Peggy. I'll show her tomorrow.'

'Well, the reason I'm callin' is . . . I have this figurine I bought in Gatlinburg. A giraffe. Made out of blown glass. Sweetest little thing – and I was thinkin' I'd give it to Canaan. Like a welcome-home present, you know? It's not much but it's the best I can do on such short notice.'

Lou Venie knew Peggy was on the verge of inviting herself over and she had to stop her. Canaan's face was a mess. When she'd called from the bus station she hadn't mentioned her condition or the reason she was coming home. Lou Venie was ashamed to think about how frosty she'd been. She'd figured Canaan was just being her usual flighty, never-stick-to-anything self. She'd always been that way. When she was six, girls had made fun of her second-hand uniform so Canaan had quit the Brownies. No thought at all about the hours her grandmother had spent scouring the classified ads looking for one they could afford or the nights Lou Venie had worked until after midnight nipping, tucking and tailoring the thing to fit her. No backbone or stamina, that was Canaan's problem. So it was only natural to assume that her granddaughter had simply hit a rocky patch in her marriage and didn't have the stomach to see it through. But that was before Lou Venie had seen her, standing on the front porch, knocking like a stranger. Before she'd seen the way the bastard had savaged that sweet face. Filled with remorse, Lou Venie had wanted to wrap her up in her arms. Knew Canaan wanted her to. Needed her to. Instead, she'd done what Southern women did best. She'd made breakfast.

'Me and Mert were thinkin' of comin' over after supper. I made one of my special Paradise Cakes. I bet she never had one of those up in New York.'

Lou Venie thought of Canaan's swollen, battered face. She could never trust Peggy with such sensitive information.

'I think you ought to let her get settled in first. She's awful tired.'

Peggy sounded disappointed but reluctantly agreed, much to her mother's relief. Then Peggy lowered her voice, almost whispering.

'So did she say? Was it another woman?'

'No, she didn't say and I don't think it's any of our business, Peggy.'

'I knew this would happen. I told Mert soon as I heard she was comin' back that you'd go right back to your old ways.'

'What ways?'

'Protectin' her. Makin' excuses. Movin' heaven and earth for your precious little princess when you won't even do one simple favor for your own daughter.'

'Are you still fussin' about last weekend?'

'We missed the biggest pre-season party of the year, Momma. Mert was up for the Golden Bama-Booster Award.'

Peggy and Mert were stalwart supporters of Alabama football, traveling hundreds of miles to watch every game in a white Winnebago with a giant red elephant painted along the side and a horn that played the first bars of 'Dixie'. They'd never had children but owned an irritating Pomeranian dog named Bear. He always traveled with them to the games, dressed in a crimson Rolltide sweater, but this time he couldn't go. The President's Party was a more formal affair. Peggy had bought a new sequined jacket from Parisians and made Mert wax up the Caddy.

'Peggy, you know I don't feel comfortable stayin' in your house, and me and that dog of yours just don't get along.'

'It was one night, Momma.'

'Well anyway – it's a good thing I didn't come over, or I'd have missed Canaan's call.'

'Oh no – Lord forbid. But you don't mind ignoring *my* phone calls, do you?'

She heaved a martyred sigh.

'If you won't let me see her, can I at least talk to her?'

'She's . . . gone out for a walk.'

It had been three hours since Canaan had disappeared into the cornfield. Lou Venie had spent that time shelling field peas on the back porch. Watching. Preparing what she might say. She wasn't good at apologies and she knew there was a good chance that she might not say anything at all.

'It's almost dark. Where on earth would she go in this light?'

'She's probably visitin' with Luke.'

Lou Venie knew immediately it was the wrong thing to say.

'Well, now don't that just beat all? I'm supposed to let her rest, let her have her privacy . . . but it's all right for her to spend time with the lunatic element of the family.'

Lou Venie's patience snapped. She couldn't argue with Peggy and worry about Canaan at the same time.

'I'll talk to you later, Peggy. I gotta go fix supper.'

It would be dark soon and Canaan would have to make a decision. She could go back to the house and face Lou Venie or she could sit in the cornfield all night and face death by mosquitoes. Or she could go to Luke's. She was close to his shack. She could see the lantern light through the stalks and she could smell the wood-burning stove. Even on the hottest summer nights, he lit the wood-burner. *To keep my coffee brewin'.*

Canaan was four years old the first time she saw Luke. Sitting on her pink suitcase in the same cornfield where she was sitting now. In those first few months after she arrived at the Old Stewart Place the suitcase never left her side. At mealtimes she balanced it in her lap, holding it with one arm while eating with the other. Lou Venie managed to pry it away from her a few times but had been worn down by the tantrums that always followed. At bedtime the case had been tucked in beside her, close enough to touch if she woke in the night, and every morning after breakfast she dragged it out to the mailbox and watched for the bus that would take her back to Memphis. Back to her mother. When the sun got too hot to bear, she retreated to the cornfield, a cool and secret place where she could pretend that the sound of rustling corn was her mother whispering in her ear late at night, when she thought she was asleep. *Love you, Candy-Cane.*

It was there, hiding in the corn and listening for the sound of a Greyhound bus on the old concrete highway, that she'd first seen her grandmother's brother, the town lunatic of Lander, Alabama. Eccentric might have been a better description of Luke Stewart but for people in Lander, lunatic was just as good a word as different. And he certainly didn't fit most people's definition of normal. He rarely spoke to others, preferring his own company and his own voice. He also had the odorous habit of searching dumpsters, ditches and domestic garbage for discarded treasure. Every day he walked from the decaying shack at the edge of his sister's farm to the town square with a burlap sack strapped across his shoulders. The bag was left over from the days when the Old Stewart Place had grown cotton. It was five feet long and sturdy. Anything Luke found of value, whether it was covered in ditch-water slime or attached to a few rancid potato peels, was added to his pickin' bag. In the summer months the stink was unbearable and people were careful to stand up-wind or avoid him altogether. He was a familiar sight to the locals, shuffling along the shoulder of the highway in his ragged bibbed overalls, the hem torn loose and dragging behind him, leaving small snake-like trails in the dirt. He was ridiculed by most people and over the generations, stories featuring Loony Luke had been passed down and embroidered. But when Canaan had first seen him ambling down the dirt road, moving in that awkward, uncertain way of someone at odds with the rest of the world, she'd simply been curious. She'd stopped waiting by the mailbox. Stopped listening for the bus and instead, spent her days following the scarecrow man around the farm, spying on him. He'd pretend not to notice but occasionally glanced up as he whittled or packed his pipe with tobacco. Each day she had followed a little closer until she'd finally gathered enough courage to sit on the corner of his front porch, tucking her pink suitcase tightly against her. They had nodded a silent greeting and she had watched him peel an apple with his pocket knife, mesmerized by the perfect, unbroken spiral that fell to the floor. He had cut the apple in two and put one half in a clean handkerchief, placing it midway between them on the porch. She had studied him as he chewed and stared out across the fields. When she reached for her half of the apple, it was to mark the beginning of a friendship and a bond that was stronger than either of them had ever known. But it was a bond she would deny when she reached her teens and she still couldn't forgive herself for outgrowing him and leaving him behind.

Luke

Her mother's predictions had failed. In spite of Myra's best efforts Emma had not taken to motherhood or to marriage with any sense of urgency. She'd refused to hold the baby, much less nurse him and her mother had been forced to take matters into her own hands. Terrified that Thom might kick them both out of his house and into hers, Myra daily sacrificed her own household and wifely duties to salvage her daughter's marriage. Each morning before sun-up she made the long trek to the Old Stewart Place, stopping on the way to pick up the black wet-nurse she'd hired. It cost her a nickel a week and a bucket of cow's milk every Friday, but she'd hoped it was a temporary solution. Just until Emma came to her senses.

But it had continued for almost three months. Every morning as the wagon rounded the sharp turn at Pig Wilson's place the high-pitched screams filled the crisp morning air, rising high across the corn. Emma rocked peacefully on the front porch, deaf to the baby's cries, as Mattie, the wet-nurse, passed unacknowledged into the house. Myra was also ignored as she headed for the kitchen to get the stove going and to start her daughter's chores. It was obvious that before long

Myra's patience and energy would slip away. One morning she stopped at the bottom of the steps.

'Where's Mr Stewart?'

'Upper north field, I reckon. He's gone 'fore sun-up. Always is.'

Myra put her hands on her hips, ready for a fight.

'Things ain't right, Lou Emma, and something's got to change.'

'Like what?'

'I've had a talk with your daddy and he agrees. I ain't comin' back tomorrow and neither is Mattie.'

Emma stretched lazily in the rocker and inspected the ends of her hair.

'Don't matter to me if you don't come back.'

Myra lifted her skirts and took the steps two at a time.

'Well, it should, missy! You got nowhere to go, Emma. And you got no money. This here arrangement is all you got so you better start takin' it serious.'

Emma's eyes filled up and she clenched her fists, shoving them dramatically into her stomach.

'I hate him.'

Myra moved quickly to the chair beside her and took her daughter's hand.

'Mr Stewart? Emma, he ain't . . .'

Emma shook her head.

'He's all right. Just leaves me alone. Lets me be.'

'Who then? You mean the baby?'

Emma hesitated as if she wanted to say something else but instead gave a slight nod.

'Well, nothin' we can do about that, but me and your daddy been talkin', like I said. We're only gonna pay Mattie to stay on under one condition. She'll take care of the cookin' and cleanin'. Take care of the baby and all.'

Emma wiped her eyes with the back of her hand and smiled. Myra frowned.

'But listen to me, Emma. She ain't comin' back 'til I know you're heavy with one of Mr Stewart's babies.'

Emma withdrew from her mother in horror.

'I can't . . .'

'You can and you will. Nothin' binds a man to his responsibilities more'n a pack of young'uns of his own flesh and blood. It's the only way, Emma. Soon as I know you've got yourself in "the way" I'll send Mattie over. In the meantime you'd better start gettin' on with chores and wifely duties. If he throws you out you ain't comin' home. That's decided.'

It only took a few days to convince Emma that she'd best follow her mother's orders. It was not an easy proposition. Thom still continued to sleep every night in the front room and spent most of his waking hours in the fields or fishing. At first she tried simple hints.

'Don't seem fair, me havin' this big bed all to myself.'

Thom had mumbled for her not to worry herself, he liked it just fine in the front room.

In spite of her best efforts, their lives remained separate. By January the winter winds had settled in, whistling around the window frames and piercing her room with shafts of icy air. She tried again to change their arrangements.

'Gets mighty cold in my room, nights.'

He nodded like he understood but the next day, she'd been dismayed to find him patching the gaps and that night to find a brick at the bottom of her bed that he'd heated in the fire. A few nights later, in desperation, she tiptoed down the hall in the dark, in her flannel nightdress with a quilt wrapped like an animal hide around her shoulders. She found him sleeping on the rag rug, in front of the dying embers of the fire and she stood watching him in the flickering light. When she gently touched his shoulders, he sat up abruptly like a wild dog expecting danger. She took his hand in hers and without a word coaxed him up from the floor. Silently he padded down the hall behind her, and the next day she moved his personal effects from the front room to her own. Their life as man and wife had finally begun.

True to her mother's words, Emma saw a change in Thom's attitude as soon as their first son, Gene Allen, was born. But even before she knew she was pregnant she discovered a weakness in her husband's character that allowed her total control. In the privacy of their darkened bed, tipsy with physical pleasure, he had confided that except for a few ageing prostitutes he'd visited when he traveled to Atlanta twice a year for supplies, he had not had much experience. The feelings Emma stirred in him were new and exhilarating.

'It just weren't that important to me before.'

The stark honesty of his confession had urged her onwards and she had been pleased to find she had a carnal talent for combining delicate innocence with passionate eagerness. In spite of his awakened desires, however, he always waited for her instigation. Too shy to touch or kiss her without invitation, he amused her with his transparent eagerness – always searching, hoping and hinting for any chance to feel her soft young skin next to his. To bury his face in her hair and feel the emotional release of long-denied passion between her sweet legs. Emma took every opportunity to nurture the sexual control she wielded over him. She knew the time would come when the promise of pleasure could be a far more powerful tool than the pleasure itself.

Canaan

The mosquitoes had feasted on Canaan's ankles and were moving up to meatier territory. She stood and made her way towards Luke's shack. The family called it the Little House – another misleading title for a piece of Stewart property. It had begun life as the corncrib; made from scrap timber cobbled together and stacked on stones to keep varmints out of the corn harvest. Her grandmother still owned the land but the corn now belonged to Mr Nathan. When Lou Venie's husband had died leaving her with two young girls to raise and a farm to manage, she had survived and still survived by renting out what few acres hadn't turned to scrubland. Over the years Luke had scavenged enough tin, chipboard and window frames to turn the obsolete corncrib into something that almost resembled a home. As she neared it, she suddenly realized that it was more home to her than any other place she'd known.

Stepping onto the porch she scratched behind the ear of a gray-and-brown mongrel, one of many stray dogs that had hung around Lou Venie's farm over the years. If they stayed for more than a year, her grandmother named them, but most of the time they disappeared after a few months before another one turned up, looking for scraps. Cannan peered in through the ripped and rusty screen door.

'Uncle Luke?'

His back was to her but she knew he was reading, lost in his own world, his head bent close to the lantern. As she stepped inside the smell hit her right away; the dark familiar smell of dirt. The fuzzy-edged smell of molded vegetables and stale pipe smoke. She closed her eyes, and for a moment she was eight years old, glancing up as she read aloud from one of his books, searching for that sparkle of pride in Luke's eyes as he stared down the stem of his pipe.

The room was furnished with cast-off junk. A table with three legs, salvaged from the city dump. An upended apple crate serving as a bedside table and on top, a candle dribbling down two sides of an old vinegar bottle, a pair of rusty spoons and a pair of ancient hair clippers. The walls were lined with scraps of cardboard, insulation from winter winds, and around the room, hundreds of books were stacked like pancakes against the walls.

She walked up lightly behind him and touched his shoulder.

'Hey, Luke.'

He glanced behind him, grinning broadly.

'Well hey there, Candy-Cane.'

He tried to get up but she wrapped her arms around him squeezing gently.

'Missed you.'

'Ain't been nowhere.'

She squeezed tighter.

'I know. I should have written.'

Luke pulled her around to the light so he could see her better and she tried unsuccessfully to hide the bruises.

'I'm a mess, ain't I?'

He shrugged.

'It'll heal.'

He pulled out a crate for her to sit on, but she ignored it. She wasn't ready to face his gently probing eyes. She turned her back to him and absently examined the stacks of books. The rich, sweet aroma of pipe tobacco was thick in the room, just barely masking the stench of sweat, dirt and decay. It was a cocktail of smells that still conjured a feeling of safety for Canaan.

'Got some chicory brewin'.'

She smiled.

'No thanks. Too hot for coffee.'

He bent over and rummaged around in a large crate. Empty bottles clinked as he searched.

'Think I got a full bottle of RC cola somewhere.'

He waved a bottle triumphantly and smiled.

'Royal Crown – the drink of Kings!'

'No. I'm fine. Really.'

A toy dog caught her eye from the top shelf and she reached for it. It was carved from a corncob and she smiled as she turned it over in her hands.

'I wondered where he'd got to.'

It was the first of many home-made gifts Luke had given her as a child. Constantly whittling, he could transform any scrap of gnarled or twisted wood into a bird or a turtle or a sleeping bear. He'd left them on her windowsill wrapped in corn husks and tied with strips of monkey grass. The corncob dog was more primitive than the others, roughly carved and badly proportioned, but it had always been her favorite.

'Where'd you find him?'

'On the ditch bank. Lou Venie threw him out with the rest of your stuff after you left.'

He watched her for a reaction but she turned away.

'She was pretty mad at you back then but she didn't mean it. You just hurt her is all. Now you're home, you can have him back.'

Canaan shook her head and returned the dog to the shelf.

'No, I'm the one who left him behind. You saved him . . . you keep him.'

She walked around the room browsing through the book titles, then held one up to her nose, enjoying the dusty smell of its pages. It was an eclectic collection. There were quite a few classics scattered here and there, but many of the titles were along the lines of teaching yourself how to tune a piano, or breast-feed a baby or spice up a dinner party with animal-shaped hors d'oeuvres. In the seventies, he'd discovered garage sales and Lou Venie had let him keep the Friday evening papers, winking at Canaan as they watched him carefully circling the ones that interested him. *I reckon he only pays a nickel or two for them books. Never has more'n a nickel or two to his name. I bet they sell him the whole lot just to get rid of him.*

Every Saturday morning while eating their breakfast, they'd seen him heading down the road towards town, the Friday paper tucked in his back pocket. Around lunchtime he usually staggered back, wrestling with a cardboard box that buckled with the weight of other people's spare knowledge.

He was a man who cherished books. Liked their shape, their smell, their weight, the various textures of the paper and the different sounds they made when he turned the pages. It didn't matter that he would never own a piano or hold a dinner party. He simply loved the words. Any words. And when she was four years old he'd passed this passion on to her. Sitting on an upturned washtub below the single dirt-smeared window of the Little House, Canaan had spent her first summer at the Old Stewart Place learning to read. Luke had been a patient teacher, giving an encouraging grunt or a firm shake of the head, taking her small finger and moving it back to the words she'd missed, nodding with a satisfied smile when she hit upon the right sounds. Each morning after the eggs had been collected from the hen house and breakfast had been picked over, she'd raced down to the Little House for a lesson, her bare feet dodging the rocks and twigs on the path.

The tantrums had stopped and the nightmares had almost disappeared. Canaan had finally begun to settle into a new life at the Old Stewart Place. But not everyone in the family had been so happy with Canaan's new-found friendship. Her aunt Peggy was still living at home and was always unhappy about something – usually about the number of times she was sent to fetch Canaan from the Little House for supper.

He's crazy, Momma. You shouldn't oughta let her go down there. 'Sides – she stinks when she's been down there.

Suffering was what Peggy had always done best. Gravely disappointed that she'd inherited the worst of her parents' physical traits, she had forced her family to endure a long and difficult transition to adulthood.

It just ain't fair. Havin' the town idiot livin' in your back yard. It's no wonder I ain't had hardly three dates to my name.

Peggy's opinion of Luke had never mellowed and she had never fully forgiven Canaan for making him the center of her world.

Luke lifted the lantern and nodded for Canaan to take it.

'You cain't see good in this light.'

'You were reading . . .'

'Nothin' important. Go on.'

He nudged it towards her and she took it, continuing around the room. She knew he was watching her. Studying her. Patiently waiting for her to make up her mind to speak. But it was different this time. This time she was on her own and childhood heart-to-hearts weren't going to help. She stopped to study a collage of photos and newspaper clippings tacked to the wall. It was a shrine devoted to Canaan. Her greatest achievements. *My only achievements.* Some were carefully preserved behind dime-store frames. Others were held in place by dry-cleaning safety pins. In the center of the wall, in a frame made of real pine and real glass, was a picture of Canaan in her cap and gown. Holding tightly to the sides of the podium, she stood on tiptoe to reach the microphone.

'Lou Venie said you give a fine speech.'

Canaan swallowed the guilt.

'I'm sorry I didn't ask you to come, Luke.'

The adoration she'd felt so strongly as a child had diminished as she entered her teens, turning to embarrassment by the time she left for college. On her few visits home, she'd spent most of her time hiding in the bathroom when she heard him calling from beyond the front porch, or darting into the Laundromat when she spied him ambling across the town square. *He only wanted to hear about college. You should've talked to him.* But she'd been young and too eager to fit in with the rest of the world. *No different than Peggy.* It was easier to hide than to risk Luke pulling a stick of Juicy Fruit gum from behind her ear in front of her peers. *What you got growing back there, Candy-Cane?* She'd been allowed to invite two family members to her college graduation ceremony, but Lou Venie had come up alone. In the end Canaan had given the extra ticket to a classmate with whom she'd had a barely nodding acquaintance. She'd dismissed her grandmother's stony silence as a simple case of awe – her first time 'up North' – but later she'd found out that Lou Venie had prematurely invited Luke herself. Had even taken him up town to pick out a brand new shirt for the occasion. She'd never known what excuse her grandmother had given, or whether he'd ever known the truth.

Luke shook his head.

'Naw. I wouldn't have fit in. 'Sides, too far for me to walk and I cain't hop trains no more.'

He smiled at her but she turned away.

'You're the one who helped me get there, Luke. You should've been there.'

She studied the clippings. They were brown and curled at the edges but the pictures and the words were still clear. And the emotions were still fresh in her heart. *Honor Student Wins Scholarship to William and Mary; Canaan Phillips Looks to the Future.*

'Readin's the easy part, Canaan. What you done – all them things you accomplished – you done that all by yourself.'

She sighed. She wanted to talk to him. Sit down on an old apple crate or an overturned washtub in their usual place and talk to him like before. Tell him about the dark demons that visited her every night in her dreams and were now venturing into her waking, daylight hours. But she also wanted to sweep the photographs from the wall, rip the clippings down and wipe that look of pride from his battered old face. *You want to know what I accomplished, Luke? You want to know what my life in New York was really like?* But of course she wouldn't. Couldn't. She was afraid if she spoke about what was in her head, it would all come gushing out and she'd lose the tiny fragment of control she'd managed to hang onto.

One of the clippings had curled up completely on itself and Canaan pressed it open with her hand, holding the lantern closer. It was a picture of herself and her high-school English teacher, Zeke Forrest. They were holding a large trophy between them and the caption read: *L.H.S. Student Wins State Championship in Debate.* Zeke smiled proudly into the camera lens while a teenaged Canaan gazed adoringly at him. Zeke had bewitched them all, sitting cross-legged on top of his desk, damning convention by wearing blue jeans, and daring to wear a ponytail in a small, deeply conservative

Southern town. Canaan had thrown herself wholeheartedly into editing the student newspaper, just to spend more time with him in the afternoons, hoping to be at the receiving end of those smiling gray eyes. She'd joined the debate team only because there were day trips out of town and if she timed things right, he'd sit next to her on the bus.

During one of her trips home, Canaan had heard that he'd finally broken many hopeful hearts by marrying a woman who'd moved to Lander to manage the new shopping mall in Garland. But Canaan still liked to believe that she and Zeke had shared something special. Something that transcended simple schoolgirl crushes. He'd made her believe she had something to offer the world. Encouraged her to leave Lander. Helped her apply for the scholarship. He'd even paid for her bus ticket and got up before dawn to wave her goodbye. Zeke was the only one who'd pushed her to look beyond Lander and the only one who could have given her a reason to stay.

'I seen Zeke up town. Told him you was comin' home.'

Canaan turned sharply.

'Why did you do that?'

'Thought you was friends.'

'You've got no right—'

She stopped and sighed, hating the hint of Lou Venie in her voice.

'Don't interfere, Luke. I got enough of that right now.'

She left the lantern on the table and turned to go.

'I gotta finish unpacking.'

'We ain't hardly talked yet.'

'I'll come back down tomorrow.'

He looked doubtful. *And so frail.* She tried to smile like she meant it.

'I promise.'

He reached for the clipping and held it up.

'You can have it if you want. It's yours anyways. I saved it when . . . when Lou Venie threw it all out.'

He waved it towards her but she smiled sadly.

'That stuff doesn't matter to me anymore, Luke. You should have just left it on the ditch bank.'

Luke

August 1912

It smelled like rain. The dark hint of damp dirt filled the kitchen where Emma stood scraping the leftovers from breakfast into two battered tin dishes. She glanced through the window across the upper fields where an early-morning storm spread like a cloud of ink towards the farm. *Good thing too*. Her tomato plants were barely hanging on and the parched, cracked complexion of the creek-bed was a daily reminder that she'd lost most of the poke salad crop she'd cultivated over the past seven years.

Thom's daddy had used the creek bank as a dumping ground for vegetable peels and fish heads and each week he'd included a few squirrel carcasses and any other vermin he'd caught pilfering the corncrib. By the time Emma married Thom, the soil along the bank had become a stretch of dark rich earth. It was the perfect spot for growing the sweet green weed – a summer staple for the poorer families in the valley. There was something deliciously dangerous about poke salad that raised it above the bitter turnip or dandelion greens. Every drop of liquid from the first boiled pot was poisonous and it had to be drained and re-boiled several times in fresh water before it was safe to eat. But Emma liked the danger and thought it was worth the trouble when it was mixed with chopped boiled eggs and onion and eaten with a fresh skillet of cornbread.

She inhaled deeply through the window, breathing in the promise of rain. On the screened porch outside the window, the boy Luke was still sleeping, wrapped in a quilt that was stained and frayed at the corners. He looked much older than his seven years. His arms and legs had grown beyond the proportions of his torso and his hair was matted in irregular clumps – as if everything about him grew at different rates. He was dressed in a second-hand pair of men's denim overalls, rolled up at the ankles and tied at the waist with a rope. They were Thom's of course. No use in wasting a good pair of overalls on a boy who was sprouting up the way he was. *No use in wasting anything on a boy like him.* The smell of sweat and dirt drifted in from the boy's corner and Emma frowned. *Filth. Pure filth. Time for a scrubbin'.* She returned to the sink, working her way through the morning dishes while Thom finished his coffee at the end of the table and read the *Lander Star*. He'd been up for hours and had tended to the daily chores before the first streaks of amber had appeared above the surrounding hills. He was leaving soon to collect the double-gauged chicken wire he'd ordered from Pete's Mercantile and Emma knew he'd consider that enough of an excuse to stay in town for the better part of the day, drinking with the boys at Duke's.

'Lou Venie, stop playin' in your gravy and bring me your plate.'

The little girl froze, her finger dripping with milk gravy, shiny with bacon fat. She paused to test the seriousness of her mother's demand and after a few seconds decided it was safe to resume her play. She wasn't a big eater, more of a mover. She transported food around her plate, sneaked a spoonful or two of scrambled eggs onto her baby brother's plate and occasionally slipped a piece of sausage into the pocket of her dress.

'Lou Venie, you want me to fetch a switch?'

Emma spoke without raising her voice but the threat in her tone was clear and her daughter quickly climbed down from her chair and carried the plate to the sink, taking great care not to spill the gravy from the narrow rim. Lou Venie's biscuit had been nibbled around the sides and her tiny four-year-old teeth left a dainty scalloped edge. Emma plopped it onto one of the tin plates and scraped the congealed gravy on top.

Their oldest child Gene Allen raced through the kitchen on his way out the back door with his two-year-old brother, John Curtis, galloping behind him. Emma grabbed the taller boy by the neck. Her children had been born close together, just as her mother had advised. *Give the man a houseful of his own young'uns and he'll move heaven and earth for you.* But once her duty was over, Emma started making new plans. The day after the youngest, John Curtis, was born, Thom came home to find his clothes and toiletries stacked neatly outside her room and the door bolted from inside. It had taken her three months to lure him into her bedroom and less than four years to move him out. She was nineteen and her family was complete. His services no longer needed. As usual he accepted whatever Emma demanded without a fight and spent the summer months building a lean-to bedroom on the back of the house, just big enough for a single bed and a small nightstand. He settled without a fuss into the position Emma created for him in the family unit, allowing her complete control in raising their children and establishing household rules as she saw fit.

Emma slapped Gene Allen on the side of the head.

'What'd I tell you 'bout runnin' in my house?'

She held him firmly by the back of his neck.

'Take Lou Venie and your little brother outside and sweep up the yard.'

Gene Allen twisted his head around and let the beginning

note of a whine escape before he caught the cold glint in his mother's eye. He slumped beneath her grasp.

'Yes, ma'am.'

As the boys scurried out, Emma picked up one of the tin plates from the sideboard and took it to the back porch. Lou Venie, squatting on her haunches beside Luke, had taken a piece of sausage from her pocket and was holding it out for him.

'Lou Venie!'

Both children jumped as Luke tried quickly to grab it from her, but Emma lifted Lou Venie by one arm and dragged her into the kitchen.

'What have I said? You stay away from him. He's dirty. You hear me?'

The little girl nodded solemnly and Emma snatched the sausage and put it on top of the plate of scraps.

'Now get out there with your brothers like I told you.'

Emma pushed her towards the front door and returned to the back porch. She opened the outer screen and whistled.

'Goldie!'

She whistled again.

'Come on, girl.'

From the upper field she could see the boisterous gallop of the shaggy mongrel that had adopted them the summer before. She put the plate on the top step then dropped a second plate of biscuits and gravy onto the floor beside Luke.

'Get up, boy.'

She nudged him roughly with her foot.

'You been layin' around enough today.'

He looked up at her, his stone-colored eyes cautious as he searched her face. She used her foot to shove the plate closer to him.

'Go on. Eat your breakfast 'fore I give it to the dog.'

By this time, Goldie had leapt to the top step, her wide body pressing against and swelling the screen door. Her tail knocked ecstatically against the door facing while she devoured her breakfast. Luke took his plate, scooping the scraps of soggy biscuits into his mouth with his fingers.

The first few months of his life Luke had wailed continually, crying less frequently and with less demand as time passed, until one day, just before his second birthday, he simply stopped crying altogether and adopted a quiet watchfulness which would define him for the rest of his life. In the beginning, he slept in the back bedroom with the other children; invisible to his mother and excluded from evening prayers and kisses. Even Myra lost interest in him, turning her attention to the offspring she considered her true grandchildren. Mute and awkward, he was moved out to the back porch soon after his fourth birthday about the same time Thom was moved to the lean-to. Folks rarely asked questions but those who did were told Luke was simple-minded and Emma didn't want him mixing with her babies. Most people knew about the boy. Where he'd come from. They reckoned the back porch was as good a place as any for his kind.

Only Thom had tried to show some compassion for the boy, but he didn't have the stomach for Emma's violent tantrums or vicious punishments. His interference usually brought more harm than good and before long he, too, was able to ignore Luke's existence. It was safer for the boy.

'You want more coffee?'

The screen door slammed behind her as she came back into the kitchen and Emma noticed the nervous, involuntary flex in her husband's shoulders. He had something on his mind. She could always tell by the way he wiggled his finger in the handle of his coffee cup. And the way the two muscles in the back of his neck stood out like steel rods. He was working up his courage for something.

'Naw, I got plenty.'

She could have gone back to the sink. Finished the dishes

she'd already started. But she didn't. Instead, she reached across the table for Gene Allen's plate, her shoulder just missing Thom's chin. She knew his entire body had gone as rigid as his neck. Knew he was breathing her in. Enjoying the smell of soap and bacon grease and that smell he said belonged just to her. That deep, dark smell that hid in the creases behind her knees, in the crook of her arm and the side of her nose. Those intimate places she rarely let him visit these days. She pulled a cloth from the band of her apron and reached again to wipe the tiny dollops of gravy from the table. Great sweeping circles that laced the air with her smell. Small urgent circles, moving ever closer to him. A strand of her hair fell from the knot at the nape of her neck and she knew he wanted to touch it. Drape it across his face. Taste it. Thom's finger moved frantically inside the handle, his fingernail tapping against the cup.

'You got something you wanna talk about, Thom?'

He looked startled.

'No. Naw. I . . . no . . . I got nothin' to say.'

She returned to the sink, smiling to herself.

'You just looked like you had something on your mind.'

'No. I was just . . . no . . . not a thing.'

She enjoyed this part. He'd stammer a few more minutes. Tap his coffee cup. Glance outside to make sure the children were out of earshot. Then, chopping his words into painful bite-sized pieces he'd ask if she reckoned he could come to her room that night. He cleared his throat.

'There was somethin' I was thinkin'. Before, I mean.'

Thom gulped the final swallow of his coffee and pushed the cup across the table.

'I run into Mizz Colt, yestidy evenin'.'

Emma stopped smiling and reached for the pump handle, heaving it furiously up and down. Water gushed over the dirty dishes, splattering gravy over the front of her only clean work dress. He might have just been making conversation but she knew by the steel rods in his neck he was planning to drag that woman and her crusade right back into her own kitchen. Miss Colt was the new teacher in Lander, a do-gooder, busybody from North Carolina who thought it was her duty to tell hard-working country folks how things ought to be done. People had been complaining about her habit of going door to door, like a Bible salesman. Stopping people on the streets. Chastising them for keeping their children out of school. Paying no mind to the fact that cotton had to be picked, and small farms depended on every living and breathing child to work during planting and harvest just to survive. And when people tried to tell her so, she always said the same thing: *Well, back in North Carolina . . .*

The year before, she'd shown up on the back porch of the Old Stewart Place, pushing a first-grade reader into Luke's hands and accusing Emma of failing in a Mother's Duty. Emma had told her to get off her porch and had gone back into the house for Thom's squirrel gun. Just to convince the woman along. But as soon as her back was turned, the teacher had followed her into the kitchen, explaining how important it was for poor families like hers to break the poverty cycle by educating their young. Emma couldn't remember much about what happened next, but neighbors told her later that she'd chased Miss Colt clear up to the Pig Wilson farm, with a butcher knife.

'She said . . .'

Thom lifted the coffee cup to his lips, forgetting that he'd finished it, hoping for one more galvanizing sip.

'Said we oughta think 'bout sendin' the boy to school when Gene Allen starts next week.'

Emma turned to let him see the full power of her fury.

'You got no right speakin' to that woman.'

'I couldn't ignore her, Emma. I was just bein' polite.'

Emma scooped out a handful of bacon fat from the lard jar and began to oil the skillet.

'The boy's simple. He ain't goin' to school.'

'He's a little bit slow but I reckon he'll do fine if you give him a chance. Might be good for him to be in the same class as his brother.'

She slammed the skillet onto the table.

'Don't you ever call him that. I ain't havin' Gene Allen tarred with the same brush as that boy.'

'You won't let me use him in the fields, Emma. You might as well let him go to school. Might find somethin' he's good at.'

'How many times I got to remind you? That boy ain't yours. You got no say in nothin' havin' to do with him. I say he's not goin' to school and I 'spect you to say nothin' more about it.'

Thom picked up his hat from the side table and settled it carefully on his head. He gave a small cough, the closest thing to a goodbye or hello he'd ever mustered. Emma continued to oil the skillet.

'Gene Allen is startin' school next week, Thom. He's goin' by hisself and that's all I'm gonna say.'

As she watched the buggy amble up the hill, the dark clouds opened and the rain poured like a bucket of dishwater. Thom pulled the brim of his hat down over his brow and hunched his shoulders forward, driving headfirst into the storm.

Canaan

She found the old blue Mustang parked behind the barn, tucked up beneath a corrugated lean-to and draped in old dust sheets. Jonathon had said having two cars in New York was an unnecessary luxury, so she had reinforced the supports that joined the shed to the side of the barn, tacked up plastic sheeting to keep out the wind and rain and packed it up like a priceless Fabergé egg. The money would have come in handy, but Canaan had not had the heart to sell it before she'd left Lander. *'Cause you knew all along you'd be back.* Her uncle Mert had dutifully cared for it while she was away, taking it out for an occasional run on the country roads to loosen its arthritic joints and to keep senility from creeping into its engine. *Give you five hundred dollars for her. Cash. Right here.* Uncle Mert had offered the same price every time Canaan came home for a visit, but they both knew she'd never take whatever was offered and they both knew that if she did, her aunt Peggy would sentence her husband to the sofa bed. A neglected Mustang, classic or not, would have clashed with Aunt Peggy's coordinated ranch house and her matching Caddy parked in her rose-lined driveway. *I will not have people thinkin' we lean on the side of poor white trash. Might as well have a sofa on the front porch.*

As her marriage had disintegrated, Canaan's visits had grown more sporadic and after a few years they'd stopped altogether. Jonathon had only made the trip once. Just after they'd married. A honeymoon he'd called it, following an impromptu wedding ceremony that seemed, at the time, romantic. Canaan had been wearing a pair of blue jeans and a tube top she'd been traveling in for three days. He'd seen the home-made Justice-of-the-Peace sign, propped against a mailbox from the New Jersey turnpike and without so much as a proposal, he'd carried her over the threshold of the small white-frame house and married her.

He didn't take well to the South during that visit, and the South liked him even less. From the first day, the sun blistered the translucent tip of his nose and pumped his lips full of water. His feet swelled like well-risen dough over the tops of his loafers and the mosquitoes flocked from all over the county to sample his virgin skin. Canaan's two-week honeymoon ended after four days, and in the years that followed she'd made her rare homeward treks alone.

The Mustang had hardly aged during Canaan's time away and as she gently pulled the covers from the car, she caressed the smooth curve of the door. She'd worked double shifts in the day and graveyard shifts on the weekends in a steamy Italian restaurant that was two blocks away from the college. It had taken every spare hour of overtime to keep ahead of her fees for the following semester. When her scholarship had finally come through, she'd blown every penny she'd saved on the car. It meant freedom. It meant she was on her way up from the red dirt of Alabama.

She slipped into the bucket seat. The smell of the cracked leather seats conjured phantom aromas and she settled in to enjoy their memories. Suntan lotion with cocoa-butter and the smell of lake water in her hair after a lazy afternoon at Crystal Springs. Stale Pall Malls. The sharp, pine-needle smell of the Avon air freshener that always rattled around under the seat – her feeble attempt to hide the smell of cigarettes from her grandmother.

She gently encouraged the engine to life and listened to the churning and chugging that had once filled her with visions of her future. Awkward and tentative at first, she was over-cautious with the gears, but old habits took over once she was on the back roads that led to town. The roads where she'd first learned to drive. She raced along, flinging chunks of Alabama clay into the rainwater ditches on either side of the road, speeding past colonies of flimsy house trailers and yards scattered like battlefields with bicycle parts, discarded mattresses, and the hollow shells of washing machines.

Hammett's Oil was the only place left that offered full service. The other two gas stations in town were self-serve and soulless. A solitary antisocial employee sat inside a coffin-sized glass booth, usually reading a Danielle Steele or a Zane Gray, and never making eye contact. They could take your money, give you change, or swipe your credit card without missing a single plot line. Even in a town as isolated and insignificant as Lander, progress had a way of sneaking in. While Canaan had been away, a Burger King had popped up at the interstate junction. It wasn't quite inside Lander city limits, but it was close enough to give the teenagers a new place to hang out on the weekends. The Old Caldwell Place, a buttery-yellow house with black shutters, where the town doctor had lived and tended to the sick, had been torn down and replaced with a dry-cleaners. A sprawling single-story medical center had been built in the middle of a field once rich with cotton and soy beans. And instead of a town doctor the town folk went to see fresh-faced doctors in crisp white coats and city-styled hair, who smiled a lot, and called everyone by their first name, without really knowing them. Even

Piggly Wiggly, that shining beacon of traditional family-style grocery stores, had revamped itself. Ditching the 1950s linoleum and the giant papier-mâché pig's head, they'd added a sleek new deli, a pharmacist, and a counter to rent movies. While Lander had progressed in many ways, its attitudes and moral judgements remained the same and nothing could transport a person back in time like a visit to Hammett's Oil. It sat on the same corner across from Lander High School and looked exactly the same as it had when Canaan was sixteen and sneaked over the road to buy a pack of Pall Malls before study hall. The Pall Malls were still there, same place, third box from the left on the third shelf. So were the peanut butter and cheese crackers she used to buy to hide the smell of tobacco on her breath.

As she drove the Mustang into the forecourt a gangly eighteen-year-old came out to greet her. He looked the car over, barely disguising his lust. His hands looked like they'd already seen twenty years of grease and oil as they moved tenderly across the bodywork.

'Ain't seen her around.'

'Been locked up in the barn for a while.'

She almost said, *Before you were born, buck-er-oo*. He nodded and continued his public caressing before lovingly lifting the hood.

'How much you want for her?'

'I don't want to sell it.'

She joined him and peered into the engine trying to see what he saw.

'I know it needs some work.'

He gave an exaggerated snort.

'You got that right.'

He lowered the hood and she followed him as he circled the car. He squatted beside the open window and let his hand glide over the seasoned leather seat.

'She's a beauty all right. Or used to be. Dang . . . I'd have loved to seen her in her prime.'

He stood up and crossed his arms.

'I can give you cash.'

'It's not for sale. Please . . . can't you just give me an estimate?'

His face slumped but he nodded submissively.

'Yes, ma'am. If that's what you want.'

'No bodywork . . . I just want to get it running. I'm planning a long trip.'

'How long?'

'I'm not sure. Few thousand miles maybe.'

He whistled.

'Sheesh, lady, I ain't no miracle worker.'

'Can you just try? I'd be very grateful.'

She flashed him what she hoped was a coquettish smile, but was immediately struck by the absurdity of flirting with an eighteen-year-old kid. She was relieved that he didn't seem to have noticed.

'Yes, ma'am. I'll sure do my best. I'll just get her up on the rack and have a look.'

She handed him the keys and he slid behind the wheel, taking a moment to savor the fit. As he drove into the dark recess of the garage, she pulled a bottled drink from the ice chest out front. It wasn't even eight o'clock yet and the heat was already working on her. Her T-shirt was sticking to the small of her back and her cotton shorts felt damp and lifeless. She wandered over to a scruffy lawn chair positioned under the only sliver of shade available and sat down. The frayed webbing scratched the backs of her legs and the aluminum frame was warm enough to feel uncomfortable. Across the road students gathered on the school lawn waiting for the first bell. The laughter and chattering brought a tightening in Canaan's stomach and she suddenly felt vulnerable and open.

The bruises had disappeared but she still imagined that people could tell. She focused her attention on reading the labels on the cans of Quaker State. She couldn't bring herself to look across the road. Not even a glance.

Zeke Forrest always looked as though he'd just tumbled out of bed and slipped into the first thing he could lay his hands on. And it was this rumpled casualness that appealed most to the opposite sex. While other men in their early forties seemed worn down by mortgages, beer guts and their children's orthodontist bill, Zeke seemed to have nothing more pressing to worry about than whether or not to comb his hair. He'd always been handsome but age had settled better on his shoulders than most and his middle-age status had certainly not deterred his teenage students from lustful thoughts. As he hurried through the morning crowd gathered outside Lander High School, he smiled amiably to familiar faces. No one noticed or seemed to care that he was carrying a dog's water bowl. He slipped around the side of the building and, checking his watch, half-jogged towards the student patio outside the cafeteria. Henry, the janitor, was hosing it down, force-spraying cigarette butts, candy wrappers and banana skins into a drainage gully. As Zeke hurried towards him he automatically twisted the nozzle to low.

'You're late, Zeke.'

He filled the water bowl.

'Overslept.'

'Late night?'

'Mid-term essays on Nathaniel Hawthorne.'

Henry nodded wisely.

'That'd sure as hell put me to sleep.'

Water spilled over the sides and Zeke turned to go.

'Thanks, Henry.'

'Hey, Zeke. When you gonna get a real dog?'

Zeke smiled and shook his head.

'I'm not gonna tell him you said that, Henry. It would crush his spirit.'

There were two things that were a constant in Zeke's life. His trademarks. One was the raggedy, badly patched VW van that he'd driven across America, back when he was sure that Jack Kerouac had all the answers. His second trademark always sat in the passenger seat of said VW van and rarely managed more than a sluggish sigh, no matter how much attention was poured on him. Stonewall was the laziest of basset hounds. Even as a puppy he'd seemed bored with the prospect of living on earth and had promptly settled in to wait for his time to run out.

'Hey, Stonewall. Henry says hi.'

Without moving his head, the dog rolled his eyes towards his master. Zeke pushed open the side door of the van and placed the bowl of water just inside.

'You ready, bud?'

He opened the passenger door and awkwardly picked the dog up in his arms, transferring him to the back of the van. Stonewall flopped down without moving an inch beyond his landing position and Zeke flipped the switch on a battery-powered fan that was clipped to the door frame. He fiddled with the controls, turning it to blow directly onto Stonewall.

'Where's your hot dog? Huh?'

Zeke searched amongst the blankets and various doggie playthings until he found the plastic hot dog. He squeaked it enthusiastically and placed it under Stonewall's paw.

'There you go. All set.'

The dog remained emotionally detached, moving only his eyes as Zeke grabbed a backpack from the front seat and a cardboard box filled with student essays.

'You free for lunch?'

The dog made no response.

'Me too. The usual?'

The dog blinked lazily and yawned.

'You got it. Turkey hoagie . . . hold the mayo.'

He slammed the front door of the van and sprinted across the parking lot trying to balance the box of papers on his hip. A cluster of girls called out to him as he passed.

'Hey, Mr Forrest!'

'Ladies.'

He nodded, a sharp, sexy little dip of his chin, which sent them giggling into a tight girlish knot. He was almost up the steps when he was stopped by a boy who was wearing a letter jacket in spite of the heat and who was tossing a football and chewing gum with equal dexterity.

'Mr Forrest . . . you comin' to the game tonight?'

'I don't know. You coming to my English class today?'

'Aw, that ain't fair. I only missed twice.'

'Hobie, school started last week. That's not what I'd call a good start to the year.'

He slapped Hobie good-naturedly on the back and took the last two steps in one go. Inside, the hallway hummed with the sound of locker chatter, lovers' spats and the enthusiasm that comes with being young and the inventors of all that's new. The walls and ceilings were crawling with crepe-paper streamers and booster banners. *Go Golden Eagles!* In his khaki trousers and red polo shirt he stood out in a walking, talking sea of royal blue and gold. A table was set up near the principal's office and Bernie Douthitt, a black woman in her mid-thirties, was busy selling spirit badges. Zeke shifted the box to another hip and tried to hurry past her. He turned the corner as she caught sight of him.

'Zeke! Zeke Forrest, don't you run from me. You know I'll catch you.'

He stopped by the water fountain and reluctantly waited for her to catch up.

'I don't suppose you'd get off my back if I bought one of those damned spirit badges, would you?'

'Come on, Zeke, break a habit of a lifetime and speak at the pep rally this afternoon.'

'Bernie . . . you know how I feel.'

'I know. But I also know that if word got around that you were giving the pep talk today we'd have to stuff 'em into the gym with a shoe horn.'

She gave him her best begging look.

'Oh, come on . . . the girls have worked really hard on a new routine for today. I want a big crowd.'

'You've already had your pound of flesh out of me, Bernie Douthitt. You tricked me.'

'Oh, you're not still sore about the reunion speech, are you? You *were* the class sponsor. It's your job.'

He looked at her accusingly until she weakened.

'Oh, OK. I know I should have told you about the Mrs Olsenbacher thing . . . but this is different.'

'I can't do it, Bernie.'

'Look, Zeke . . . you owe me.'

'How do you figure?'

'Do you have any idea how hard it is to teach on the same English course as you? I can't compete with you. I mean, you're the reason I became the cheerleader sponsor to begin with. Had to do something to make me feel worthwhile, didn't I? Please, Zeke.'

She smiled eagerly up at him and he smiled charmingly back.

'No.'

He continued down the hall as she called after him.

'But they love you, Zeke.'

'No!'

In the staffroom Zeke poured himself a cup of coffee and joined his friend Jimmy at the window. Jimmy sighed as he stared at the pageant of teenage girls on the grass outside.

'God . . . I love the smell of young flesh first thing in the mornin'.'

Zeke took a sip of his coffee.

'You're disgusting.'

'Well, at least I have the decency to pretend. You've got 'em layin' at your feet and all you can think about is their SAT scores.'

He nodded towards a group of freshly scrubbed beauties.

'I mean . . . look at that.'

'Out of bounds, Jimbo.'

'I know that . . . but why can't you just once act like every other self-respecting divorced man around here? Lie. Let us no-hopers pretend somebody's scorin'.'

Canaan's car pulled into the service station across the road and Zeke watched her as she talked to the mechanic.

'You remember Canaan Phillips? Class of '84?'

'Nice legs. Hair you'd wanna run barefoot in?'

Zeke smiled patiently.

'Honor student. Scholarship to William and Mary.'

'You remember what you want, I'll remember what I want. Why you askin'?'

He nodded over to where she was sitting. Jimmy sucked in a big mouthful of air.

'Whoa now. Hold on. I know that look.'

He glanced at Jimmy who was smiling back with a big goofy, know-it-all grin.

'Don't tell me Mr Straight-and-Narrow is interested in a student?'

'Ex-student.'

Jimmy rubbed his hands together.

'Well, well! The boy ain't perfect.'

He sidled up closer.

'So was there? . . . you know . . .'

'No, nothing happened.'

'R-i-i-ight!'

'Oh hell, Jimmy. I was a kid myself, too scared of losing my first job.'

'Yeah, but I bet she was hot for you.'

'The only thing Canaan Phillips was hot for was gettin' out of Lander. So when she got her chance I gave her my address and wished her luck. The End.'

'Did she write?'

'Sent me a wedding announcement.'

'Youch.'

The bell rang for class.

'Showtime!'

Jimmy guzzled his coffee and left.

Across the road, Canaan seemed to be studying the pyramid of oil cans and a scrap of her hair had slipped from its ponytail to obscure her features. Zeke watched her a few more moments, hoping she'd look his way, before finally following Jimmy to class.

Luke

Luke was good at being invisible. Blending into the background was the only way to survive his mother's tantrums and in the first eight years of his life he had perfected a talent for keeping as low a profile as possible in the corner of the back porch where he lived. The issue of going to school or not going to school had never been that important to him. It was just another emotive topic that seemed to bring him more attention and stirred up his mother's wrath. Judging by Gene Allen's whining complaints the year before, Luke had come to equate learning with a form of punishment anyway and had shown little interest. His attitude had changed, however, this year when Lou Venie came home from her first day at Lander Elementary clutching her Reader's Primary and bursting with detailed accounts of classroom life. For the first time in his young life, he ventured from the safety of his secret cocoon to listen when his sister practiced her reading skills. He eavesdropped on homework lessons and became obsessed with the words he knew were locked away inside the library books that Lou Venie brought home for Thom to read to her.

It was spring before he first dared enter the house to whisk one of the books away for a few hours of frustrating study. In the fields each night, under the rustling canopy of corn, he had burrowed between the rows working relentlessly by flickering lantern light. Understanding was just beyond his grasp and each time he fought the inevitable disappointment as he returned the book to Lou Venie's satchel before sunrise.

His mental restlessness was soon matched by his need to test his physical boundaries which subconsciously confined him to the farm. He began by exploring the outer edges of his world and beyond by choosing a visible landmark, and upon reaching it, choosing another; the creek bank one day, the line of trees above the upper north field the next. His paths continued to spread in a full circle, like spokes in a wagon wheel, around the farm, until one day he had been aiming for a water tower he had seen in the distance, and had discovered the railroad line.

The tracks provided a wealth of oddities like animal skulls, rusty spikes and shotgun shells. Most importantly, it proved to be a valuable map that allowed Luke to explore at safe distances, always leading him back to the farm. It had eventually led him beyond the bend of White's Gap Ridge and it had been on that day that he had seen the tree house for the first time.

It was a simple platform, with timber half-walls on four sides, safely balanced in the ample arms of the tree. Strips of wood had been nailed to the trunk of the tree to form a ladder and it disappeared into a hole in the middle of the floor. Consumed with curiosity, he had crawled through the high grass on his belly for a closer look.

'Hey!'

From his prone position in the grassy trench he had carved across the field, he looked up to see the face of a young girl peering down from the platform. He ducked down as if it would hide him from her eyes.

'What you doin' down there?'

He looked up, peeping through the curtained safety of the waving blades of grass.

'You can come up here if you like. Come on. It's all right.'

Her name was Estelle Patterson and she spent most of that first day telling him her life story, along with every scrap of information on life that she had managed to gather in her nine years. She was the only child of the shipping manager at the cotton mill and her mother had been a debutante in Montgomery. He didn't know what a debutante was, but based on the reverence in Estelle's voice it was pretty important.

Luke sat cross-legged for hours while Estelle told him about the hundred or so toys and dolls she owned, listing and naming them all for him. The tree house had been a birthday present from her father, she'd said, but her mother didn't like it much; thought it wasn't ladylike and didn't want it too close to the house. Estelle liked to talk and Luke liked to listen. She attempted a few questions, but he had either ignored them or shrugged as he hugged his knees tighter to his chest. She didn't seem worried, but was content to gabble endlessly about whatever entered her head.

Every day after that, he waited for her, squatting in the high grass, until she waved him up the ladder. In the beginning she had invented a new game for each day, delighted to have found such an agreeable and malleable playmate. He said little and submitted to Estelle's wishes without question, patiently fanning her with a make-believe palm leaf while she lounged in decorated splendor as the Queen of Sheba. On other days, he allowed her to dress him in a crumpled shawl and a straw hat with droopy flowers and tattered netting. Barely flinching when she screwed the pearl-drop earrings onto the fleshy part of his ear lobes, he sat quietly in Estelle's dress-up clothes while she gossiped about dinner parties and new fashions, nibbling invisible cake and drinking make-believe tea.

They would have continued in this way had she not eventually suggested they play school. Luke's reaction was immediately animated and she was delighted with his eager acceptance. It was even better than tea parties as far as Estelle was concerned. She basked in Luke's open admiration and she devoted the remaining days of summer to teaching him to read. She took her role seriously, giving him black glass beads from her mother's button tin as rewards and scolding him if he forgot to raise his hand before answering a question.

One day in late August, she let him begin a new book but had grown weary of his stuttering attempts over difficult words and insisted that she should read the remainder of the story. Estelle liked to play teacher but she liked to show off even more. Luke sat glumly by, waiting for her to get bored and let him have another chance.

'Estelle?'

Estelle's mother shouted from below, making them both jump. In all the time he had spent in the tree house, he had never seen Mrs Patterson, only heard her call from the porch or the kitchen window.

'Essie, honey – you up there?'

'Yes, ma'am. We're playin' school.'

'You got somebody up there with you?'

'Yessum.'

'Well, come on down and I'll fix you some lemonade. You can have some sugar cookies if you want.'

'Yes, ma'am! We sure do!'

Estelle jumped up and started down the ladder.

'Come on. You like cookies and lemonade, don't ya?'

He nodded, having no idea what they were and as she disappeared like a rabbit down the hole, he looked longingly at the discarded book but followed behind her.

'You should have told me you had company, Estelle. You know I always like to meet your friends.'

As Luke glanced down in search of the next step, he could

see Estelle's mother staring at his calloused feet, black with layered dirt. When he reached the ground she continued to stare, taking in the lanky, unwashed hair that hung to his shoulders and he self-consciously tucked one long strand behind his ear. As her eyes moved critically down his thin frame and grimy overalls he dropped his eyes and used his big toe to drill beneath the soft layer of dead pine needles to the dirt below.

'You one of Estelle's school friends?'

He shook his head. Estelle, who was accustomed to doing all the talking, chimed in with answers.

'He don't go to school, Momma.'

'He "doesn't" go to school, Estelle.'

Estelle rolled her eyes.

'Doesn't, doesn't, doesn't.'

Mrs Patterson circled around him.

'You visitin' somebody?'

'He lives on the other side of the ridge, Momma.'

'What's your name?'

'His name's Luke. Can we go get our cookies now?'

Mrs Patterson ignored her daughter and continued to stare at Luke, a false smile frozen on her face.

'What's your folks' name?'

For once Estelle couldn't answer for him. She'd never bothered to ask him his last name. He dug his toe deeper into the dirt, almost losing his balance.

'S-S-Stewart.'

Her look of polite puzzlement disappeared as recognition dawned in her eyes.

'You're that idiot boy of Emma Stewart's, aren't you? I thought she kept you locked up. Like father, like son . . .'

She stopped as if she'd lost her breath and spinning around, grabbed Estelle by the shoulders.

'What were you doin' up there, Estelle?'

'Playin', Momma.'

Mrs Patterson sank to her knees and faced her daughter. 'Did he touch you?'

The little girl looked confused.

'We were just . . . he wanted . . .'

A darkness swept over the woman's face and gripping Estelle roughly by the shoulders, she shook her until the girl's head jostled from side to side.

'Essie, tell Momma what he did. Momma won't be mad. Just tell her the truth. Where did he touch you?'

Her mother's voice rose to a hysterical screech and Estelle burst into tears. Mrs Patterson let go of her daughter and stood, swinging around to face Luke.

'Get out of here, you filthy piece of trash. If I find out you've hurt my little girl . . .'

She stopped to search the ground and picked up a thick branch. Luke stumbled backwards, falling against the tree as she lunged at him, waving the branch and screaming.

'Get out of here. Don't you ever let me see you here again. You hear me?'

She picked up stones and branches, hurling them at him as he stumbled down the incline and ran across the field and through the tall grass. Her screams tore at him and followed him as he continued to run, long after he was out of range of her angry missiles. It was the last time he saw Estelle, but not the last time he saw Mrs Patterson.

Canaan

Canaan dozed in the late September sun, lulled by the gentle
lapping of lake water against the flat boulder she was lying
on. Patterson Lake wasn't the most popular waterside spot
in Lander. It lacked the depth that lured serious fishermen
and it hid enough stumps just below the surface to ward
off speedboats and waterskiers. The water's edge was either
a tangled mess of brambles or an assault course of rocks and
boulders, so with Crystal Springs and Holt Lake to choose
from, swimmers and families had never bothered with
Patterson. The big plus for Canaan was that she could walk
there without going near the highway. She'd been walking a
lot lately. Ever since the mechanic had laid her one-and-only
escape plan to rest. She'd suspected it all along but now it
was confirmed. It was going to take a lot of money or a
major miracle for her Mustang to get her as far from Lander
as she wanted. She'd be lucky if it got her to the state line, the
boy had said. *Good enough for gettin' around town. Long as
you ain't in no hurry.* She'd taken it out the night before for
one last fling, but now it was parked in the barn, waiting
for her to make up her mind.

From the Old Stewart Place, the walk to Patterson Lake
meant battling through a few acres of overgrown woodland

but there was no chance of running into anyone she knew on the way and once she was there, she was almost guaranteed solitude. It was the perfect place to skinny dip if you had a mind to. Not that she did. Not these days anyway. But there had been plenty of humid nights and scorching afternoons when she'd sneaked down to this same spot to enjoy the adolescent sexual pleasure of cool water on her naked flesh. The cut-off shorts she was wearing were the same ones she'd worn when William 'Bill' Stanford Junior of the Stanford family lumber dynasty had taught her to waterski on the boat his parents had given him for his sixteenth birthday. They were the same shorts she'd been wearing when his mother had asked if she wasn't that 'Phillips' girl, as if it was the name for an infectious disease. Over the years, the shorts had unraveled beyond decency, leaving little to the imagination but they were the best option in the leftover ragbag of clothes she'd found in the top of her closet. She'd cut the T-shirt off at the midriff when she was sixteen. It had been the height of fashion at the time but gravity had worked just enough on her breasts so that now it was a close call in the cover-up department. Not that Canaan cared. The boulder was fairly well protected from prying eyes and at this moment in her life she didn't give a shit whether she shocked or embarrassed some unsuspecting peeping tom.

She'd already been in for a swim and the water was still dripping from her body and clothes, trickling lazily towards the edge of the rock. She turned her head and inhaled deeply into her damp hair. It smelled like moss, rich and dark. She was on the edge of dozing again when she heard the voice.

'C'mon, bud. Fetch it. Get your hot dog. Go on.'

She knew before she opened her eyes that it was Zeke. Even when he was making idiotic demands of his dog, his voice still dripped with the rich, Southern drawl of a gentleman scholar. His voice had a deep, molasses-like tone that made you want to wade into it and lick it from your fingers.

It was the voice she'd fallen in love with as a teenager and the voice she'd carried in her head long after she'd left Lander, the one that had admonished her during her most troubling episodes of self-doubt. She scrambled down and ducked between the rocks where she could watch him without being noticed herself. He stood on the other side of the lake trying to coax an indifferent basset hound into the water. A few feet away floated a plastic hot dog. He gave the dog's backside a shove but the animal didn't budge.

'Damn it, Stonewall.'

He shook his head in disgust then pulled his cotton shirt up over his head. When Canaan realized that he was unbuttoning his blue jeans as well, her immediate reaction was to look away, but she turned back, rationalizing that he was too far away for her to see any details that might keep her awake at night. His lean torso was tanned and, she noticed, absent of tan lines. He had obviously discovered the private advantages of Patterson Lake for himself. She watched him hobble across the sharp rocks towards the water before diving in. He took a few playful dives, turning a gorgeous backside sunnyside up, before snatching the plastic toy and waving it above his head.

'C'mon, Stonewall. Come and get it. C'mon, boy!'

The dog stayed resolutely still while his owner bobbed and waved and squeezed the squeaky toy to no avail. When Zeke started playing an imaginary drum, slapping the surface of the lake using the hot dog like a drumstick and singing 'Smoke on the Water' at the top of his lungs, Canaan decided it was time to leave. She had managed to overcome her initial feelings of intrusion but somehow it was easier to see him naked than to see him making such an uninhibited fool of himself.

On the way back, she took the left-hand fork in the path and headed towards the Little House. She'd seen Luke leaving that morning, a cane fishing pole in one hand and a bucket of freshly dug worms in the other, but she knocked just the same.

'Uncle Luke. You here?'

She knew he wouldn't have minded her coming inside, but she still felt uncomfortable. She'd been avoiding him for the last two weeks. Going back to old patterns, but not really sure why. She went straight to the shelf where she'd seen the clipping of Zeke and tucked it into what was left of her jean pocket. She was about to leave when she noticed an old envelope that had slid between the wall and the shelf and she pulled it down to take a look. Inside, she found a large photograph, torn into note-sized pieces. She moved them around trying to put the jigsaw together, totally absorbed in matching limbs and heads. When the screen door suddenly flung wide open, Canaan jumped, ready to apologize for snooping – but it was Lou Venie.

'Lord, Lou Venie, you scared me.'

'Thought you were goin' down Patterson's Lake for a swim.'

'Did. Too crowded, so I came back. What's all that for?'

She nodded towards the stack of supplies her grandmother was unloading. A wire brush, a bucket, a bottle of bleach and a wad of plastic bags held tightly under her arm.

'Oh, I come down here every few months and clear out all the food he hides around the place.'

She pulled the bed away from the wall and picked up a burlap flour sack that was underneath. She opened it and wrinkled her nose, squeezing it closed again and dropping it into one of the plastic bags.

'I don't reckon I'll ever get the stink out of here. He's been hoardin' food for too long now to make any difference.'

She splashed a puddle of bleach on the damp spot where the sack had been and began to scrub with the wire brush.

'I been feedin' him three meals a day for over fifty years.

You'd think he'd have gotten the idea by now that he ain't gonna starve. Did it when he was a boy too. Momma used to find shriveled-up carrots and taters stuck all over the back porch. He dug 'em up from the fields, when nobody was lookin'. Never did grow out of it. I seen him out there not more'n a month ago. Middle of the night.'

Canaan continued to piece together the fragments of the photograph. Slowly a family portrait appeared and she recognized her grandmother as a young girl standing with her parents and siblings. Canaan's great-grandparents, Thom and Emma Stewart, sat stiffly on ladder-back chairs under the crab-apple tree that still grew in the front yard. Lou Venie stood between them, a sunken-eyed little girl with her small hand resting on her father's knee. Her hair was cut in a lopsided bob and her fingers toyed with a string of pearls around her lace collar. In the grass below, her brothers sat stern-faced, their chins lifted in an exaggerated pose for the camera. A few feet behind them, Luke stood between Emma and Thom with his chin lowered, his eyes lifted shyly upwards.

'Have you seen this before?'

Canaan nodded towards the fragments and Lou Venie pulled her glasses up from her chest for a closer look.

'Not since I was a girl.'

'Who tore it up?'

Her grandmother shrugged.

'Probably Momma. Always tore up the ones she didn't like.'

They shared an uneasy glance and Canaan resisted saying anything about her grandmother's own similar tendencies. Lou Venie picked up the corner of one of the pieces, squinting through the cheap plastic glasses, and studied Emma's rigid features.

'Momma was always pretty, even when she started gettin' on in years, but she was vain when it came to pictures. Never thought they did her justice.'

She tossed it back on the table.

'What you doin' down here, Canaan?'

'Lookin' for Luke.'

'Well, he's gone fishin'. Same as he does most days.'

Lou Venie went back to scrubbing, but Canaan could tell by the rhythm of her movements and the tensing of her jaw that her grandmother was gathering her wits for something else.

'Saw Kyle up at the Piggly Wiggly this mornin'.'

With all of her weight behind her the force of the wire brush left deep, narrow scars as it scraped the hide of the floorboards.

'Said you never came by last night.'

She paused and glanced at Canaan who had begun to put the fragments back into the envelope.

'Said he waited at the store all evenin'.'

Lou Venie listened for an answer, then threw the brush into the bucket.

'You left here like you was all set to see him. Where'd you go?'

'Driving.'

'Where drivin'?'

'Just driving. I wanted to think.'

It was a safe but simplified truth. She had gone to Piggly Wiggly. Parked on the other side of the square and watched as the last of the box boys had bounced out the front doors, grinning with pleasure at the fistful of dollar bills she'd seen Kyle Bernard count out into their eager hands. As the overhead lights had snapped off one by one across the store, she had seen the cashiers leaving in a small protective huddle. As they had rounded the corner, headed towards the parking lot behind the store, each of them had reached to massage their own private aches. She had seen Kyle lock the door and flip over the 'Closed' sign as he searched once more around the quiet streets. She had hunched down in the seat, relieved when he had turned and headed towards his little office at the back of the store, his white shirt illuminated by the fluorescent lighting of the frozen food cabinets.

She sat for over an hour, vaguely aware of the drunk who used the benches as guide supports to stagger across the square, taking one swig after another from his brown paper bag. The shouts and squeals of teenagers, flirting in small packs beneath the lampposts, had drifted somewhere along the edge of her consciousness. She couldn't remember what, if anything, had triggered the tears that had blurred the street lamps, so that they joined in one continuous circle of light around her, but she could remember the crushing pressure in her chest as she screeched the Mustang around the square on two wheels and headed towards White's Gap Ridge.

It had seemed easy enough at the time. The drop was substantial and there were no wide spots in the winding road, no verges where teenage couples looking for a quick feel in the back seat of their car might catch sight of her flying past and raise an alarm. No one would find her until the next day when the afternoon train from Chattanooga came through, and only if one of the two engineers happened to look out as they rounded the ridge.

The speed she had reached on the stretches of back roads had dwindled considerably as her old car had climbed the hill. At the peak, she had taken a deep breath as the car pointed downward, poised like the front seat of a fairground roller coaster, and she had been overcome with an insane desire to hold her arms above her head and squeal with excitement.

The blackness at the edge of the road had raced past her as her hands had gripped the steering wheel. She had concentrated so hard on jerking the wheel to the right, that several times she thought she had done it and that her dulled senses had simply not caught up with her actions. It could have been so easy. Just one quick jolt. Then it would have been out of her hands. She wouldn't have had time to change her mind or jerk the car back onto the road.

At the bottom of the hill, she had parked under a tree and turned off the lights. With her head tilted back and her arms crossed over her chest, she had cried until it seemed her nose and eyes would close up completely and suffocate her. Her arms and legs felt as heavy as rain-soaked sandbags. Finally, exhausted, she had driven home.

'Why'd you lie to me, Canaan? You never were plannin' to see him, were you?'

'I've got plans of my own.'

Lou Venie went back to scrubbing.

'I ain't seen much evidence of plans. They so special you gotta keep 'em secret?'

Canaan returned the envelope to the shelf and faced her grandmother with tired, vacant eyes.

'I don't want to spend my life standing at a cash register in Piggly Wiggly wearin' a pink polyester dress and white orthopedic shoes because those are the only shoes I can get over my corns. I don't want to get so used to wearing a God-damn hairnet that I wear it at home to keep my gray, brittle hair from falling out.'

'He's offerin' you good money, Canaan. Not even askin' for experience, just doin' it as a favor for me. Nobody ever said it had to be permanent.'

Canaan sat down on the floor next to her grandmother and searched her eyes for some sign of understanding.

'But it would be permanent. Can't you see that? I'd start off with this idea of doin' it for a while, and then I'd get a little raise, and then another one, and then before I knew it, I'd be lookin' forward to my free Thanksgiving turkey and my Christmas bonus ham.'

'There's nothing wrong with honest work. You think you're so much better than hard-workin' folks around here?'

'No . . . of course not . . . but—'

'I figured you'd learned your lesson, after crawlin' back, but you're still just as stuck in your high-and-mighty ways as your momma was.'

Canaan's anger was fierce and sudden.

'Don't talk about her that way. She was unhappy and alone.'

'Your momma was selfish. Always was.'

Lou Venie pulled herself up by the bed-frame, clumsily gathering her cleaning supplies.

'Selfish and high and mighty . . .'

She stormed out without looking back. Canaan stared after her long after the screen door had stopped vibrating on its hinges. In the distance she could hear the train whistle as it came around White's Gap Ridge from Chattanooga. She pulled her knees up, wrapping her arms tightly around them and rocked gently as the whistle came closer.

Luke

It was another two days before Luke saw Mrs Patterson again. He was sitting in the shade of the barn watching his siblings playing a game of statues when he heard her on the road. The children were suffering from the bored listlessness that comes at the end of a long hot summer. They had played every game their small brains could remember or invent, and had exhausted themselves with wading, climbing, and fishing in addition to their usual summer chores of snapping beans, peeling apples, and helping their mother with the canning. There was an anxious edge to their boredom now, an awareness that time was running out, that school would soon start and it wouldn't be long before they were cooped up inside for the long winter that lay ahead. They were desperate for change but also desperate to hold on to the pleasures and freedom of summer. When they heard the automobile come over the ridge, they all stopped the game to see who was coming and hurried up to the house, excited to find something more interesting than yet another game of statues.

It wasn't the first automobile they had seen. There had been dozens to gawp over during their few trips to Atlanta. They had even seen one or two in town, but the prospect of getting a personal, up-close look at one was more than they had dreamed of.

Once they saw the driver, however, their exuberance vanished immediately. There would be no touching, no staring, and certainly no ride along the back roads of Lander. Mrs Patterson ignored the children who had automatically lined up along the path and marched past them towards the front door. They knew who she was, but had never spoken to her so they stood silently, heads bowed, because it seemed the right thing to do. They'd seen her in town, always wearing what Lou Venie called 'nice lady' clothes. Their mother always went out of her way to greet the woman but tended to take a step back when she spoke as if Mrs Patterson deserved a larger portion of space to walk amongst them. They knew she lived in the big white house on the other side of the ridge and that it was the only house in town with three balconies and six white columns.

They knew that her daughter Estelle only came to school in the mornings because she had a private tutor in the afternoons who taught her French and deportment. No one at the school knew what deportment was exactly but generally they believed it had something to do with foreigners.

Luke watched as Mrs Patterson slammed her gloved hand against the Stewarts' front door. His heart seemed to rise, throbbing and pulsing inside his neck as soon as he saw who was in the car, but he felt tied to the place where he sat, unable to run or hide or do what he did best – disappear. He saw his mother open the screen door, heard Mrs Patterson's voice, raised and sharp, and saw his mother ask her inside. He wanted to come closer, to sit beneath the window and listen to their conversation, but his legs were numb and heavy so he sat very still, trying to sink deeper into the shadow of the barn.

*

Inside, Emma offered Mrs Patterson a cup of coffee and realized with dismay that she'd used the last of the sugar for the jam she'd made that morning. She didn't have long to worry.

'I don't have time for coffee or chit-chat, Mrs Stewart. I'm a busy woman and my business is urgent and serious.'

Emma tried to remain calm, but her insides were churning away. A visit from Mrs Patterson was something she had daydreamed about many times, but it had become more of an obsession in the last month. Mrs Patterson was the fundraising chairman for the Lander Ladies Circle and the highlight of the fundraising season in October was the harvest festival Cake Auction. Only the best cooks in the county were invited to submit entries and the competition to win the highest bid of the season was fierce. Emma had never been asked to submit before but her mother and her friend Dovie had always said, 'Emma, there's not a woman in Lander can come close to your hummingbird cake.'

For the last few months, Emma had tried every way possible to get Mrs Patterson's attention. She took cakes and pies to the funeral gatherings of people who were barely acquaintances, just because she knew Mrs Patterson would be there. Emma imagined the great lady tasting her peach and strawberry pie, or her lemon pound cake and asking who had made such a divine dessert, then seeking Emma out, begging her to join their elite band. She crossed her arms hoping to calm the nervous shudder she could feel inside her.

'Of course, Mrs Patterson . . .'

'You have a simpleton son?'

Emma looked confused. Was this part of the suitability interview?

'Yes, that's right . . . but I . . .'

'And his name is Luke?'

'Yes, it is, but . . .'

'Plain and simple, Mrs Stewart – he has molested my daughter Estelle on several occasions. She has not been able to give me details as yet, but considering where he's come from, I know I'm right.'

Emma sank down in a chair.

'I'm sure you must be mistaken . . .'

'There is no mistake. I was concerned when we first bought the house, when I heard that there was . . . But I have been assured by others in the past that he was no threat. I was told that he was kept under constant watch, so you can imagine my horror to find him hidden away in my daughter's tree house.'

'I am so sorry, Mrs Patterson. I had no idea he'd been wandering. He usually stays close to the house.'

Mrs Patterson opened the door and walked out onto the porch.

'Well, that's not good enough. I will expect you to keep him under more careful guard from now on and if I find proof that he has damaged my little girl in any way, I will move heaven and earth to make you pay.'

The children were still on the path and she pushed them aside on her way back to the car. Emma watched until the plumes of dust had evaporated over the hill before moving. The children watched her carefully, fearful of the way her neck had turned a deep burgundy red creeping up to her jaw-bone, and the way her lips had stretched to a razor-sharp line. They had seen these signals before.

'YOU!'

She didn't even have to call his name. They all knew who 'you' was.

Luke rose from the shadows. He started towards her, in small uncertain steps. She stared at him for a second or two, her eyes burning and filling with blood, before moving towards him, one large step, then another – a longer stride, faster and faster. In seconds she had hiked up her skirt and was sprinting towards him until she met him head on and hit him with a backhand so powerful it knocked him off his feet.

She grunted and screamed with each kick and slap, finally dragging him by one leg to the crab-apple tree at the top of the road.

'Gene Allen, fetch me your daddy's rope from the barn.'

The boy stood rooted to the ground, too terrified to move. Lou Venie nudged him and whispered.

'Go on, Gene Allen. We're all gonna get it if you don't.'

He carried the rope across his shoulder, tripping over it and stumbling over the clumps of dirt as he crossed the field. His mother was standing under the tree, her foot stamped firmly on Luke's leg. His eye was already swollen shut and his lip, nose, and knuckles were bleeding.

She snatched the rope from her son and slung it over the lowest branch. Gene Allen scrambled back down the incline wanting to get as far away as possible from the scene. Luke had started to wriggle out from under her foot and she stamped down hard on his chest, holding him in place while she tied a noose. Slipping it over his head she pulled with all her might, lifting him to a standing position.

'You're here 'cause I let you be here, you got that?'

He tried to nod but she gave another tug of the rope until he was standing on his tiptoes. His face was a deep crimson and his eyes felt as though they were going to pop out of his head.

'There ain't no reason why I shouldn't string you up just like they did your daddy. Nobody would think nothin' about it if I did.'

Down the hill he could hear the other children crying. He clutched at his neck. His chest felt as though a heavy stone was slowly crushing him. She leaned in close to him, pulling the rope with her.

'You play by my rules. Don't you forget that.'

She released the rope and Luke fell to his knees, loosening the knot around his neck and sucking in more air. She slung the rope once more around the branch then tied it off.

It was the most visible spot from the main road so that everyone could see him. Lou Venie was allowed to take a plate up to him once a day and Gene Allen was given the less desirable job of taking him the bucket to use for a toilet.

She left him there for three weeks.

Canaan

Canaan used a piece of bacon to stab at the eggs. The edges were dark brown, hard and crispy, but the yolk was almost raw – thin and vulnerable. The first stab burst its transparent skin and her plate was flooded with the bright yellow flow, heading towards the barely nibbled biscuit.

'You gonna be ready by ten?'

Lou Venie eyed her granddaughter who was sitting at the kitchen table in a shabby pink bathrobe.

'I said I would be.'

Lou Venie wiped down the counter tops, being careful not to drag the sleeve of her best and only Sunday dress in the wake.

'I don't want to be late. I'm never late. Brother Blackman always mentions my promptness.'

Canaan shoved the plate back. Lou Venie gave her a disapproving look but said nothing as she picked it up and carried it to the counter.

'Used to be, church was a time for families. It's been hard all these years goin' by myself.'

'You've got a brother living a hundred yards from your back door.'

Lou Venie ignored the remark and pulled a tin pie-plate from the cupboard.

'Shame to waste this. You ain't hardly touched it.'

She put the biscuit and egg on the pie-plate and scooped the blob of congealed cheese grits next to it. She poured hot bacon gravy over the top of it.

'So you think that old car of yours is gonna get us to church and back?'

Canaan shrugged.

'It'll be nice – like old times – you goin' with me this mornin'.'

Canaan pushed the chair back from the table and pulled her robe tighter around her before heading for the bedroom.

'Don't get used to it, Lou Venie.'

By the time Canaan was dressed, Lou Venie had finished the dishes, scrubbed down the table and put the plastic flower arrangement back as the centerpiece. Her black patent-leather handbag was sitting on top of her Bible on the corner of the table and she was holding the pie-plate, now piled high with the breakfast leftovers. She looked up when Canaan came in and frowned at the black trousers and black sleeveless over-blouse she was wearing.

'You don't have nothin' better than that? You look like you're fixin' to bury somebody.'

'I'm fresh out of ruffles and white gloves, Lou Venie. If you want me to go, this is what you get.'

Her grandmother sighed and took the pie-plate onto the back porch. She placed it on the top step and rang a large cast-iron bell beside the door.

As she came back in, she took off her apron and hung it on the hook.

'He'll probably complain about the grits. He likes 'em plain.'

'Then why'd you put them on his plate?'

TERRI WILTSHIRE

'They'd just be throwed out if I didn't. Shouldn't go to waste.'

She picked up her purse and Bible and started for the door. Canaan didn't move.

'Why do you still feed him like a field-hand?'

'It's what he's used to. He likes it that way.'

'You feed him leftovers.'

'He gets regular meals. Better than he'd get if he was on his own.'

'You treat him like he was a stranger, not family.'

Lou Venie clasped her Bible defensively to her chest.

'I treat him better than most.'

Canaan laughed, rolling her eyes to the ceiling.

'Have you ever let him in the house? Has he ever sat down at your table for supper? Your own brother?'

Lou Venie stiffened.

'I promised Momma.'

'You promised the devil.'

Her grandmother glanced around as if she was afraid someone might hear.

'Hush that. You oughta show more respect.'

Canaan picked up her car keys from the counter and pushed past her grandmother.

'I have trouble respecting a woman who pretends her own child never existed.'

The Sunday crowd at White's Gap Baptist were gathered by the front steps, dressed in a variety of go-to-meeting clothes that ranged from designer labels to Simplicity pattern number 238. It was a barren-looking building. Short and narrow. Red brick. With the sort of windows that belonged in a factory. And there was nowhere to hide. Canaan hung back, wondering what had possessed her to agree to such naked exposure. Lou Venie waded in with confidence and Canaan

98

tried to drift further from the faithful and closer to the get-away car.

'Canaan Phillips! Is that you?'

Canaan turned to face an exquisitely dressed young woman with a massive mane of hair, power-styled into place. Her nails were expensively manicured and her make-up expertly applied.

'Hello, Mim.'

Mim Simpson had been Homecoming Queen at Lander High School their senior year; the object of fantasy for every male and the envy of every female. She had also been the ring-leader of an elite gang of bullies who had made Canaan's life hell.

Mim hugged her tightly as if they were long-lost friends. As if she'd never filled Canaan's locker with moldy cafeteria garbage to remind her that no matter how many votes she might get for the Spring Queen, she'd still be Trash.

'I just about didn't recognize you.'

She gave Canaan enough of a once-over to let her know she'd noticed that her sandals were K-Mart plastic.

'I heard you were back. How'd you talk that good-lookin' Yankee husband of yours into movin' down here? I thought he hated the South.'

'I didn't. We're getting a divorce.'

Mim tried her best to look sympathetic but her face, more accustomed to pouting or flirting, filled with pleasure at unearthing this tidbit of gossip.

'Oh, I'm sorry. I am so lucky to have my Nathan and my girls. I just don't know what I'd do if I was in your place.'

'Well, let's just hope it doesn't happen to you.'

Canaan smiled politely and tried to move away but Mim stopped her with a patronizing tap. Her pretty chin tilted upwards as a dainty laugh slipped from between her pearl-perfect carnivorous teeth.

'Oh, I really don't think that's likely. I mean, Nathan is

completely devoted to me. He would never leave me for another woman.'

She hesitated.

'Was it another woman?'

Was it another woman? No. It was many women. Or maybe it wasn't. Maybe it had all been in her head. She'd never known. Besides – it wasn't women, real or phantom, that made her leave.

'No.'

Mim looked disappointed.

'Oh. I heard . . .'

She crossed her arms and settled into a front-porch, rocking-chair chat.

'So where are you livin'?'

'I'm back at my grandmother's. Look, I—'

She tried again to leave but Mim was on a roll.

'You probably heard we live up on Mimosa Ridge now.'

She paused, waiting for Canaan's reaction. Mimosa Ridge was a new development of overblown, overpriced antebellum-style houses perched on the east side of Green Mountain. The hillside had once been scattered with cramped wooden shacks, built to house the families who worked at the cotton mill. When Canaan had been in school, the area had been known as the Mill Village, and the village kids had been the only ones who were considered lower on the social ladder than non-commercial farmers' kids like her. When the mill had closed down, the village itself had remained, and the unemployed families had found menial work where they could and continued living in the same two-room shacks they'd been born in. But it didn't take long for a developer to notice that the shacks had exceptional views of the river and town below, so the bulldozers came in and leveled the village in a single cleansing swoop. Views like that belonged to the very rich.

Disappointed in Canaan's lack of reaction she pressed on.

'So have you got a job yet?

'I'm not planning to stay long. Look, Mim, I really need to go in. Find my grandmother.'

'Oh sure, sure. We'll talk later. And I'm sure we'll see you at the reunion.'

The invitation had remained unopened for four days until Lou Venie could no longer stand it and ripped it open herself. She'd followed Canaan around the house reading it aloud and when there was no measurable response, she took to propping it in plain view. Leaning against the jam jar at the breakfast table. Tucked inside the TV guide as a bookmark. And on the windowsill of the bathroom, held in place by four shell-shaped soaps that Peggy had brought her from Gulf Shores. Canaan had ignored the hints. Refused to be drawn in when her grandmother tried to discuss it. *I didn't have anything in common with them when I was in high school, Lou Venie. I'll have even less in common with them now.*

But with Mim she decided to play the game. Anything to get away from the false coziness.

'Maybe. We'll see.'

Before Mim could launch into the plans she'd made for the reunion, Canaan hurried around the corner and up the concrete steps. Her grandmother was waiting for her in the foyer.

'Canaan, you remember Kyle, don't you?'

Kyle had been studying the bulletin board. He turned and grinned.

'Well, Miss Canaan Phillips. How in the world are you? Sister Lou Venie told me you were back. I was hopin' I might be seein' a whole lot more of you.'

He looked much as she remembered him, but the round baby face and flushed cheeks that had always made him look like a toddler who'd just finished an enormous bowel movement was made even more absurd with age. Her grand-mother nodded.

'Kyle was just sayin' that the job at the deli is still open.'

Canaan looked at her watch.

'Everyone's going in. Shouldn't we find a seat?'

'Everybody knows my seat. But we ought to go on down. Don't like to leave things to the last minute.'

She turned to Kyle.

'Why don't you sit with us today, Brother Kyle?'

'Yes, ma'am, it would be a pleasure. A real pleasure.'

Lou Venie led and they followed. Reluctantly, Canaan slid into the pew, with Kyle sliding in beside her. He opened a songbook for them to share and winked as he whispered into Canaan's ear.

'I believe your grandmother is tryin' a little matchmakin'!'

The preacher smiled down at the congregation.

'It's good to see so many of you here this mornin' and we're especially blessed to have Sister Lou Venie's grand-daughter, Canaan Phillips, back with us. Sister Canaan has had some difficulties of late . . .'

He turned a benevolent smile on Canaan and she tried to remain impassive, fighting the urge to glare at her grand-mother. She could feel everyone's eyes on her. Brother Black-man nodded.

'And I just want you to know that we're all prayin' for your husband to leave that sinful relationship and come back to you.'

The service dragged on beyond the limits of Canaan's sanity. She suffered through the sermon and sharing a song-book with Kyle who slyly touched his fingers to hers and stroked his elbow against her waist. She even managed to get through the unbearable ritual of 'greeting your neighbor'. Every person within twelve feet insisted on hugging her, taking her face in their hands and gazing meaningfully into her eyes. *We're prayin' for you, Canaan. I just know he'll see the light.* She tried to keep control of the blue-flame anger that danced away inside her. She didn't want to release it. Didn't want to count to ten or waste it. She wanted to nurture it, expand it, hold it close until she could unleash it in all its fury in her grandmother's direction. By the time she'd fought her way through the happy throng and down the steps to the parking lot, she felt dizzy with the effort. Lou Venie shook a few hands, gave a few grateful nods but made her way quickly to the car. The engine was sputtering and coughing as Canaan tried to get it started. Lou Venie buckled herself in.

'Give it more gas.'

'That has nothing to do with it.'

'Just try it.'

'When was the last time you drove a car, Lou Venie?'

Her grandmother sighed and looked out the window.

'You're mad at me.'

Canaan slammed both fists against the steering wheel.

'Why can't you just tell the truth?'

'I was only tryin' to stop some of the gossip before it got started.'

'So you made up some of your own?'

Lou Venie reached out to touch her hand but Canaan snatched it away and shrank further into the corner of her seat. A mustard-colored hatchback pulled up beside them and Kyle grinned from his window.

'You ladies need some help?'

Canaan snapped impatiently.

'No, Kyle. We're fine.'

For a moment he looked as though he might insist, but he glanced from Lou Venie to Canaan and shrugged.

'Well, OK then. Hope I'll see you again soon.'

He drove off and they sat in silence.

Lou Venie turned and reached again for Canaan's hand.

'Canaan, you know good as I do that adultery is the only biblical grounds for divorce there is.'

Canaan pulled her hand away and crossed her arms.

'What about broken ribs and black eyes or seven trips to the emergency room? Those don't count?'

'Folks 'round here are raised to believe in *for better or worse.*'

Canaan's eyes filled with tears as she turned to face her grandmother.

'. . . *'til death us do part*?'

She stared out the window.

'I guess it would've been better for me and you both if Jonathon had just finished the job.'

'Don't say things like that.'

Lou Venie's voice sounded more judgemental than re-assuring. Nearby, a family piled into a station wagon and Lou Venie waved when they caught her eye. Canaan tried again to start the car but it groaned and died.

'Damn!'

'I hope you weren't plannin' to make your big escape in this thing.'

'It's been sitting too long, that's all.'

The father of the station wagon pulled alongside.

'Can I help y'all with that?'

Lou Venie smiled.

'Well, I think . . .'

Canaan leaned over her grandmother and snapped aggressively.

'No! We don't need help. We're fine. OK?'

The man looked surprised.

'Well . . . all right then.'

They drove off and Canaan wrestled again with the gear-box.

'I thought you took it to get fixed.'

'Costs too much.'

'Well, you know what you can do about that.'

'Don't start.'

'You were sittin' right next to him. Jobs ain't that easy to come by 'round here.'

'Lou Venie, stop it! I'm not taking that job. I'll fix the damn thing myself if I have to.'

Her grandmother sat quietly for a moment.

'So when you plannin' on leavin' again?'

Canaan shrugged.

'Few weeks. Maybe another month or so.'

Lou Venie snorted in disbelief.

'You were never any good at makin' decisions. Always needed to be forced into it. If what you told me about Jonathon is true—'

'What do you mean *if*?'

'*If* what you said is true . . . I don't know why you stayed with him as long as you did.'

Canaan closed her eyes and whispered.

'Because he made sure I had no place to go but back here.'

There was another long silence. A woman got into the car across from them and waved. Lou Venie smiled and waved back.

'I could say it serves you right. You only married him to get out of Lander and get back at me.'

Canaan laughed.

'. . . and how many times have I heard your voice all these years in my head? *You've made your bed, missy miss!* I didn't go to New York to punish you, Lou Venie.'

Her grandmother shifted in her seat, pulling her dress further over her knees.

'Well, it did the job just the same.'

Canaan turned the key and the car suddenly shuddered to life. She shoved the stick into gear and backed out. As they passed the front steps, Brother Blackman waved and gave

Canaan a thumbs-up sign. Lou Venie gave him an OK signal and smiled.

'And I'd rather you didn't call me Lou Venie in front of my friends. It ain't respectful.'

Luke

His mother's voice took on a different quality when she read. It wasn't warm, exactly, but it wasn't tinged with the usual bitterness and it had a rhythm that he found soothing, especially when he closed his eyes. Luke wrapped his knees tighter into his chest, squeezing himself further into the small, dark corner outside the front room.

'Daddy always grumbles like a bear when he reads that part.'

Emma stopped reading and Lou Venie sank anxiously behind her quilt.

'Your daddy ain't here to read though, is he?'

The little girl shook her head.

'No, ma'am.'

'You want me to read or not?'

The children exchanged nervous glances and nodded.

'Yes, ma'am.'

Saturday was story-night. Thom started the ritual the year before, tagging it on to the children's weekly bath. Every Saturday, late afternoon, Luke waited impatiently for the clinking of supper dishes to stop and for Thom to appear on the back porch, lift the old tin bathtub from the railroad spike that suspended it from the rafters and drag it beside the fire in the front room. It was an hour filled with infectious giggles and energetic splashing. In the shadows, Luke watched as Thom's usually solemn face was transformed. When the children had been wrapped and dried with large sheets of flannel they were dressed in nightclothes that had been warmed on a wire strung across the fireplace. Then Thom gathered them around and read a few chapters from one of Lou Venie's library books or one of his own favorites that he kept stacked beside his bed. He read until one by one they nodded off and then he carried each of them to their beds in the back room. Luke had never been included but it had still become an important part of his week.

Tonight, Thom wasn't there for story-night and only Luke and his mother knew why. The night before, Luke had been awake, listening from his corner on the back porch.

'Don't try lyin' to me, Thom. Shug Bolton said she saw you plain as day.'

'Shug Bolton sets outside Mizz Philly's cathouse regular these days, does she?'

'Said you was huggin' on some young whore's neck. A girl, Shug said. Downright lascivious she called it.'

Luke raised up, peering through the screen and into the parchment-colored light of the front room.

'You talk to me, Thom Stewart. Don't you look away in your whiney, spineless way. You visitin' that whorehouse or ain't you?'

'I only went down there with Duke, the one time's all.'

She hurled herself at him, palms slapping and feet kicking as she screeched and spat.

'Low-life, no-good, nasty-minded filth . . .'

Thom had raised his arms over his head, twisting like a snake in water to avoid her hammering fists.

'He supplies Mizz Philly with liquor, Emma. I went down to help him unload it. That's all it was, I swear.'

She flung a coffee cup, catching him just above his right

eye and leaving a crimson half-moon cut as it shattered on his forehead. He pulled a handkerchief from his pocket and held it to his head, while Emma fought to control her uneven breathing. She glared at him.

'I don't want you near Lou Venie and the children no more.'

'What are you sayin'?'

'No stories, no Saturday nights, no fishin'. You can get on with your work, you can sleep out there in your room and I'll bring you a plate at mealtimes, but I don't want you havin' nothin' to do with 'em.'

'Now come on, Emma. I know you're mad at me. But don't take it out on them.'

'I cain't trust you no more and I don't want you touchin' Lou Venie.'

'Oh my Lord, Emma. How can you . . .'

Emma's smile curled to one side, dark and malicious.

'You like 'em young, don't you, Thom. That whore was no more'n fifteen, if a day.'

His voice had sounded tired and sad as he shook his head.

'You're a vile woman, Emma.'

He had pushed past her and Luke heard the front door slam. A short time later he heard the wagon heading over the hill. Luke knew from that moment that there would be no more bedtime stories. His mother would soon grow tired of the task and the other children would find other things to fill their time.

Luke stretched his legs and moved closer to the crack in the door. He could see Lou Venie's eyes drooping to a half-closed state. His mother nudged her roughly.

'You asleep, Lou Venie?'

'No, ma'am.'

'Then sit up. I ain't botherin' if you don't pay attention.'

Lou Venie wriggled to an upright position and her mother continued. Ordinarily, on story-night, Luke listened to every last word but his mother's voice had become so mechanical and lifeless, he decided to make for the cornfield early. He crept from his hiding place and headed to the back of the house to his father's room. Sidestepping the creaking floorboards, he picked one of the books from Thom's stack and slipped it down the front of his overalls. He lifted the lantern from the nail above the bed and crept quietly out the back door. He knew that getting caught inside the house meant a beating but he felt he was safe. He could hear his mother's voice droning on in the other room and he knew that Thom would not be home that night or possibly any night again.

He eased the back door shut, raced across the yard and into the fields. Settling himself deep within the corn he opened Thom's book and started another long night's battle trying to teach himself to read.

Lou Venie was the first to see Gene Allen's head drop to one side in a sluggish doze. She hoped her mother wouldn't notice until she had finished the chapter, but as she started the next paragraph, she glanced up and without completing the sentence, she slammed the book.

'Wake your brother up and y'all go on to bed. And don't dawdle.'

Lou Venie herded her brothers into the back bedroom and crawled into her small single bed. She knew that something wasn't right. Her mother had that edge of un-erupted anger that they had all come to look for and dread. She lay in the dark until she heard the steady breathing of her brothers in the other bed then tiptoed down the hall. Her mother had fallen asleep in the chair, the basket of mending at her feet and a half-darned sock limp in her hand. Lou Venie watched her from the dark before crossing the kitchen to the pie safe. She reached behind it and pulled out a sliver of ham with a nice fat ridge of well-cooked fat. She'd hidden it after supper that night, while her mother had been busy at the sink and when she was supposed to be finishing her turnip greens. Listening for signs of her mother's sleep, she crept to the back porch and slipped through the screen door to give Luke the treat. But Luke wasn't in his corner. She felt around his quilt in the dark as if he might be lost in its folds, then stood looking out over the fields. In the center of the north field she saw the lantern light – and her heart pounded with fear. He had not gone beyond the rise like he usually did. In his eagerness and impatience he'd stopped short on the wrong side of the rise and now he was clearly visible to anyone who happened to glance his way. Outside, a crab-apple dropped from its branch and noisily rolled along the tin roof of the back porch. Lou Venie heard her mother stir and without thinking hurried back inside through the screen door. She was almost to the hallway when the screen door slammed behind her and her mother cried out.

'Thom? That you?'

Lou Venie hurried into the bedroom and scrambled under her covers, her heart racing, trying to hold her breath. She could hear her mother in the kitchen, imagined her checking the back porch, seeing it empty, and catching sight of the light in the cornfield. She heard the screen door slam again and the sound of her mother pounding down the back steps. She tiptoed to the window and watched as the shadow of her mother headed for the cornfield. She began to moan softly, twisting her fingers in the folds of her nightgown. Suddenly the light in the field began to move eerily through the corn and as Emma emerged holding the lantern in one hand and dragging Luke with the other, Lou Venie felt the warm trickle of urine running down her leg and onto the wooden floor. She began to whimper, frozen to the floor. Only the sound of the door slamming broke her fear and she plunged back into her bed.

Emma burst into their bedroom.

'Gene Allen, get your brother and sister and bring 'em outside.'

She groped beneath the tangled heap of quilts and blankets, grabbing arms and legs and jerking the boys roughly to the floor. Lou Venie joined them at the bottom of the bed and as Emma stormed out of the room, they followed closely behind, clasped pitifully together.

In the kitchen she pulled the rug beater from the nail beside the canning shelves, and as she turned to face the children Lou Venie began to whimper again in a thinly controlled panic. Emma pushed her towards the door and shoved the lantern into Gene Allen's hands.

'Take this and do what I say.'

She dragged the children down the back steps and out to the yard where Luke was cowering near the well. Lou Venie's sporadic whimpers had evolved into a chant-like moan and the two boys stared, wide-eyed and ashen, in the lantern light. Emma glared at Luke.

'Stand up.'

Luke slowly stood with his head down. His mother held up the book.

'Where'd you get this?'

He looked at Lou Venie whose teeth were chattering as she shivered in the warm night air. He looked down at the ground.

'You been in my house, haven't you? You been stealin' from my own house!'

His voice was almost a whisper.

'No, ma'am. I was borrowin' . . .'

She took two giant strides towards him and slapped him backwards.

'Halfwits don't read. Ain't I said that? Ain't I told you?'

'Yes, ma'am.'

'Gene Allen?'

'Yes, ma'am?'

'You hold that lantern up good and high, so I can see what I'm doin', you hear me?'

'Yes, ma'am.'

'And if you don't I'm gonna give you some of the same, you understand?'

'Yes ma'am.'

Against all his best efforts, Gene Allen had begun to cry, and with his eyes and nose streaming, he wiped the sleeve of his nightshirt across his face and held the lantern high above his head.

Emma turned to Luke.

'You know what to do. Get over that well.'

Luke hesitated and his eyes pleaded with her before filling with tears. He stumbled towards the well and leaned across it when his mother screamed.

'Don't mess with me, boy. Get 'em off.'

The ribbons of tears on Luke's face glistened in the lantern light and he looked desperately at the other children. Lou Venie stuffed her small fist into her mouth to stop the convulsive sobs that rattled her shoulders and Gene Allen struggled to hold his arm up, his muscles burning and quivering, causing the lantern to dance and swing like a marionette, casting eerie shadows on their small family circle.

'Do it now!'

Lou Venie let out a small gulping cry as John Curtis clung to her and buried his face into her nightgown. Luke unfastened the hooks on his overalls and dropped them to his ankles. Stretching over the roughly splintered lid that covered the well, he grabbed hold of the spike on the other side that held the bucket in place. The first swing of the rug beater came sooner than he expected and his breath became tangled in the scream that tried to explode from his lungs.

'I want to hear you say . . . *I'm a halfwit . . .*'

She hit him again and Lou Venie screamed in unison with her brother.

'Say it!'

'I'm a halfwit.'

She hit him again.

'. . . *and halfwits don't read.*'

He tried to speak but the force of her continued blows caught him each time and all he could manage were half-whispers and gasping swallows. She stopped to catch her breath.

'I'll beat you 'til sun-up, boy. Say it.'

Except for his mother's labored breathing, the whole world seemed to go quiet around him. Then from somewhere he could hear the wailing sobs of his sister and beyond the secluded veil of the night, the crickets chirped in unconcerned harmony. He rested the side of his face against the rough wood and his lips quivered, the words scalding like bile in his throat.

'Halfwits don't read.'

He started to cry again and Emma swung the rug beater with both hands. As the rushing surf in Luke's head collapsed around him, the night moved in to engulf him and he felt the first trickle of blood run down his leg.

Canaan

The zipper in the pink polyester uniform was heating up and sweat was trickling down the small of her back. By the time she got to the Piggly Wiggly her face would be as swollen and pink as the embroidered pig on her left breast pocket. She shifted her purse from one shoulder to the other and lifted her ponytail off her neck, hoping for the slightest of breezes. She'd promised herself that it would be worth it. Six weeks' work at the deli and she could get the car in running condition again and then she never had to set foot in Lander again. Her grandmother had been overjoyed when she heard she was taking the job. She'd been up at the crack of dawn to press her uniform, as if it wouldn't stand up crinkle-free on its own, and had cooked an enormous breakfast that made Canaan nauseous just thinking about it. The biggest drawback would be the daily walk to town. The Mustang was tucked up safely in the barn, awaiting its surgery. Now as she drew closer to the town square, Canaan wasn't so sure she shouldn't just have sold the car to the mechanic and bought a one-way plane ticket to Anywhere, USA.

Kyle was waiting for her at the front of the store, manically clicking his ballpoint pen as if he was counting customers. Canaan imagined him pacing back and forth, watching the square for her, straightening his tie, and checking his watch.

'Well, howdie-do! Right on time. Now if you'll come on back to the office with me, we'll get you ready for the noon rush. The high-school crowd can be vicious.'

He walked with an air of commander-in-chief towards the back of the store and Canaan followed, aware of the curious stares. A young girl was stacking jars of Bama Jelly and Kyle snapped his fingers with authority.

'Aline . . . labels to the front, please.'

He looked back at Canaan to see if she was impressed and gave her a 'see what I have to put up with?' sort of look. He opened the door and nodded for her to enter. His office looked like the dorm room of a giddy Freshman girl – shelves filled with a menagerie of stuffed toys, a desk cluttered with mini-statuettes, *World's Best Boss* and a bulletin board plastered with witty bumper stickers: *It's lonely at the top, but you eat better*. He nodded Canaan into a chair before taking a clipboard down from behind his desk.

'Let's see now . . .'

He opened a drawer and pulled out a name tag already stamped with her name, a hairnet that swelled and expanded like a living, evil thing when he released it from his grasp and a pristine time card. He checked each one off the list with a flourish.

'That's the necessaries taken care of.'

He moved them towards her but stopped just short enough to force her to lean over to retrieve them. He gave her an appreciative stare.

'Looks like I got the uniform size right on the button.'

'Yeah . . . uh . . . thanks for taking care of it.'

'Not a problem.'

He looked down at her sandals.

'You got steel-toed shoes?'

She shook her head.

'No problem. I'll call Harry over at Shoe City.'

He looked again at her feet and Canaan self-consciously tucked them beneath her chair.

'Hmmm . . . I'd say a size six?'

She nodded and he slapped his hands together enthusiastically.

'Yes-siree! I have a real gift when it comes to the female form.'

He walked around the desk and sat on the edge, his leg brushing Canaan's knee.

'I was thinkin' once you get the hang of the deli counter, we might just have to move you up to the cash registers. Don't want to waste that pretty face in the back of the store, do we?'

He waited for a response and then leaned forward, his mouth inches from her ear.

'You know when we were in school, I had a crush on you.'

Canaan smiled politely. He continued.

'Course, you were a senior and I was just a sophomore. Never in a million years thought I might be your boss one day.'

Canaan stood and moved towards the door.

'Shouldn't I . . . you said . . . the noon rush?'

His grin wilted but he bounced up and followed her to the door.

'Oh right. Guess we oughta get you on out there. Dot and Juanita can fill you in on most things . . .'

He opened the door for her.

'. . . but anything you want or need . . .'

He stabbed her arm with his finger, accentuating each word.

'You-just-come-to-me.'

She squeezed between Kyle and the door but forced herself to turn back. Whether she liked it or not, her future depended on this job.

'Thanks, Mr Bernard.'

He shook his head.

'We're old buddies, Canaan. You can call me Kyle when we're alone.'

He pointed the way to the deli, insisting that she walk ahead of him and she knew he was watching her ass moving smoothly beneath the pink polyester. At the counter he clapped his hands together like a Sunday-school teacher and urged the two women to drop what they were doing and pay attention.

'Dot. Juanita. This is Canaan. I want you to treat her right and welcome her into our cozy little family, all right?'

He gave Canaan one more wink before leaving her on her own. She tucked her hair into the hairnet and smiled nervously at her co-workers. Both women were in their fifties. Dot's uniform had obviously been nipped, tucked and altered to highlight as many curves as possible and the front zipper was plunged low enough to show off an ample sun-leathered bosom. She offered a half-smile through lips that looked as if she'd been sucking on Marlboros since she was twelve years old.

'Well, well. So you're the "Miss Harvard" girl Kyle's been braggin' about.'

The other woman grinned.

'I'm Juanita . . . and that's Dot.'

Juanita had the broad hips and exhausted eyes of a mother-of-six. The two women were busy making submarine sandwiches for the first five students who'd beaten the others to Lander's favorite lunch spot.

'Slide down this way, Dot. Give the girl room to work.'

Canaan moved into place and looked with confused panic

at the stacked containers of meat and condiments. Juanita winked.

'Don't worry, Sugar. Just follow us.'

Canaan smiled warily at the next customer, a teenage boy dressed in K-Mart's version of California Surfer Dude.

'I want a ham hoagie. No mustard.'

Canaan nodded, then turned to study the board above her head. She tried to follow the other two women, but the more she tried to keep up the further behind she fell. Unfortunately she'd mistaken Dot's earlier smile for genuine friendliness and asked her for help. It was obvious that Dot didn't have the patience for training new staff. She rolled her eyes and pointed to the correct containers, then watched and judged every move, criticizing Canaan's novice techniques.

'Uh-uh-uh . . . tomatoes last . . . tuck the ham in like a blanket.'

Canaan struggled to pick up the pace and finally put what looked like an explosion of shredded lettuce, mangled tomatoes and seeping mayonnaise on the top counter. Surfer Boy stared at it and frowned.

'Have I got to pay for this?'

Juanita glanced over at the pathetic excuse for a sandwich and smiled sympathetically at Canaan. With a quick flurry she added another handful of maple-cured ham and shoved it towards the boy.

'It may not be purty, hon, but it's bustin' with personality!'

Canaan smiled to show her gratitude, but Juanita had already plunged into rapid-fire banter with the next customer. The crowd of students was now jostling six deep on the other side of the glass and as their shouts for attention grew more demanding, Canaan's ability to focus on more than one task at a time diminished. A strand of hair managed to work its way out of the hairnet and as she lifted her head to sweep it from her eyes with her forearm, she caught sight of Zeke Forrest coming through the front door. She finished the next order, nervously watching as he stopped to talk to a student. As she slammed the next order onto the service counter he disappeared behind the cereal shelves and in a panic she turned and pushed her way through the double doors into the back storage room. She snatched the hairnet from her head, trying to salvage some element of attractiveness, but caught sight of herself in the metallic door of the meat-storage locker. She sank down onto a tomato crate and decided to wait it out.

Dot was the first one to see Zeke and shouted over the heads of the students.

'How's my luck runnin' today, Zeke? You gonna take a chance? Try somethin' new?'

He smiled and played hard to get.

'I don't know, Dot. I'm pretty set in my ways.'

'Come on. Somethin' hot and spicy?'

'I'm not a spicy kind of guy.'

'You don't know what you're missin'.'

'Maybe next time.'

Dot sighed.

'All right then . . . turkey and Swiss it is.'

'Oh and a—'

'I know. A plain turkey – no mayo.'

She shook her head in good-humored disgust.

'Best-fed dog in Lander, Alabama. Hell, probably in the whole damn state.'

She handed him the order and couldn't resist tickling the side of his wrist as he took it from her.

'I'm gonna keep tryin', you know.'

He lifted the hoagies in thanks and smiled as he forced his way back through the crowd.

'I'm countin' on it, Dot.'

She grinned at Juanita and fanned herself with a napkin.

'Lord, what I wouldn't give for private lessons from that man.'

Canaan was sitting on the crates trying to decide whether it was safe to go back when Dot barged through the doors. Her face was streaked in a variation of hard-working pinks and reds and her black eyes flashed.

'You workin' here or not? Get your butt out here and start hustlin'.'

Canaan hurried out and took the next order. She cut the hoagie roll lengthwise and after carefully placing the slices of salami she tried to arrange the olives in a neat, orderly way. Dot threw an empty roll at her.

'Hey! Miss Harvard! You gotta do more than one at a time.'

Canaan looked confused and Dot shouted in exasperation.

'Take another order!'

A student saw her opportunity and moved over from Juanita's huddle.

'I want a Tex-Mex, no jalapeños.'

Canaan sliced another roll and lay it beside the other one, twisting to read the menu board behind her. Dot shouted again.

'Three! Three! You can do at least three at a time.'

Another student pushed his way through the crowd and put his hoagie on the counter.

'Is this pastrami? Looks like roast beef to me.'

Dot scowled at Canaan and snatched the order from the boy.

'Start usin' your eyes, Harvard.'

She made a new roast beef sandwich in seconds and shoved it back to the boy.

'Next!'

Surfer Dude was back.

'You put mustard on this.'

Canaan was still trying to finish the salami and Tex-Mex.

'I'm sorry – what?'

'Mustard. I said no mustard.'

Canaan took the sandwich from him and laid out another bun to start again. The rumble of complaints grew as Canaan's heart raced and her hands became clumsy strangers. *I can do this*. Juanita shouted a few encouraging words from her end of the counter, but Dot seemed to revel in Canaan's incompetence and joined the side of the students.

'Don't mind her, kiddos. Miss Harvard ain't used to gettin' her hands dirty.'

For the next thirty minutes Canaan fought to keep from crying. Especially in front of Dot. She had a feeling that tears would have the same effect as rolling over and exposing a pink, vulnerable belly. Dot would tear her apart. The work didn't get easier, but eventually she managed a steady if slow-paced rhythm. Then, as quickly as they'd come, they seemed to disappear. Juanita handed over the last order.

'Thanks, hon!'

Dot tossed her sponge onto the counter-top and looked at the chaotic mess that Canaan had created along one-third of the deli.

'I think you got clean-up duty today. I'm goin' out back for a cigarette.'

Juanita patted Canaan on the shoulder.

'It'll get better, Sugar. I'll go get the mop.'

Luke

Emma dropped the packages on the table and turned to the children who had quietly and obediently followed her in from the wagon. Her voice rumbled up from somewhere deep inside like a growl.

'Get out. All of you. I don't want to see or hear you anywhere near this house 'til this afternoon.'

The children had endured a dangerously hushed ride from town, and they obeyed without a fuss, filing out the kitchen door and waiting until they were well past the barn before allowing a single syllable to escape their lips.

When the distant sound of the children's shouts had faded completely, she knelt beside the stove and reaching underneath, pulled out a small tin that had once stored cherry-flavored cough drops. She took it to her bedroom, bolting the door behind her.

Inside were a few trinkets and a stash of dollar bills rolled snugly into a cigar. The tin had followed her from her parents' home and every week, even during the heaviest days of her pregnancies, she had crouched to deposit the pennies and coins she had managed to hide from Thom. When the coins multiplied sufficiently, she took them to town in a little velvet pouch and traded them for a crisp new dollar bill.

In the beginning the purpose had been clear. She had never expected to stay, certain that there would be some sort of signal, a sign from God, that would release her from the old man she had married and the screaming baby she despised. But the sign had never come. Just the babies, and the dollar bills had continued to pile up in the tin.

She placed the roll of bills on the dresser and rolled it absently from side to side with her finger, then took a neatly folded scrap of tissue paper from the corner of the tin and unwrapped it. The locket inside was the size of a baby's fingernail. It was only just big enough for a dainty pair of initials, one on each side, but she had never bothered to have it engraved. She fixed the latch behind her neck, opening her blouse and pulling it down around her shoulders so that the locket nestled like a drop of dew between her breasts. She stared into the mirror, as her small chin fought to remain steady and tears rose above the banks of her eyelids, spilling down from the outer corners. She had known for a long time, before Doc Caldwell had made it official, but the words had still knocked the wind from her lungs and all she had wanted to do was to get out of his office and away from his inane babbling.

'Not surprisin' really, Emma. It's been six years since John Curtis was born and you're still young.'

He had patted her shoulder in a grandfatherly way and she had wanted to scratch the understanding smile from his face.

'You can be grateful that your momma didn't pass on her female problems to you. You got nothin' to worry about. You're a strong, healthy young woman with plenty of fruitful years ahead of you.'

She touched the locket, then her hands moved to her breasts, her fingers spreading like a fan to measure the tender new swelling. She put her head into her hands and cried, her whole body shuddering in continuous waves of grief. She should have known, should have been more careful.

The punishment Emma had meted out for Thom's visit to Miss Philly's cathouse had not worked out as she had planned. She had figured he'd stay away for a few days then slink around the house for a few weeks, sticking close, in the hope that she would relent and allow him more time with the children, but instead Thom had spent more time in town. On the few nights he had come home, it had been late and he'd been drunk. She'd heard him staggering up the porch and down the hall to his room. For months afterwards he had drifted in and out of their lives, coming home only to take care of those things that were absolutely necessary to the feeding and safety of his family, and in the cold darkness of her room, Emma had suffered with the images of the whores she knew he was touching.

In early spring, Alabama had been hit by a freakish heat-wave more lethal than the worst day in recent Augusts, and Thom and Emma had spent many long hours of planting, side by side in the parched fields. There had been no conversation, not even a glance or a nod, as they had passed one another like blinkered mules in the dusty furrows. During planting season a bucket of sugar water and a ladle always sat at the edge of the field to fight dehydration, but on one especially scorching day, they had guzzled it dry by early afternoon. Afterwards, Emma had trudged back to the house, fighting the dizzy nausea of heat sickness that had suddenly come over her. At the side of the house she had held her face under the pump head, dampening her lips and tongue with the puny stream of sun-warmed water.

From her room, she had heard Thom scrambling around on the back porch and she had watched him drag the wash-tub down to the barn, angry that he had thought of it first. In a fit of heat-fevered insanity, she had stripped her sweat-drenched clothes from her clammy body, and soaked a cloth in the tepid water left in the enamel basin. The water had been edged with the black, bobbing bodies of thirsty flies that had lost their grip on the slippery sides of the bowl, but she had barely noticed them as she squeezed the liquid down her arms and her chest, watching it turn to a muddy trickle. The shallow puddle of water had allowed no more than a dispersal of the grime that covered her body and in desperation, she had jerked the quilt back on the bed, searching for a pocket of protected coolness and collapsed, face down on the sheets.

Thinking back, she had no memory of bolting the door or even closing it, only the rabid determination to relieve the sweltering heat, and there had been no warning, no creaking floorboard or the usual nervous cough. She had wondered how long he had watched from the doorway before silently crossing the room and tracing his calloused fingers down her spine. She rolled over in a panic, groping unsuccessfully for the covers that had been thrown to the foot of the bed, then cowered against the headboard. As he sat gently on the side of the bed, he had touched her shoulder, letting his fingers drift slowly down her arm and she had been horrified to recognize the unmistakable flutter in the pit of her stomach.

'I fixed a cold bath for you, down in the barn.'

His words had been soft and his eyes kind, and though the dark, luxurious coolness of the water beckoned, she had moved ever so slightly, closer to him. He smelled of earth and sweat, tempered with a sweet, musky smell that made her want to bury her head in his neck and breathe deeply. With a painful slowness she had leaned towards him like a bobcat circling the bait of a finely built trap, its natural warning system muffled by its hunger. He made no move toward her, his eyes controlled and steady, forcing her to come to him; and she hated him for it.

The passion had been terrifying, a power struggle ending with an unspoken truce. When it was over he had gone quietly back to his room and that night he had joined the family at the supper table, instead of taking a plate of leftovers to the barn. Although his return to the fringe of their lives had been limited, his overnight trips to town immediately stopped. Since then, she'd been careful always to bolt her door, but in spite of feeling safely in control again, she had not been able to shake the growing fear that her lapse would cost her dearly.

She put the tin of treasures away and washed her face. She hoped the swelling around her eyes and the pinkness that flared around her nose disappeared before Dovie Calhoun showed up.

As Emma's only childhood friend, Dovie was bothersome but harmless; a lumpish girl whose fawning worship of Emma had always made her easy to boss. Emma's mother had loathed the girl when they were younger, considering Dovie far too homely and dim for her adored daughter, and her opinion had not softened over the years.

That morning in town, as Emma had been settling the children down in the wagon with stick candy before going to see Doc Caldwell, Dovie had called out from across the road.

'Why, Lou Emma Stewart, the Lord must've set you down right where I needed you.'

She had waddled across from the dry-goods store and by the time she had said goodbye, she had invited herself over for the afternoon, brushing aside Emma's excuses and hinting that it sure had been a long time since she'd had any of Emma's delicious ginger cake.

Considering Dovie's meager brainpower, she had created a comfortable existence for herself, picking and choosing the elements of married life and motherhood to suit her needs and limitations. No one had ever expected Dovie to marry, but much to everyone's surprise, especially Emma's, she eloped less than two years after Emma's wedding. She set up house, thrilled with the prospect at first, but she soon recognized that cooking and cleaning were two things for which she had neither the talent nor the desire to pursue.

The few times Emma had visited the Calhoun home, it had taken all of her willpower to sit in one of the heavily stained armchairs. Dishes, caked with abandoned meals, had been stacked around the room, and dirty clothes were piled and draped randomly, the fermentation of body odors heavy in the air. Emma had not been eager to return and Dovie had not encouraged it. Dovie's days were spent visiting neighbors on the east side of the ridge and sometimes, depending on the state of her stumpy legs, she ventured over to the west side, sampling her neighbors' home baking on spotless plates and enjoying the pleasant shade of their front porches.

Emma dampened the corner of a linen cloth with witch hazel and held it to her right eye, keeping watch through the window with her other. Dovie had never been one to stick to prearranged schedules, and Emma dreaded the sight of her, rising up over the hill with her daughter Della Mae in tow, swaying from side to side with the plodding gait of a milk cow.

The witch hazel performed its magic, absorbing the puffiness from around her eyes, and she twisted a few stray wisps of hair into place, taking several deep breaths before unbolting the door. The house was quiet. The children would be hungry soon, but she knew they wouldn't dare come back for lunch until the sun was in a position she defined as afternoon. A movement on the back porch caught her eye as she passed through the kitchen and she picked up the broom on her way out.

'Get up, boy! You think you can lay around here all day?'

She prodded Luke in the side with the broom handle and he squirmed to protect his ribs.

'Go on. Get out of here.'

He stumbled down the back steps, and she picked up his quilt with the end of the broom handle, carrying it like a dead snake to the back door and slinging it towards him.

'I want you to scrub this nasty thing and them overalls too. Stinks to high heaven out here. Drag the tub down by the pump. Lye soap's in the bucket down in the barn.'

She propped the broom in the corner and reached for the mixing bowl on the top shelf, then pinned the corners of her apron in place and tied the sash behind her. She hoped baking a ginger cake would help subdue the thoughts that had been gestating in her head since she'd seen Doc Caldwell that morning.

Dovie Calhoun's hips tumbled over the sides of the old ladder-back chair where she sat with her legs spread wide, creating an awning of skirt to catch the crumbs of cake that escaped her lips. She had worked her way through a third of Emma's ginger cake and showed no signs of slowing her pace. Dovie had never been an attractive girl but the last few years had been especially unkind and at twenty-five she looked a good twenty years older and a good forty pounds heavier than she had when they had been teenagers.

Emma sat across from her, mending a torn sash on one of Lou Venie's dresses. From a distant field, the echo of children's games floated back to the coolness of the shaded porch where they sat.

Dovie shoved another piece of ginger cake into her mouth and propped her fleshy arms across her belly.

'Said my body just ain't made for havin' babies.'

Her words splattered soggy cake over her arms and she pinched each morsel between her fingers and tucked it back inside her bottom lip.

'Said I'm lucky to have my Della Mae.'

She had seemed unusually cheerful since she arrived, but Emma noticed a hairline crack in Dovie's voice that sounded ready to fracture from the pressure inside. Emma rolled the thread between her thumb and forefinger until a neatly tightened knot appeared magically at the end.

'Havin' babies ain't all that special, Dovie. Sometimes it's a downright curse.'

Dovie brushed the remaining splatters of cake from her arm and turned her head away as if to study the progress of the honeysuckle vine at the end of the porch.

'But I was so sure this time, Emma.'

They sat quietly until Dovie recovered her jovial optimism.

'I reckon he's right. And Della Mae means the world to me. She does. But . . .'

Her voice seeped through the crack again.

'I know David-Wayne sure wanted a boy.'

Emma said nothing, her needle darting in and out like a dragonfly on a stagnant pond.

'It's the one thing I know he always wanted. I mean, he loves Della Mae and all, but he don't know how to talk to little girls, growin' up with all them brothers. I reckon he'd have made a real fine daddy if he'd just had a boy.'

Dovie looked up in time to see the scowl on Emma's face.

'Now Emma, I know you don't like David-Wayne, but he's treated us just fine. Never once laid a finger on neither of us and you can't say that about too many men these days.'

Emma held up the sash she was mending.

'That look straight to you?'

'Me and David-Wayne been married for near on nine years now. Ain't you ever gonna back down?'

'You shoulda asked me first, Dovie. You didn't know him like I did.'

'Shoot, Emma, we both knew David-Wayne since we was kids.'

Emma threw the dress into the basket at her feet and

walked to the edge of the porch, folding her arms fiercely across her middle.

'You didn't know him, Dovie.'

Dovie shrugged and reached for another piece of cake, chewing thoughtfully while Emma stared out over the fields. The children had moved closer to the house and were playing a game of statues, and nearby, Luke knelt beside the washtub in his underpants, still scrubbing the quilt and overalls. Emma called across the yard.

'Ain't you finished yet?'

She came down the steps, advancing slowly and deliberately towards him.

'Smelled like every dog in the county took a pee on that old quilt – didn't it, boy?'

The children's game slowed to a halt as they stopped curiously to listen.

'Cain't hold yer pee-water, can you, boy?'

Della Mae giggled and turned to share the laugh with the others but Emma's children stood perfectly still, their faces frozen and fixed on their mother.

'Every night, just like a helpless little baby, he pees all over his quilt.'

Della Mae giggled again.

'Della Mae!'

Dovie's voice smacked her daughter into a reluctant silence. Emma suddenly bolted back to the edge of the porch and slapped the floorboards with the palm of her hand.

'Dovie, pass me that mendin' basket. I reckon I got just the thing.'

Dovie's voice was quiet.

'Emma, what you doin'?'

'Go on. Pass it over here.'

Dovie shoved it over with her foot and Emma dug around until she came up with a large scrap of flannel.

'Come 'ere.'

Luke looked up but didn't move.

'I'm almost done . . .'

'I said get over here.'

He dropped the quilt into the water and crossed the yard where his mother stood unfastening the pins on her apron.

'I reckon if you're gonna pee in your britches like a baby, we oughta dress you like one.'

She pulled him towards her and he squirmed, trying to get away.

'Please . . .'

She clipped him hard across the ear and jerked him towards her again, pulling the flannel between his legs and pinning it in place.

'There now. That's more like it. You got your own little pee-pee pants.'

She turned towards the silent children, her face smiling and encouraging, and her own children followed her cue, making soft but hesitant gurgles of laughter. Della Mae joined in and the laughter built as Luke returned to the wash-tub.

She could feel Dovie's disapproving eyes on her as she joined her on the porch.

'Oh stop it, Dovie. It ain't gonna hurt him and I ain't gonna make him wear it all day.'

'Seems to me like you enjoy treatin' that boy the way you do. Ain't his fault he's simple.'

'I don't treat him no different than nobody else would. You think he'd be treated any better in the county home? I coulda sent him there, soon as I knew about him, but I didn't. He's lucky he's got what he's got, so you can get off your high horse, right now, Dovie Calhoun.'

Dovie pushed the crumbling ruins of the cake away from her and Emma slumped down in the chair. She watched Luke hunched over the tub, his scrubbing interrupted only by a quick swipe of his arm across his eyes. She settled back with satisfaction and listened to the distant chants of a new game, the splash of water as it spilled over the side of the tub and the scraping of Luke's knuckles on the washboard.

Canaan

Canaan's head was still buzzing as she cleared the prep table and wiped down the condiment containers. She was only vaguely aware that there was a commotion at the front of the store, but as it grew louder, it drew her attention.

'You ask her. She'll tell you.'

'Sir! Sir! I know they're returnable, but I can't take 'em up here.'

'Six eight ten. That's plenty enough for them cakes, 'ain't it?'

Canaan's heart sank as she recognized Luke's adamant voice. Reluctantly she headed towards the front. She could hear the agitation in the girl's voice as she neared the register.

'No . . . now . . . Sir! Sir! I'm sorry. You're just gonna have to take these outside . . .'

Canaan saw Luke lining up a dozen or more glass bottles on the conveyor belt. Some of them were slimy with ditch water and soggy leaves. The girl desperately reached for the microphone.

'Mr Bernard. We have a problem on register three.'

Canaan hurried over and Luke grinned when he saw her. 'There she is. That's her.'

Canaan quietly and quickly started putting the bottles back into his bag.

'Put these away, Luke.'

'This is Aline. I was tellin' her about you.'

Luke smiled proudly at the young woman who seemed relieved that someone else was dealing with him.

'Canaan was valedictorian.'

Canaan snapped at him and shoved a bottle into his hands.

'Luke, help me with these – now!'

Obediently he returned the bottle to the bag.

'But how'm I gonna buy my Dolly Madisons?'

Canaan looked at the girl and nodded towards the cakes he'd brought up to the counter.

'How much?'

'Seventy-eight with tax.'

Canaan reached into her pockets and fished out a dollar bill. The girl gave her the change as Kyle rounded the corner, his shoulders squared in self-importance.

'We got things under control here?'

Aline nodded and pointed to Canaan.

'Yes-sir. They're related.'

Kyle gave a parental 'I'm disappointed in you' smile.

'Well, I sure hope this isn't a sign of things to come, young lady.'

Canaan shoved the last of the bottles into the bag and dragged them off the conveyor belt.

'No-sir . . . I'll take care of it.'

She led Luke outside the store and handed him the bag.

'Why do you always have to make a fuss, Luke?'

'I didn't. It was Aline made a fuss.'

She handed him the cakes.

'Please just go on home, Luke.'

'I will soon as I eat my cakes. You want some?'

She could feel her temper rising.

'No, I just want you to . . .'

She hesitated.

'. . . not talk to people about me.'

'Makes me proud to tell 'em.'

'I know but it's hard enough for me without . . .'

He gently pulled her arm.

'Why don't you come sit with me? I got my own bench.'

She pulled away, exasperated.

'I can't . . . I'm . . .'

She took a deep breath.

'Luke, I don't want you coming around here when I'm working. I can't just stop and talk to you. Do you understand?'

He nodded.

'Like with Lou Venie.'

'Lou Venie?'

'She likes me to pretend I don't know her when she's uptown.'

Canaan's heart melted.

'No, Luke, that's not . . .'

He patted her arm and started across the street.

'It's OK. I don't mind.'

She called after him.

'Luke!'

As she tried to decide whether to go after him, she heard another voice from across the square.

'Canaan!'

Zeke was standing by his van. He waved cheerfully and, dodging the cars, jogged over to her. There was nowhere for her to run.

'Hi, Mr Forrest.'

He hugged her and she responded awkwardly. He laughed.

'We're both grown-ups now, Canaan. You can call me Zeke.'

She smiled sheepishly.

'Sorry.'

'I heard you were back. You been avoiding me?'

'No. Of course not.'

'So how are you?'

She glanced down at her uniform.

'What does it look like?'

'Well, pink was never your color.'

There was a heavy, uncomfortable pause and Canaan turned as if to make her get-away. Zeke blurted something out trying to hold her back.

'Are you goin' to the reunion?'

'Oh God . . . no. Are you?'

He shrugged.

'Part of my job description. Class sponsor, remember?'

She smiled.

'Do you get hazard pay for that sort of thing?'

They both laughed, more of a half-laugh than a real one and Canaan took a small, hesitant step away from him.

'Look, Canaan. Why don't you go with me?'

She shook her head.

'I really hate those things.'

'Me too. Sounds like a good match to me.'

'I'm sure your wife would rather . . .'

He laughed.

'How did you miss that bulletin? She left me in a cloud of dust. Almost five years ago.'

She started to feel panicked.

'No but really. I need to get back to work. It was good to see you.'

He reached out and touched her arm and she felt the same teenage flutter in the pit of her stomach.

'Look, they've roped me into making a speech. Mrs Olsenbacher is finally retiring.'

'Gummy Bear?'

'Mrs Toothless Wonder herself.'

Canaan smiled. Mrs Olsenbacher had been the reigning dame of the school cafeteria. She was a beefy country woman of solid German stock who soaked her teeth in a glass on the condiment shelf while she slapped healthy portions of macaroni casserole onto green plastic plates. Her lips were flabby and oversized and without the support of her dentures, they flapped across her gums when she spoke. And she spoke constantly to every student who passed by on their way to the cash register. She prided herself on knowing something about each student and had not seemed concerned that she sometimes repeated the same questions day after day.

Your momma workin' hard at the bank?

Bet your brother's enjoyin' hisself at A&M.

The students always nodded politely, pretending that they hadn't already told her the answer many times before, then shared winks with anyone in the line who could share the joke. For Canaan, however, Mrs Olsenbacher's daily question had created a ripple of sniggers around her.

How's that Looney Tune uncle of yours?

On days when Mrs Olsenbacher had been especially talkative the harmless but insensitive old woman had elaborated on some hilarious thing she'd heard Luke say or seen him do when she'd been in town the day before.

The humiliating episodes had eventually thrust Canaan into the welcoming fold of the brown-baggers, a group of students who braved the rain, cold and sweltering heat to eat under the metal awning optimistically referred to as the Student Garden. It consisted of a small patch of grass, sliced down the middle by a bald dirt-trail short cut and a scrawny bush usually decorated with sandwich wrappers and banana skins. The concrete slab had supported a shabby collection of splintered picnic tables and was carpeted with cigarette butts. Zeke had been the only staff member to choose the same dining option, much to the irritation of other teachers who considered it treacherous that he would renounce the inner sanctum of the teachers' lounge. The B-Bs had filled their oasis hour with laughter and discussion, the likes of which Canaan had not known since. She wondered, with a touch of jealousy, if there was another, similar group that met there now and if Zeke still joined in.

'I can't believe old Gummy Bear is still alive. She still keep her teeth by the ketchup bottles?'

'Last few years they moved up by the cash register. Word is she's donating them to the trophy case in the library.'

He took Canaan's hands.

'Please come with me. It would be a real treat to talk to somebody about something besides the football team for a change.'

'Oh, Zeke. I don't know.'

'There's a bet goin' 'round about me slippin' old Gummy Bear the tongue when I give her my farewell kiss . . .'

Canaan cringed and he smiled, encouraged.

'Come on. You can't pass up a chance to see that! Go with me.'

'I don't know if I'm ready to face . . .'

She hesitated and shrugged. Zeke squeezed her hands.

'The past? I'm part of that past too, Canaan. It was an important friendship for me. I've missed it.'

She was suddenly overwhelmed by an old, comfortable feeling of belonging.

'Me too.'

'Go with me.'

She took a deep breath and smiled.

'OK.'

There was a loud rapping on the window. Canaan turned to see Kyle frowning from the store window. She pulled away from Zeke.

'Sorry, I have to go.'

She hurried inside and Kyle gave Zeke a disapproving smirk before scuttling back to his office.

Luke had settled on his bench under the deep shade of the magnolia tree, arranging his bag of bottles on the seat beside him. Zeke wandered over with Stonewall and two sandwiches from the deli.

'Hi, Luke.'

Luke tipped his hat.

'Mr Forrest.'

Zeke had tried to get him to call him by his first name for years, but the old man had always insisted on formality. After Canaan had left for New York he'd taken over as guardian – partly because he was genuinely fond of him and thought he was far more interesting than most of the people who lived in Lander, and partly because he'd hoped it would keep him in touch with Canaan. It hadn't.

'Mind if I join you?'

Luke slid along the bench hugging his pickin' bag tightly against him. Zeke unwrapped the sandwiches and Stonewall flopped down at his feet. He tore off a part of the turkey sandwich and fed it to the dog.

'No luck with your bottles today?'

'Nope. Gotta clean 'em up. People don't like things dirty.'

They ate silently for a while – Zeke and Stonewall their Piggly Wiggly hoagies and Luke his Dolly Madison cupcakes. When Zeke had finished his last bite he reached into his backpack.

'I've got something for you, Luke.'

He pulled out a second-hand book and handed it to him. Luke's eyes danced as he took it.

'*Treasure Island*!'

'You said you wanted it.'

'Never had one of my own. What you want for it?'

They'd been through this same routine for years. Zeke looked at the sack between them.

'How many bottles you got in there?'

''Bout fifteen.'

'All returnable?'

'Yes-sir. Every dang one.'

Zeke smiled and pulled the bag towards him.

'Well, I figure that oughta pay for it.'

Luke

She had known, as soon as the pregnancy had been confirmed, where she would go. It wasn't the sort of information that ordinary folk usually kept at hand, but she had stumbled upon it, accidentally, years before. She had been helping arrange flowers at the church for Gussie Harper's wedding to the new vice-president of the bank, when a visiting cousin of the bride had confided that Gussie had been pregnant the summer before.

'She don't think I know about it, but her momma all but told my momma it was so. I can bet you the groom don't know nothin' about it though.'

She had continued to unload her secret to Emma, in hurried whispers, explaining that her aunt had seen to it that Gussie had been taken care of before anyone had grown suspicious.

The day after her visit to Doc Caldwell Emma called on Gussie Harper, on the pretense of discussing church plans for the spring picnic, but wasted no time in stating her true purpose. The color drained from Gussie's powdered cheeks.

'Who told you that?'

'That don't really matter, now does it? What matters is that you don't want people around here to get wind of it.'

Gussie picked up a paper fan with a picture of Jesus at Gethsemane on one side and 'White's Gap Baptist Church' printed in Old English letters on the back. She fanned frantically, turning her back to Emma as she walked to the window.

'I never took you as somebody who'd stoop this low for money, Emma.'

'Oh, I don't want money. I want to know where it is you went to take care of it.'

Relief flooded Gussie's face and without a word she crossed to her writing desk. Taking out a piece of stationery, she quickly scribbled a few words across the delicate paper and handed it to Emma.

'I don't know the name of the man who does it, but if you go down to a place called Pete's – it's down by the railroad yard – just ask for Pete and give him this. He'll tell you what to do.'

On the paper she had written, *Tilly needs some fixing*.

Emma's face wrinkled with suspicion.

'Who's Tilly?'

'She was one of our maids when I was in trouble. She sent me down there with a note, said the same thing. She takes care of a lot of girls that way.'

She looked at Emma curiously.

'Who's this for?'

Emma stood and shoved the note into her bag.

'I think I'm holdin' some information that's a little too important for you to be askin' questions, Missus Harper. Just keep that in mind. You have a lot more to lose than I do.'

She smiled sweetly.

'I'll show myself out.'

The following day, she drove down to the railroad yard and found Pete Hibbett sitting in an armchair in a dark corner of his hardware store. The floor was dirt and what little light found its way in revealed an odd collection of farm tools, funeral caskets, and fishing tackle. The room smelled of damp dirt and earthworms and she walked carefully through the clutter of nail kegs and pyramids of rope as she handed him the note. His shirt was open and his bare belly, creased with angry red stretch marks, rested on his knees. He looked up at her from bulging bullfrog eyes, one of which wept steadily from the corner.

'Tilly send you here herself?'

She glared at him, refusing to be intimidated.

'Good as.'

He smiled and she tried not to recoil from the sight of brown tobacco juice that oozed between his teeth and dribbled down his chin. He pulled himself up with a walking stick and limped closer to her.

'Might take me some time to set it up.'

He was close enough for her to smell the stench of decaying teeth on her face.

'My doctor friend is pretty busy these days.'

He grinned and hobbled a little closer, forcing her to take a step back, then led her to a small office in a lean-to at the side where they finally settled on a price.

A few days later she sent the children on a fishing trip with Thom. She packed enough food and water for them to get through the day and a set of dry clothes for each of them, then at three o'clock in the morning she waved them goodbye from the front porch. When they were safely out of sight she pulled her own bundle from under the bed and set out on foot around the outskirts of town, carefully traveling along the tree line in the pre-dawn shadows. Pete met her at the door, leading her across a darkened store and into the office that was lit by a single deformed candle. She laid the roll of money down on the small desk and he counted each dollar bill, looking at her periodically with his weeping eye.

'That's about it, I reckon. He's waitin' for you in the back.'

He pulled aside a stained and shredded bedspread that

had been hung like a curtain, and led her into a room that evidently served as his living quarters. A man sat on the side of the bed sorting through a leather suitcase that lay open beside him. He was slight of build, no bigger than a teenage boy but his face was creased like a well-cured ham. He looked up as they entered and motioned towards the wooden table that had been pulled to the middle of the room, below a lantern that hung from a hook in the ceiling.

'Take off your step-ins and get on up there. I don't like takin' no longer 'an I have to.'

She had looked hesitantly at Pete and the other man glanced up and smirked, pushing his glasses up on the bridge of his nose.

'Pete, go make us some coffee. Hot and strong. This won't take long.'

She crawled onto the table and laid back, staring at the shadows the lantern cast on the ceiling and walls. The man selected a few instruments from his suitcase and pulled a stool towards the table.

'Lord's sake, lady, how you think I'm gonna get to you way back there? Scoot down here to the edge.'

She raised up on her elbows, trying to obey, but one of the table legs was shorter than the others and it wobbled from side to side with her efforts.

'And pull them skirts out of the way. Unless you want a real mess on your hands.'

She pulled the skirts from underneath her and held them in a wad across her chest. He lifted her legs and propped her feet on the edge of the table and she turned her head to one side, taking a deep breath that shuddered more feebly than she wanted. When she opened her eyes, Pete was standing in the door watching, holding back the curtain as he leaned on his stick. She bolted upright, covering herself.

'Get him out of here. You hear me? Get him out right now.'

The small man sighed and sat up from his crouched position.

'What do you want, Pete?'

'Coffee's ready.'

'Well, go drink it, then. I'll be out there directly.'

'You usually let me watch.'

'They're usually a lot younger.'

He looked up at Emma whose eyes were shiny with hate.

'I think this'n has a mind of her own, Pete. I don't want no trouble.'

Pete's bulging eyes never left Emma's.

'She ain't gonna talk. I'd bet my mule on it.'

'She may not, but if you don't get out of here she's gonna make my job a lot harder and you know I don't like missin' my breakfast. Now go on. Get outta here and stay out 'til I'm finished.'

After Pete had gone, the man gave her a leather belt to put between her teeth and started work. She remembered very little of the operation itself. It was as if she had disappeared for a while, and the final hour before sunrise was now a hazy collection of uncertain memories. She remembered sipping coffee that tasted like bark and she remembered being trundled into the back of a wagon and being propped in one of the chairs on her front porch, as the sun was coming up.

Thom found her in the same chair in the late afternoon, her skirt stuck to her legs with dried blood and he carried her to her own bed before fetching the doctor.

Doc Caldwell was silent throughout the examination, but spoke in a low voice as he washed his hands in the basin.

'You didn't tell him about the baby, did you, Emma?'

He looked at her with his steady, no-nonsense eyes and she shrugged.

'Didn't see much point.'

He began to pack his bag, refusing to look at her.

'Well, I don't know if you did this yourself or got somebody else to, but in case you're wonderin', it's done the job. And more than likely it's done it for good.'

He picked up his bag to leave.

'You could've died, Emma. Still could over the next couple of days.'

'I'm gonna be fine.'

He stared at her then shook his head.

'Yep, I reckon you will.'

He stopped at the door before going out.

'I'm tellin' Thom you had a miscarriage. He's a fine man and he doesn't deserve the heartache of knowin' the truth.'

Canaan

The pain started in his hips and lower back and stretched down the backs of his legs to the balls of his feet. His upper torso had not yet caught up with the burning, aching sensations in the lower half of his body, but instead felt heavy and numb. He hobbled across the gravel parking lot. Trying to walk erect. Trying not to let others know. Jimmy limped up beside him.

'Zeke, tell me again why we decided to do this one more year.'

They were making their way to Zeke's van as swarms of high-school students whooped and hollered around them.

Zeke's shorts were caked in mud and one sleeve of his jersey was ripped from its armhole. His knees were covered with grass stains and if it was possible, Jimmy looked worse. Zeke waved his hand above his head.

'Talk later. Just get to the van.'

They had almost made it when a student slapped him on the back. Zeke tried not to wince.

'Good game, Mr Forrest.'

Zeke turned and smiled but kept moving. Painfully.

'Two points, Hobie. We'd have won it with overtime.'

Hobie grinned and tossed the football in the air, walking, practically skipping, backwards as he talked.

'Whatever you say. Too bad I won't be back next year so I can prove it wasn't just luck.'

Zeke stopped and pointed a swollen finger he'd jammed in the very first play.

'Be careful now, Hobie. I'm the one person in this world who could make sure you come back next year.'

Hobie laughed.

'Yeah, well, you did OK, Mr Forrest . . .'

He trotted off to join his friends but turned back with a wicked grin.

'For an old guy.'

They reached the van and Jimmy crawled into the passenger seat.

'I don't know about you, son . . . but I'm about ready to retire the old jersey.'

Zeke dug his keys out of the glove compartment, moaning deeply as he reached a little too far.

'I don't remember hurtin' this bad last year.'

Jimmy leaned back against the seat.

'We won last year. There's no better pain relief than the euphoria of middle-aged victory over youth.'

On the drive back to Zeke's apartment, they were silent except for the soft little groans or sharp intakes of breath as they rattled over railroad tracks or dipped into potholes. As they pulled onto the patch of hard-packed dirt that served as Zeke's parking space, they both sat for a moment, dreading the jarring drop from the van and the long climb up the steps to Zeke's front door.

The apartment sat over the top of an old wooden garage that hadn't seen a lick of paint in more than thirty years. The double barn doors didn't quite join but leaned against each other like two drunks working together to stand upright. What might have been considered a yard was overgrown with ragweed and cow thistle. And at the base of the stairs were the leftover remnants of a herb garden planted by one of the few hippy couples who'd lived in Lander in the sixties. The fourteen steps had been patched together over the years, rotted planks replaced by whatever scrap of wood Zeke could find to nail into place. It left a ragged facsimile of a staircase, randomly dangerous with no handrail to support the inevitable stumble along the way.

Inside, the apartment was surprisingly comfortable – with a perfectly good if not modern kitchen and bathroom and a recently painted living room and bedroom. It was furnished with cast-off furniture, sofas from second-hand shops and chairs – bottomless and abandoned at the city dump – lovingly restored in the garage below.

Jimmy collapsed on the old leather sofa.

'Just bury me with my cleats on, that's all I ask.'

Stonewall took his usual place, curled up in the wingchair, his jowls hanging over the faded tapestry arm. Zeke appeared with two beers and Jimmy took one and sighed.

'It wouldn't be so bad if it wasn't flag football.'

They clinked bottles and Zeke headed down the hall towards the bathroom as Jimmy continued.

'I mean, it's a girl's game really. Not a real sport.'

Zeke returned and handed Jimmy a tube of Deep Heat rub then headed back to the kitchen, letting his friend ramble on. Get it out of his system.

'And it's not like they're even that good.'

Jimmy took his jersey off and started to rub the Deep Heat into his shoulders.

'Jesus, Zeke, we got beat by the B team. The same pimply-faced sissies I used to pick on for being in the band.'

Zeke carried in a tub of hot water and put it down in front of Jim.

'I warned you, Jimbo. Payback is hell.'

Zeke brought the second tub of steaming water in and sat

beside Jimmy. They peeled off their socks and slipped their feet into the hot baths then took a big swig of beer and stared out through Zeke's screen door to the moonlit jungle below. The muffled sound of an old Phil Collins song, played on a car stereo, passed by and disappeared into the night leaving the cheerful hum of crickets making love in the tall grass. Jimmy took another satisfying gulp of his beer.

'Bernie says you turned down that fellowship again.'

'Don't start, Jimmy.'

'What'd you tell 'em?'

'I don't have time.'

'Bullshit. That's the same thing you said ten years ago. You shouldn't still be teachin' high-school English, Zeke.'

'I like teaching high-school English.'

'But it's not what you planned. Lander was just a stoppin'-off place, remember? You weren't supposed to stay.'

'There's nothing wrong with the life I've had here.'

'No. Not for people like me. And not for people like you either if that's what you set out to do.'

'Places like Lander need teachers just as bad as places like Vanderbilt.'

'Yeah, but places like Lander don't pay you to finish that God-damned book you've been writing for fifteen years. They don't pay you to finish that PhD you've only got two years left to finish.'

'Money isn't everything.'

Jimmy grabbed his jersey and pulled it on over his head.

'Very noble, Zeke. But you know what, bud? That's not the reason you said no.'

'Oh really?'

'Yeah really.'

'And you think you know the reason?'

'You bet I know the reason.'

'Well, enlighten me, Mr Wizard.'

'You said no because you're a chicken shit and it's too

easy to sit back on your smug ass and soak up all this small-town adulation.'

Zeke sat up, defiant.

'I'm proud of what I do.'

Jimmy stepped out of the footbath, sloshing water over the sides.

'Awww hell, Zeke. You're really pissin' me off.'

He picked up his shoes and socks and headed for the door, leaving sloppy footprints across the floor. He turned back before he left.

'They won't ask again, Zeke.'

Zeke picked up the spirit badge and threw it at the screen door.

Damn, he hated Homecoming.

Every lamppost in the square was festooned in royal blue and gold and in every store window home-made posters joined forces with flashing signs and declared undying pride in the high-school football team. As the Indian summer neared its end, some of the shoppers still clung to shorts and T-shirts while others hurried the promise of fall with corduroy and three-dimensional sweaters in the muted colors of turning leaves. It was Homecoming weekend and the town was dizzy with Golden Eagle pride.

Canaan examined the school and business supplies at the back of Lucille's Five-and-Dime, trying to ignore the bubbly high-school students who were choosing blue-and-gold decor-ations from the wall of crepe-paper streamers and pom-poms. She had hoped to avoid the Homecoming hysteria that led grown men to dig out their old varsity letter sweaters and wear them around town, seeking out the peers from their past in barbershops, drugstores and diners, to re-enact in glo-rious detail the winning point of the winning game of the winning year they had played for the Golden Eagles. The women were as bad: swapping trinkets of gossip about the color, the cut and the cleavage of the evening gown the Homecoming Queen planned to wear and comparing it to the good old days when beehives and nineteen-inch waists defined style and elegance.

She would never have ventured out into such mania if Lou Venie hadn't insisted. She said she had a stack of utility bills to take care of and 'complaints to see to'. Canaan didn't ask for specifics. Her grandmother kept an ongoing list of other people's shortcomings and oversights and was only too willing to share them in long, drawn-out detail if you made the mistake of asking, 'Why's that?'

Canaan had also promised Luke that she'd buy him a new ledger. *One with gold letters on the front.* So instead of waiting safely in the car for Lou Venie to run her errands, she'd been forced to mingle with the Homecoming zombies. For the last few weeks Luke had been working day and night on his newest project, cataloguing his thousands of books, writing down not only the title, author and ISBN code but where he'd bought it, how much he'd paid for it and a few paragraphs on why he loved it. He'd always been a list maker. There was one corner of the Little House reserved just for the stacks of ledgers he'd kept over the years. He'd kept detailed accounts of every town he'd visited, every job he'd been paid for, every boarding house he'd stayed in and every meal the various landladies had prepared for him. He even had a list somewhere of his weight, which he'd measured on the first day of every month for the past seventy years. Now it was books. The only surprise for Canaan was that he'd never done it before.

She headed to the front of the store, dodging two determined cheerleaders who'd obviously been sent for more crepe-paper supplies. The woman at the checkout had hair the color of red licorice and it was swept into a gravity-defying confection of loops and curls.

'You bought your spirit badge yet?'

She held up a badge the size of a saucer that showed a swooping eagle with talons dripping with blood. A blue ribbon emblazoned with *Champion Eagles* hung below it.

'No, thanks.'

She grabbed the bag and her receipt before the woman had a chance to sell her a blue-and-white shaker for the football game and joined the gathering mob of people outside who were watching workmen as they set up the grandstand in front of the courthouse. Lou Venie emerged from the post office, a glow of satisfied accomplishment on her face. Canaan wondered what sin some poor mailman had committed. She waved discreetly to get her grandmother's attention and Lou Venie hurried over.

'Look at this. Found a goldmine in there!'

She waved a stack of brochures and flyers then fanned them out like a deck of cards.

'I was thinkin' . . . all you really need is to get out and start socializin'. That was your problem in high school. Always had your nose in a book. Made people think you was too good to have a good time.'

Canaan blushed as complete strangers listened in to their conversation. She tried to speak low and close to Lou Venie's ear.

'Can we talk about this in the car, please?'

Neither Lou Venie's excitement nor her voice level wavered.

'Just look at these, Canaan. Coffee mornings, craft clubs, quilting circles . . .'

She pulled out a handwritten index card.

'And a bowling league is looking for another member. Course you'd have to go to Garland for that one . . . over to the Super Bowl . . . but look here . . . they play twice a week with tournaments on Saturday . . .'

Canaan tried to pull her grandmother away from the hub of the crowd.

'Will you stop it? I don't bowl, I don't make macramé planters, and I don't sew. I do not need you to find me a social life.'

She took her grandmother's arm to lead her across the road.

'Now come on. I want to get away from all this craziness.'

Much to her relief Lou Venie followed without arguing, but as soon as they were safely across the road she started again.

'Well, you ask me, you'd be a lot better off if you got involved in some of this "craziness". You had a perfectly good chance to meet some of your old friends at the reunion . . . but you think you're too good . . .'

Canaan hadn't planned to tell her, but she couldn't stand the pious tone in her grandmother's voice.

'For your information, Miss Social Secretary, I am going to the reunion.'

Lou Venie's face lit up and she pulled Canaan to a stop.

'Well now, that's about the best news I've heard in a while. You meetin' some of your friends there?'

'I'm going with Zeke Forrest.'

Her grandmother's jaw turned to iron and her eyes narrowed. She turned and marched towards the car.

'And that's just about the worst news I've had in a while.'

Canaan caught up with her.

'Why? I thought you'd be happy.'

'Wasn't there enough gossip goin' 'round your senior year? You got to add fuel to the fire?'

'What gossip? What are you talkin' about?'

'You think I didn't know what people were sayin' about you? It was all over town. Wasn't right a teacher showin' so much attention to a young girl.'

'Nan . . .'

She rarely called her grandmother Nan. It was a throwback to her early years at the Stewart farm and it usually signaled that she was feeling vulnerable. She turned Lou Venie to face her.

'Nan. Nothing happened back then. Never has and never will.'

'I saw how many times he brought you home late.'

'We were working on the newspaper.'

'Gallavantin' all over the state. Stayin' overnight.'

'The whole debate team was there. There were three other girls in my room.'

'I saw the way you looked at him in that picture.'

Canaan moaned and raised her hands in the air in despair.

'It was a schoolgirl crush! For God's sake, Lou Venie, what is your problem?'

The old woman turned and snapped at her.

'I'll tell you what my problem is, missy. That man sent you away. Filled your head with silly ideas. Made you think you were special and better than all this. He good as nailed me in my coffin when he put you on that bus.'

She hurried towards the car and stood waiting for Canaan to unlock the door. Next to the Mustang, a dumpy woman, dressed in a royal-blue sweatsuit and covered in spirit badges, was helping her teenage daughter to mummify their car in crepe paper and balloons. Canaan waited impatiently for the woman to move out of the way so that she could unlock her car. At last she cleared her throat and the woman smiled as she squeezed to one side.

'Sorry, hon. You want us to decorate your car too? We got way more than we need.'

Canaan didn't look at her but shook her head and slammed the car door. God, she hated Homecoming.

Luke

John Curtis climbed down from the chinaberry tree and raced across the yard, his face pink with excitement.

'The togger's comin', Momma. Togger's comin.'

Emma applied the last lick of spit to Gene Allen's unruly hair as he grimaced and tried to inch away from his mother's grasp.

'Photographer, John Curtis. Stop talkin' like you're stupid. Now get over here and let me comb out that rat's nest.'

She let go of Gene Allen and he streaked past his brother and out the kitchen door.

'Gene Allen, if I see a speck of dirt on you before we get this picture done I'm gonna whip you within an inch of your life.'

She pulled John Curtis between her knees and began to yank at the tangles with her comb. He winced but continued to jabber about the photographer's big black car in breathless half-sentences.

Harvel Jenkins had been the first photographer in Etowah County to take his business to his customers. Previously, families who could afford a portrait had been forced to travel to a studio in one of the larger cities, so Harvel's idea of home portraits had spread quickly among the rural and town population of Lander. As he had grown more successful, he had celebrated by purchasing a big black motor car and the smoky trail he created on the dusty farm tracks signaled to gossiping neighbors that someone must have been laying aside extra egg money to pay for a 'Harvel Jenkins Home Portrait'.

John Curtis had been up in the chinaberry tree all morning watching for the plume of dust heading their way. He squirmed in his mother's grasp as the sound of chugging grew louder. Gene Allen yelled from the front porch.

'He's here, Momma! He's here!'

John Curtis squealed and made a lunge for the front door. Emma sighed and stood up, brushing the knotted fluffs of hair from her skirt as the sound of sniffles rose from the other end of the back hallway.

'Lou Venie, get on out here. Poutin' ain't gonna do you a bit of good.'

For the last few days, Lou Venie had been practicing for the photographer in the mirror, tossing her long hair over one shoulder and smiling demurely from a side pose, then dividing it down the middle and bringing it forward to cascade down her chest in a wispy froth. She had practiced with bows and her mother's pins and combs, trying to get just the right sweep. That morning, in the excitement of choosing her dress and freeing the ringlets of hair from the rags that had bound and trained them during the night, she had forgotten to gather the eggs. Emma's bellow, when she'd found the empty egg basket, had sent them all scurrying, and she told Lou Venie she wouldn't be included in the picture-taking until her chores were done. In a desperate hurry to finish before the photographer arrived, Lou Venie had carelessly dropped the basket, breaking all but two of the eggs, and Emma had dragged her into the yard and tied her to the kitchen chair with one of Thom's shirts. Deaf to the little girl's screams, Emma chopped without mercy, holding each ringlet above Lou Venie's head and dropping it to the grass below.

'You take somethin' from me that's mine, Miss Venie, and I'm gonna take somethin' from you that's yours.'

When it was all over, Lou Venie had been left with a short, jagged bob that sprouted over her ears like tufts of crab grass around a sapling, and she spent the morning hidden away in the back room.

Emma straightened a few strands of her own hair and checked her profile in the mirror above the sideboard, then stood on tiptoe as she smoothed her skirt over the flat slenderness of her waist. She should have been showing by this stage, but that was all over with now and she smiled, pleased with what she saw. In the months since he'd found her, half bled to death on the front porch, Thom had been tender and attentive while she recuperated. The last few weeks she had felt stronger and better than ever. She smiled again at her reflection. Things were finally back to the way she wanted them. She straightened the bow at her neck and caught a glimpse of Lou Venie lurking at the edge of the door.

'You stopped your snivelin' yet?'

Lou Venie nodded and wiped the small patch of dampness that glistened under her nose.

'Come on then.'

She grabbed Lou Venie by the wrist and pulled the reluctant little girl outside to where the others were waiting.

Harvel Jenkins was busy setting up his equipment, looking official and talking himself through his checklist so that everyone could admire his technical know-how, and Gene Allen sat in the grass, at his feet, studying every move. John Curtis was a few yards away, inching closer to the black automobile as Thom set up the chairs in front of the apple tree. Emma came down the steps dragging Lou Venie behind her.

'Mighty fine day for a family portrait, Mizz Stewart. Perfect light, I'd say. Why don't you and your husband take a seat in them chairs and I'll start placin' the young'uns.'

He clucked around them like a meddlesome aunt, moving the children from standing to sitting positions and back again.

'Almost missed you, boy. Slide on in the back there between your ma and pa.'

He stepped back and formed his hands into a square.

'That's gonna balance ever'thing out just fine.'

Emma twisted in the chair in time to see Luke step into the space between them. He was dressed in his usual ragged overalls, but underneath the bib he wore a crisp new shirt and his hair had been combed and tucked neatly behind his ears. She turned with venom towards Thom and he lowered his eyes.

'The boy oughta be in the picture too, Emma. It's supposed to be a record.'

She continued to stare at him and he stumbled on.

'I give him one of my shirts and cleaned him up a bit, make him presentable.'

Her anger danced just below the surface of her eyes.

'I ain't havin' that boy in my family picture.'

Thom slowly looked up and met her glare with an uneasy calm.

'Well, we ain't havin' a picture without him.'

Harvel flapped in blissful ignorance behind the camera.

'This is gonna be just fine. Move on up a little bit, young man, and you two boys look up this way.'

Thom gazed with unwavering determination at his wife.

'Don't make a scene, Emma. You don't want Mr Jenkins spreadin' tales.'

Emma opened her mouth to say something but stopped as the photographer stepped from behind the camera.

'Mister Stewart, look this way. You too, Mizz Stewart.'

Thom turned and faced the camera, straightening his back against the chair.

'Sugar, why don't you put your hand on your daddy's knee? There you go. That's fine. Mizz Stewart, let's see that pretty face.'

Slowly she turned to face the camera, her teeth clenched and her eyes vacant and empty.

'Now hold real still 'til I tell you to move.'

Lou Venie lay awake in the dark and listened to the steady whistled harmony of sleep across the room where her brothers shared the big bed. She twisted the short snippets of her hair between her fingers and stared out the window. The moon was full, the night cloudless and the landscape beyond shone with a pearly-blue haze. On the clothesline the remnants of a white shirt, hung with clothes pins by its shoulders, jerked and shuddered in the breeze.

As soon as the photographer's car had dropped over the hill and out of sight, her father had gone to the barn to work on the chicken coop he was repairing and her mother had grabbed Luke by the ear, slapping him around the yard. Lou Venie and her brothers had sought refuge on the front porch, watching nervously as the two of them danced in clumsy circles.

'Take it off. Take it off right now or I'm gonna rip your arms off myself.'

Amid the slaps, Luke managed to pull his arms from the shirt and Emma wrenched it from the rest of his body, ripping away the bottom two buttons and leaving gaping holes where they had been. She grabbed her sewing basket from under the porch swing and the three children hurried out of her way, cowering in the corner at the far end. Pulling out a large pair of scissors, their mother began to slash the shirt into ribbons and they watched as the sweat popped across her forehead and top lip. By the time she had pinned it to the clothesline, a flag of warning for all to see, Luke had disappeared.

It had been a short tantrum, compared to most, and although things had quickly returned to normal, the afternoon had been a difficult one for Lou Venie. The boys had been unmerciful in their taunting, following her and teasing her to tears.

'You look like a nappy-headed squirrel, Lou Venie. Mizz Colt's gonna make you sit with the boys at school.'

They had spent the day tormenting her and when she had complained tearfully to her mother, Emma had joined in.

'I reckon they're right, Venie. We might have to change your name to Henry or Travis before school starts. What do you think, boys?'

The boys had agreed amid giggles.

'And you sure ain't gonna need all them dresses no more. I think we oughta buy you some britches.'

They had continued the persecution, until Lou Venie locked herself in the back bedroom, crying herself into a fitful nap. When she finally ventured outside, the boys seemed to have forgotten her and were content with their own game. She felt fairly safe playing with her doll under the weeping willow tree, until they suddenly appeared with their hands behind their backs.

'Got somethin' for you, Venie.'

She stepped from behind the sweeping branches and eyed them suspiciously.

'What is it?'

'Somethin' to make your hair grow.'

In an instant Gene Allen knocked her to the ground, straddling her and pinning her down. The boys had collected handfuls of the broken eggs that Lou Venie had dropped that morning, scooping them up from the compost on the creek bank where they had laid, for hours, spoiling in the hot sun. The boys smeared the stinking goo into her hair and over her face, squealing with gleeful enthusiasm as Lou Venie squirmed and screamed beneath them. Her mother sent her down to the creek with a towel and a bar of lye soap because she didn't want the smell to get into the house and Lou Venie cried pitifully all the way down to the clearing. She had always been scared of the creek, even in broad daylight, but as the evening shadows crept closer, she had been overcome with terror at what was hiding in the undergrowth a few feet away.

Even now, safe in her bed, surrounded by the reassuring snores of her tormentors, she felt uneasy. She missed the comforting feel of her hair on her neck; she felt naked and exposed.

In the darkness, she heard the familiar squeaking of floorboards from the other end of the hallway and she sat up in bed, terrified, pulling the quilt to her chin. As she stared into the black tunnel beyond the door, Luke seemed to materialize. He crept across the room, making one careful step at a time then stopped at the end of the other bed and looked over at her. Putting a finger to his lips, he pulled a king snake from behind his back and lifting the covers at the bottom of the boys' bed, he dropped it underneath. At the door he looked back over his shoulder and they exchanged small conspiratorial smiles.

She waited nervously for the impending spectacle, grateful to be awake, the trauma of her day forgotten in her excitement. Through the window, she saw Luke saunter casually across the yard. He reached up and pulled the white shirt from the line, and tucking it under his arm he melted into the night just as the screaming started in the next bed.

Canaan

Luke's directions had been easy to follow. She pulled the Mustang alongside the ditch and turned off the engine. The small white frame house had been recently painted and the shutters, trimming the windows, were a glossy black. The yard was a haven of shade, protected by four large magnolia trees and enclosed by a chain link fence. Along the side of the house, within spitting distance of the porch, the railroad track lay napping in the sun, guarded by a regiment of mimosa trees. She picked up the book Luke had given her. He'd been busy with his cataloguing project when she'd brought down his breakfast. He'd barely raised his head from the table but before she'd left, he'd asked her to get him another ledger and handed her a battered copy of *The Adventures of Huckleberry Finn*.

'That'n ain't mine. Wonder if you can deliver it back to its rightful owner fer me?'

There was a torn corner of newspaper stuck inside like a bookmark with a name and an address scribbled across the newsprint. She pulled it out and checked the address with the number on the chain-link gate. She was halfway to the porch when a black woman in her late fifties came around the corner of the house with a clothes basket propped on one hip. She saw Canaan and in three long strides was on the porch. She opened the screen and glared at Canaan.

'I'm tired of you people botherin' me. I told you last week I go to Grove Chapel Methodist. Always have and always will, so you can do your preachin' someplace else.'

Canaan took a few steps forward.

'No, ma'am, I'm not door-knocking. My name is Canaan Phillips. I'm looking for somebody.'

'Who's that?'

'Squeaky James. I think his real name is Titus.'

'Why you want him?'

'My uncle, Luke Stewart – well, my grandmother's brother – was his friend, when they were kids.'

'Luke Stewart?'

'He lives at the Old Stewart Place.'

'Can't say I know him.'

'Well, he asked me to return a book that belongs to Squeaky – er – Mr James.'

'Nobody calls him Mr James 'less they want money or they lookin' for a soul to save.'

She looked at Canaan for a minute, trying to decide.

'You say they were friends?'

Canaan nodded and held up the book for her to see.

'Luke said Squeaky knew my granddaddy too. Woody Phillips?'

The woman's scowl lifted slightly and she walked to the edge of the porch.

'Woody Phillips – worked at Garland bus depot?'

'Yes, ma'am.'

The woman smiled and the basket relaxed on her hip.

'I'm Treva. Squeaky's my daddy. Come on up and have a seat.'

She stepped aside, motioning for Canaan to sit in one of the metal lawn chairs clustered on the front porch.

'He ain't here right now. Went fishin' this morning but

he's usually back 'round about now. You want some iced tea while you're waitin'?'

Canaan nodded and Treva disappeared through the screen door. The shrill blast of cartoons vibrated from inside the house and when Treva appeared a few minutes later with two glasses of iced tea, she stuck her head back in the door and hollered.

'Casey James Douthitt, you better turn that junk off and get dressed. If you're not ready when your daddy comes, you're gonna miss the parade.'

She smiled at Canaan, handing her the tea and sitting in the chair beside her. A small boy in Batman pajamas burst out the door, then retreated shyly to Treva's side when he saw Canaan.

'Casey, this is Canaan Phillips. She's a friend of Paw-Paw's. Say hello.'

He mumbled something that resembled hello and buried his head in Treva's shoulder. Treva rolled her eyes and laughed.

'You oughta come 'round more often. He's not usually this quiet. Daddy says he's the only boy he knows gets his tongue sunburned in the summertime.'

She rubbed her hand lovingly across the top of his head.

'He loves his Paw-Paw though. Would've gone fishin' with him this mornin', but Casey's daddy is takin' him to the Homecomin' parade.'

She nudged the little boy in the ribs.

'Ain't he?'

The little boy perked up, his eyes twinkling.

'I'm gonna ride on the football float.'

Treva winked over his head.

'I made him a football uniform like the big boys.'

She hugged him to her.

'Casey here's gonna play football for the Golden Eagles when he grows up, ain't you, C.J.?'

The little boy squirmed uncomfortably but his sideways grin gave away his pleasure.

'Now run on in and get dressed. Your daddy's gonna be here any minute.'

He zigzagged across the porch and through the door, blocking invisible linebackers in his path. Treva and Canaan laughed and settled back in their chairs.

'His momma and daddy are always busy this time of year. Homecomin' and all. His daddy's one of the coaches at the high school and my daughter teaches English.'

'Bernice?'

'That's right. We call her Bernie. You know her?'

'We were in the same year. We graduated together.'

Bernice, like Canaan, had been one of the faceless students whose names had appeared frequently on the honor roll, but whose identity had remained in the shadow of the brighter stars at the school.

'Well, ain't it a small world? She's Bernie Douthitt now.'

They both turned as the sound of loud complaining rumbled from the side of the house. Treva sighed.

'Sounds like Daddy didn't have much luck.'

His voice was high and scratchy like a choirboy fighting off puberty and as he came around the side of the house, some of his words disappeared altogether in a high-pitched squeak.

'Dad-burn waste of my time. Waste of good minners. Been better off sittin' of the porch, danglin' the damn thing in my iced tea.'

The old man was small, with a wiry frame and a snow-white sprinkling of fuzz encircling a shiny black head. He was dressed in a pair of work pants that hung well below non-existent hips and were trampled beneath old Brogans that were dusty and cracked. He marched along, alone in his aggravation, with a cane pole slung over one shoulder and a bucket that trickled steadily from a badly patched hole, leaving a trail in the dirt behind him.

'Daddy, you got a visitor.'

He stopped in mid-stride and eyed Canaan suspiciously. Treva raised her voice and exaggerated her words.

'She's Woody Phillips's granddaughter. You remember him, don't you? Worked with you down the bus depot.'

'Course I do. I ain't senile.'

Canaan stepped forward and smiled, adopting the same exaggerated projection as Treva.

'How are you, Mr James? I'm Canaan Phillips.'

He nodded as he passed her on the steps.

'I'm fine. And I ain't deaf neither, but you can't tell my daughter I ain't.'

He leaned the pole against the house and turned to take a better look at her.

'Well, you might as well come in outta the heat. I gotta put these minners in somethin' else or I'm gonna lose the whole dang bunch of 'em.'

He opened the screen door and she followed him inside.

'Treva, best set another place for lunch. I got a lot of catchin' up to do with Miss Canaan Phillips.'

The kitchen was small with a green Formica table filling most of the floor space. An electric fan sat on the top shelf, looking down on them and rotating from side to side like a priest nodding his blessings on those below. Earlier, Canaan had joined in to catch Casey and get him dressed and ready to go with his father. Then she'd helped Treva mash potatoes and chop turnip greens. Treva grilled some pork chops and cooked a skillet of cornbread and while they ate Squeaky entertained them with stories about Canaan's grandfather.

'Now me . . . I can take 'em or leave 'em, but your granddaddy, he hates snakes like nobody I ever seen, and when he looked up into them yeller eyes . . . biggest dern rat snake you ever saw . . . draped all the way 'round the door facin' . . . probably crawled down there from the Cobb Farm . . . you know they usually keep a snake or two in their barn to keep the rats out of the feed . . .'

He paused to catch his breath.

'Well, missy, he pulled up his shotgun and shot every dang thing in that barn. Your grandma had over a hundred cannin' jars in there and he blasted every dern one of 'em to smithereens. Peaches and green beans and home-made jelly all over the place. Biggest mess I ever seen.'

They were all doubled over with laughter, not so much at the story itself but the animated way that Squeaky told it. He was a natural actor who liked to make faces and got up often to do an imitation. Canaan enjoyed hearing stories about her grandfather. She knew hardly anything about him. Her grandmother had never forgiven him for dying on her before their girls had even reached high school. He was another part of Lou Venie's past that she'd chosen to bury and forget.

Canaan took a deep breath and dabbed at her eyes with the cuff of her sweatshirt. Squeaky's eyes were also streaming from the laughter and he wiped them with the paper towel that Treva handed him.

'I never laughed so hard in all my days.'

He took a bite of cornbread, and began to choke between hoots of laughter. Treva rushed over to pound his back and he waved her away impatiently.

'What you doin', girl? Stop fussin' and get me some water.'

She held a glass under the faucet and brought it to him. They watched him drink it down. Waited until the coughing spasms slowly subsided. He glanced at Canaan and smiled.

'It's a real shame you never knew him. He was a fine man.'

Treva began to clear the table.

'What was that book you said you had?'

Squeaky looked up.

'Book?'

Canaan scrambled into her purse.

'Yeah. It belongs to you.'

She pulled out the copy of *Huck Finn* and pushed it over to him. He picked it up and studied it, the smile dropping from his face.

'This ain't mine.'

'Are you sure? Luke said . . .'

'Luke Stewart sent you over here?'

'He's my great-uncle. He said it belonged to you. Gave me your address.'

She pulled out the scrap of paper and showed him Luke's handwritten directions. Squeaky shook his head.

'You tell him it ain't mine. Never was.'

Canaan flipped open the front cover.

'But it has your name in it.'

The writing was childish and unpracticed but it was still clear. Treva leaned over the table.

'Daddy, you sure? That sure looks like your signature to me.'

He stood up and slammed the chair under the table.

'I said I don't want it.'

He shuffled out the door.

'Treva, I'm goin' for my nap.'

Canaan turned to Treva to apologize.

'I'm sorry . . .'

Treva shrugged and smiled.

'Don't pay him no mind. He goes off like that ever' once in a while. It don't last.'

She filled the sink with soapy water.

'Just leave the book on the side there. He'll come 'round directly.'

Canaan was helping with the dishes when they heard the front door slam.

'Momma, we're back.'

Casey came bounding into the kitchen with a miniature football nestled in the crook of one arm, his chin tucked low on his chest. His mother Bernie followed, gracefully stylish in a jean skirt and checked cotton blouse, her black hair swept softly from her face with a silk scarf. Her smile was gentle and relaxed and the casualness of her clothes could not mask her willowy elegance.

'Hi, Canaan. Bobby said you were here when he picked up Casey this mornin'. I was hopin' you'd still be here.'

Casey tackled his grandmother around her knees.

'Whoa, boy. Slow down. Ain't you gonna tell us about your big day in the parade?'

Treva glanced up at her daughter and Bernie grinned.

'Oh, Mee-Maw, he was the best-lookin' football player on that float. You should've seen all the cheerleaders fussin' over him. Isn't that right, C.J.?'

The little boy shrugged shyly and ran from the room.

'Momma, I appreciate you takin' care of him again tonight.'

Treva brushed her off, and Bernie looked over at Canaan to explain.

'The game won't be over 'til eleven, and he gets so hyper with all the excitement. I don't know what I'd do without her.'

She gave her mother a hug. Canaan dried her hands and slung her purse over her shoulder.

'I need to get home, Treva. Thank you for a wonderful lunch. And tell Squeaky I enjoyed meeting him and enjoyed his stories.'

'It was a pleasure meetin' you.'

Canaan gave her a shy peck on the cheek and Bernie picked up her car keys.

'I'll walk out with you. I've still got to pick up some banners for the fences.'

Bernie stopped her on the front porch.

'You goin' to the reunion tonight?'

Canaan nodded reluctantly, hoping she wouldn't ask if she was going with anyone.

'Oh, good. I'll see you there then. Bobby can't go. Has to get the boys all psyched up, you know.'

She shrugged.

'Personally, I hate those things, but if you're going we can have a good gossip about it over coffee next week.'

She rummaged in her handbag and handed Canaan a spirit badge.

'I've got these comin' out of my ears. One of the hazards of being a coach's wife and sponsor of the cheerleader squad.'

As Canaan got into the car she tossed the spirit badge into the passenger seat and looked up at the house. She caught a glimpse of Squeaky peering from behind the bedroom curtains. The gap grew smaller as she stared, but she could tell he was still there, watching as she drove away.

Luke

Emma took the biscuits out of the oven and put the pan on the table. With nimble quickness and precision she sliced each steaming disc, smeared butter on each side and closed it around a slab of country ham. She placed each biscuit into the bottom of a basket, safely layered with tea towels to trap the heat and keep them warm until they reached their destination. Lou Venie sat at one end of the table, transferring the forks from her mother's box of silverware and carefully rolling them inside a clean pillowcase.

The smell of baking filled the kitchen. A chess pie cooled in the center of the table, its golden brown surface still bubbling in small dark eruptions around the edge. Gene Allen chased John Curtis around the table using a black armband as a slingshot, laughing with sadistic glee when he managed to snap the elastic on bare skin. With each snap, John Curtis yelped, then giggled as he tried to outrun the next one. Without interrupting her biscuit buttering, Emma took a long wooden spoon from the table and whacked each of them on their backsides as they passed.

'That ain't nothin' for you two to play with. Now put it over there with your pa's shirt.'

Gene Allen did as he was told while his brother tried to rub away the sting his mother had delivered.

'Why's Pa gotta wear armbands, Momma?'

'Respect.'

Gene Allen sat at the table, catching the dribbles of butter that escaped from the sides of the biscuits and sucked his fingers as he talked.

'We goin' the funeral, Momma?'

She slapped his hands away from the biscuits.

'No. We're takin' you over to Granny Myra's. Funerals ain't the place for young'uns.'

'Della Mae's goin'.'

'It's Della Mae's daddy that's died, Gene Allen. Now fetch me a jar of apple butter off the pantry shelf. John Curtis, help him. And get me down a jar of bread-and-butter pickles.'

The boys dragged a chair to the shelves and Gene Allen passed a jar to his brother.

'Danny Holt says Della Mae's daddy was butt-naked when he died.'

John Curtis giggled.

'Butt-naked.'

Emma grabbed the jar from Gene Allen and pulled him down from the chair, pushing him towards the back door.

'Go on outside, both of you, and don't come back in here 'til we're ready to load up the wagon.'

The boys left and Emma began to stack plates in the bottom of a bushel basket. A plate slipped from her hands and would have crashed into the stack below had she not caught it between her palms. Her knees felt as if they would dissolve beneath her and she glanced over at Lou Venie, who was painstakingly rolling another pillowcase with spoons.

'Them knives need polishin' before you roll 'em up and finish stackin' these plates when you're done.'

She wiped her hands on her apron as she hurried down the hall and bolted her bedroom door, sinking down, as her knees finally gave way. Her hands and shoulders shook and she clenched her fists to her chest as she tried to force her body into submission, determined to gain control.

Thom had given her the news two days before, on a cool spring morning when there was nothing more pressing in life than wringing out the last load of bed sheets.

'They found David-Wayne this mornin' down by the railroad yard.'

She didn't look up from her work but cranked the handle, guiding the sheets through the rollers.

'Ain't nothin' new. Dovie finds him down there most mornin's these days, stinkin' drunk. He's never been good for nothin' but drinkin' and whorin' if you ask me.'

'He ain't drunk, Emma. He's dead. Walked into a train.'

The shock had stopped her cold, but she immediately went back to cranking the handle.

'I suppose I should be sorry.'

'I know you didn't like him much, that's your own business, but Dovie's your best friend. You gotta think of her and her little girl at a time like this.'

Emma nodded, pretending to work loose a stubborn roller.

A few hours later she reluctantly visited Dovie with a pot of chicken and dumplings, and the nervous grinding in her chest was made worse the closer she came to the house. The doctor's buggy was outside and she was aware of an uneasy stillness that made it difficult to take a breath. Inside, the curtains had been drawn and she found Dovie teetering erratically in a rocking chair. Della Mae was curled like a startled kitten on one end of the sofa, watching as Doc Caldwell put away his stethoscope and syringe.

'Sedative should start workin' in a few minutes, Dovie, make things a little more bearable. Why don't you try gettin' some sleep now?'

He nodded towards Emma.

'Emma's here. She'll look after Della Mae for you. You get some rest.'

Dovie was still wearing her nightgown, her hair a mesh of matted straw around her shoulders. Her nose ran steadily across her top lip and down her chin and although her words were slurred she turned with relief to Emma, trying desperately to relay a sensible order of events.

'He was quiet at supper, but then, he usually is. And when I woke up this mornin' about four and he wasn't there, I just thought he'd decided to get to the mill early.'

'Didn't he go to Duke's last night?'

Dovie shook her head and wiped her nose with her sleeve.

'He was home all night. Said he was tired and turned in before I did. He was sleepin' sound when I came to bed.'

She shuddered and closed her eyes.

'I wish he had been drinkin', Emma. Just this once I wish he'd been drunk so's I could explain it to folks. Understand it myself. But he was sober, Emma . . . and . . .'

She started rocking again.

'Took all his clothes off. Why would he do that, Emma?'

She started sobbing again softly. Emma glanced at the doctor, then followed him as he nodded her towards the front porch. He shuffled his feet in embarrassment.

'It's probably not decent to talk about such personal things, but everybody's gonna know sooner or later and Lord knows Dovie's gonna need somebody to help her through this.'

He looked at Emma as if he was having second thoughts about telling her, then sighed and continued.

'They found his nightshirt and his long johns folded up, neat as a pin, about half a mile from where he was hit. Looks like he just stripped naked and started walkin' right down the middle of the track 'til the train came along . . . carried him more'n five hundred yards 'fore they could get the thing stopped.'

'Maybe he was sleepwalkin' and he just tripped.'

He shook his head.

'Driver said when he came 'round the bend and his lights hit David-Wayne, he just stood there, stretched out spread-eagle-like. Driver was shaken up somethin' awful. Wasn't a thing he could do. Said David-Wayne kept his eyes open, stared right at him, the whole time. Said it was the scariest thing he'd ever seen.'

She watched as Doc Caldwell climbed into the buggy and nodded when he asked if she'd stay with Dovie for the day. When she went back inside, Dovie was staring with dull eyes into an empty space above the fireplace and Della Mae had started whimpering, her bottom lip quivering pitifully as she called *Daddy* over and over. Emma hurried outside to get the pot of dumplings from the back of the wagon, then set it on the kitchen table, and left without saying another word.

The shivering had finally stopped but a deep sob worked its way up into her throat. Emma shoved her apron into her mouth, forcing the sob back down. She took several deep breaths as she leaned her head against the bedroom door. Lou Venie knocked softly from the other side.

'Momma, I finished what you said.'

Emma wiped her face with the hem of her apron.

'You go on. I'll be out directly.'

She washed her face in the basin and sat on the edge of the bed until she felt fully composed. A few minutes later she walked onto the side porch and yelled for Thom to come load the food into the wagon.

The funeral was mercifully short. Emma had a lot of food waiting in the wagon and she didn't want it spoiling while the preacher tried to sidestep the difficult issues of David-Wayne's public and embarrassing demise and the blatant sin of taking his own life. The preacher decided to take the easy route and say very little beyond the 'earth to earth' speech. It's always hard to talk about the glory of heaven when mourners are picturing the deceased in the fires of hell. Emma was grateful, not only for the sake of her prize-winning chess pies, but for making it easier to hold the granite image she only just managed to maintain.

On the drive to the Calhoun house Emma was quiet and for once she was glad for Thom's silence. If he'd felt inclined to fill the silence or ask her questions she was sure she would have collapsed into an emotional heap. She sat in the back, holding onto a collection of platters and jars, trying to keep them steady as the wheels of the wagon bumped along the rain-washed gullies. As they turned down the road towards the house, there was a sign on the side of the road: *Slow – Death*.

It had been painted with a wide brush on a scrap of timber and it was propped up with three large stones. She could see the small gray house across the field as Thom reined in the horse and the wagon slowed to a crawl. There were already several wagons hitched to trees near the house and it was obvious that a few of them had not heeded the *Slow* sign, because a ghostly cloud of white, chalky dust was gradually creeping across the yard where the tables of food lay.

Thom tied up the horse and helped Emma down from the wagon. There were clots of men mingling under the shade of the trees, smoking and speaking in low whispers. The women gathered around makeshift tables made from doors taken off their hinges and laid across ladder-back chairs. The tables were already groaning with plates of fried chicken, mounds of mashed potatoes, and a stepping-stone path of fruit pies down the middle. Emma found spaces for her own contributions, but stayed to herself. She didn't want to be drawn into the funeral talk. She didn't want to start combing through the tiniest details of David-Wayne's death, or the half-remembered things he'd said that gave some clue to his state of mind or the tea leaves someone had read the very morning of his 'accident' that clearly warned that something awful was bound to happen. She didn't want to hear the funeral gossip or superstitions or old wives' tales, so she shut it out. She filled her head with the clatter of serving spoons and the job of arranging the table just so, being careful not to make eye contact in case they dragged her in against her will.

The time soon came when she'd done all that she could do and she knew she had to find something else quick or the old hens would swoop in on her. She was Dovie's best friend, after all, she would surely know some new and unexplored bit of information. Dovie was sitting on the front porch swing, wrapped up like the charred remains of a Sunday roast in a black gunnysack dress. Her eyes were small red dashes in puff-pastry sockets, and women were taking turns in the seat beside her, holding her lifeless, pudgy hand and crooning like pigeons in her ear. Emma took her place in the line and waited for her dutiful turn with the widow. She hated David-Wayne for putting her through this.

Canaan

Canaan found several old tubes of lipstick in the back of her dresser drawer and had already wasted twenty minutes trying them. They smelled like dead flowers and their texture was distinctly grainy, but for some silly reason she felt she should at least make the effort. Finally in a fit of exasperation she smothered her lips in Vaseline and scrubbed off the layers of color before moving on to jewelry, another minefield. Jonathon had bought her a few token pieces while they were married but she had never had the confidence to accessorize the way Southern girls were supposed to. She tried several plain studs before settling on a simple pair of cameos she'd found years before in a box of her mother's things. She examined them in the dresser mirror and tried once again to fluff some life into her hair. She had been sitting in her slip for the last two hours trying to remember what the 'getting ready for a date' routine involved. Not that this was a date exactly. At least, that's what she constantly told herself to help combat the nerves. It was nothing more than two old friends joining forces. Endurance under stress, nothing more.

She used a pair of nail clippers to remove the sale tags from her new dress. The color was nice – periwinkle blue – but the material was too clingy and the neckline too plunging for her taste. Shopping had never come easy for Canaan but the task was even more troublesome in Lander. Most people either drove to Atlanta if they wanted something special, or to the Walmart in Garland if they wanted more variety. The old Mustang would never have made it, even to Garland, so Gracie-Lee's had been her sole choice. It was the only dress shop in Lander, a compact little store with yellow film taped to the front windows to keep the sun from fading the merchandise. Gracie-Lee herself had not worked there in twenty years but her taste was still very much in evidence. Canaan had searched through the racks of old-fashioned dresses picking out the only two she could find in her size that didn't look like something Lou Venie would wear to a church function. She had initially dismissed the periwinkle dress because of the deep V-neckline and the clinging curves, but the one she preferred, the black summer-wool with classic lines and timeless appeal, cost almost two and a half times more. So she'd settled for the knit dress with deep side pockets in the seams. Periwinkle blue looked good next to her skin, although she didn't know it was that color until she got it home. Through the yellow-filmed windows, she'd thought it was a dark lilac.

She pulled it over her head and smoothed it down over her hips, then stood on the end of the bed trying to create a full-length view with a half-view dresser mirror. As she hopped down onto the rug she caught a glimpse of something on the windowsill and opened the sash to inspect it. It was an acorn, its cap painted a bright blue and a smiling face painted below. One eye had been drawn open, the other in a straight line – to wink at her. She smiled and took it over to the dresser to look at it more closely under the lamp. It was from Luke – to wish her luck. She was five years old when he first introduced her to the Acorn Elves. They'd come across the first one sitting at the edge of a tree hollow filled with rainwater. *This one ain't much of a runner, is he?* It was all he had said, but it had been enough to drive her wild with curiosity. She had listened wide-eyed and still while he had told her about the elves who turned into acorns when they were seen by humans. Each one they found had its own story. One had been wedged between two stones. *Must've got his foot caught, poor ol' thing.* Another had been propped in a tree limb. *Didn't think we'd look up this high, did he, Miss Candy-Cane?* Their magical appearance and the stories that Luke attached to them had kept her entertained for many years but by the time she turned twelve, she found them silly and childish. It hadn't stopped him from sending them to her anyway. They started appearing outside on her windowsill, usually when she was troubled or there was something to celebrate. *Must have wanted to wish you luck,* he'd say, or *Probably just dropped by to cheer you up.* The morning after Mim Simpson and her gang had dumped the cafeteria garbage into her locker there had been one, and the night she'd graduated, the day she'd had the letter from William and Mary and even the morning she'd packed her bags to leave for good. He'd always seemed to know when her moods were significantly up or down.

She put the acorn in the side pocket of her dress. She could use all the luck she could get tonight. In the living room, Lou Venie was on her hands and knees laying out the carpet she'd spent most of the day scrubbing by hand out in the back yard. The October sun had been warm enough to dry it out and she now tried to wrestle it back into place. Canaan slung her purse across her shoulder.

'I won't be late.'

Lou Venie glanced up at her and frowned.

'That teacher of yours picking you up?'

'No. I'm driving.'

Lou Venie choked back a laugh as she smoothed out a hump in the carpet. Canaan tried not to sound defensive.

'It's been drivin' fine the last few days. Besides, I'm not going that far.'

Her grandmother raised up and sat back on her haunches.

'You goin' out like that?'

'Like what?'

Lou Venie pointed.

'Like that. Low-cut.'

'It's a plain cotton-knit dress, Lou Venie.'

'Don't matter if it's silk or cotton. Still makes you look like a slut.'

Lou Venie went back to the carpet. She waited for Canaan to react, to shout at her. But she didn't make a sound. Ruthie would have shouted. And screamed. Lou Venie thought about all the times her daughter had accused her of having an ugly, suspicious mind. *Just before she left me. Just before she walked out of my life for good.* She sat up again and whispered as she turned around.

'I'm sorry, child.'

But Canaan had already left.

The sun had set somewhere between White's Gap Baptist and the old water tower and the sky had turned from tarnished gold to ripening blueberry. As Canaan drove into town the street lamps buzzed to life and created bright white pathways along the sidewalks. There were no street lights in front of Zeke's apartment but a large lamp, stuck on top of a utility pole, lit the waist-high weeds and provided a playground for the last of the summer moths. Canaan pulled in behind his old van and got out as Zeke waved from the top of the stairs and made his way down. He hopped past the step with the broken board and she shook her head.

'They were trying to condemn this place when you moved in twenty years ago.'

Zeke laughed.

'They still are. My ex-wife tried to get it in the divorce settlement just so she could burn it down herself.'

Canaan locked the car door and caught Zeke smiling at her. No one in Lander locked their car doors, or their front doors for that matter. In small towns everyone knew who was who and at any given moment where they were and what they were doing and with whom. When most people knew what your great-grandmother's middle name was, locks weren't really a necessity. But after fourteen years in New York with three chains, two deadbolts and an alarm system on the windows she had forgotten there were places in the world where they laughed at precaution. She shrugged.

'Habit. You sure my car will be all right here?'

'It'll be fine. And you're gonna be fine. You ready to face the masses?'

She nodded nervously and he put her arm through his and gently guided her to the sidewalk.

'This time tomorrow you'll wonder what all the fuss was about.'

The reunion was at Buddy's Pit Bar-B-Que that sat just over the railroad tracks on Zeke's side of town, only a few blocks from his apartment. It was the only place to eat out in Lander besides Betty Ann's Diner and the McDonalds they'd built a few years before at the interstate junction. It had started life as a roadway shack that covered a concrete pit, where a whole hog simmered under a canopy of heavy gauged foil, its own juices mingling with Buddy's secret barbecue sauce. Two generations of Buddies had continued the tradition and the secret sauce, and its hefty, two-fisted sandwiches had become a popular local treasure. Almost a year before, however, progress had beckoned and it had closed down sprouting a sign that promised great things to come. The granddaughter of Buddy the first, having finished a catering and restaurant management course in Atlanta, took over the humble building and proceeded to rip out its soul. She tore down the shack where visitors had sat for years on rickety stools resting their elbows on narrow ledges that surrounded and overlooked the pit. She turned the pit itself into a centerpiece with gingham-dressed windows, for modern diners to sneak a peak at the past. Then she built a cedar-framed restaurant around it that encouraged customers to *Enjoy the taste of the good-old-days*. The dining area was scattered with wood-block tables stenciled with chubby little boys in overalls and straw hats and bell-shaped little girls in pinafores and bonnets. Steps covered by a barn-wood awning led down to what was called the Social Room, where guests mingled around pot-bellied stoves, chatting from picturesque rocking chairs and tossing their peanut shells to the floor to add to the ambience of times past.

When Canaan had been a teenager, Buddy's had been a high-school hang-out on weekends, the perfect place to stop after a night of backseat necking. By day it had been filled with good-old-boys with gun racks in their pick-up trucks. But since its conversion, the clientele of Buddy's consisted mostly of young businessmen, back-slapping their way up the social ladder, and their well-groomed, empire-building wives. Canaan had taken her grandmother to Buddy's for supper soon after its grand opening, but Lou Venie had not been impressed and couldn't be persuaded to stay for Buddy's famous chocolate rolls. She had marched out, her nose tilted in an offended manner as the sound of peanut carcasses crunched below her. *Good old days, my foot. They think we went around throwin' garbage on the floor? My momma would've skinned us alive.* Canaan had agreed with her, but had adopted a 'told you so' smugness for the drive home. Her only reason for going in the first place had been to satisfy her grandmother's curiosity and she had never expected to return. Especially not for a class reunion.

Zeke cleared his throat like a bashful teenager.

'You look nice.'

'Thanks.'

They walked silently for a while as a few weather-hardy crickets squeezed a few more notes from the October night. Zeke shoved his hands in his pockets.

'Great the way we're able to just pick up after all these years, isn't it?'

Canaan felt her face go hot and was glad of the dark. She reached into her pocket and rubbed the acorn Luke had given her between her thumb and forefinger.

'Sorry. I'm out of practice.'

'So how does it feel to be home?'

'Even worse than I thought.'

'Are you nervous about tonight?'

She nodded and clutched the acorn tightly in her palm.

'People aren't as bad as you think, Canaan.'

'Well then, I guess I've never mixed with the right crowd.'

They could see the restaurant now, lit up and glowing. A wide porch wrapped itself around three sides of the building and diners-in-waiting rocked patiently behind enormous fern baskets and beneath a flock of twittering ceiling fans. There was a low hum of animated conversation and laughter as they drew nearer and Canaan tensed up. Zeke squeezed her hand.

'Don't show fear. They can smell it.'

Luke

Luke sat on his haunches in a corner of the barn as Thom finished one of the shelves that would eventually store Emma's canning jars. He had been watching the progress for hours, silently observing and rushing for a hammer or dropped nail to hand to Thom when he sensed they were needed. When he heard his mother calling, he retreated into the shadows. He wasn't afraid of retribution, but of losing the small amount of cherished private time he had with his father. After his twelfth birthday, Luke grew so much that he towered above his mother, and although her tongue had not relinquished its sharpness, the whippings and random slaps had dwindled considerably. His brother Gene Allen, however, showed more of his mother's mean streak as he grew older, and had willingly taken up the banner of persecution against Luke, enlisting the help of his younger brother who was weak and easily led.

Thom lifted a two-by-ten onto the brackets, then stood back cocking his head to one side.

'Boy, you reckon you could do me a favor?'

Luke looked up and nodded, his eyes eager.

'I wanna finish this job up this evenin' and I'm gonna need

some more penny nails. Ain't got time to get 'em myself. You reckon I can trust you to get 'em for me?'

Before Thom had finished his sentence Luke was on his feet. Thom reached into his pocket and handed him some coins.

'I need about two dozen. Can you remember that?'

Luke nodded and carefully placed the coins in his front bib pocket.

'Just follow the railroad tracks that-a-way. When you get to the railroad yard, you'll see a little place called Pete's across from the platform where they load the cotton. He'll get you what you want.'

Luke grinned and dashed towards the barn door.

'Hey, wait a minute.'

Luke's heart sank. He was afraid Thom had changed his mind, but instead he handed him another nickel.

'You been a big help today, boy. Get yourself a RC cola while you're down there. Pete's got an icebox full of 'em. You ever had a ice-cold RC before?'

Luke shook his head.

'You better go on then. I won't be here when you get back. Just leave the bag on the bench.'

Luke stood motionless, until Thom shooed him out the door, then he galloped away from the house and towards the railroad tracks.

He found Pete's easily and was proud that he'd been able to remember and follow his father's directions. As he stepped over the raised lip of the door, the bright sunlight blinded him to the murkiness of the store. The dirt floor felt cool to his feet and he blinked with uncertainty before taking another step inside. A weedy man, with a few greasy strands of hair slicked over a bare patch of head, leaned on the cold pot-bellied stove and eyed Luke curiously. The cavity of the man's sunken chest was clearly visible above the stretched neckline of a badly stained undershirt, and in one hand he clamped a

Mason jar filled with brown slime. From behind the counter a mountainous figure of bare flesh rose up and balanced on a cane.

'You got business here, boy?'

The man leaned over the counter, his belly flattening against it like rolled biscuit dough, and Luke swallowed before nodding and reaching inside his pocket for the coins.

'Penny nails.'

The man leaning on the stove laughed and spit into the jar.

'Hell, Pete, I think you got yourself a customer.'

Pete limped around the end of the counter on his cane. His overalls were unhooked, the bib flapping below his enormous belly like an Indian loincloth. He squinted, closing his weeping eye and piercing Luke with the other one.

'You aimin' to build somethin'?'

Luke shook his head.

'My pa.'

'What's yer name, boy?'

'Luke. Stewart.'

Pete's smile spread slow and deep across his face.

'Yer momma Emma Stewart?'

He nodded and Pete chuckled.

'Well, I'll be damned. She done sent her idiot boy out into the world.'

Luke looked away as Pete waddled towards the other man.

'You remember little Emma Scott, don't you?'

The man nodded and Pete continued, settling in for a good, long session.

'Purtiest little thing you ever saw. Her momma was always spoutin' high-falutin' muckity-muck, 'bout how her daughter was gonna marry this doctor's son friend of theirs, Georgia way or somewhere such.'

A string of brown saliva hung between the other man's lips and the jar. He wiped it off with the back of his arm.

'Ain't she the girl spoilt by that nigger hobo?'

Pete stared at the boy and Luke shifted his eyes uncomfortably from side to side.

'That's the story I heard.'

'What was his name . . . Cody, Coony . . .'

'Corny. Cornell Dobson they said his name was. You ain't heard his name before, have you, boy?'

Pete fixed his eye on Luke.

'You're the bastard son of Nigger Corny, so they say.'

He let out another ugly, snorting laugh.

'I bet it sure put a hitch in their gitter when you came along.'

Pete flipped his hand towards the far corner of the store.

'Nails are over there; barrel in the corner. Bring me a handful and I'll count 'em out fer you.'

Luke gratefully disappeared behind the shelves and boxes, but Pete's voice crawled over the top and mocked him from above.

'I'm tellin' you, Stringer, you shoulda seen her. That little girl was ripe for pickin' 'fore she'd even put down her baby dolls.'

From the cracks between the shelves, Luke saw Pete slap Stringer on the back, then lean closer to him as if to whisper a secret. Instead he lifted his chin and raised his voice.

'And last time I seen her, looked to me like that fruit was just as plump and ready for harvestin' as ever.'

Their laughter was shrill, like shards of glass, and Luke tried to concentrate on counting the penny nails. He had hoped to count them out himself, but the lessons he'd had in the tree house had faded over the years. At last he plunged his hand into the barrel and carried a fistful to the counter.

'How many you need?'

'Two dozen.'

Pete counted them out and put them in a bag, scraping the change from the counter. Luke held up the extra nickel.

'Pa says I can have a RC.'

'Your pa says that, does he?'

There was an ugly burst of laughter from the two men and Stringer choked on tobacco juice. Pete pointed to the ice-box and after sniggering at Luke's attempts to twist or pull the top off, he showed him how to use the lever at the side of the ice chest. Luke grabbed the bag of nails and hurried out the door with the RC. As he stepped into the bright sunshine he heard Pete call after him.

'Tell your momma we said howdy, now.'

Their laughter followed him outside and down the ramp. When it had faded to silence he stopped and took a swig from the bottle. It was cold and sweet and the best thing he'd ever tasted in his life. He took another swig and tilted his head back, savoring the sensation as it chilled and tingled his parched throat.

'Hey, you.'

He looked around but saw no one.

'Under here.'

It was an unusual voice, high-pitched and broken.

'No – behind you . . . down here.'

Luke squatted, turning his head to one side, and stared into the face of a young black boy sitting cross-legged in the dirt under one of the derailed boxcars. The boy grinned.

'Lot cooler down here. I'll share my space with you if you give me a swig of that RC.'

Luke stared uncertainly and the boy grinned again, waving him over, so he crawled under to join him. Trying without success to fold his long frame into a comfortable position, he resorted at last to a crumpled contortion that left his head and body twisted to one side.

'Name's Squeaky James. Glad to meet you.'

He stuck his hand out and Luke handed him the bottle of RC. Squeaky laughed.

'Well, I'd a been satisfied with a handshake but you won't catch me sayin' no to a swig or two.'

He took a long guzzle, then wiping his mouth with the back of his hand he sighed.

'Royal Crown cola . . . the drink of Kings!'

He handed the bottle back to Luke then eyed the paper bag clutched in his other hand.

'What you got there?'

Luke nervously pulled the bag of nails closer to him, and Squeaky chuckled.

'You don't say much, do you? Don't matter. I got so much to say, you wouldn't have no time left no how. Come on, let me see what you got in there.'

Luke slowly relinquished the bag and Squeaky eagerly opened it. His face fell.

'Oh, hell. I thought you'd bought some goober peas off old Pete. Fat old bastard won't let me come in. Says I run off all his customers with all my talkin'. You like goober peas? Now me . . . I love goober peas, floatin' in the top of an ice-cold RC. Nothin' better in the whole world. You got a name?'

'Luke.'

'You live by here?'

Luke pointed in the general direction and Squeaky nodded.

'We live down the line that-a-way. Right next to the tracks. My daddy's a sharecropper. Grows cotton mostly and sugar cane. Makes the best sorghum syrup in the county. Hell, practically in the whole South. You ask anybody. You like sorghum? Now me . . . I hate sorghum, but ever'body else sure does love it. Waste of a good biscuit if you ask me. Give me milk gravy ever' time. I been trying to get my daddy to grow somethin' decent, like goober peas, but he says peanuts don't sell as good as cotton.'

Squeaky's conversation was fast and continuous as if every word was linked to the next, and Luke realized that his own mouth had been slowly creeping upwards into a smile.

'You ever hopped a train?'

Luke shook his head.

'I aim to hop trains the rest of my life. See them men over there? Hobos. They been all over the world. Stop somewhere. Do a little work. Stay a little while or keep goin'. That's what I'm gonna do. Your momma know you're down here? My momma don't. She'd jerk a knot in my tail if'n she knowed I was down here. She don't like me hanging around hobos. Sometimes they let me sit with 'em over there and listen to their stories. You ever been to Chattanooga?'

Luke shook his head and handed the RC back to Squeaky for another drink.

'That's gonna be my first trip, I reckon, Chattanooga. But I ain't sure my legs are long enough to haul myself up in there when the train's movin'. I mean, one slip and a man could lose both his legs. Now me . . . I'm kinda partial to my legs. They might be stumpy, but they get me where I wanna go, you hear what I'm sayin'?'

He threw his head back and laughed and Luke felt his own smile broaden.

'I been waitin' for that growin' spell my momma keeps sayin' I'm gonna have any day now. You sure got long legs, don't you?'

Luke looked down at his legs bent awkwardly in the shape of an S.

'Guess so.'

'You like fishin'?'

Luke shrugged.

'Never been.'

'Hell's bells. You never been? Well, Squeaky James is the

man to teach you. Ain't nobody in these parts good as me at catching crappie and ain't nothin' as good as crappie fried up by my momma.'

The baritone pealing of a distant cast-iron bell brought Squeaky scrambling from under the boxcar.

'That's my daddy. I gotta help him with the plantin'. He's gonna be mad as the devil too, 'cause I was supposed to be there to help him 'fore dinner.'

Luke followed him out and Squeaky stretched, thrusting his chest up like a rooster.

'Lordy me. I'd stretch from here to Georgia if it weren't so far to walk back.'

He winked.

'Thanks for the RC. Next time, thought, don't forget them goobers.'

He started across the rail yard kicking dirt as he walked, then turned back, squinting into the sun.

'Hey, you wanna go fishin' with me in the mornin'?'

Luke nodded.

'Meet me at the water tower, sun-up. You'll have to swear a sacred oath that you won't tell nobody where my fishin' spot is, though.'

Luke nodded solemnly.

'All-righty then. See you in the mornin'.'

Luke sipped his RC and watched Squeaky weave between the boxcars, running gracefully along the track lines like a tightrope walker. He watched until he could no longer see the small black head bobbing above the tall grass in the field beyond. Wedging the empty bottle into his pocket and gripping the bag of nails tightly, he set off for home. It was the first time he'd ever been given a proper responsibility and he didn't want to be late.

Canaan

As they made their way up the center sidewalk, people on the porch turned to watch them. Canaan could feel the surprised glances and hear the curious whispers. Zeke squeezed her hand into the crook of his arm but she instinctively pulled away. On the porch he opened the door for her and she hurried through, eager to get away from the low hum of the gossiping huddles.

Inside, a hostess came bounding up, her smile toothy and uncomfortably sincere.

'How y'all doin' tonight? You stayin' for supper or you visitin' our Social Room?'

Zeke took over.

'Class of '84?'

The girl nodded.

'You bet. They're down in the Social Room.'

She leaned over the church podium that served as the hostess stand and hunched her shoulders, wrinkling her nose with a bubbly cuteness.

'That was a good year, you know. I was born in '84 on the fourth of July, so my daddy named me Liberty, but all my friends call me Libby.'

She smiled proudly as she presented her name badge as

proof. Canaan was still surprised by how often and how easily people in the South could offer complete strangers unsolicited and irrelevant personal details. The girl obviously didn't expect them to exchange their own stories with her. Shame. She had a doozy of a comeback when the time was right. *Well, my mother got knocked up when she was seventeen, killed herself in Memphis when she was twenty-two and left me alone with her rotting corpse.* The girl turned quickly on her heel, inviting them to tag along by wiggling her little finger. They followed her bouncing ponytail across the dining room and Zeke leaned forward to whisper in Canaan's ear.

'You surviving so far?'

'Depends. My heart hasn't stopped if that's what you mean.'

The hostess stopped at the top of the steps leading down to the Social Room.

'There's plenty of hot coffee and soft drinks over there and there's a table full of goodies in the corner. Y'all enjoy yourselves now.'

The soaring rafters hummed with cheerful conversation and the occasional squeal of recognition. As they descended the steps Bernie Douthitt bounded up to them.

'Two friendly faces. Your timing is perfect.'

'Bernie, hi. Do you know . . .'

She smiled and squeezed Canaan's arm like an old friend.

'Course I do.'

She leaned closer to Canaan.

'Have you heard anything scandalous yet?'

Canaan shook her head.

'We just got here.'

'Oh, you're here together?'

Canaan shifted uncomfortably on the stairs and Zeke put his arm around her shoulders.

'I forced her into it. Canaan's here under duress.'

Bernie laughed a deep hot-caramel laugh.

'Ain't we all, Sugar, ain't we all?'

They followed as she continued down to the bottom of the stairs.

'You know, everybody claims to hate these things but they don't dare miss it in case they miss some good gossip.'

Zeke nodded.

'Or to make sure they aren't the ones being gossiped about.'

Bernie grinned.

'You got that right.'

A woman in a vibrant blue sweater appeared on cue with a felt-tip pen and a roll of self-adhesive stickers. She smiled enthusiastically at the trio but immediately twisted her lips in concentration.

'Now don't tell me. They gave me this job 'cause I'm good at remembering names and faces.'

She looked at Bernie.

'Now, I'm pretty sure I know you. You work at the high school, don't you?'

'That's right.'

'Still at good old LHS.'

'You bet.'

The woman looked suddenly serious.

'I hope these cutbacks haven't affected you. It's such a shame to have to lay off hard-workin' folks. But it's happenin' all over, I hear.'

'Lay-offs?'

'The new cleanin' contracts. I think it's criminal bringin' in that big business group from California.'

Canaan watched Bernie's expression closely, expecting a flash of anger or at least a stab of sarcasm. Instead she saw a warm smile spread patiently across her face.

'I teach English at LHS. I'm Bernie Douthitt.'

'Douthitt? Coach Douthitt's wife?'

Bernie nodded.

'Well, of course you are.'

The woman dropped her eyes in embarrassment and hurriedly wrote her name on the badge. She slapped the sticker on Bernie's blouse and Canaan jumped in with her name before the woman could start trying to place her.

'Canaan Phillips.'

Zeke leaned over and started to give his name.

'Zeke—'

The woman smiled flirtatiously.

'Oh, don't be silly. You don't have to tell me your name.'

She handed Canaan her sticker without looking at her, focusing instead on Zeke. He thanked her for her help and she tugged at a loose strand of hair at her neckline before bustling away in the manner of a woman with too much to do. Zeke grinned and ushered the two of them into the room.

'Well, we've survived the welcome wagon. Only an hour and a half to go.'

He playfully tapped the spirit badge on Bernie's blouse.

'See you're busy playin' the coach's wife, Bernie.'

'And cheerleader sponsor. You keep forgetting that.'

'No, I don't. I just choose to ignore that particular weakness in your character.'

She nudged him in the ribs with her elbow.

'I didn't think you liked these things, Zeke.'

'I don't, but it keeps me in a job.'

Bernie winked at Canaan.

'Don't let him fool you. This man has always been able to do exactly what he wants. From what I can figure Zeke Forrest can do no wrong.'

She adjusted her spirit badge and straightened her back.

'Much as I hate to, I have some minglin' to do. Bobby needs some new B-team equipment and I've just spotted somebody with more money than sense.'

She smiled and disappeared into the masses. Suddenly they were alone again in a small corner of a crowded and noisy room. People kept bumping into them, apologizing and then, recognizing Zeke, giving him an energetic handshake or a friendly slap on the back. Zeke turned to Canaan.

'Can I get you a Bar-B-Q plate?'

'No, I'll just practice breathing if you don't mind.'

Secretly he reached down and squeezed her hand. It made her heart leap but made her angry at the same time and confused. She wasn't sure why she should feel angry. Perhaps because she felt invisible next to him and she couldn't decide which was worse, being invisible or being the focus of curious stares. A short stocky man came up and punched Zeke playfully in the ribs.

'Zekie boy!'

'Jimmy! You remember Canaan Phillips?'

'Yeah.'

He hardly glanced at her to begin with but there was a sudden realization and he took her hand and held it in both of his.

'Oh, sure. Yeah!'

He grinned at Zeke.

'He's told me plenty about you.'

Zeke blushed.

'Sorry as I am to admit this, Jimmy is one of my oldest friends.'

'And dearest.'

Jimmy was still holding her hand, rubbing it like a rabbit's foot. Zeke pulled her hand away and smiled.

'He's also going through a mid-life crisis.'

'Not a crisis, definitely not a crisis. A quest.'

Zeke nodded like he'd heard it all before.

'So how come you haven't moved on Chrissy Ledbetter?'

'Where? Where'd you see her?'

'On the veranda.'

'Was she . . . oh, never mind. I'll find out for myself.'

He forced his way to the double doors leading onto the veranda. Zeke shrugged.

'He's not as shallow as he seems. He's actually got an exceptional mathematical mind.'

She laughed.

'For remembering phone numbers and vital statistics?'

'It was a nasty divorce and out of the blue for Jimmy. He was crazy about her.'

'So you're saying he used to be different?'

He chuckled.

'Uh no, come to think of it he's always been obnoxious. But he hasn't always been a womanizer.'

There was a medley of screams at the bottom of the stairs as more arrivals spotted long-lost friends.

'Well, Canaan, fill me in. I've been waiting years to hear the details.'

'Details?'

'You had plans to set Manhattan on fire. What happened?'

'I forgot my matches.'

She looked away, pretending to watch Bernie who was working her charming magic on an old fart in a royal-blue-and-gold sweatsuit.

'Well, I wouldn't worry about it. There's plenty of matches lying around if you know where to look.'

She gave a sarcastic laugh.

'In Lander?'

'Sure.'

She turned to challenge him but a bevy of young women engulfed them.

'Hey, Mr Forrest.'

They moved in unison like a synchronized swim team.

'Now ladies, you know it's too late to change your final grades now.'

They giggled and gathered around him. Canaan listened

as they all explained who they had married and where they had moved to and how they were all having a slumber party that night for old times' sake.

'You must have very understanding husbands.'

'Oh, we left them behind with the kids. Sherry still lives here, so we're campin' out on her den floor.'

One of the women stepped forward.

'You still live in that old garage apartment, Mr Forrest?'

He gave them one of his endearing looks of suspicion.

'Now why would you want to know that?'

They shared a knowing look and broke down into giggles again.

'Oh, nothin'. We were just thinkin' of rollin' a few yards tonight.'

'Well then, I'm definitely not tellin' you where I live. I've torn down my fair share of toilet paper out of trees, thank you very much.'

They exchanged a few more memories then hurried off en masse when they caught sight of the former basketball coach who had caused uproar at the end of their senior year when he got one of the cheerleaders pregnant and married her.

'Why *do* you still live in that old garage apartment? I know you could afford to live somewhere else.'

'I like it. Closest thing to Bohemia I could find in Lander.'

There was a whisper of cashmere as Mim Simpson swept past her. She ignored Canaan and took Zeke's arm.

'There you are, you handsome thing you. Are you all ready for your big speech?'

'Ready as I can be.'

'Well then, consider this your ten-minute call.'

She turned and pretended to finally notice Canaan.

'You know somebody told me you two came together, but I just didn't believe it.'

Zeke smiled.

'Well, you never know, Mim. Some things you hear in Lander are actually the truth.'

'I guess so.'

She took his hands in hers and looked earnestly into his eyes.

'I wonder if you'd be sweet and do me a big favor? I've been so busy getting things organized . . . I haven't had a minute. Could you get me a plate of buffalo wings?'

Zeke looked uncertainly at Canaan. She smiled and nodded.

'Go on. I'll be all right.'

He turned to Mim.

'Anything else?'

'No. That'll do me fine.'

She called after him.

'Not the spicy ones now!'

She waited until he was out of earshot before taking Canaan's arm and turning her away from the crowded room. Her queenly smile was gone.

'I'm only tellin' you 'cause I think you ought to know what people are sayin'.'

'About what?'

'About you . . . and how pathetic it is to see you throwin' yourself at Zeke Forrest.'

'Throwing? I'm not – I didn't want to come.'

'Then why did you?'

'I don't know . . . he asked me . . .'

'And you were flattered?'

'No . . . I . . .'

Mim flipped her hair over her shoulder and smiled knowingly.

'I'm not really all that surprised that he asked you. He's always been attracted to the seedier side of life. I mean, look at that old place where he lives. You fit right in.'

Canaan could feel the anger in her rise and suddenly she felt like fighting.

'Zeke and I have been friends for a long time.'

'Oh, Canaan. He's friends with a lot of people. Look around. That's his way.'

Canaan could see Zeke heading back. Mim leaned closer and whispered in her ear.

'I just thought you'd want to know, seein' as you've already tried once to climb out of that ditch you were born in.'

Zeke handed Mim the plate of buffalo wings and Mim absently passed it on to Canaan.

'What am I thinkin'? We've gotta get you up onstage.'

She turned Zeke around and playfully pushed him towards the stage. Canaan moved towards an empty table and put the plate of wings on the corner. Zeke's friend Jimmy had obviously bombed out with Chrissy Ledbetter and was standing with another teacher in front of her. Onstage Mim tapped the microphone.

'Can y'all hear me all right?'

Jimmy whistled and Mim put her hand over her eyes to look out over the audience.

'Buddy Johnson, is that you? Now y'all be quiet! I mean it.'

When things had simmered down, she cleared her throat and flashed her perfectly straight teeth to an admiring crowd.

'Way back in 1980, when we were just innocent little ninth-graders . . . can anybody remember back that far?'

A voice shouted from near the door.

'I can't remember breakfast.'

There were ripples of laughter and Mim continued.

'Well, that was the year that a certain young teacher first came to LHS.'

The microphone was set just low enough so that Mim had to lean forward, giving an ample view of her cleavage.

She clasped the microphone stand firmly in one hand and swiveled her hips from one side to the other, her knit skirt clinging to every curve. Men around the room softly groaned in quiet ecstasy. Jim joined them.

'God almighty. Makes you want to join the PTA, don't it?'

The other teacher, in his fifties, nodded without taking his eyes off her.

'I hear ya. You remember the pep rally when she—'

Jim put his hand up to stop him.

'Don't ruin it for me. I've got it memorized just the way I like it.'

Mim flashed her famous vote-winning smile.

'So here he is, our own Prince Charming and Class of '84 sponsor . . . Mr Zeke Forrest.'

The room exploded in applause and whistles and the sighs and groans changed to female murmurs of approval. Jimmy shook his head.

'Listen to that. Lucky bastard.'

Canaan tried not to listen but Jim and his companion were less than an elbow length in front of her. She'd thought he might turn and see her but he had been too engrossed with what was going on in front of him. His friend mirrored his disgust.

'All those ragin' hormones . . . wasted.'

Canaan could see a quarter of Jim's face as a wicked grin curled across his face.

'Not tonight.'

'Tonight?'

'He told me this afternoon.'

'No shit?'

'Said it's a sure thing. Not gonna look a gift horse in the mouth.'

The other guy was aglow with disbelief. Thrilled with the possibilities.

'No shit?'

Canaan fought her way through the crowd, her face raging hot and rigid. She heard Zeke's voice rise over the crowd.

'Thank you, Mim. It's hard to believe . . .'

At the top of the steps a man in a Class of '84 sweatshirt stopped her.

'You're Cathy, right?'

Canaan shook her head and tried to continue on her way but he pulled her back.

'Katy?'

'No.'

'I'm close though, right? You were on the pep squad?'

She pulled her arm back roughly and glared at him.

'No, I wasn't! Now get lost. I'm not who you think I am – OK?'

The guy backed off.

'Hey, sorry. Just tryin' to be friendly.'

She glanced over her shoulder and saw Mim standing on tiptoe to give Zeke a peck on the cheek. She looked away and hurried across the restaurant. She walked back to Zeke's apartment, trying to decide if she wanted to cry, scream or set his house on fire. She felt humiliated and sick to her stomach. How could she have been so stupid? She was nothing more to him than a new diversion in this small, claustrophobic town. Something else to place a bet on. *A sure thing*.

Safe inside the car, she slammed the door and turned the key. Nothing happened. *No!* She tried it again. Over and over. She banged her fists against the steering wheel. The dashboard. Finally, she locked up and waded through the tall grass towards the sidewalk. Shoving her hands into her pockets she felt the small painted acorn Luke had given her. She took it out and threw it into the weeds, then started the long walk home in the dark.

Luke

Lissie James plunged the chunks of apple below the boiling water with a spoon, holding them down long enough to allow the plump, frothy pieces underneath to bob up and take their place. Her daughter Willa perched on a stool nearby, her tongue lodged in the corner of her mouth, as she concentrated on peeling another apple for the pot. Mrs Patterson from the other side of the ridge brought over several bushels every year, and paid Lissie to make 'the best apple butter on God's green earth'. Payment usually came in the form of a small basket filled with the more damaged fruit of the crop; bruised but suitable for making enough applesauce to last until Christmas. In recent years Mrs Patterson had also included a handful of change, enough to buy a few extras for the children; but this year the extras would have to wait. The two-roomed share-cropper shack where they lived needed repairs before the heavy winter set in. The newspaper that insulated the inner walls hung in tattered shreds, battle scarred from winter winds that had whipped through the gaps in the boards. The loft where the children slept was starting to leak and the tin roof of the porch had begun to curl and warp, weakening the entire structure. The money that her husband, Jaspar, brought in from his share of the cotton crop usually paid for the bulk of their necessities, but they had lost an entire acre to boll weevil that year and the sorghum syrup they made from the sugar cane wouldn't be enough to make up the loss.

Pig Wilson, the owner of the land, had approached Jaspar in the spring, offering him the chance to buy the old shack from him and with hindsight, Lissie was afraid they had jinxed the prospect by making plans that were too grand and unpredictable. Late at night they had whispered like excited teenagers about the possibility of leaving a piece of property to their children one day. By September they had both known that money for a deposit was out of the question and that it was a dream that was best forgotten.

Lissie rubbed her lower back, trying to ease the thudding ache that had started a few hours before.

'Willa, sit up straight or you ain't gonna make it 'til we finish this last batch.'

Lissie arched her own back and crossed to the table where a bowl was piled with apples stripped of their skins, their buttery flesh tanning to a golden brown in the steamy air of the kitchen.

'He still out there?'

Willa nodded and Lissie leaned over the table, peering through the window as Luke paced up and down the railroad track, stopping to dig something from between the boards with his toe.

He had appeared, as usual, right after breakfast, standing by the tracks with his hands in his pockets, waiting patiently for someone to see him. Lissie had called to him from the front porch.

'Squeaky's got homework to do, Luke. Might be a couple of hours 'fore he's done.'

As always, she had offered him a chair at the kitchen table, but he had refused, content to stroll up and down the tracks. He had left his post only once that morning, when the train from Chattanooga had come through, stepping back to wave at the engineers as they passed.

Lissie moved an apple from the top of the pile and began to core and slice it.

'I wish to goodness he'd come inside.'

In the six months since her son Squeaky had first brought the tall young man home with him, Luke had never set foot in their house. Night after night, he had been invited to join them for supper and each night he had declined, sitting quietly on the embankment that supported the tracks, waiting for them to finish. Lissie always took a plate to him which he accepted eagerly, but often times, they would come out to find that he had gone, leaving the empty plate on the corner of the porch. Squeaky had explained that Luke didn't like going inside houses but it didn't stop her from feeling guilty.

'He shown up anymore at the school?'

Willa shook her head.

'Sometimes he walks with us as far as the water tower.'

Lissie frowned as she chopped.

'It ain't right what they done to him. He wasn't botherin' a livin' soul.'

There was a small creak as the door of the back room opened and Lissie stopped her chopping as she waited for the small pleading voice she knew would follow.

'Momma, I read enough yet?'

'Where'd you get to?'

'Pretty far.'

'Did you finish the chapter?'

There was silence and she smiled as she imagined him weighing out the possible answers and consequences in his head.

'No, ma'am.'

'Well then, I'd say you ain't read enough.'

The door slammed and Lissie and Willa exchanged

amused smiles as they heard the sound of stamping feet and a whine that resembled a braying donkey as he complained to the four walls that would imprison him for a while longer.

Squeaky had never found school a worthy pastime and Lissie and Jaspar had fought an uphill battle since the first day they left him at the Lacy Stone School for Coloreds. He was whittling a new fishing pole on the front porch by the time they got home. From that day onwards, no amount of begging or threatening could persuade Squeaky that sitting in a classroom was the thing to do when the fish were biting.

Luke's friendship and ardent interest in learning temporarily improved Squeaky's outlook on the ordeal; not that he ever considered school anything but a trivial diversion of his valuable time, but for a while, he tolerated the daily discipline for Luke's sake.

Lissie visited Mrs Locklear, the county-appointed teacher at the school, to discuss the possibility of Luke attending summer classes with Squeaky. The woman had always been kind to Lissie, even during her son's worst behavior, and Willa – who had always been a good student – idolized her. She was a widow who had taught for many years at the white school, well respected and known for her generous, caring and enthusiastic methods. When her husband died and her children moved away, she shocked and dismayed her family and devoted admirers, by choosing to spend her twilight years teaching the colored children of Etowah County. True to her reputation, she had been eager to help when Lissie asked her about Luke, and had agreed that anything was worth trying if it meant Squeaky might spend more time on his education.

Mrs Locklear stopped by every few weeks to report on Squeaky's progress and to let Lissie know how Luke was getting on. In the beginning, Luke resisted coming into the classroom, choosing instead to sit on the front steps, listening through the open door, but venturing as far as the cloakroom when it rained. Mrs Locklear encouraged Luke to join the weekly nature walks, but he refused, remaining behind. Minutes later he was usually spotted, following at a safe distance. When she stopped to discuss a new discovery with the other children, she was amused to see him inching closer, hiding behind nearby trees. She learned to raise her voice so that he could hear without revealing his hiding place. She finally won him over with a stack of shabby books with loose bindings and soiled pages, a collection she had salvaged from a storeroom in the courthouse that had been destined for the incinerator. She cleared a small back room, allowing him to read undisturbed while Squeaky struggled with arithmetic and writing in the adjoining classroom. At the end of each day, Luke ignored Squeaky's complaints, staying on to help Mrs Locklear clean chalk boards and erasers, stack books and sweep the classroom floor. Gradually, he was lured further and further into their circle. By the end of the summer session, he had taken his very own desk in the back corner of the room.

In spite of Luke's peculiar ways and guarded behavior, Lissie had grown fond of the boy and his presence had brought a welcome improvement in Squeaky's restlessness. She had never met Luke's mother or anyone else from his family but she never asked about them. She had heard ugly stories from friends who had suffered the brunt of Emma Stewart's nasty temper; her reputation was well established in Lander and few people sought her out without good reason.

In August Lissie and Jaspar had asked Luke to join them for a family picnic at Cypress Creek, and although hesitant, Luke had hardly been able to contain his excitement on the long journey by wagon. Lissie had contemplated asking Emma's permission, feeling guilty that she might cause another mother to worry, but late that day she had been grateful that she had let her fear of the woman override her desire to do the proper thing.

Squeaky and Willa stripped to their underclothing and their shrill screams of delight echoed around the clearing as they swung out over the shallow water of the creek on the rope swing their father had fixed two summers before. It had taken their best efforts to entice Luke into joining them, but when he finally removed his overalls, Lissie stifled a gasp at the sight of his scrawny back and spindly legs. They were criss-crossed with welts and scars of open wounds that had been left to heal on their own. As she watched the awkward boy drawn into the unfamiliar world of children's play, she vowed that as long as she had anything to do with it, his time with her family would remain a secret.

In September, on the first day of the new school year, she waved Luke goodbye along with her own two children and wished him luck. He had been waiting for them before sun-up.

Jaspar had made him his own lunch pail, to match Squeaky's and Willa's, and Lissie had filled it with cornbread and crackling. Luke sat on the front porch and examined every inch of it, grinning to himself and looking up every few minutes to show his appreciation. Before the three set off, Jaspar handed Luke his first book with a leather strap that he'd made from one of his old belts. Luke ran his fingers across the lettering, awestruck, and Lissie put her arm around his shoulders.

'It's *Huck Finn*. We were hopin' it might encourage Squeaky with his readin' but he ain't touched it since we bought it. We decided you oughta have it instead. Mrs Locklear will give you more books. Then you can strap 'em all together.'

They watched as the boys made their way down the dirt road. Squeaky kicked stones a little more light-heartedly than usual with his friend by his side and Luke held his new lunch pail and book gingerly by his side as if he might break them.

The transformation in Luke had been slow but seemed

complete and Lissie had been proud to see a spark in his eyes that she'd never seen before. In spite of towering above his classmates, he looked like any other student, and the children had accepted his oddities with ease, gently persuading him into their playground games.

A few weeks into the new term, two men from the county board of education appeared at the front doors of the school. A nervous murmur had spread through the classroom, but it had quickly subsided and the children had remained very still as they tried to hear. Mrs Locklear left the room, joining the men in the cloakroom. There had been a few quiet words, inaudible to the children inside, but the men's voices had suddenly raised in anger and the normally calm Mrs Locklear had shouted in protest, trying in vain to hold the men back with her frail, elderly arms. They pushed past her and came into the classroom, dragging Luke from his desk. He made a flimsy attempt to resist, but quickly surrendered, passively allowing them to shove him along between rows of students and out the door. The children gathered at the windows to watch, then slipped out in small trickles to surround their teacher like a protective cloak. Mrs Locklear followed behind the men, heaping shame on their actions and one of them dropped his grip on Luke's arm and turned to face her.

'Look, ma'am. We're doin' our job, just like you are but you've got no business teachin' a white boy with the coloreds.'

She moved closer to him, placing a grandmotherly hand on his arm.

'Tell me who's complainin'. Can't you tell me that? Let me talk to 'em?'

He shook his head.

'There's more complaints than you have excuses, ma'am, so I'd just back off from this if I was you.'

'Are you at least gonna let him go to the junior school? He's a little behind but he'd catch up in no time.'

The man looked uncomfortable.

'The boy's simple, Mizz Locklear. He's better off stayin' at home where people can take care of him.'

'He's happy here. What's the harm in him stayin'?'

'It just don't look right. People won't stand for it.'

They climbed into the buggy and took the reins, waving Luke towards the road.

'You go on now, boy. Get on back to where you belong and don't let us catch you hangin' 'round here again, you hear?'

Luke looked to Mrs Locklear for confirmation and she nodded.

'You go on, son. I'll see what I can do.'

Squeaky and Willa watched Luke shuffle down the dirt road. He glanced back at them, then darted into the woods. A few days later Squeaky and Willa came home to report that Mrs Locklear had not come to school that morning. Lissie heard later that people had taken to openly ignoring the teacher when they met her in town, and a few of the less restrained citizens had shown their contempt by spitting at her feet. There had been rumors of much worse and the old woman's health had deteriorated rapidly. The story that circulated after her disappearance had been that she'd gone to Georgia to live with her eldest daughter.

A pickle-faced man in a severely cut black suit had taken over at the school and Squeaky had returned to fishing. The new teacher was fond of caning and Squeaky had suffered several severe lashings for playing hooky and for falling behind in class. Hoping to protect her son, Lissie forced him to study an hour every day and two hours on Saturday.

The back door creaked again and Lissie looked up to see her son peering into the kitchen.

'You done this time?'

'Yessum.'

She searched his face, then smiled, satisfied that he was

telling the truth. She carried the carving board of chopped apples to the pot of boiling water and dumped them in. Squeaky picked up one of the freshly peeled apples and Willa slapped his hands.

'Momma, tell Squeaky to eat the apples I ain't peeled.'

Lissie pushed the new apples down into the pot with a spoon.

'Squeaky.'

He scowled at his sister then licked the apple and put it back in the bowl just as his mother looked up from her work.

'Titus James, eat the rest of that apple.'

He smiled smugly at Willa and took a bite as his mother joined them at the table with the carving board.

'Then peel me another five apples to take its place.'

The smile melted from his face and Willa grinned with satisfaction. He slumped and grimaced at his sister as she handed him the knife. Lissie ignored them and continued chopping.

'Luke's been waitin' for you all mornin'.'

'Where is he?'

'Where do you think?'

He stood up and stretched to look out the window.

'Can I go see him?'

'Not until you finish your peelin'.'

He slouched back in his chair.

'He might go off again.'

'No, he won't. And if he does, he'll be back.'

The day Luke was banished from the school had been the last they'd seen of him for several weeks. Squeaky had waited in vain each day at the water tower and Lissie had tried to dismiss vivid tapestries in her head, spun from threads of gossip she had heard over the years. The mailman had sworn up and down that he had seen the boy tied to a tree in nothin' but his all-together on a day when the ground hadn't yet thawed from the night's frost. Others had claimed to hear the

sound of wailing, and low animal-like moans carried across
the fields on still nights. She had been wrestling with the
notion of visiting the Stewarts' farm to make sure he was all
right, when he suddenly appeared one morning just before
breakfast. Lissie and her family had greeted him with quiet
acceptance and he had turned up every morning since, van-
ishing just before the children left for school and returning in
the afternoon like a pet with a sixth sense, when Squeaky and
Willa came home from lessons.

Lissie squeezed her son's shoulder.

'Finish the one you're peelin' and go on out. I'll finish up.
Willa, you too. You've been sittin' there almost three hours
now. I can manage the rest.'

They made a few perfunctory scrapes across the apples
and tossed them into the bowl. Squeaky licked his fingers and
hustled out the door, almost tipping his chair over in his
haste.

Through the window Lissie watched as Squeaky scrambled up the embankment to join Luke and she saw the boy's
shoulders lift and his face light up. She reached into the
bushel basket and tossed an apple to Willa.

'Here, take him this and ask him to stay for dinner.'

Canaan

Dot picked up an industrial-sized jar of mayonnaise and yelled from the other end of the counter.

'Hey, Harvard! You finished with this?'

The jar was missing its lid and there were great globs of mayo along the side going translucent. Canaan stopped wiping down her station and reached for it.

'Oh yeah. Sorry.'

'Nobody taught you 'bout puttin' things away?'

Canaan hadn't slept much the night before. The conversation she'd overheard at the reunion wouldn't leave her alone and she'd spent most of the night reinterpreting things Zeke had said to her.

'I said I was sorry!'

She'd never lost her temper before. Juanita took the jar and started cleaning it up. She smiled at Canaan.

'Go on. Take your lunch break.'

'Are you sure?'

'We can manage. You feelin' all right?'

Canaan nodded.

'I'm just tired.'

Dot snorted as she refilled the ketchup bottles.

'I'm not surprised after the night you had.'

'What?'

Juanita nudged Canaan towards the swinging doors.

'Don't pay any attention. Dot's just jealous.'

Canaan was too exhausted to ask questions. She just wanted to find a corner, get off her feet, and close her eyes for a few minutes. She was getting her purse from the locker when Kyle stuck his head around the office door.

'Miss Phillips?'

'Yes-sir?'

'I've had three calls this mornin' from Zeke Forrest askin' to speak to you. Now I'm sure I made the policy on personal calls clear.'

'Yes-sir.'

'So I expect you'll make sure it doesn't happen again.'

'Yes-sir.'

He checked around to see if there was anyone else lurking in the back room before sidling up to Canaan, like a gossiping crab.

'Exactly how personal are these calls?'

'They're nothing.'

He looked relieved, but troubled.

'Good. Glad to hear it. Personally, I don't care who you sleep with, but I don't like it when you drag your love life into my grocery store.'

Canaan's fatigue suddenly waned and she snapped defensively in the face of his rudeness.

'I have not slept with Zeke Forrest.'

She wasn't sure if it was a smile of disbelief or perverted pleasure, but the right side of his mouth twitched when he spoke.

'Well, maybe not – but half of Lander saw your car there this mornin'. Course, that sort of thing doesn't bother me. I mean, you gotta have some fun now and then . . . let your hair down.'

She didn't bother to wait for him to finish. She charged

through the store and out the front door towards the phone booth outside the drugstore. She took a scrap of paper out of her purse and dialed the number scribbled in the corner. A boy answered with a lazy-day drawl.

'Hammett's Oil.'

'This is Canaan Phillips. I have a Mustang on Parkville Road. You were supposed to send a tow truck over first thing this mornin'. Right away, you said.'

She could almost see his shrug.

'Wadn't me.'

'All right, maybe it wasn't you but it was somebody there.'

'Well, I don't know who'd that be.'

'Then who would know?'

'My boss maybe. You want me to get him?'

'Yes, please!'

Nearby a teenager waited to use the phone. Canaan turned her back to him and tucked the mouthpiece as close to her mouth as possible.

'They did? When? Who sent it back?'

She slammed the phone back on its cradle, then muttering under her breath, she set out on foot to Zeke's apartment.

The hood was up on her Mustang. As she got closer she could see a pair of tattered blue jeans, stamped with oily fingerprints, leaning far into its throat. The jeans were old and worn enough to have begun ripping and unraveling at strategic stress points and in spite of her anger Canaan couldn't help admiring his stress points. He was wearing a white T-shirt with fingerprints that matched the ones on his jeans and a few smeared oily palm prints. He stood up and grinned happily, proud of his work.

'I figured I owed you one after last night.'

She scowled, taken aback by his confession.

'I don't need your help.'

'My way of sayin' sorry. I shouldn't have forced you to go.'

She crossed her arms. *So he wasn't confessing after all.*

'You had no right to send the tow truck away.'

He grimaced with disapproval and added another palm print to his right hip.

'Do you know how much they charge to drag a car three blocks?'

'I'll have to pay them anyway for wasting their time.'

He dove back under the hood.

'Naw, don't worry. I took care of it. You scared me last night. I looked everywhere.'

'Is the car ready? Can I drive it now?'

He made another tweak.

'Almost. I called. Your grandmother told me you'd made it home safe.'

'I didn't feel like staying.'

'She doesn't like me much, does she?'

'She doesn't trust you. Look, I need to get back to work.'

He motioned her over to his side and nodded towards a wrench he was holding.

'Here, hold this.'

Reluctantly she obeyed. Hating the closeness of him.

'Tight. To the right.'

Their hips were touching and the smell of engine oil combined with his sweat and effort made her dizzy, almost nauseous, with anger and residual passion.

'OK. I got it. Now get in and start it up.'

It sputtered to begin with but almost immediately started up, sounding stronger than it had in years. He lowered the hood and smiled proudly.

'I don't know how long it'll last, but at least it'll get you home.'

She slammed the car door and put the car into reverse. She couldn't look at him.

'Thank you.'

'You got time for coffee? Or iced tea? I've got some mint growin' around here somewhere.'

He searched among the waist-high weeds. She shook her head without looking at him.

'No, I have to get back.'

She accelerated quickly so that she wouldn't have to hear him say goodbye or worse yet to suggest they get together again.

Dot pounded on the bathroom door.

'Hey! Harvard! This ain't your own private john, you know. You listenin'?'

'I'll be right out.'

Canaan splashed more water on her face. And dabbed it off with the stiff blue paper towels. It had started with the engine oil. But it was the smell of him too. She'd felt the same giddy weakness in her guts when they'd worked late on the school paper and she'd caught a whiff of him. But then when she'd come back she'd wolfed down one of Juanita's leftover Tex-Mex hoagies. They were hard on the old innards at the best of times, but going down into an angry stomach – it was bound to come back up again. She wiped the corners of her mouth one more time and gave the toilet a final swipe.

She found Dot and Juanita at the back door, smoking. Dot took a deep drag and blew it forcefully out her nose and mouth. Canaan imagined it coming from her ears as well and her eyes turning dragon red.

'Did you finish the front before you took up residence in the bathroom?'

'Yeah, it's done.'

'Did you stand the mop outside the bucket?'

Juanita sighed.

'Oh, Dot, it don't really matter.'

'Course it does. It won't dry if you leave it in the bucket. Then when I go to use it – it's stinkin' and moldy.'

Canaan nodded.

'I stood it outside the bucket. Head up like you said.'

Juanita was sitting in a chair that propped open the door. One leg was crossed over the other one as she massaged her calves. Canaan had never noticed the dark blue veins that twisted and bulged their way around her legs. Juanita caught her staring and smiled.

'Concrete floors.'

Canaan nodded awkwardly and hurried over to punch out. She found an envelope clipped to her time card and she eagerly ripped open the side. Juanita grinned.

'First paycheck?'

Canaan nodded.

'Welcome to the meat market, Sugar.'

Dot blew another smoke ring into the night air.

'Welcome to the rest of your life.'

Canaan pulled the check out and glanced quickly at Dot.

'I'm not staying long. This is just temporary.'

Both women burst out laughing. Dot flicked her cigarette into the alley.

'Yeah, I hear ya. Temporary.'

Canaan frowned, studying the check.

'This can't be right.'

Juanita looked over her shoulder.

'Your shoes. He deducted for your shoes.'

'I thought . . . I mean . . . I had no idea they . . . Oh, never mind.'

She opened her locker and pulled her sweater and purse out. Dot stood and stretched.

'The first twenty years are the hardest. After that it's smooth sailing.'

Juanita patted Canaan on the back and opened her own locker.

'Don't let it get to you. It's always hard . . . at first. You'll catch on.'

Dot slung her saddlebag purse over her shoulder and stood with one hip cocked to the side.

'Don't guess they taught sandwich-making at Harvard.'

Canaan slammed her locker.

'William and Mary, not Harvard.'

'What?'

'I went to William and Mary.'

Dot headed towards the door.

'Honey, do I look like that matters a sack of shit to me?'

She waved over the back of her head.

'See ya tomorrow, Harvard!'

As much as she wanted the car to race home, to spin loose gravel and make a point to those she passed on the way home, the old Mustang just wasn't up to it. It moseyed home at its own speed ignoring her need to play the petulant teenager. She pulled into the barn, nosing her way deep into the darkness and left the car running. The tears had already started to burn her eyes as she'd come over the hill and she tilted her head back and let them freely run down her face. The engine chugged and the fumes drifted up from the exhaust. She closed her eyes and imagined going to sleep. Just curling up in the leather back seat and dozing off.

'Shouldn't run the car inside like that.'

Luke leaned down into the car window and smiled. Canaan opened her eyes and reluctantly turned off the engine.

'Just resting. I've had a hard day.'

She grabbed her purse and shoved the car door open. She was almost to the door, hoping he wouldn't question her.

'Did you forget?'

She stopped and sighed.

'What?'

'I think you forgot somethin'.'

He was smiling his idiotic 'I've got a secret' smile.

'What, Luke? Just tell me.'

She wasn't in the mood to play games. He moved closer to her.

'You forgot to wash behind your ears.'

He reached for the side of her head and she pulled away impatiently as he pulled a stick of Juicy Fruit gum from behind her ear. He tried to give it to her but she shoved it away.

'I'm not eight years old anymore, Luke.'

She turned again to go.

'You take that book back like I asked you?'

All she wanted to do was soak her feet.

'I thought you said you were friends.'

He nodded.

'That's right.'

'Well, he didn't act much like you were.'

'No. Don't reckon he did.'

'Well, are you friends or aren't you?'

'He was my best friend 'fore we fell out. But we're workin' towards makin' up. I run into him ever' now and then. I usually nod. He usually turns away.'

'That's not what I'd call eager to make up.'

'It's just a stage he's goin' through.'

'How long you expecting it to last?'

''Til he's over his hurt.'

'You hurt him?'

'He thinks I did. So I reckon I did.'

Her legs were throbbing and her feet felt like they would start screaming if she didn't get them into a hot tub in the next ten minutes.

'Well, I'd appreciate it if you didn't put me in the middle of your feuds. I've got enough problems.'

She slung her purse over her shoulder and headed out into the dark towards a hot, soapy bath.

Luke

Luke watched from the lower branch of the mimosa tree for a sign; a wave or a nod from the window to let him know he'd been seen. The gray and pink layers of sunrise were merging to become daylight and though he had seen Lissie moving around in the kitchen and had heard the sound of the oven door grating against its hinges, there had been no other stirrings in the hour since he'd arrived.

Squeaky was usually up and waiting for him on Saturday mornings, but the last few days had been long and hard and Luke figured the whole family was taking a well-deserved rest. Everyone, that is, except Lissie. She was always there; the last one to turn the lantern out in the evening and the first one to light it in the morning. He sometimes came late at night when everyone else had gone to bed and watched her work until after midnight. He had never been much of a sleeper anyway and sitting in the dark, cradled in the branches, he found it comforting that someone else was awake while the rest of the world slept.

Jaspar would be up soon to go into town. The wagon stood ready, under a nearby tree and Luke felt a ripple of pride as the gathering light shimmered across the tins of syrup stacked neatly in the back, tied down with rope. He had helped load the wagon the night before, the final task in a difficult but rewarding effort.

When he arrived at daybreak a few days before, he'd been surprised to see the large group of friends and relations of Squeaky's family, who had gathered to help with the sorghum harvest. He and Squeaky had worked alongside Lissie and half a dozen women to strip the razor-sharp leaves from the sugar-cane stalks. By mid-morning his hands had been cut and bleeding but he continued without complaint. In spite of much pleading, the boys were excluded from the more dangerous work of clearing the cane while Jaspar and the older men hacked away with machetes. Within hours, the field had been flattened, the cane heaped like splinters in a tornado-ravaged forest. The boys worked all afternoon clearing and hauling it to the edge of the field where Willa and her cousins chopped off the seed heads and collected them in gunnysacks for cow feed. Throughout the day the women and young girls moved from group to group with baskets of food and buckets of water. As the sun began to set they all joined forces, dragging the decapitated stalks another five hundred yards, stacking them in bundles beside Jaspar's syrup mill, where the men were busy digging trenches and filling them with hickory chips. The following morning Jaspar was up before the sun to light the chips, so that by the time the other workers arrived, they were glowing, deep burgundy and white. While the stalks were fed into the drum press, Squeaky and Luke took turns urging the mule in a well-trodden circle, resting in between to watch the juice as it oozed from the cane and flowed down a series of pans positioned over the hot coals. Jaspar flitted from one pan to another skimming the light green froth from the top and slinging it into an open pit nearby. Occasionally, he allowed Luke a small taste of the thick mahogany-colored syrup and Squeaky showed his friend the secret pleasure of sucking the sweetness straight from the sugar-cane stick. The syrup-making continued well into the night. Luke helped Lissie hang kerosene lanterns in the tree branches and set up tables where everyone worked in assembly line siphoning the syrup into sterilized cans and hammering the lids into place.

They had put aside a few cans of syrup for their own consumption to spread on hot buttered biscuits; a comforting remedy for the cold winter mornings that lay ahead. Luke could see them now in the morning light, stacked like paint cans along the front porch. The screen door opened and he straightened up, his feet dangling below the branch, as Lissie came out and picked up one of the cans. She waved.

'Mornin', Luke. I heard Squeaky stumblin' 'round upstairs. He oughta be out any minute now. Biscuits are almost ready. I'll bring you out a couple.'

He scrambled down from the tree and through the window he saw Squeaky emerge from the loft, a slow-moving clump of quilt descending the ladder. Luke watched as Lissie gave her son a one-armed hug while lifting the can of syrup onto the table. Squeaky's eyes were puffy with sleep but when his mother motioned outside to where Luke was waiting, he flung the quilt from his shoulders, the cloak of grogginess gone. He lifted his overalls from a nail above the fire and pulled them on over his long johns, then ignoring his mother's warning, he slammed the door on his way out. Hopping from the end of the porch with the elastic flexibility of a tree frog, he strolled over to Luke and saluted.

'Reportin' fer duty, capt'n.'

Luke smiled shyly and flipped his hand up in a half-snapped salute.

The boys sat down on the bank.

'You brung it?'

Luke nodded and pulled a lovingly whittled slingshot from his pocket as proof. Squeaky pulled out one that matched and they touched them ceremonially like swords.

Squeaky stuck the slingshot into his front pocket and rubbed the back of his neck.

'Lands' sakes, I got muscles achin' I didn't know the Lord God give me.'

They were comparing cane cuts and blisters when Lissie came out with an old flour sack tied at the neck.

'You boys headin' off soon?'

They nodded and joined her at the porch. She smiled down at them, then looked off in the distance.

'Reckon you're goin' very far today?'

Squeaky crossed his arms and lifted his chin playfully towards his mother.

'Shoot, I figure we can make it to Chattanooga by ten, be in Chicago for supper.'

'Don't say.'

'I do say.'

Lissie smiled, placing a gentle hand on Luke's shoulder and he felt his ears go red with a warm comfortable glow.

'I guess with all that travelin' you two'll get mighty hungry.'

'We can grab us a pot of hobo stew on the way and I hear they got steaks the size of Tennessee up in Chicago.'

Lissie laughed and patted Luke's shoulder.

'Well, just in case, why don't you take these biscuits with you. Might tide you over if you run into trouble.'

She handed the flour sack to Squeaky and he looped it through his shoulder strap.

'They ain't floatin' in sorghum, are they?'

'No. Just a few for Luke. Yours are all plain.'

He looked satisfied and motioned for Luke to follow him. Lissie called after them, her face more serious.

'Squeaky. I want you back before sundown now.'

He turned and kept walking.

'I know.'

'And all jokin' aside, I don't have to tell you to stay away from those hobos.'

Squeaky acknowledged her with a half-hearted wave over his head and Luke grinned over his shoulder as Lissie waved them off.

'You two be careful, now.'

Luke waited until they were out of earshot before he spoke.

'We really goin' to Chicago?'

Squeaky hooted with laughter and Luke ducked his head in embarrassment.

'Lord no, son. It'd take us a week to get that far.'

Luke followed in silence.

'Where we goin' then?'

Squeaky grinned.

'It's a surprise.'

They trampled through the woods and across fields that were unfamiliar to Luke. When they reached a small hill Squeaky put his finger to his lips and pulled Luke to the ground.

'We gotta stay low, so nobody'll see us.'

Luke followed obediently, copying Squeaky's crab-like crawl up the hillside. Halfway up, he stopped, surprised by the billowing tip of a white tent that suddenly appeared above the peak. As they reached the top, they lay on their bellies and watched the activity below. The flaps of the tent had been lifted all the way around and tied to the frame. A sign was propped against a post that said *Holy Lamb of God Revival*. Makeshift benches were set up in rows fanning out around a simple wooden stage. An upright piano stood to one side and a thin woman with her sleeves pushed up to reveal sharply pointed elbows rattled out a tinny version of *Bringing in the Sheaves* while flocking pilgrims took their seats, shaking hands and humming along with the tune.

They watched as the final stragglers took their seats and a

man in a white shirt and string tie held his hands up, like Moses parting the sea, to get everyone's attention. The crowd hushed as he welcomed them. A few hearty amens drifted up from the audience and as the preacher gave a nod towards the woman with the pointy elbows, she pounced on the keys with a rousing gospel song and everyone rose to their feet, waving their hands and clapping as they joined in the chorus.

Squeaky began collecting pebbles, placing them in a pile between the two of them. Luke strained to hear the sermon, but the shouting from the congregation blocked most of the words. Squeaky nudged him excitedly as a group of men who had been milling around a pick-up truck lifted two large sacks and headed towards the podium. A handful of believers had taken their places in front of the stage and were swaying from side to side while others in the audience encouraged them. The preacher plunged his hand into one of the sacks as a woman on the front row shouted 'Glory!' and he pulled out a rattlesnake, holding it aloft to screams of delight. Luke watched in fascination as the preacher weaved between the believers. Squeaky grabbed Luke's arm just as the preacher shook the tail of the rattlesnake high above his head and Luke jerked as if the snake had lunged for his own neck.

Squeaky stifled a giggle.

'It's time.'

He pulled out his slingshot and picking up the first pebble he aimed carefully towards the tent. He let it go, shaking his head as it fell six feet short.

'Damnation.'

He picked up another one and looked over at Luke.

'Don't just lay there like a lump of dirt, help me out.'

His second shot hit a man who was sitting in the back row and Squeaky gave a whispered shout of victory as the man reached for the spot as if swatting a fly. The next one was more controlled and powerful and it struck a large woman who was sitting at the side, on an upturned fruit crate. The woman jumped up and shouted as it hit her plump backside. They continued to pelt the congregation and across the tent people began to leap into the aisles, until Squeaky could no longer control his convulsive laughter.

They didn't stop running until they reached the water tower, then collapsed in giggles at the side of the train tracks. They devoured the biscuits, retelling with hilarity the sights they'd just witnessed, as if the other one had not been there to see it themselves. Squeaky complained bitterly about the syrup that had seeped out of Luke's biscuits and ruined his own, but for the first time, Luke didn't take it personally. As they lay against the embankment, arms crossed behind their heads, Luke looked up at the sky, his eyes still watering from the laughter, his stomach full and the sweet taste of syrup still lingering on his lips – syrup that he had helped make. In the distance he could hear the faint sound of a train whistle. Squeaky sat up, listening, then forced Luke to his feet and started running alongside the track.

'Come on! I reckon we could catch that thing if we make it to White's Gap. It's level there, easier to catch on.'

Luke's long legs caught up with him easily and he lumbered along beside him.

'What are we doin'?'

'Hoppin' a train, of course. It's the one to Chattanooga, but we can hop off at Fort Payne, make it back in plenty of time for supper.'

Luke grabbed Squeaky's arm and held him back.

'Your momma told us not to.'

'No, she didn't. She said she didn't want me hangin' around them hobos. Well, we ain't.'

Luke looked skeptical but continued to walk briskly beside his friend.

'I don't think she'd want us to do this neither.'

Squeaky stopped and put his hands on his hips.

'Hell's bells, Luke. Ain't you got a bit of gumption in you? Momma ain't gonna know. I ain't gonna tell her. Are you?'

Luke looked confused.

'Well, are you?'

He shook his head.

'Well, there you go. There comes a time when you cain't listen to ever'thing your momma tells you.'

'I like your momma. Don't like lyin' to her.'

'We ain't gonna lie. We just ain't gonna tell her every little thing we done, that's all.'

The whistle blasted again, closer, and Squeaky looked over his shoulder impatiently and back at Luke.

'Now, you gonna be a baby all your life or you gonna come with me and see what's out there?'

'We'll be back 'fore sundown?'

Squeaky spit in his hand and held it out to Luke.

'I swear. And Momma won't ever know.'

Luke hesitated then shook Squeaky's hand. They made it to the level patch at White's Gap and managed to catch their breath before the train appeared around the bend.

'Now just wave at 'em like we always do and let it go on by a little ways. Then when I give the signal, you start runnin'.'

Luke could feel all the life drain from his face, but he nodded, his stomach churning as the train got closer.

The engineers waved, making Luke feel like a liar, but when Squeaky gave the signal he stumbled blindly towards the front of the train, wondering what he would do if he caught it.

'CATCH ON! CATCH ON!'

Squeaky's short legs were pumping furiously to keep up, as Luke reached for the ladder on the side of a boxcar. Squeaky yelled.

'NO! NOT THAT ONE.'

He pointed frantically above Luke's head.

'THE DOOR'S BOLTED. GET THE NEXT ONE!'

Luke glanced back as the next car came bearing down on him and he lunged forward, latching onto cold steel with both hands. For a few seconds, his feet bounced along the ground like rocks across a pond and his stomach leapt into his throat as the wheels made grinding, chewing noises, sucking greedily at his flailing legs. With a monumental heave, he hoisted himself up, and positioning his feet firmly on the bottom rung, he held tight and reached for Squeaky. The small boy was losing speed and Luke's own muscles ignited as he forced his shoulder into an unnatural twist to move his fingers closer to Squeaky's outstretched arms. He had a horrible vision of losing his grip and falling head first, but he readjusted his hold, and stretched a little bit further.

Squeaky's face wrinkled with abject failure and Luke felt his heart shrink, frightened that his friend had given up and that he would now be alone in an adventure he hadn't wanted to begin with. As a frustrated scream burst from Squeaky's lungs, a great surge of determination pushed his small body forward and Luke was suddenly grasping him by the wrist. He pulled him upwards and Squeaky scampered up his back. With a choking fear he clung to Luke's neck like a baby possum. Slowly, his muscles quivering from the added weight, Luke worked his way up the ladder. He swung one foot across to the open door, creating a bridge for Squeaky to cross. Once he was inside the boxcar, Squeaky anchored himself against the door and held out his hand for Luke to pull himself in.

When the danger was over, the two boys collapsed against one another on the solid floor, overcome by nervous, insane laughter. As the giggles died down and they wiped away the tears that accompanied the relief, their eyes began to focus on their shadowy surroundings. Squeaky tugged at Luke's arms and they scooted into an empty corner, their backs stiff against the swaying rhythm of the boxcar.

Nearby a man lay on his side with his head propped in

one hand and he watched them with amphibian eyes, daring them to blink or look away. His clothes were stiff and waxy with dirt, and the fingernails that protruded from finger-less gloves were black with grime, but the most fascinating thing for Luke was his beard. It was the color of wet slate and dozens of ornate buttons were threaded onto wiry gray strands of hair and braided like the beards of pirates Luke had read about. The pirate hobo grunted and Luke looked away quickly, embarrassed that he'd been caught staring, but the man laughed and rolled over, turning his back to them.

The other men slept in protective circles, bunched tightly together in the corners of the boxcar, but some allowed them-selves the luxury of a full stretch, their heads resting on pillows of their worldly goods.

Squeaky was unusually quiet and had jammed himself between Luke and the wall. He looked up and gave Luke a shaky smile, then hunkered down even lower, until his eyes barely peeked above Luke's shoulder. The crooning thump of the boxcar as it swayed provided a simple melody for the bari-tone snores and rattling coughs around them. The man on the other side of Luke rolled over and looked up through crusted eyes. A damp, stringy cough rumbled low in his chest, building to a crescendo, and shuddering through his body. He held his fists tightly across his middle, as if he could forcibly restrain the spasm. The man looked once more at Luke, his eyes beyond caring, then spit the blood-stained phlegm onto the floor, inches from his leg.

Luke looked away and staring out through the open door, he watched the fields of Alabama pass him by.

Canaan

The letter H wasn't lit at the Thunderbird motel and truck stop. Canaan pulled in and parked under the neon claws of the five-foot Aztec bird that flashed on and off to welcome road-weary travelers. She was about thirty miles from Lander on a dark stretch of concrete highway just off the interstate. Few people traveled the old highway these days except for the truckers who were happy to take a short detour if it meant a hot shower at the Thunderbird and a big bowl of Gertie Keller's Brunswick stew.

Zeke's repair work had turned out better than he'd predicted. She'd made it all the way to Chattanooga that day and if her luck held out it might take her the rest of the way home. If her luck held out. What a joke.

Inside the truck stop, the waitress greeted her before the little gold bell on the door finished announcing her entrance.

'Hi, hon! You want a booth or a table? Or you just wanna sit at the counter?'

'Booth, please.'

'All-righty.'

The woman flashed her a congratulatory smile, as if Canaan had just chosen the correct door on a TV game show, then sashayed a path to a corner booth. She handed Canaan a plastic menu speckled with dried droplets of gravy and ketchup.

'You just holler when you're ready to order, all-righty?'

Canaan nodded and the woman headed over towards a small clutch of plaid-shirted men with greasy baseball caps who sucked on toothpicks and made sly glances in Canaan's direction.

'You fellas ready for some more coffee?'

One of the men wrapped an arm around the waitress's hips and pulled her towards him.

'I'm always ready for somethin' hot, if you're givin' it out, Annie Bell.'

They laughed and Annie Bell playfully knocked his hat over his eyes.

'Sugar, you cain't handle nothin' hotter than my coffee.'

Canaan studied the menu and lit a cigarette. She'd bought three packs at a gas station just outside of Chattanooga and had already finished one of them. The first puff had tasted surprisingly good, and she had welcomed it like an old friend she hadn't seen in years. But it wasn't long before, like some old friends, she'd remembered why she'd let them fade from her life in the first place. It hadn't stopped her from lighting one after another, relishing the harshness of the smoke as she forced it down her throat, letting the ash fly wherever it wanted.

The waitress showed up with a glass of water and cutlery wrapped in a paper napkin.

'Thanks.'

'You're mighty welcome. You ready to order?'

Canaan nodded and the waitress pulled a pad from her pocket and a pen from behind her ear.

'What can I do you for?'

'Coffee. Meatloaf platter with a side order of onion rings and peach cobbler with ice cream.'

Lou Venie would be proud. The waitress smiled again, plucking the menu from her hands.

'My goodness. You eat awfully big for such a little thing.'

The irritating phrase, *eatin' for two now*, kept running around in Canaan's head like a rat in a wheel. She took a long hard drag and watched the smoke curl around her reflection in the window.

Lou Venie thought she was going to Chattanooga to see an old college friend. She'd found the number in the yellow pages at the library. Dismissing the family practices, she'd chosen a teaching hospital full of transient medical students who were all on their way to somewhere else. The doctor had looked as though he should still be wearing a high-school varsity jacket. He'd been thorough and efficient but appeared to have flunked Bedside Manners 101, which suited her just fine. She couldn't have handled a Southern dose of over-friendliness. He'd given her a stack of pamphlets on pre-natal care and she had dumped them in the silver trashcan outside the parking lot.

'You want ketchup, Sugar?'

The waitress had returned with an oval platter piled with three chunky slabs of meatloaf and encircled with five small bowls of overcooked vegetables. Canaan shook her head as she unrolled her fork and the waitress left her to the mountainous meal in peace. She hadn't eaten all day, or for that matter several days. Each morning, she'd stayed in bed with the quilt pulled over her head trying to protect her churning stomach from the smells and sounds of sizzling bacon, the visions of slimy egg yolks swimming on a bed of grease. When the nausea had risen to dangerous levels, she'd thrown on a pair of jeans and hurried out through the kitchen as Lou Venie called after her. *Breakfast is almost done*. Canaan waved on her way past. Not daring to look her grandmother in the eye. *Not hungry. Just leave it. I'll eat it after a while.*

Then she had headed towards the barn, in a race to reach the backside, away from the house, and heave the meager contents of her stomach over the side of the creek bank a few yards beyond. The retching usually lasted no more than a few minutes. Afterwards her stomach muscles ached with the effort it took to stop the sound from carrying across the morning air and through the kitchen window.

There was nowhere in town she could have bought a home-pregnancy test. Not without everyone knowing and piecing together whatever stories they wanted to believe. She'd made the appointment from a pay phone across from the library, waiting for the next three days to drag by and avoiding Lou Venie.

'More coffee?'

Canaan nodded and waited for the waitress to leave before scooping the few remaining bites of her dinner into her mouth. Confronting the reality of her situation had brought on a vengeful hunger. She took another bite of a corn muffin and washed it down with fresh coffee.

The waitress had moved back to the men in the plaid shirts and the four of them were engrossed in a game of sexual theatrics. One of them offered her a cigarette and another one lit it for her.

'Thing is, Annie Bell, you've spoiled us. We don't hanker after nobody but you. Nobody else can measure up.'

Annie Bell nudged him with her elbow and leaned seductively towards the ashtray so that her cleavage was in clear view of one of the men and her shapely behind brushed against the shoulder of another.

'Buford, you lie like a dog. You'd say anything to get in my panties.'

'Naw, I mean it. Ain't that right?'

He looked to the others for confirmation and they shared a smiling nod.

'The T-bird ain't exactly convenient. We only come this way to see you every week.'

The men all grunted their agreement.

'Whaddya say? Come on out with us tonight. We'll see you get home safe.'

One side of Annie Bell's face relaxed slightly, and the air around the table was spiked with a measurable excitement as they waited for her answer.

Canaan's nausea rose with such velocity, she knocked over two chairs as she lurched towards the ladies' room on the other side of the diner.

'Sugar, you OK?'

The waitress took a few steps forward, just as Canaan caught the first eruption of her dinner in her hands and slammed through the bathroom door. The force of the second and third retches brought her to her knees as she tried unsuccessfully to make it to the toilet. By the time the waitress followed her inside, chunks of meatloaf and green beans hung from Canaan's hair and splattered the floor and wall. The woman held the door open, shaking her head in sympathy.

'Well, bless your heart. I don't reckon you're gonna want that cobbler and ice cream, are you?'

From inside the restaurant, the men twisted in the chairs for a better look.

'See there, Annie Bell? We been tellin' you 'bout Gertie's meatloaf.'

They laughed and went back to their toothpick sucking.

'Y'all hush. Cain't you see the poor little thing's sick?'

She squatted down beside Canaan.

'Are you pregnant, Sugar?'

Canaan scrambled to her feet and wiping her hands on her bluejeans, she staggered past the waitress and out of the restroom. She picked up her purse from the booth and the little gold bell jingled as she opened the door.

'Hey, wait a minute!'

As Canaan backed out of the parking space, her tires spitting gravel, the waitress came running out waving her check in the air.

'You cain't leave without payin' just 'cause you don't feel good.'

Canaan could see her pleading face in the rear-view mirror, but her need to escape far outweighed any sense of remorse.

'Come on, lady. I've already had to pay for one stiff this week.'

In the mirror, Annie Bell's face appeared to throb as the red-and-blue Thunderbird sign flashed above her. Canaan turned her eyes towards the black stretch of highway that loomed ahead of her and stepped on the gas.

A ghostly blue haze shimmered through the gaps of the curtains and Canaan crept quietly across the porch, inching forward in the dark to keep from tripping over misplaced lawn chairs. The door was mercifully silent as she slipped inside. Lou Venie was asleep in the vinyl recliner, a small table lamp spotlighting a crossword puzzle book that was propped over her middle. A few feet away, an old black-and-white movie pulsated from the television. Canaan moved quickly down the hall and straight to the bathroom where she locked herself in. Stepping under the shower fully clothed, she let the hot steamy water wash away the vomit. She slowly undressed, kicking her clothes to the back of the tub and lathering her skin to a solid froth of foam.

In her bedroom, she dug around in the back of her closet until she found an old terry-cloth bathrobe and put it on. It had been a high-school graduation gift from her grandmother and it had lovingly seen her through her college days. There were threadbare patches across the backside from hours of late-night cramming sessions and one of the pockets had been ripped off when she'd caught it on a doorknob, but it offered the same security as a cherished teddy bear with a ragged ear.

She squeezed the excess water from the clothes and laid them over the windowsill, letting them hang half-out in the cool night air. Sitting on the bed, her back against the headboard and her legs tucked inside the robe, she stared at the puddle that was collecting below the window.

About ten weeks. I take it you're not married.

It had been an obvious guess. She'd burst into tears when he'd told her. Even though she'd known all along what he'd say.

I'm separated . . . soon to be divorced.

She'd been grateful for the doctor's bluntness and his casual acceptance. No disapproving looks or tightening of jaw muscles.

Well, you've got a little time to think about it, but I wouldn't put it off.

She scrambled off the bed and listened at the door before groping her way down the dark hall. In the living room, Lou Venie's chin had dropped and was gently vibrating with the soft snore of a deep sleep. Canaan knelt beside the sideboard and unplugged the phone. Carefully grabbing the cord so that it didn't drag across the floor, she tucked the phone close to her chest and tiptoed out of the living room. The only other outlet was in the hallway, so she plugged it in and pulled the cord taut along the baseboard as she crawled inside the coat closet and closed the door.

It took several tries to remember the number, so easily had it been erased from her memory. She listened as it rang. It sounded hollow and cold in the darkness of the closet.

'Hello?'

His voice snapped like someone who had been interrupted.

'Hello?'

She could almost see Jonathon's lip curling into the snarl she knew so well.

'God-damn it, who is this?'

There was the sound of movement and faint mumbling as he turned away from the mouthpiece.

'I don't know who it is. Will you just shut up?'

His voice slurred with booze and he shouted down the line.

'Who the hell is this?'

Canaan hung up and held the phone in her lap. Before she could think rationally, her heart pounding, she dialed another number. She'd memorized it years before but it was still as easy to remember as her own birthday.

'Hello – Zeke Forrest.'

She slammed down the phone as soon as she heard his voice. Maybe it was hearing his name, so close. It sounded so intimate in her ear. The light from the bathroom filtered through the crack in the closet door and she coiled further into the corner, looking up at generations of discarded winter coats. Her heartbeat raced around in her chest and she took several deep breaths to slow it down. As she inhaled, the smell of damp dogs and mothballs worked its toxic magic on her nauseous insides. She pulled the old robe tightly around her as her shoulders shook and her sobs grew more violent.

Luke

The cotton blanket clung rigidly to the clothesline, frozen in mid-flap. Lissie struggled to pry it away with fingers stiff with cold. The first north wind of the winter had blown in the night before, glazing everything with icy crystals, but Lissie had been too tired to notice until now. A few yards away, Squeaky poked his head out of the barn door and called to his mother.

'When we eatin', Momma?'

It was late in the afternoon, several hours away from their usual suppertime, so she knew that his question was prompted by boredom and not hunger. She tried folding the blanket but it crackled in her arms and she sighed.

'Not for while, yet. Doc Caldwell's comin'. I cain't do nothin' 'til he gets here. Tell your daddy, 'less he got a squirrel today, it ain't nothin' but bread and tuit tonight.'

He looked disappointed but nodded and shut the barn door. From the window in the top loft, her daughter waved and gave a wistful smile.

'Willa, get back inside near the stove.'

She watched until Willa disappeared then walked slowly back to the house, as the wind snapped at her aching joints.

In the kitchen, she lowered the drying rack and untied the

bundles of herbs she had carefully preserved over the summer, then draping the blanket stiffly over the top, she hoisted it above the fire. The water in the cook pot had still not come to a boil so she opened the stove door, poking the sleeping embers until they flared up. Within minutes, the water began to boil and she pinched off a few mint leaves and dropped them in. Using the edge of her apron to hold the iron handle she carried it, steaming, into the back bedroom and set it on the bedside table. The dim light from a gauze-covered afternoon sun cast a single shaft of light across the iron bed and the sweat on Luke's face danced like water in a hot skillet. She used her hand to wave some of the steam towards him, then rinsed the cloth hanging on the bedpost with fresh water from the basin.

'Come on, Sugar. Doc'll be here soon.'

She bathed his face with the cool cloth, then lifted the covers to check the dampness. Over the last few days, it had been a constant battle to keep dry blankets and sheets on his bed and the fire had been stoked throughout the nights to keep fresh steam circulating for his raspy lungs. Her arms ached from the constant washing and wringing and her eyes felt heavy and filled with grit in spite of the few naps she had managed to steal at the kitchen table. It had been three days since they had found Luke, feverish and incoherent, on the corner of their porch. They didn't know how many hours he had been there or how long it had taken him to find his way to them, but they had moved him into the back room and Jaspar had made a makeshift shelter in the barn for himself and the children.

The knock on the front door sounded tired and listless and when she answered, Doc Caldwell didn't look much better than the patients he'd been tending. He did little more than touch Luke's forehead and lift the blankets to feel his skin, then forced open one of the boy's eyelids to reveal pale eyes that roved unfocused in their sockets. He took one of the multicolored vials from his bag and tapped a sprinkle of powder into a small square of white paper. He folded it and handed it to Lissie.

'Don't know if this is gonna do much good and I don't know that he's gonna last more'n twenty-four hours anyway, but mix a pinch of it with tea. Give it to him every few hours.'

He closed up his bag and smiled with exhausted eyes, patting her on the shoulder.

'Looks like you've had about as much sleep as I have, Lissie.'

She nodded and tried to smile back.

'Can I fix you some coffee? Jaspar keeps a tin of it special.'

He shook his head.

'No, thanks just the same. I got too many people to see yet.'

He sighed and rubbed the bridge of his nose, his shoulders slumping further under the weight of his duties.

'In all my years, I've never seen influenza like this. I'm buryin' more healthy, young people 'round here than I've got comin' home in boxes from the war. There just doesn't seem to be an end to it. And nothin' I do seems to help.'

Lissie cleared her throat as she crossed to the kitchen shelves.

'We don't have no ready money, but I can give you some jars of my applesauce and some of my dried herbs.'

He nodded and gratefully accepted her offerings.

'Nobody's got much in the way of ready money these days. Iler Mae will appreciate havin' these; she spends most of her time fussin' at me for not eatin' properly. Not a day goes by that she doesn't threaten to go cook for somebody else, but since my Eula died, I haven't had much interest in eatin'.'

As Lissie walked him to the door, he turned to ask the question she'd been dreading.

'His momma know where he is?'

She shuffled uncomfortably and shook her head but when she looked up, she was surprised to see that his expression was filled, not with reproach, but understanding.

'Won't be easy, I know . . . but I think you oughta tell her, Lissie. Soon as you can. He's in a mighty bad way, and I think it best you tell her before anythin' happens.'

She nodded reluctantly and shut the door behind him.

She made tea to the doctor's instructions and patiently held it to Luke's lips, waiting until the whole cup had been emptied one tiny sip at a time. She left a newly rinsed cloth on his forehead then went into the kitchen to fix her family their supper. The slab of smoked bacon had been finished off the day before, but she had been saving the drippings after each meal. She warmed it up in the skillet and crumbled half a loaf of stale bread into it, stirring until every drop of fat was absorbed and the crumbs were golden brown and crispy. She raked a few potatoes from the oven into a bucket and put a plate on top of the skillet to make the trip across the frozen yard to the barn.

The children scurried around to lay the table, throwing a cloth across a bale of hay and collecting their plates from the top of the kerosene stove that Jaspar had rigged up for warmth. They shoveled the fat-soaked bread into their mouths, enjoying the warming comfort it brought, lulled by the sound of scraping tin plates and the gurgling of sleeping hens that cozied together in the chicken coop a few feet away. Jaspar reached over and touched his wife's hand, his calloused fingers brushing tenderly across her tensed fist.

'What's Doc say?'

She glanced uneasily at the children who had suddenly stopped their hurried feeding and looked at her expectantly.

'Doc thinks we might lose him.'

Squeaky's face creased with pain and Lissie held out her arms to him. He collapsed, sobbing in her lap as she rocked him gently.

'I'm sorry, Momma. I'm so sorry.'

She soothed him, pressing her cheek into the soft nap of his hair.

'Now, Titus James, don't you go blamin' yourself. It ain't your fault.'

The week before, she had not been so generous, her fear having stripped her of all reason. The night he and Luke hopped the train, he had returned home close to midnight to face the panic-driven anger of his parents. Jaspar had been out for hours in the wagon searching for the boys and by the time Squeaky had walked through the back door, his mother had reached the point of hysteria. He had confessed his sins and taken his punishment with a quiet acceptance, which led Lissie to believe that Squeaky's experience had been more frightening than the adventure he'd imagined. She had never seen him so shaken and so unwilling to brag of his endeavors even days afterwards. Something told her that his wandering days had ended on the very day they had begun.

On the night they found Luke unconscious, Squeaky had hovered at the bedroom door, his eyes stricken with worry and his fingers twisting nervously around each other. She found him later, shivering on the front porch, his face streaked with guilty tears. Between sniffles he told her about the raspy, feverish sickness of the hobos he had been so keen to meet, and slumping beneath her arm, he heaped all the blame on his own shoulders.

The tears he shed now were even heavier.

'I made him go, Momma. I made him sick.'

She pulled him up, cradling his chin in the cup of her hand.

'This flu's killin' people all over the country, Doc says. So Luke coulda caught it anywhere.'

She nudged him back to his plate and they finished their meal in silence. That night she made out a pallet beside Luke's bed and tried to get some sleep. She knew she'd need as much strength as possible the next day.

In the morning she felt better rested, and Jaspar agreed to watch over Luke while she made the trip to the Stewarts' farm. Jaspar had wanted to go himself, but she had convinced him that as a mother, it would be better if she relayed the news.

She wrapped up in a cape and set out across town, practicing in her mind what she would say. The roads were quiet and the front yards empty of children at play. Pale lights from inside the houses gave notice that there was life beyond the locked doors, but those within seemed suspicious, shut off, and watchful. Many of the windows displayed blue stars, a message to those who passed that someone they loved was fighting in the war. A few of the stars were gold, a badge to the ultimate sacrifice, to say that their son or husband had died for their country.

Over the last year, Lissie had seen plenty to make her grateful that Jaspar's crippled foot had kept him from the war. He had lost most of the toes on his left foot a few years before, while clearing the sugar cane and although it had seemed an unfair setback at the time, she now saw it as a blessing. Of the few Negro men who had been conscripted from the area and shipped to the Western Front, most had come home with missing limbs or gelatinous eyes, or not at all. Many of the young black men who had been left behind had migrated North when word had spread that there was plenty of well-paid work in munition factories. Not a day went by that Lissie didn't thank God that her husband had decided to stay in spite of the hardships; hardships that might have been alleviated with the money Jaspar could have sent home each week from a steady paycheck. It had meant extra work for all of them, but it had kept them together.

Lissie had taken in laundry to make ends meet, and while collecting and delivering other people's shirts and linens, she had come face to face with the realities of a war that had mercifully bypassed her own family. She had seen the coffins lying in the front rooms. She had heard the quiet sobbing from various corners of the houses as she waited to be paid for the crisply starched tablecloths that would lie beneath the mourners' feast later that day. Worse still were the sounds of young men in the front parlors, who had come home to die from the mustard gas that slowly poisoned their bodies, coughing chunks of their youthful lungs into their mother's lace handkerchiefs.

From a distance, the Stewart farm looked desolate and forbidding in the frozen gray sky and Lissie's heart thumped nervously as she came closer. She was halfway up the dirt path that led to the back porch, when Emma suddenly appeared from inside and latched the screen door. In her fist, she held a broom that looked prepared to do battle with the slightest provocation.

'What you want here?'

Lissie stopped where she stood and looked down at the ground.

'Mizz Stewart?'

'Yes.'

'I'm Lissie James. Your boy, Luke? He's been stayin' with me and my family the last few days.'

'Well, if you're wantin' money, you ain't gettin' any.'

'No, ma'am. It's . . . you see, Luke's sick . . . real sick and the doc, well . . . he says he may not make it.'

'That so?'

'Yes, ma'am. So I thought you'd want to know. I thought you might want to come back with me . . .'

Emma snorted.

'Why on God's green earth would I want to come back with you?'

'To . . . see him. Doc says he might not live another day, but we're prayin' for the best.'

'Well, you just go on prayin' for the best and I'll go on prayin' for what's best for me.'

Shock burned Lissie's face but she made no move to leave. Emma's voice was firm and hostile.

'I think you better go now.'

'We live just past Willow Junction . . .'

'Don't you people listen, or you just too stupid to understand? Now get out of here and don't come 'round here again. You're lucky I don't get the squirrel gun after you. Now git.'

She waved her hand in the air like she was shooing a pesky dog from her hen house and for the first time Lissie straightened her shoulders and looked Emma in the face. She took a step forward, the nervousness gone and her eyes steady and calm.

'You ain't gonna see me 'round here no more, Mizz Stewart. I can promise you that.'

Emma shifted the broom to her other hand, her knuckles white as she squeezed the handle nervously. Lissie continued to stare brazenly, a strength rising from her anger.

'And if that boy gets better, you can bet he won't be back here again, not if I can help it.'

Emma retreated towards the back wall.

'My husband's just inside. You git outta here now.'

There was a flicker of uncertain fear in Emma's face and Lissie slowly and deliberately turned her back on her and walked away.

Relief that she had faced and overcome her fear of the woman, made Lissie's walk home easier in spite of the increasing weariness she felt with each step. Her ribs rattled with a permanent shiver as the cold found its way into the folds of her cape and the muscles in her neck throbbed as she hunched them against the wind.

The children were waiting for her in the front yard with eager faces and in an instant her discomfort was forgotten. While she'd been away, Luke had awakened and asked for water. She went into the back room and sitting beside his bed, she brushed a strand of his hair, dry but stiff with sweat, from his forehead. He opened his eyes and she smiled.

'Well, Mister Luke, you sure give us a scare. We been fussin' around you for days and you slept right through it.'

He smiled feebly and she took his hand.

'You reckon you could eat some soup if I fix it?'

He nodded and swallowed.

'Thirsty.'

'I'll send Squeaky in with some water. He's bustin' a gut to see you.'

She tucked the blankets around him and picked up the pan of water, now cold and still, beside the bed.

Canaan

The frenzy of Homecoming had finally died down and the town was getting geared up for Halloween. All week at Piggly Wiggly she and the other employees had been forced to wear rubber pig noses and pink floppy pig ears on a headband. She'd put her foot down when Kyle suggested they also attach the curly tails to the backs of their aprons and she wasn't alone. Only Dot had agreed to wear the tail. She seemed to enjoy making an issue of waving it around when male customers were present. Canaan figured it was the closest Dot would ever get to a Playboy Bunny suit.

It was Canaan's first Saturday off and much as she would have preferred to stay as far away from town and Piggly Wiggly as possible, she needed to cash her first paycheck. She drove uptown early, hoping to beat the late sleepers, and Friday night partygoers. The car had behaved admirably since Zeke had tried his hand at mechanics, but she couldn't believe it would last much longer. She was determined to squirrel away as much as possible to pay for the work on the engine but her first priority was to find something loose and shapeless to wear. It wasn't likely that she'd start showing in the next eight weeks but she wasn't taking any chances. Everything she owned was tight and figure-hugging and would give away her condition much sooner than she wanted.

As she crossed the road, she saw Luke carrying his trademark burlap sack. With every step he took, the sound of aluminum cans clanked behind him. She stood outside the drugstore and watched as he stopped a young couple on the street who were holding canned drinks.

'You almost finished?'

The girl giggled nervously.

'What?'

'Your can. Can I have it when you're finished?'

The boy moved menacingly towards him and shouted something abusive. Luke scurried along the sidewalk but then stooped down to retrieve a crushed Dr Pepper can from the curb. As he stood up he looked in Canaan's direction and she ducked quickly into the store. She hid behind a spinner rack as Luke cupped his hand against the glass and stared through the window, trying to find her inside the store. He finally gave up and catching sight of someone else with a half-finished drink can he hurried down the sidewalk towards them. It was only then that Canaan realized that she was in the mother/baby corner of the store. The spinner rack was filled with books on every subject from natural birth to milk pumps. She tentatively reached for one called *The New Mother* but was suddenly aware of the number of people waiting for their prescriptions nearby. She hurried next door to the dress shop.

The sales assistant was determined to follow Canaan around offering the standard, and often misguided, fashion advice.

'That would look fantastic on a figure like yours. Why don't you try it? The color is perfect with your eyes.'

Canaan was in the dressing room trying on a selection of loose-cut blouses and dresses. She turned sideways, staring at herself in the mirror, then rolled the other clothes into a ball and stuffed them under the blouse. She was studying her profile when the sales assistant called out.

'Aren't you kin to that loony guy?'

Canaan pulled the clump of clothes from under her dress and jerked the curtain back.

'His name is Luke.'

'Well, whatever his name is he's in some kind of trouble out there on the square.'

As she tried to cross the road Canaan could see the fear on Luke's face. Two teenagers were circling him on the square. One was holding his hat, taunting him with it before throwing it like a frisbee to his buddy. Luke stumbled towards them each time they held it out to him, clinging protectively to a paper bag clutched to his chest, the sound of cans rattling in the sack he had strapped to his back. Nearby, two more boys sprawled across the hood of a beat-up pick-up truck, watching, before plodding like playful hunting dogs in Luke's direction. They joined the other two, forming a circle around the old man. By that time it was clear that Luke was more concerned about getting out of the circle and keeping hold of his paper bag than getting his beloved hat back.

'Havin' trouble there, Looney Tune?'

The tallest of the four, a gangly boy with a pointed weasel-like face, did most of the talking, but the other three winked and slapped their hands in mid-air as Luke became more and more flustered.

A crowd of curious onlookers had gathered but no one looked interested in intervening.

'Come and get it. Come on . . . you want it? Huh?'

Luke tried to make a break for a gap, but his slow shuffling steps were no match for the youngsters.

'Gotta move them feet a little faster, retard.'

He began kicking the backs of Luke's heels until he fell with a thud. They laughed and the chubby boy with the pendulous belly that protruded from between the checked curtains of his unbuttoned shirt, waved the hat under Luke's nose.

'Come on, Looney. We'll give you your hat. Show us what you got in the bag.'

He reached for the paper bag and Luke tried to twist away.

'It's mine. Paid for it myself.'

'Ain't you gonna share with your new buddies?'

The force of Canaan's tackle knocked the boy backwards and the surprise knocked the wind from his lungs. She stood between Luke and the boys, her eyes flashing and her hands fisted at her side.

'Get away from him, you little shits.'

The fat boy struggled into a sitting position trying to catch his breath, but the others strutted towards her with a nervous bravado.

'Ooo-hoo! Ain't you tough?'

Canaan took several determined steps towards them.

'He hasn't done anything to you.'

She glared at the crowd who were watching.

'He hasn't done anything to any of you. Now get away from him and leave him alone!'

The boys shrugged and tossed the hat to the ground.

'Don't matter to us. We was gettin' bored anyways.'

She watched them help their friend up from the ground and saunter towards the drugstore. A handful of onlookers whispered among themselves and Canaan stood defiantly until the last one had trickled away. She knelt beside Luke.

'Are you all right?'

He didn't look at her. Just stared at the bag that was crushed against his chest.

'My cakes.'

His Dolly Madison cupcakes had exploded from their wrappings and he tried unsuccessfully to fit the crumbs back into the package. Canaan took his arm.

'Let me help you up.'

He continued to look at the ground.

'Thank you, ma'am.'

'Do you want me to take you home now?'

'No thank you, ma'am. I don't live far.'

He glanced up and Canaan saw for the first time a deep sadness in his eyes. He looked away again and Canaan felt a sickening ache in her chest.

'Oh God . . . Luke . . . you don't have to pretend you don't know me.'

He looked relieved and nodded. She helped him up.

'Come on. I'll walk you home.'

They stopped at Hammett's Oil on the way home. Luke had insisted that they collect cans and bottles along the way to pay for the replacement cupcakes and Canaan had tried to be patient as he wandered out into fields and down into drainage ditches to add to his collection. She told him to wait on the forecourt so he wouldn't see her toss the cans in the trash can and pay for the cupcakes herself. Outside, she handed him a soft drink.

'Sorry. They didn't have RC.'

'But they had my Dollys?'

She nodded as she handed the new package to him and they walked across the forecourt towards the main road. She was in the middle of helping him open the wrapper when Zeke's VW van turned in and pulled up beside them.

'Hi! You two need a ride?'

Luke shook his head.

'Don't take rides.'

They both continued to walk and Canaan glanced at Zeke, trying not to notice that he was wearing the blue chambray shirt that she'd first seen him in uptown. The one that gaped just enough for her to see his collarbone.

'He doesn't feel safe in cars.'

'But Luke knows me.'

She shrugged but kept walking. She didn't want to stand around and make idle chit-chat.

'He won't even go in my car. I left it uptown so I could walk him home.'

Zeke pulled his van onto the shoulder and slowly rolled beside them.

'You want me to get it for you?'

'No. I'll just walk to work tomorrow.'

She speeded up her pace.

'Wait up, Luke! I'm coming with you.'

Zeke rolled ahead of her trying to talk to her through the window, lowering his head to catch her eye.

'I can pick you up in the morning if you want. What time do you—'

She let him see the flash of anger in her eyes.

'I don't need your help. I've been walking most of my life. That's what girls from the wrong side of the tracks do best. No matter what you and your buddies think.'

'Canaan, what's wrong with you?'

'Nothing – just stop interfering with my life, Zeke.'

'Interfering?'

'It's what you're best at, Zeke. You can't help it. You sit all safe and snug in your so-called bohemian apartment – always on the lookout for some poor sucker like me who desperately wants to believe they're special and deserve better.'

'You do deserve better.'

Luke was a good fifty yards ahead of her by now. She stopped walking and slammed her fist against the side of the van.

'Did you think I was so desperate? Did you think I'd be so grateful for somebody like you to pay attention to me?'

He put the handbrake on and jumped out of the van.

'What are you talking about?'

She squared off with him. Ready to fight.

'A *sure thing*.'

He looked confused and that pissed her off even more.

'That's what you called me. A *sure thing*. God-damn it! I can't believe I let you . . .'

He took hold of her wrists.

'Canaan, I really don't know—'

She pulled away.

'At the reunion, Zeke. Don't pretend you don't know. I heard your friends talking about it. *Zeke's onto a sure thing tonight. Said so himself.* Damn it! How could I be so stupid?'

She stomped off down the road, but Zeke hurried after her.

'Canaan! Canaan! Wait a minute! Please listen to me.'

He took her by the shoulders and she suddenly felt small and vulnerable and tired. Her eyes filled with tears.

'I can't believe I actually thought you might be different from the assholes in this town . . . might actually care . . .'

'Canaan . . . it was Gummy Bear.'

'What?'

'Mrs Olsenbacher was the sure thing.'

She looked uncertain for a minute.

'No. No. I know what I heard. I'm not stupid, Zeke.'

'I told you about it! Don't you remember? They had money bet on it . . . Gummy Bear's goodbye kiss? Jimmy started callin' it my *sure thing*.'

'But I heard him say—'

'Is that what you really think of me?'

She pulled away from him.

'I don't know what to think anymore. Nothing in my life has ever been what it seemed or what I expected.'

'I'm sorry you were hurt.'

'I'll get over it. It was probably for the best anyway. Made me realize . . .'

She turned from him and headed towards home, suddenly aware that she'd said far more than she wanted to.

'Anyway . . . I'm sorry I . . .'

She waved her hand as if that would finish the sentence for her.

'You sure I can't give you a lift? Luke can find his own way home.'

'No. He's had a rough day. I want to stay with him.'

'Can we try this again, Canaan? Start from scratch?'

'It's not a good idea.'

'Don't I even get a second chance?'

She turned to give a sad smile.

'No. I don't think so.'

She caught up with Luke a few yards down the road and fought the urge to wave at Zeke when he passed them.

'Haven't you got those cupcakes opened yet?'

'Waitin' on you.'

She opened the packet for him and handed it back.

'Enjoy. You deserve it.'

Luke offered one of the cakes to her.

'No thanks.'

He held it there in mid-air until she looked at him. He winked.

'Chocolate with cream in the middle.'

She reached up and took it.

'I haven't had a Dolly Madison in years.'

'Good for what ails you.'

They shared a knowing look, then at the same time shoved the whole cupcake into their mouths. They both started to laugh, spraying chocolate crumbs and blobs of cream into the air. Canaan put her hand in Luke's and they walked the rest of the way home.

Luke

The fading afternoon light turned the driving rain the color of dirty bathwater. Luke sat, wrapped in a blanket, on the front porch, his legs drawn up for warmth against the wall of water that cascaded off the porch roof. He was still weak but he had not moved from his position all day, as he waited with the rest of the family. Squeaky sat on a stool, gazing through the waterfall to the distorted world beyond, and Willa rocked gently nearby, staring at the abandoned dirt-dobber nests under the porch roof.

Doc Caldwell had been by that morning, his second visit in three days, since Jaspar had carried Lissie to bed and sent Squeaky racing across town to fetch him. That night Luke had moved with the rest of the family out to the barn. Squeaky had hollowed out a patch on the opposite side, and over the next few days, he had slept and eaten alone, building the walls of his own solitary exile. During their long vigil on the front porch he had not spoken to Luke or Willa or allowed his eyes to meet theirs.

The hinges of the screen door creaked and they all turned to see Jaspar in the doorway. He moved like a man taking his first steps on artificial legs and his eyes, raw from exhaustion, searched for something solid to focus on. His lips parted, allowing a few whispered sounds to escape as he struggled to form the words.

'She's gone.'

He held out his arms as Willa bolted from her chair, grabbing him around the waist and sobbing into his chest and Squeaky walked, trance-like, until he was absorbed into their embrace. Luke watched through swimming eyes. He desperately needed to join them, but a deep invisible chasm separated him from their private grief. Jaspar buried his face in his daughter's hair.

'It was so fast. I wadn't ready.'

He squeezed the children tightly to him, as if some almighty Hand might rip them from his arms. He raised his head and cried up to the rafters.

'Oh, my Lissie. I ain't ready, baby. I ain't ready.'

Willa continued to cry softly, but Squeaky stood stiff and lifeless then pulled away, brushing his father's arms from around him. He bounded off the porch and through the waterfall of rain, his feet slipping clumsily beneath him as he made his way across the muddy mire of the yard. Luke dropped the blanket and followed him.

He found Squeaky in the barn on his knees, small and helpless, making strangled noises as he rocked back and forth on the floor. Luke crossed to him, taking tiny cat-like steps, his hair and shirt saturated with rain that dribbled down the back of his neck and between his shoulder blades. As he drew near, his shadow spread over the crouched figure and gathering his courage he gently touched his shoulder. Squeaky jerked backwards with the spewing force of a volcano, his eyes black and molten.

'Don't you touch me.'

Luke stepped back.

'I'm sorry . . .'

'You're sorry?'

Squeaky lunged forward, grabbing the straps of Luke's overalls and slinging him to the ground.

'Is that all you can say, you son-of-a-whore? You're sorry?'

He straddled Luke, his fists knotted and raised.

'You couldn't go home to your own momma. You had to come to my house . . . make my momma take care of you.'

Luke raised up, confused by a hatred he'd never seen in his friend.

'I . . . I—'

His sentence was cut off as Squeaky kicked him in the stomach and he felt the air rush upwards from his gut.

'You didn't go home 'cause your own momma don't want you.'

He kicked him again and Luke rolled into a tight ball to protect himself.

'Well, let me tell you somethin', you halfwit white-boy, my momma didn't want you neither.'

'Squeaky, please . . .'

'She just felt sorry for you. Like a poor mangy stray dog. That's all you was to her.'

A deep bellow erupted from Squeaky's throat as he threw himself on Luke's back and they rolled across the straw floor. Luke remained passive, allowing the small boy to punch and scratch in a frenzied attack.

'You killed her.'

Luke staggered to a standing position, flailing his arms as he tried to free himself from his friend's clawing hands. Squeaky fell backwards, through the door of the chicken coop and, as the chickens squawked and flapped hysterically, he grabbed an egg from the nesting shelf and threw it at Luke. It landed with a sickening thud on the side of his head, oozing down behind his ear and Squeaky rummaged through the straw for more.

'She's my momma. Not yours.'

Luke dodged the eggs, trying to inch closer, but was forced back each time. Suddenly Squeaky stopped in mid-aim and his eyes flickered with an unreachable sorrow.

'You stay away from me, you sorry piece of white trash. I hate you. I'll always hate you.'

Holding an egg in each hand, Squeaky sank to his knees, his head bowed as if all the strength had drained from his body.

'You killed her . . . you killed my momma.'

Luke wiped his own tears away with the back of his hand, then silently slipped out the barn door and into the growing darkness.

The rain had created gullies in the road, streamlets that churned with chalky deposits of sandstone on their way to the nearest creek. Luke stumbled along, trying to see through the downpour as the rain pelted his face. At the water tower he sat shuddering beneath its protection, until he heard the clear piercing whistle of the train. In the deep shadows of the landscape he saw the light as it broke through the trees, and he started to run. It was not as easy as it had been before. The darkness and the rain made it difficult to see and his recovering lungs and aching limbs were weak and puny in the face of such physical danger. The solid ground beneath him had turned to mud and even when he grabbed hold, the rungs of the boxcar were slippery. He held on, trying to build up his strength, moving inch by inch until he was safely inside. He stood at the door of the empty boxcar and watched as the lights of Lander twinkled in a blanket of rain, and finally disappeared from sight.

Canaan

Canaan tied a hooded sweatshirt around her waist and wandered down to the Little House. The weather was still so mild, it felt like a warm spring day in New York. After years of staring out over heavy gray clouds and cold, slate skylines and trudging through the dirty black slush of city snow, she never thought she'd so look forward to cold weather. She was sure her morning sickness wouldn't be so bad if the air was frozen. Everything seemed to smell stronger in warm air.

She could hear her grandmother mumbling to herself as she stepped onto the porch. The door squeaked as she opened it.

'Help me with this, will you?'

Lou Venie was using all the strength in her wiry frame to move Luke's bed. Her face was pink with the effort and her elastic hairband had slipped up over her ear and looked dangerously close to popping off her head entirely and shooting across the room like a slingshot.

Canaan lifted the other side and they moved it to the far wall.

'I wanna get this stink cleared out of here while you're gone. Try to keep him out as long as you can, will you?'

She poured a bucket of soapy water onto the floorboards and started to scrub. She looked up at Canaan.

'Did you want me for somethin'?'

'I was looking for Luke.'

'I threw him out so I could get started. Gonna take me the best part of a day.'

'You know where he went?'

'Down in the barn. Stringin' the poles. Never seen him so excited. Even made me give him a haircut this mornin'. *You're just goin' fishin'*, I said. *You think the fish give a flitter 'bout whether you got a haircut or not?* But he wouldn't have it. Said he was gettin' too shaggy-headed.'

Luke's haircuts were another of his odd habits, like collecting books, and squirreling food away in the Little House until it rotted away to nothing. He had a knack for showing up when Lou Venie was busy with something else and would follow her around, holding his rusty pair of hair clippers and shuffling his feet impatiently until she gave in. The pattern was always the same. She'd mumble to herself as she dragged a kitchen chair out to the yard and draped a tablecloth around his shoulders, then she'd complain about how stiff the clippers were and ask him why he didn't let her use the scissors. Canaan had watched over the years as Luke sat with eyes watering and his mouth drawn tightly as the old clippers yanked and pulled more hair out than they cut. But he put up with it and never gave in to the scissors no matter how much Lou Venie complained.

'You'd better get a move on. He'll be back up here huntin' you 'fore long and I don't want him interferin' with my work. He'll start tryin' to salvage half of what I'm tryin' to throw away.'

Canaan sighed.

'I wish I hadn't promised him. I haven't been fishing since I was fifteen.'

'Well, don't get all carried away and bring me back a mess of fish to gut and clean.'

'Not much chance of that.'

'I got a deep freeze full of crappie and catfish. I tell him I got plenty, but ever' dang time he brings me back a string of 'em. Guess he figures it pays his keep. But it just makes more work for me.'

She stopped scrubbing and sat back on her haunches.

'You find your breakfast all right? I left it in the oven.'

'Wasn't hungry.'

'You ain't been eatin' right since you got back.'

'You mean I haven't been eating what you think is right.'

Lou Venie threw another splash of suds on the floor.

'What's that supposed to mean?'

'Lou Venie, I've been trying to tell you . . . I've never liked *good ole country breakfasts*.'

'You used to eat 'em.'

'Because you made me.'

'Well, it ain't just that. You're sleepin' all the time. Cain't be good for you.'

'It's nothing. It always takes time for my body to get back to normal.'

'Will you go to the doctor? Make sure there's no damage needs takin' care of?'

Canaan wasn't very good at lying to her grandmother. The radar in the old woman's head always seemed to trip her up.

'Nothing's wrong, Lou Venie. I've been through this before.'

She opened the screen door to leave.

'I'll keep Luke out 'til sundown. And I'll make him throw the smallest ones back.'

'Throw 'em all back. I don't want 'em.'

*

On the walk to the lake Canaan was glad she'd agreed to go. The leaves had turned their deepest hue of the season. They'd been clinging to the branches much longer than usual this year because of the mild spell, but one good wind would strip the trees bare. They looked as though they'd been painted. It was the kind of beauty in nature that couldn't be ignored, even in Canaan's self-absorbed state of mind.

Luke set up the lines while Canaan set up 'camp'. Luke had complained and refused to bring lawn chairs or a cooler with them. *That ain't fishin', that's homesteadin'.* But Canaan wasn't going to put herself out any more than she had to. She'd stuffed her old backpack with a blanket and a pillow. Roughing it was one thing but she wasn't sure how long she could take sitting on a rocky slope. If she got bored at least she could find a grassy patch somewhere and take a nap. Lou Venie had been right. She seemed to be sleeping all the time these days. She opened the top of the backpack and found a thermos of coffee and a plastic bag full of sandwiches that her grandmother must have slipped in while she was taking her shower. It was only ten in the morning, but she was already feeling hungry. She took out one of the sandwiches and started to take a bite. She knew it was tuna but her hormones had mutated its smell to something resembling the sweet putrid smell of black-eyed peas that have been left to mold in the back of the refrigerator. All she'd eaten that morning was dry toast and black coffee, but she could feel it rising in her throat. She scrambled down the embankment towards a small peninsula trying to make it as far away as possible. She was aiming for a small clump of reeds where she was hoping to hide, but her body betrayed her and she went down on her knees at the water's edge. She sat there for a while, trying to compose herself, fighting the need to cry. When she turned, Luke was sitting on a small boulder watching her. She tried to make light of things.

'Must have eaten something that disagreed with me.'

He smiled and held out his hand for her to join him on the boulder.

'You must've been eatin' things that disagreed with you for goin' on two or three months now.'

She turned to look at him and there was something so deeply kind and understanding in his eyes that she collapsed in sobs as he wrapped his arms around her. When she was finished crying, they sat for almost an hour, her head on his shoulder. Quietly staring at the water.

She made the first move.

'Guess we better go check those lines.'

He nodded then took her hand.

'You gonna keep it?'

She filled up again, but nodded.

'Lord knows why. The women in my family aren't exactly known for handling motherhood very well.'

'They weren't bad mothers.'

Canaan laughed as she wiped her eyes.

'Are you kidding me?'

He patted her hand again and stood up.

'They were just scared. That's all. And there wadn't nobody there to tell 'em not to be.'

He helped her up and they headed back to the fishing lines. For most of the afternoon, Canaan slept on her blanket, exhausted from the hormones and emotions and lulled by the gentle lapping of the water. The sun was low in the sky when she finally opened her eyes and noticed Luke's line bobbing in the water. She sat up.

'Luke! Luke! You got one!'

Luke scrambled down to the edge to bring it in and she squealed just as she had when she was eight years old and Luke had brought her fishing for the first time. She slapped him good-naturedly on the back.

'I knew it. You always get the first one.'

Luke grinned, pleased with himself.

'He's a good'un, ain't he?'

'He sure is.'

'Lou Venie's gonna like him, I bet.'

Canaan bit her lip.

'Luke, why don't we throw him back?'

'Aw, naw. He's a good size. Better than any I caught last week.'

She tried again.

'You know, we don't really need to take any back with us.'

'Can't let Lou Venie down.'

'Well . . . she told me she doesn't want anymore.'

He nodded as he dropped the fish in the bucket.

'Uh-huh.'

'Says she's got plenty.'

'Yeah, I know.'

'Are you just trying to cause trouble?'

He smiled.

'Lou Venie needs people to fuss at. It's what keeps her going.'

Canaan shook her head and sat back down. Luke finished baiting his line then headed into the weeds.

'Where you off to?'

'Gotta relieve myself.'

'I thought you just did that.'

He shrugged.

'Not havin' much luck lately. You watch my line now.'

There was something in his voice that worried her.

'Luke? Are you . . .'

'I'm fine, Candy-Cane. Just fine. Havin' a little trouble with my waterworks, that's all.'

He disappeared over the ridge and Canaan lay back to watch the changing colors of the late-afternoon sky. She wasn't sure how long she'd dozed, but she was startled awake by Luke's shouts.

'Canaan! Canaan! Come here! Hurry!'

She stood quickly, feeling dizzy and disoriented.

'Luke?'

'Hurry, Canaan! Over here!'

She followed his voice, running, stumbling down the embankment. She saw him huddled on his haunches at the water's edge.

'What? What's wrong? Are you hurt?'

He put his finger to his lips.

'Ssshh!'

'Luke . . .'

He touched her arm to stop her talking then pointed a few yards out on the lake. A turtle was swimming towards a log and on its back was a bright yellow butterfly.

'Ain't that the purtiest thing you ever saw?'

Canaan felt a mixture of relief and annoyance.

'Luke, for cryin' out loud. You scared me half to death! For what? That? Damn it!'

He took her hand and pulled her down.

'Sit down with me.'

She resisted, feeling irritable and angry by the fear he'd stirred up in her.

'I left the lines.'

'They'll wait.'

She plopped down beside him in the dirt as he continued to watch.

'Must be the last butterfly of the season.'

He turned to her and smiled and she was struck again by the deep kindness in his eyes.

'Bet there ain't any two people in the world seen that same thing.'

She couldn't help but feel moved by his childlike joy. She slipped her arm in his and they watched as the turtle crawled up onto the log and the butterfly flitted to an upright branch.

'I'd say we was pretty dang lucky, wouldn't you, Candy-Cane?'

She squeezed his arm.

'I guess so, Luke. Pretty dang lucky.'

Luke

They'd been hunkered down in the undergrowth for almost an hour and Luke's legs were burning from staying still so long. But he didn't dare move. He'd seen first-hand the Major's habit of silent backhanded slaps to make his point. Luke wasn't much of a talker anyway, but in the two days he'd been traveling with the Major he'd figured his silence kept him safer than most who crossed the man's path.

Luke was thirteen when he left Lander and started traveling the lines and after a year he finally felt it was where he belonged. The brotherhood of hobos accepted the tall sickly boy without questions or judgement, providing him with a network of protection wherever he roamed. In the beginning he stayed on the periphery, eating alone, sleeping at a distance. Before long, a few of them managed to coax him into their circle and accepted his quietness the same way they accepted every other man's oddities and quirky behavior. The faces he came to know changed every few days, as work or itchy feet led them in different directions. He learned to accept the friendships as they came along and to move on after a few days when he woke up and found they were gone.

They were a varied group. There were the fast talkers and the braggarts, the storytellers and the philosophers. They came from all over the country and from all different back-grounds, some with families to feed back home, some with families they'd decided were better off without them. There were moonshiners on the run from revenuers, thieves on the scam, children who'd been dumped out of orphanages when they turned eighteen, former teachers who yearned to see the world instead of read about it. There were men on their own who were frightened of settling down, who had either aban-doned the shackles of family life or had never started in the first place. And there were some who just didn't fit in with the rest of the world and never would.

Major Clancy Maddux had never been an easy fit. He was not a philosopher or a storyteller. His scathing remarks were carefully crafted to make people squirm. He was barely in his thirties but his barking commands and bullying ways had earned him the nickname Major. As he'd spent time in the army his promotion from foot soldier suited him just fine. He'd survived his time in the trenches, but his family had not survived without him. He'd come home to find that his wife had died in the Spanish Influenza pandemic and his two chil-dren had died of starvation. He hopped a train the week after and had dedicated every minute to taking back what he felt the world owed him and punishing anyone who got in his way.

He'd hooked up with Luke two days before and con-vinced the boy to travel up to North Carolina with him. Luke had followed his lead, never questioning his decisions on destination or direction. But now he wished he'd asked a few more questions, backhanded slaps or not. They were hid-ing in the undergrowth watching a farmhouse as the late-afternoon shadows gobbled up the landscape. The farmer was a small wiry fellow, with a straw cowboy hat pulled down to shield his eyes from the low-setting sun. Not long after they'd taken their positions, they'd seen him heading back from the lower field, his work boots caked with mud.

As he put one muddy boot onto the first step of the porch he reached out and examined the side trellis, heaving with honeysuckle, which had pulled away from its supports. One more job before supper. They watched as he sauntered down to the barn and came back dragging scrap timber and a handful of nails, a hammer tucked into the back of his work jeans.

A few minutes later the man's wife came out from the kitchen, her hairline damp from boiling turnip greens.

'You tell them boys where they could clean up?'

'I showed 'em. Could probably use a towel or two, though.'

'They work out all right?'

Her husband nodded.

'Good workers. Got the last hunnerd yards of the fencing finished.'

'Well, I made a extra mess of cornbread and beans. Should fill 'em up.'

She opened the screen door to return to the kitchen.

'I'll send Mary Louise down with the towels soon as I finish with her.'

The Major winked at Luke and whispered.

'This place is lookin' like a good bet, boy. A real good bet. We'll sit tight here for a little while longer . . . wait'll it's too dark to start any work. Get some good hot grub, a place to stay and be off before mornin' light.'

So Luke sat on his haunches for another twenty minutes waiting obediently, but uneasily, for the Major to give the signal. It came soon after Mary Louise came out with a basket of towels and a bar of soap. Her father glanced up as she came down the steps.

'Just leave it down by the pump. They'll be up directly.'

Luke watched her closely as she crossed the yard and seemed to be coming straight for them. She was around sixteen years old and her hair was a deep mahogany color. Her face was broad and open and friendly with a generous scattering of freckles. The Major watched the boy's blatant admiration with a knowing smile.

'This is definitely the place, boy. You notice the dress that little girl was wearin'? Store bought. Not home-made calico. Yes-sir, this is the place for us.'

He patted Luke on the shoulder and stood up, motioning for him to follow. They ambled up to the front gate where the farmer was mending the trellis. The Major slid his hat from his head, chin down and eyes to the ground.

'Sir, I was wonderin' if you might have some chores we could help you with in exchange for a night in your barn? Me and the boy – we're hard workers. Could really use one night's sleep that's dry and warm.'

Just as the Major had anticipated, it was too late to start anything new, so the farmer told him they could have supper with the other two and share the barn with them. Then, he said, he'd find them some work to do in the morning. The Major put on a big show of gratitude and humility that made Luke feel uneasy. He made up his mind that the next morning when the Major left he'd stay long enough to pay off both their debts then head out on his own, make his way back down towards Chattanooga.

'Told the other two to wash up down yonder. You go join 'em and we'll bring you down some vittals. I'd appreciate it if you'd bunk down on the east side of the barn. Got a pregnant cow that's skittish.'

Luke followed the Major down towards the water pump where two old hobos in their sixties were stripped to the waist and scrubbing away in a big washtub. One was tall and skinny, the other one wide and bald. They grinned good-naturedly.

'Well, you boys showed up just in time for the heavy work . . . grab that bar of soap and scrub my back, will you?'

The Major scowled and headed for the barn.

'Let me know when they got grub ready.'

Luke smiled a half-apology to the other two, then rolled up his sleeves and started scrubbing the dirt and axle grease from his arms. The tall one grinned.

'That old boy's sure got a hitch in his gitter. He your kin?'

Luke shook his head.

'Saw you two sitting in the weeds over an hour ago. Afraid you might have to work for your supper?'

Luke looked up, embarrassed.

'I'll do my bit, and the Major's.'

The wide, bald one laughed.

'Looks like the Major's got himself a good deal. Plenty to eat, safe place to sleep and a boy to do all his work for him.'

Luke lowered his eyes and kept scrubbing. The tall one laughed.

'Don't look so worried, boy. We ain't bothered. We seen plenty like your buddy.'

'He ain't my buddy.'

His words snapped back more forcefully than he intended, but the two men just chuckled.

'This here's Cooter. I'm Spoons.'

'Luke.'

With introductions out of the way, the two launched into a long and colorful story about the tornado they outran near Dothan, Alabama. Luke continued scrubbing but his shoulders relaxed and he found himself smiling in spite of himself. He had learned to be wary, and guarded with his emotions, but there was something about the two old friends that made him forget to be careful. Cooter leaned in close.

'Hey, boy . . . that young girl's got the eye for you.'

He nodded towards the house where Mary Louise was watching him closely. Luke blushed and bent lower over the washtub.

'Pretty little thing, ain't she, Spoons? Ain't taken her eyes off the boy since she saw him.'

Luke was only fourteen but he was over six feet tall and

had begun to fill out with a few boyish muscles. His hair was long and not very clean and his face was layered in rail dust, but underneath the dirt there was a sweet kindness in his eyes. As he scrubbed away the muck, she watched with growing interest and the two men took every opportunity to point it out.

When they finished washing up, Luke followed them back to the barn where they continued to talk non-stop, to the annoyance of the Major, who was stretched out on a bale of hay trying to sleep. They were in the middle of another story, one that concerned a hornets' nest, when Mary Louise showed up with supper. Her father was tending the pregnant cow at the other end of the barn and Cooter hurried to help her with the heavy door.

She carried two bowls of pinto beans and a basket of cornbread over her arm. She handed the bowls to Cooter and Spoons and turned shyly to Luke.

'I got two more and a jug of milk if you want to come help me. Momma made some cobbler too.'

Luke looked at the others as if he needed permission. The Major had a strange set to his lips, not a smile exactly, but not a frown either. Spoons laughed.

'Well, don't that beat all. Go on, son. She won't bite you. If you don't mind though, me and Cooter's gonna get started. I'm so hungry I could eat the southern end of a northern-bound mule.'

Luke nodded and reluctantly followed the girl up to the house where her mother was waiting to load them up. They were halfway back to the barn before either of them said a word.

'How far you been?'

Luke shrugged.

'Don't really know.'

He knew she wanted him to say more, but no matter how hard he tried he couldn't force another single word out. They continued to walk in silence. Once they were inside the barn, the Major seemed more interested than usual in what was going on. He watched closely as the girl took extra care around Luke, noticed how her eyes flashed brightly when she looked up at him, how the color in her cheeks rose every time his hand brushed hers in the exchange of plates and corn-bread and spoons. She probably would have stayed and watched them eat if her father hadn't intervened.

'Mary Louise! Get on back to the house. I'm sure your momma still needs your help.'

She left reluctantly and the men dug in to enjoy one of the few hot, hearty meals they'd had in weeks. When they were finished Cooter stacked the dishes up outside the barn door and they sat around the lantern light telling more tall tales. The Major set up camp in the far corner and made it clear he didn't want to be bothered with socializing. They kept their storytelling to a low murmur and eventually curled up in their own patch to get some sleep.

When Luke felt the harsh shake of his shoulder and the whisper close against his ear, he tried to wake up enough to get his thoughts clear. It wasn't going to be easy to tell the Major he was staying.

'C'mon, boy. The back window's open. Looks like the dining room. Saw a big chest in the corner. More'n likely that's where they keep the silver.'

Luke sat up.

'What . . .'

'C'mon, boy. Sun-up's in two hours. Gotta be long gone before then.'

He grabbed Luke by the arm and pulled him to his feet.

'I'll hoist you up through the window, then I'll keep an eye out.'

Luke looked confused.

'I can't . . . No . . .'

The Major grabbed his head and held him in a vice grip, his calloused whisper hot in his ear.

'You can and you will, buddy boy. I seen the way you made eyes at that little girl. You don't do this, I'm gonna make all kinds of a ruckus and make sure her daddy knows you were planning to show his little girl a good time. He'll have the dogs after you so fast you won't have time to sit up and beg.'

Without waiting for an answer, the Major dragged Luke towards the barn door.

'Don't reckon the boy wants to go.'

The voice drifted up lazily from the shadows.

'Stay out of my business and I'll stay out of yours.'

Another voice from the other side of the barn chuckled.

'Well now, we can't rightly do that. We've kinda taken a shine to the boy.'

'Go back to sleep, old man. There ain't nothing you can do.'

'Oh, I think there is.'

Luke heard a sharp intake of breath and felt the Major release his grip on his arm. As he watched, Spoons emerged from the shadows with a pitchfork pressing against the Major's ribs. He smiled in the moonlight.

'Well, don't that beat all? Looks to me like I've drawn a little blood. I'm willin' to draw a lot more if you don't get goin' right now before we start raisin' a ruckus ourselves and see who he believes.'

The Major said nothing at first, testing the strength of the threats, but Luke saw him wince as the tines dug deeper into his flesh. He took a few steps back and nodded.

'Fine.'

He slumped towards the door.

'C'mon, boy.'

Luke stood frozen, staring at the raised pitchfork then back at the Major. He felt Cooter's hand on his shoulder.

'The boy's with us now.'

The Major growled and started to argue, but Spoons stepped forward, raising the pitchfork to the man's neck.

'You'd better act a little more grateful. He's gonna stay to pay off both your debts.'

He grumbled something under his breath but disappeared out the door.

Spoons and Cooter looked at Luke and smiled.

'Well, I think that worked out purty good. How 'bout you?'

Canaan

She had completed her first trimester and most of the sickness
was passed, but certain things still set her off. That morning
it was her deodorant. When she came out of the bathroom
Lou Venie was in the kitchen, cooking cornbread for the
Thanksgiving turkey she'd be baking the next day. Canaan
sat at the table feeling shaky and weak, tentatively trying a
few sips of coffee before getting dressed for work. Lou Venie
plopped a plate on the table in front of her.

'I made you a biscuit with sorghum. It was the only thing
I could keep down when I was pregnant with your momma
and your aunt Peggy.'

Canaan closed her eyes and braced herself for Lou Venie's
interrogation.

'How long have you known?'

'A few weeks.'

Lou Venie returned to the dishes in the sink. Canaan
knew there was more to come, but she didn't want to be the
one to start it rolling. She could tell by the color of her grandmother's ears that things were stewing inside her. At last Lou
Venie slammed the frying pan on the draining board.

'You been back over three months. You couldn't figure it
out no sooner than this?'

'I'm used to things not working, Lou Venie. I stopped paying attention to periods after my first trip to the emergency room.'

Lou Venie picked up the coffee pot from the table and pushed the plate towards Canaan like she was a picky three-year-old.

'Eat your biscuit. A baby can't live off air.'

The biscuit was floating in syrup and the sight of yellow butter swirling in the dark pools made her feel sick again. Lou Venie dumped the coffee grounds into the trash.

'A woman still knows. You can't tell me you didn't know.'

'What difference does it make?'

'We could've done somethin'. There's a clinic in Anniston.'

'It wasn't your decision. It's not your problem.'

'That's just what your momma said. Ruthie didn't care about nothin' 'cept how it affected her. Never thought of nobody else.'

Canaan couldn't take any more. She usually let Lou Venie's tirades wash over her. It took less effort that way and most of the time it meant that the lashing was over in less time. But when Canaan's mother was used as ammunition it always pushed her to fight. For some reason she felt she owed it to her to defend her memory.

'She didn't have a whole lot of options back then, did she?'

Lou Venie had gone back to chopping celery for the corn-bread dressing. She waved the knife in the air.

'There were options. If you knew where to look for 'em.'

Canaan laughed sarcastically.

'Oh right. And you would've done that, would you? Taken Momma to a backwoods butcher, just so she wouldn't embarrass you?'

Lou Venie turned her back to Canaan and dropped a handful of chopped celery into the mixing bowl. Canaan stopped as the silence filled the room. She crossed to her grandmother and turned her around, searching her eyes for denial or truth.

'You did, didn't you?'

Lou Venie wouldn't look at her. Canaan stood closer and whispered.

'It's why she ran away. That's it, isn't it?'

Lou Venie looked defiant.

'It would've made life a lot simpler for both of us without—'

'Me.'

Canaan turned to leave. Her head felt suddenly too big for her shoulders and she felt as though she needed to lie down. Lou Venie reached out for her.

'Canaan, I didn't mean . . .'

Canaan pulled away.

'Don't. Don't. Some things you just can't take back, Lou Venie.'

Canaan left her grandmother in the kitchen, surrounded by chopped celery, mounds of sage, and a small frozen turkey trying its best to defrost in time for Thanksgiving the next day. Canaan picked up her name badge from the sideboard and Lou Venie tried again to apologize.

'Canaan, I'm worried about you. I never meant—'

'I'm late for work.'

She wasn't late for work. She'd agreed to work the afternoon and evening shift so that Juanita could start cooking for her huge family gathering the next day. Canaan wasn't expected until lunchtime, but after the morning's events she had things to do. She didn't look up as she drove off, but she knew Lou Venie was watching her from the front porch.

She went straight to Betty Ann's Diner to reserve a table for the next day. The building was a skinny sliver of brick on the town square, wedged between the shoe-repair shop and the taxicab office. And it was the only place of business open on Thanksgiving Day. Betty Ann had lost her husband years before and her children had moved too far away to make the trip worthwhile. So every year she opened her doors to those who didn't have families to eat with, serving up platters of turkey, cornbread dressing and her famous sweet-potato casserole steeped in rum and topped with brown sugar and pecans.

When she left Betty Ann's she headed out to Herbie's Fashion Barn to do some shopping. It was a strange place, inside a disused National Guard armory and it sold every-thing, clothing-wise, that had been rejected by someone somewhere along the line. There were end-of-the-line clothes, flawed clothes from manufacturers, second-hand clothes and shoes, and an unusual corner that sold retread tires and thirty to fifty plastic funeral wreaths. The odd thing to Canaan was that no one seemed to think this was unusual. Canaan had only been inside Herbie's a couple of times in her life. It always gave her the creeps – a graveyard for unwanted goods – but she knew it was the only place in town where she could get what she needed.

Throughout the day, Lou Venie's words revisited her, but she was surprisingly calm about it. It was almost as if she'd known the truth all along and there was a certain relief in hearing it said out loud at last. Piggly Wiggly was busy with last-minute shoppers, but they were mostly those buying one or two items that had been missed off the original list. A jar of cranberry sauce. A pack of chicken livers for extra giblets in the gravy. The deli made only ten sales all day so Kyle put Canaan to work clearing out the stockroom which suited her just fine. She wasn't in the mood to socialize or to put up with Dot's abusive banter.

Just before she drove over the hill, she turned her car lights off and slowly coasted down the drive. She sat in the car for over an hour, watching Lou Venie through the cur-tains. When she saw the bathroom light go on she sneaked in and got undressed in the dark. About thirty minutes later she heard Lou Venie ease her bedroom door open. She pretended to be asleep and she could sense her grandmother watching her. Finally she heard her moving through the house, turning off the lights and locking all the doors. When she heard her bedroom door close, she finally rolled over and went to sleep.

Luke

They were camped under an old railroad bridge not far from Johnson City, hoping to wait out the bad weather, but the storm system had been hammering the South for four days with no sign of letting up. They'd been cooped up in a boxcar for the last few hours, unable to open the doors for air because painful bullets of rain pelted their bodies and turned the floor into a slippery, muddy mess. Spoons remembered a railway trellis that he said would be a good place to stay the night, so he talked Luke and Cooter into jumping off when they reached the Riverside bend. Cooter had cussed as they scrambled down the waterlogged embankment, up to their ankles in muddy sludge.

'Where the hell you takin' us? Feels like the whole county is slidin' into the river and takin' me with it!'

'There's nowhere else in Johnson City we can keep dry, boys. I'm tellin' you – this place is the best we're gonna get tonight.'

And he'd been right. Once they got a fire going it was the warmest and driest they'd been in days. Spoons grinned at his companions, holding his hands closer to the flames.

'Don't this beat all? Coot, you're a magician when it comes to fires.'

Luke had always been amazed by how Cooter was able to conjure a fire in such impossible conditions. No matter how wet, how dark, or how lacking in suitable material, he could get a fire started in less time than it took most men to open a can of beans. Cooter shrugged it off.

'Two things the good Lord give me when I was born . . .'

He rubbed his shiny bald head and winked.

'A headful of hair old Samson would envy, and a talent for fire.'

Spoons laughed.

'The Lord giveth and the Lord taketh away.'

Cooter got his name in his late twenties, when the last patch of hair on top of his head disappeared and he was left with a slick baldness that encouraged a constant bombardment of teasing from his traveling companions. Bald as a Coot was the name that stuck and for years he carried an old pair of hair clippers with him, habitually taking them out to shave the narrow strip of stubble that stretched around the back of his thick, bulldog neck. While he clipped, he told anyone within earshot about the luxurious mass of thick hair that had crowned his head before one fateful night of passion. When he had their attention, which he always managed, he continued with wide-eyed seriousness to tell the story of a night spent with a gypsy prostitute called Medusa. How he'd paid for his passion with his hair, because he didn't have enough money to pay her. How she'd screeched and cursed him and how he'd woken the next morning without a hair on his head except for the small patch at the base to remind him of what he'd lost.

Cooter liked to weave tidbits of fables and myths into his own past and he took particular delight in hearing his stories passed on by others as 'gospel truth'.

Spoons, his traveling companion for more than thirty years, was over six feet tall with a forward stoop. He was a musician and if he'd lived another life, been raised in another household, he might have played the piano, banging out tunes with the playful snappiness that defined his nature. But a piano was not the best instrument for the road. Instead he carried a pair of spoons in his back pocket, always ready to pull them out and play a rhythmic percussion to another man's mouth harp or the occasional banjo or guitar.

The spoons were warped and battered and tarnished, but he would never replace them. They'd come from his momma's house, and as he was fond of telling others when they tried to convince him to replace them with some shiny new ones, 'These boys are the only things my momma left me 'sides my good looks.'

Then he'd smile his radiant toothless grin and tap another tune on his thigh while the men around him hummed and whistled.

From the first day Luke joined Cooter and Spoons, he was accepted as one of a threesome. There was never any hint that the arrangement was temporary or that Luke hadn't always been a part of the team. It was as if they'd been expecting him all along and he was just running a little late. He settled in very quickly under their wise tutelage and they taught him the rules and showed him the shortcuts that had helped them to survive. The two men were on the weary side of sixty but they were the most energetic and good-natured vagabonds on the rails. They had never known any other life and, because they saw their living arrangements as a choice and not the consequence of bad choices, there was no sign of regret or despair. Wherever they stopped for the night or whichever train they hopped, the two characters quickly earned the admiration of others with their wildly imaginative stories and their worldly wisdom. Luke, quiet and shy, was accepted right along with them.

They protected him from bullies, always able to defuse a situation with their comic antics. Entertainment was rare on the lines and if a stranger tried to pick a fight with Spoons or

Cooter, or more commonly with Luke, the weaker target, the other hobos made it clear they would take their side in any argument. They needn't have worried. The two men were masters at disarming most anyone, even those hell-bent on spilling blood.

They were good teachers, both on the handling of human behavior and the basic skills of survival. They taught Luke to read the signs that other hobos carved into wooden trestles, on fences, and along the tracks; a secret code that ordinary people, bound to the restraints of what hobos referred to disdainfully as a 'settled life', passed by without noticing. The small carvings allowed others to benefit from the lessons learned by those who had already traveled that way. It told them which houses would give them food, or a bed in the barn. A dagger warned of dishonest men who would offer work, then threaten the law when time came to pay the wages. There were signs that warned of dangerous dogs or angry bulls and signs that told them there were people with home remedies if they were sick.

It was Cooter who gave Luke his nickname Feets and Spoons who worked out the little carved sign that Luke would later use as a signature of his work in the heading mills. He crisscrossed the country with them, sitting amongst a new circle of faces each night, scooping his own tin cup into the iron pot of bubbling stew, and listening as the men swapped tales of narrow escapes and daring exploits.

For four years he'd been an integral part of the threesome – a permanent member of a family that defended each other and watched each others' backs. He believed in them. Trusted them. So, on the train that night, when Spoons said to jump, Luke didn't ask questions. He just jumped blindly into the pounding rain and scrambled down the embankment towards the abandoned railroad bridge that ran parallel with the new line. Now, safe and dry, he settled around the fire, while Cooter told a story about how an acquaintance from his early days on the line got his name.

'I was nineteen, just a little older than you, Feets, when I hooked up with this old guy who always thought he knew better'n ever'body else. He hadn't been on the lines all that much longer than me, didn't even have a nickname yet, but 'cause he was older and all, he thought he knew better. Well, we was trying to get to Rome, Georgia, one night – people said the peaches were ready for pickin' and if you got there early enough you could get on one of the fruit trucks, end up with two, three days' work at least.'

Spoons threw some more wood on the fire and Luke lay back against the bridge embankment watching the smoke and ash curl upwards towards the rotting timber cross-ties. Another train rattled by on the next line and the bridge they were under shook in unison. On either side of them, the rain continued to pour and rivulets of slick muddy water raced its way to the river's edge, but the men didn't notice. They were dry and warm and they huddled back, ready to enjoy one of Cooter's stories.

'Well, sir, we'd been travelin' for a couple of hours since we'd changed trains. I didn't see the need for changin', but he always had to prove he was in the know. Said he knew just what to do and to leave it to him. Well, I got bored after a while and I fell asleep, just to block out his moanin' and com-plainin'. All of a sudden this old boy is half draggin' me, half kickin' me to the door and shoutin'. *We missed our spot, boy. Missed it! Gotta get off now or we'll never make it by morn-in'*. Well, I gotta tell you, I was half dead to the world and it was black as tar-in-summer-heat outside and I stood there lookin' out the door and I couldn't see a damn thing.'

He started chuckling to himself the way he always did when he told a story that tickled him. It was part of his charm that he got so carried away with his story that he sometimes couldn't finish it for laughing.

'*Tuck and roll, boy!* he yelled out to me. *Soon as you hit the ground. Tuck and roll.* 'Fore I knew what'd hit me, he'd grabbed me by the neck and shoved me out the door. Next thing – we were both fallin' . . . and fallin' . . . and fallin' . . . and not hitting anything remotely resemblin' dirt. I'm tellin' you, boys, I was all ready to tuck and roll, but there was nothin' there to roll on, and my ass was too damn scared to tuck. All I could hear was this old guy cussin' up a storm and the sound of water rushing towards us. When we finally hit the water, I came up madder than a rabbit in a straitjacket.'

The other two joined in with Cooter's laughter.

'Worse thing of all? We weren't anywheres near Rome, or even Georgia. When we changed trains, the stupid jackass put us on the wrong train . . . one that doubled back on us. After all that travelin' we ended up about two miles from where we started.'

By this time Cooter was wiping his eyes with the corner of his coat-tail.

'The boys who'd been with us started callin' him Cross-Tie, and that was the name that stuck, but I had my own name for him. I called him Tucker. *Tuck and roll, boy! Tuck and roll!*'

The laughter of the men filled the muffled space below the bridge as the rain pounded around them and the sound of another train and the shudder of the bridge above them added to the roar. Spoons walked to the side of their shelter and leaning on the upright support of the bridge, he peed into the wall of water.

'Hey, this thing is moving.'

Cooter laughed.

'Nothin's movin' but your eyeballs, son.'

Luke joined Spoons and put his hand up against the thick support.

'See? See there? You feel it?'

Cooter called to Luke.

'Don't get drawn in, boy. It's the white lightnin'. He'll be seein' elephants swimmin' upriver 'fore you know it.'

Luke felt a strong shudder where his hand touched the support and he turned back to Cooter in alarm. A deep, guttural moan seemed to erupt from the earth below him, and the sound of collapsing timber and iron spikes, wrenched from wood, filled the air as the bridge twisted and collapsed around them. Something hit him hard from behind, knocking the wind from his lungs and flinging him several feet away. He landed face first in the mud, and tried to rise up on his knees to catch his breath, but Spoons was lying across his legs where he'd tackled him and knocked him out of the way. He looked back at the wreckage and tugged on Spoons' shirt.

'Where's Cooter?'

Spoons was suddenly alert, holding his arm across his chest and scrambling back towards the rubble. He started digging with one arm.

It was Luke who saw him first – about two yards out in the shallow part of the river. Cooter had tried to run when he realized the bridge was collapsing but he'd run in the wrong direction. His head and chest were just above water. He was arched across a sleeper and pinned by a girder. Luke waded out to him. Spoons was splashing wildly behind him trying to get to his friend. Luke thought he was dead.

'Cooter?'

Cooter opened his eyes and smiled weakly.

'Lost my bearin's. Couldn't tell which way was up. Spoons?'

'I'm here, you old bastard. What you doin' way out here?'

Cooter tried to chuckle but bloody bubbles spewed from his lips.

'Just waitin' for a elephant to come swimmin' by.'

It took an hour to get him free and another hour to get him to a nearby barn. There wasn't a farmhouse in sight, and the barn hadn't stored anything but kudzu in at least ten years, but there was enough hay and old feedbags to make a bed for their friend, until they could get help. Spoons left to find a doctor and Luke promised not to leave their friend's side. Not long after Spoons left, Cooter asked Luke to help him sit up.

'I need to make my finals eye to eye.'

Luke helped him up and waited for him to get the strength to speak.

'You're a good boy, Feets. But don't you go lettin' nobody take my things when I go.'

He groaned and Luke propped him up higher to help with his breathing.

'You and Spoons can sell my shoes. Ain't gonna fit them boats you call feet no how.'

His attempt to chuckle made him croak in pain.

'You keep my clippers, though. You keep 'em so's you don't forget ol' Cooter.'

He died minutes later and Luke wrapped the clippers in the rag bundle and tucked them in the front bib of his overalls. He wrapped his arms around Cooter and held him until Spoons got back.

The doctor told them there was nothing he could've done, even if he'd been standing on the bank when the bridge collapsed.

'All his insides were crushed. Looks like he took the bulk of the weight. It's a miracle he lived as long as he did, especially movin' him all this way.'

But Spoons was not willing to relinquish his guilt. He continued to moan softly, holding his friend's lifeless hand.

'Sorry, Coot. I hurried fast as I could . . .'

His grief was raw and painful to watch. But the doctor noticed that Spoons also held his arm tightly against his chest and that his breathing came in short raspy wheezes.

'Looks like you've broken some ribs. You may have pierced something. Why don't you let me have a look.'

But Spoons refused and a few days later when he and Luke were on the road again, it was obvious things weren't right. Luke regretted that he hadn't insisted the doctor take a look at his friend. He wasn't the insisting type, but he couldn't help feeling that since he'd suddenly been put into the position of strongest, he should have taken the lead. Cooter would have insisted. And so would Spoons if it had been Luke who'd been injured.

At first Luke thought his friend's prolonged silence was due to simple grief, but after a while he realized that Spoons found it difficult to draw enough breath to speak more than a word or two. When he did say something his face was pinched with pain. He stopped eating and over the next few weeks, the wheezing and rattling got worse and he was too weak to walk much less catch a train. Luke stayed with him, enduring day after day of silence and trying his best to get his friend to eat. He lay awake at night listening to the shallow half-breaths, wishing Spoons would suddenly sit up and tell another story or say, *Hell, I've had enough of this . . . let's go hop us a train.*

Finally, one night, he did just that. He sat up slowly and with great effort and said he was tired. With the few words he could manage, he begged Luke to help him make one more hop. In the middle of the night Luke lifted Spoons' frail, bony frame into a stationary boxcar and cradled him until daybreak, with no idea as to the train's destination. In the darkness, Luke felt a feeble nudge and he bent down so that he could hear Spoons' faltering whisper.

'Don't this beat all?'

An hour before dawn, Spoons took one last breath and died and Luke added his traveling spoons to the bag with Cooter's hair clippers. Luke was alone again and he had no idea where the train was headed.

Canaan

She woke to the smell of turkey drippings and the sound of her grandmother banging around in the kitchen. When she came out an hour later, Lou Venie looked surprised to see Canaan dressed.

'Thought you might sleep in today. Must've been crazy at work . . . all those last-minute shoppers.'

She looked down at the Fashion Barn bag Canaan was carrying and noticed the purse on her shoulder.

'If you're lookin' for somethin' to do, I could use some help lifting the turkey. I like to get ever' last scraping out of the bottom. Gives the dressing a special kick.'

'I'm not staying for lunch, Lou Venie.'

'What do you mean? I—'

'I'm taking Luke up to Betty Ann's.'

'Not today.'

'Especially today. I'm treating him to a real family Thanksgiving dinner. Not a day eating alone in the Little House with a plate of leftovers that's gone cold.'

'Please, Canaan. Can't we just put things aside for today?'

'I've been puttin' things aside for too long.'

'But what'll I do with all this?'

'Give it to the dog.'

She slammed the door on her way out, even though she knew she didn't have to. She had made her point.

Luke was already on his third cup of chicory coffee by the time she knocked on his door. He was bent over his table, surrounded by stacks of books – carefully and methodically cataloguing each one in an old ledger.

'You still workin' on this?'

He didn't look up, just kept writing.

'Important to remember where they come from.'

She rummaged in a small cardboard box that was on his bed. He looked up for a moment and smiled proudly.

'Only give a quarter for all of them. It was . . . a yard sale over on Oak Avenue. Lady said I could have the whole box for a quarter if I'd just go and not touch her Irish lace tablecloths.'

He chuckled and Canaan picked up a copy of *Treasure Island*.

'Mr Forrest got me that one.'

'Zeke Forrest?'

He nodded.

'Good man. Likes to talk about books.'

He returned to scribbling and she sat down next to him.

'I've got a surprise for you.'

He grunted but kept working.

'I'm taking you up to Betty Ann's for a Thanksgiving dinner. Just the two of us.'

He stopped and looked up at her.

'Lou Venie always makes me a nice dinner.'

'She's . . . uh, I've decided that I'd rather spend the day with you.'

He frowned.

'Lou Venie goin' with us?'

'No. She's . . . I thought this time it ought to be just you and me. What do you think? I bought you something special for today too.'

She took out a shirt she'd bought at Fashion Barn.

'It's a hundred percent wool. You'll have to wear a T-shirt underneath it. But it's a nice color, don't you think?'

He nodded and let her help him put it on. Then she took out a pair of second-hand wing tips.

'Don't like shoes.'

'Well, you've got to wear something on your feet. It's too cold and they won't let you in the restaurant barefoot.'

She led him to the side of the bed and tried several times to get the shoes on him.

'Stop squeezing up your toes, Luke.'

'Dern things don't fit right.'

'Well, they were the biggest size I could find.'

'Why can't I wear my work boots?'

Nine months out of the year, Luke went barefoot, rain or shine. And in the winter months it had to be below freezing before he'd succumb to wearing an old pair of work boots that he'd found flung over a cattle fence. They had more holes in the soles and toes than a pair of sandals, caked in mud and no laces, but it was the closest thing to shoes she'd ever seen him in. She stood up, putting her hands on her hips in an exasperated way.

'You can't get all gussied up and not have decent shoes.'

She tried to hurry him along. She half expected Lou Venie to come charging down to the Little House. But when they left, walking arm in arm, she noticed that the curtains had been drawn.

It was a thirty-minute walk to Betty Ann's Diner and most of it was done in silence. Canaan tried to start conversations but she was aware that she sounded too cheerful, too forced. The square was deserted, the only flutter of movement coming from inside Betty Ann's. The windows were steamed over with the residue of the early morning's cooking and baking and the dark shapes of customers pulsated behind the frosted glass. Inside, the tables had been pushed together and draped with paper tablecloths. Small wax pilgrims stood amidst centerpieces of autumn leaves and dried ears of Indian corn. The customers were mostly single men, bachelors by destiny or by design, creating their own makeshift family gatherings around the tables. They glanced up as Canaan and Luke entered, but returned to feasting.

'Two platters. Phillips.'

While Betty Ann sculpted two pyramids of food on the oval plates, Canaan turned to Luke who was working one shoe against the counter trying to get a better fit.

'Where do you want to sit?'

He pointed towards the window.

'On the square.'

'No, I mean in here.'

'Don't want to eat in here. Want to eat at my place. On my bench.'

'Luke, we can't eat out there, it's too cold.'

Betty Ann stopped serving and smiled at Canaan.

'I can put these in take-out cartons if you want.'

'No, that's OK.'

She took Luke's hand.

'Wouldn't you rather sit in here where it's warm?'

He shook his head again, more firmly.

'Out there. That's where I always sit.'

Canaan sighed and turned to Betty Ann.

'Better make that two to go.'

They sat on the bench nearest the Civil War memorial cannon. Luke settled down quickly and grinned at Canaan like a young boy showing off his tree house.

'See? Best view of the square and I can watch the trains when they come through.'

Canaan handed Luke one of the Styrofoam cartons. Her fingers had not had enough time in the diner to warm up from the long walk. They felt numb and unmanageable. She fumbled with the plastic-wrapped forks and spoons and pulled her coat tighter around her. Luke took the fork from her and eagerly dug in. She took a few bites in silence as Luke made satisfied hums and murmurs while he chewed. This wasn't quite the family dinner she had planned. As she flipped her collar up with one hand, balancing her food on her knees, the doors of the Lander Methodist church suddenly opened and people poured out from the Thanksgiving Day prayer service. They filed out, shaking hands with the minister but hurrying past each other as they made their way to their cars parked around the square. The women of the congregation tossed their best smiles of goodwill from side to side as they scurried down the front steps, but their minds were obviously at home with the basting turkey and the cranberry sauce they'd forgotten to get down from the top shelf of the pantry. Canaan's gaze followed a group of churchgoers as they crossed the square to Betty Ann's. They were husbands mostly, a few teenage sons, sent to pick up an extra pecan pie or a loaf of pumpkin bread to bulk up the family dinner. As Canaan watched, Zeke came out of Betty Ann's, holding the door open for them with one hand and holding his own plastic carton in the other. He headed towards his van and helped Stonewall out of the back, before ambling over to them, the dog reluctantly following him. Canaan tried to swallow the mouthful of sweet potatoes that seemed to be swelling in her mouth. He smiled down at them.

'Well, this is what I call a traditional Thanksgiving meal. I doubt the Pilgrims ate off Styrofoam, though. Mind if we join you?'

The uncomfortable lump of sweet potato had lodged in her throat but she smiled and motioned for him to sit. Stonewall fell into an exhausted heap nearby. Zeke opened the carton and the steam rose into the crisp November air. He took a bite then smiled with the pleasure of a contented man.

'Yep, this is definitely better than sittin' by the space heater with nothin' but football to watch on the tube.'

'Don't you have dinner with your family?'

He shook his head and took another bite.

'Only family I ever had belonged to Catherine. They were good enough to adopt me, or maybe I should say tolerate me, on these occasions. But the invitations dried up after their daughter had the good sense to leave me.'

Canaan blushed.

'I'm sorry, I didn't mean to pry.'

'Oh, it's not a problem. I don't regret havin' a fling at marriage and all that. But when it came down to it I wasn't cut out to own a weed-eater and go to cookouts with the neighbors. Cathy was a career woman, a good one too and I knew that when I married her so I can't complain. When she was offered a big promotion in Chicago, we decided she should take it and I should stay here.'

The three of them ate in silence. Above the tart smell of cranberry sauce melting in hot gravy, she could smell Ivory soap. It was the smell she remembered when she was in high school, standing close to Zeke while he leaned over the day's proofs, his neck exposed and inches away. A train whistle sounded and they all looked towards the tracks that lay across the road behind the church, waiting for the train to rumble by.

Luke nodded in recognition.

'The 232 to Chattanooga. Must be one o'clock.'

Zeke smiled.

'You know your trains, don't you, Luke?'

'Spent a lot of time on the 232.'

'You worked for the railroad?'

'Nope. Rode the rails. Just after the first big war. Lookin' for work.'

Zeke moved eagerly towards Luke squeezing Canaan between them, his leg pressed tightly against hers. A part of her was thrilled with the closeness, but disappointed that it was unintentional.

'Well, well. All these years I've known you, Luke, and I never knew you were a hobo. Always thought I'd like riding the rails myself. Where'd you go?'

Luke's eyes shone excitedly over his cup of coffee as he took a sip.

'Up as far as Philadelphia once. As far west as Baton Rouge, but mostly I stayed 'round Alabama and Tennessee – Chattanooga mainly. Spent almost a year in Georgia. Work wasn't too good over there, but I liked the boardin' house I lived in. Landlady was a good cook. Wore men's clothes and smoked a pipe, but she was a lady all right. All the men liked her.'

Zeke's neck was within nibbling range and Canaan felt an overwhelming urge to get away. She shifted her weight to signal her discomfort. Zeke smiled briefly at her, moved down a few inches then turned his attention eagerly back to Luke's story.

'Her name was Miss Nedra and she didn't take no disrespect, no-sir. She could throw a grown man out the front door with one arm if he was makin' trouble. But she was a good woman. Looked out for all of us.'

Canaan noticed that the bacon fat in Zeke's green beans was congealing as he listened. She looked down and was embarrassed to see that Luke had slipped off his shoes and his cracked, road-worn toes were protruding through the gaping holes of his white socks.

'Luke, for crying out loud, get your shoes back on. Your toes are gonna drop off with frostbite.'

She picked up one of his shoes and tried to replace it, but Luke wiggled his foot out of the way.

'Don't like wearin' shoes. On the line if you was barefoot, people left you alone.'

'Well, you're not on the line now. Come on. Straighten out your foot so I can put this back on you.'

She felt a soft tap on her arm. Zeke gave a gentle,

reproachful smile and she slinked back to her seat, her face flushed like a scolded child. He leaned closer to Luke.

'So you never wore shoes at all?'

'Nope. Couldn't find none to fit me anyways. They called me Feets. Feets Stewart. Ever'body had nicknames. Whistler, Stinky Stein, Cross-Tie . . .'

He hesitated.

'. . . Cooter and Spoons.'

He took another sip of coffee.

'I seen a man stabbed for his shoes once. And another beat to a pulp for a pair of boots. 'Most every man had a buddy to watch his back, 'cause when a man died on the line, if he didn't have nobody to watch out for him, all the others picked him apart like beetles on a dungheap. Shoes were the first things to go. Didn't even matter if they didn't fit. They knew they could sell 'em on. Pay for a couple months' tobacco or a jug or two of moonshine.'

Canaan studied the changes in Luke's face. Before her eyes, he'd turned into a stranger, full of unfamiliar stories about a life, a man she'd never known. Suddenly she felt left out. Zeke urged him on.

'What sort of work did you do, Luke?'

'Heading mills. Built the lids that fit in the top of barrels, headers they called 'em. They still got one of my headers on one of the barrels in Hincey's Hardware. Think so, anyway. Might have thrown it out by now. I used to check on it when I was able.'

'How'd you know it was yours?'

'Always carved a little foot on one end. Like this.'

He took his plastic knife and carved a stick drawing of a foot in the lid of his Styrofoam carton. Zeke admired it.

'Well, now that I know your signature, I'll keep my eye out for your handiwork.'

Luke grinned with pleasure and Canaan forced her way from between them.

'Time to head back, Luke.'

She grabbed the empty carton he'd been carving and threw it in a nearby garbage can.

'Tell Mr Forrest goodbye. We gotta get going.'

Zeke stood up and pulled Stonewall to his feet.

'Could we walk back with you two?'

'Your van . . .'

He shrugged.

'What else have I got to do today? I'd enjoy the walk, Stonewall could certainly use the exercise and I'd certainly enjoy the company.'

'I don't think so. This was supposed to be just for me and Luke today.'

'Oh, sure. I'm sorry. I just thought . . .'

He backed away before turning to go.

'Look, I'm really sorry for buttin' in.'

She wanted to change her mind, tell him that of course he could walk back with them, but instead she watched him cross the square.

Luke said nothing as they started home. She tried several times to start conversations, but he answered with one syllable and kept walking. When they arrived at the Little House they could see Lou Venie sitting on her front porch. She stood up to go inside and Canaan noticed how stooped she looked. And small.

Canaan turned to Luke.

'How about fixin' me some of your famous coffee and havin' one of our good, long talks?'

Luke shook his head.

'Thought I'd take a nap.'

She turned to go, but he put his hand gently on her shoulder.

'Candy-Cane – it's 'bout time you decided who you're mad at.'

Luke

Over the next year, Luke traveled a large portion of the Eastern United States, making a few transient friendships along the way, but most of the time keeping to himself. He slept rough as he'd always done, in fields and old boxcars. Occasionally in the winter months, some farmers took pity and gave him a corner in their barn in exchange for odd jobs. Then, just after his nineteenth birthday, he followed rumors of steady work at a heading mill in Georgia and stumbled upon Miss Nedra's boarding house. For the first time in his young life he learned what it felt like to have a place to come home to every night and the satisfaction of sleeping in a real bed.

Miss Nedra's coarse and eccentric habits prevented her from attracting respectable boarders, but her rooms were always fully booked by skittish men who didn't like rules that were too confining or landladies who were hell-bent on taming their wanderlust. They never questioned Miss Nedra's insistence of payment up front and in return she never questioned them or grew worried if they disappeared in the middle of the night.

The house was on a large corner lot, a rambling two-story place with peeling paint and broken boards on the front porch. A splintered swing trailed along the floor by a single mangled chain, the result of a drunken fight over a woman who had not feigned interest in either of the suitors anyway. In spite of the potential hazard in housing such a large collection of festering manhood, there had rarely been a problem that Miss Nedra couldn't handle.

She'd been surrounded by men since she was thirteen when her mother died leaving her to take care of her father and five older brothers. She cooked for them, kept the house repaired and running smoothly, scrubbed their muddy work clothes, and even turned her hand to plowing, picking, and fence-mending during the busy times.

In her younger days Miss Nedra was considered a beauty of sorts, more handsome than pretty, with a strong jaw line and steely-gray eyes, but a hard life in the wind and sun, and a few farm accidents that loosened her teeth and scarred her arms, left her battered and old before she hit her mid-twenties. It didn't help that she only wore men's work pants and flannel shirts, mostly hand-me-downs from her brothers, or that she kept her hair short. Women in the town seemed to think they'd be contaminated by her manliness and avoided her whenever possible. In spite of the questions over her sexuality, there were still rumors of the sexual favors she offered her odd, socially-misfit boarders and of orgies she organized on the weekends. She knew about the whispers, understood the stares, but Miss Nedra didn't bother much with what other people thought. She knew that as long as the brawls didn't flow into the nicely manicured lawns of her neighbors, and she paid her bills at the dry-goods store, they left her alone.

Luke first showed up on her front porch late one evening after the supper dishes had been washed and put away and Miss Nedra was having her evening smoke. Her hair was spiky and sharp, and the way she sat with the pipe clenched between gritted teeth made her seem fierce and angry, but there was something in her eyes that told Luke he would be safe with her.

'Heard you got a place for people like me.'

She stared him down.

'I got places for people who work. You got work?'

He nodded.

'Foreman over the heading mill said I could start tomorrow.'

'I get paid every week. In advance. You got enough to do that?'

He nodded and she smiled.

'Well then, we'd better drag out some leftovers. Get you fed up 'fore the big day.'

He followed her into the house and she took him up to his room. It was small and sparse, but the iron bed was painted bright blue and there were clean sheets and a fresh towel by the basin. She handed him the key.

'Breakfast at six. Supper at five. I can make you ham biscuits to take with you to the mill, but it'll cost you extra. I'll go whip you up some supper. Won't be fancy, but it'll be hot. Come on down when you've settled into your room.'

He sat on the bed and took a look around. It was the first room that someone had called 'his'. He unfolded the rag bundle he always carried under his arm and laid out his worldly treasures on the dresser: a tin cup for scooping hobo stew, the *Huck Finn* book that Lissie had given him many years before, Cooter's clippers, and a battered pair of spoons. He laid them out with great pride, then sat for a short while admiring them.

When he came down later, Miss Nedra was just heaping a pile of sweet potatoes onto his plate next to turnip greens and a chunk of smoked ham. She handed it to him and nodded towards the screen door.

'Already got the table set for breakfast. Go on out on the porch to eat. I'll keep you company.'

He sat on the steps and she watched him eat while she puffed on her pipe. It was the best food he'd tasted since he'd eaten with Squeaky's momma and he took his time with each bite. When he was through Miss Nedra offered him a puff of her pipe, but he declined. She leaned back in the rocking chair and sighed.

'Settles me down in the evenin's. Belonged to my late husband. Never quite fit his face, I said, but he thought it made him look distinguished. Never saw it myself. Some faces are just built for a pipe and his weren't.'

It was the start of a daily ritual for Luke. He felt vulnerable eating at the table each night with the men, so he waited until they'd had their fill and Miss Nedra made a special plate for him to eat on the back porch while she enjoyed her 'settlin' down' smoke.

The first morning he came down early and had his coffee and a ham biscuit on the same porch. Miss Nedra poured him another cup of coffee and looked down at his feet. She frowned.

'Lloyd Bundrum ain't gonna let you near the machinery if you show up without shoes. He tell you to wear shoes?'

Luke nodded.

'You got any?'

He lowered his eyes.

'Stay right here. I got some I can loan you.'

He sipped his coffee, dreading the scene. He knew whatever shoes she brought wouldn't come near to fitting him. But when she came back he was surprised to find that they slipped on.

'They were my daddy's old work boots. He bought a new pair just 'fore I left home, so I brought these with me. Kept 'em on my bureau to remind me where I come from and where I gotta go back to if I don't make this place work for me.'

The boots were stretched beyond recognition. There were

no laces and the leather bulged over the sides of soles, a molded imprint of her father's pudgy, calloused feet.

'They ain't purty, but they'll pass muster with Lloyd, I reckon.'

She gave him a pair of old shoestrings but he only used them to tie the boots together. As soon as his shift at the mill ended each day, he kicked the shoes off and set out for the boarding house with the old boots draped across his shoulder.

He hadn't planned to stay very long, but there was something comforting about this new, more settled life. He missed Spoons and Cooter and missed the life he'd led with them, but without them, life on the line had been a lonely place. The men at the heading mill and the men who came and went at Miss Nedra's were never going to replace his old friends, but his landlady's simple, no-fuss companionship gave him a sense of belonging and a purpose. He became an expert at repairs and painting and cleaning gutters. He picked cooking apples from the three bent and gnarled trees out back for Miss Nedra's famous Apple Crunch Cobbler and he kept her company when she made jar after jar of hot apple butter. But the times he enjoyed most were first thing in the morning and last thing at night. When the other men were still in bed and the breakfast biscuits were baking in the oven, he and Miss Nedra sat on the porch with cups of coffee and watched the sky turn pink or amber. There were times when they didn't say a word to each other and that was fine with Luke. It was enough to know they were sharing something special. Then in the evening, when the supper dishes were put away, Miss Nedra took out her pipe and they'd take up the same positions – Miss Nedra in the rocker, Luke on the steps – and they'd listen to the crickets and breathe in the night sky. It was times like that made Luke believe he'd finally found home.

Canaan

As Andy Williams crooned 'Silent Night' on the car radio, Canaan fought to breathe.

'Lord, Lou Venie. What'd you do, bathe in that crap?'

Canaan pointed the fresh-air vent towards her face as her grandmother's perfume gobbled up every ounce of air in the car.

'Your aunt Peggy gave it to me.'

She offered it as a logical explanation and Canaan accepted it. Peggy always gave Lou Venie her present early, a few days before the big party. The year before it had been a sequined sweater, a flashy expensive garment with a silvery snowman chasing a shiny black top hat across her chest. Lou Venie only wore it once, to the party, but it had served Peggy's purpose, allowing her to show off her generosity towards her elderly mother in the company of her impressive friends. This year it had been a bottle of overpriced, overpowering perfume in a collector's bottle and they both knew Peggy expected her to show up reeking of the stuff.

In the weeks following Thanksgiving there had been a temporary and silent truce with Lou Venie but Canaan had spent most of the time at work or in her room. Agreeing to go to Peggy's annual Christmas Eve dinner party was Canaan's first gesture of reconciliation.

The houses on Peggy's street were decked out like whores at Mardi Gras, each one trying to outdo the other with flashing lights and gaudy cheer. Mert met them at the door with his usual elfish good humor and Canaan handed him a bottle of expensive French wine. The day before, she'd driven across the state line to a package store in Rome, Georgia, choosing one that had been a favorite luxury in New York. She had stayed away from booze since coming home – not a difficult thing to do in the dry counties that surrounded Lander – but she had decided a simple gesture of goodwill was better than a box of talcum powder and a new fishing lure. There was also a selfish motive. She couldn't stomach an evening of Peggy's home-made eggnog swamped with artificial rum flavoring. Mert peeked inside the wrapping paper.

'Is this wine?'

He glanced uneasily over his shoulder.

'I don't know, Canaan. I don't think Peggy would like you bringin' wine in the house. She's got a lot of her church friends here, you know. Maybe you oughta just leave it out here. Keep it for yourself.'

He took their coats, hiding the bottle behind a basket under the parson's bench and ushered them into the living room where guests were sipping eggnog from football-shaped punch cups. A small group swarmed around the tree admiring its decorations. It was a six-foot evergreen gasping for breath under a blanket of fake snow. A herd of red felt elephants dangled from its branches along with collector's ornaments commemorating bowl games from the past twenty years.

'Did you see the one Mert gave me this year? The little football?'

Peggy had appeared with a tray of sausage balls, wearing a battery-operated apron alight with a giant poinsettia. She put the tray down on the table and squeezed between the admirers to point out the ornament.

'If you tilt it up it plays *We wish you a Merry Christmas*. Isn't that cute?'

She turned and caught sight of Canaan and Lou Venie and squealed with exaggerated delight.

'Momma! You look beautiful. And don't you smell wonderful.'

She smiled modestly to her audience and gave a self-deprecating shrug.

'I bought Momma a bottle of Armand Villenci for Christmas.'

There was a murmur of approval and she turned to Canaan.

'Well, don't you look mysterious, missy miss? You goin' for the lady-in-black look this year?'

Canaan nodded and waited with growing agitation for Peggy's attention to flit onto someone else, but her aunt's eyes settled on Canaan's feet.

'Shame we didn't have a white Christmas this year. Those boots would've come in real handy.'

Canaan's winter boots had fought their way through plenty of New York blizzards over the years, but they were the only shoes, other than sandals or tennis shoes, she'd had to wear. To Canaan's relief Peggy spun to face the other guests.

'There's hot sausage balls on the table, now, everybody. Don't let 'em get cold!'

In an instant she had disappeared through the swinging door that led to the kitchen. While the others continued debating the weakness of the new line coach at the University of Alabama and the merits of flying to Korea to do their Christmas shopping, Canaan and Lou Venie stood alone in the corner by Mert's expensive music system.

'You want eggnog?'

Lou Venie shook her head.

'I told you not to bring that wine. Peggy's funny about that sort of thing.'

Canaan picked up a carrot stick and swirled it around a bowl of ranch dip.

'I didn't think it would be a problem. Mert drank a whole case of beer when he came over to help us trim the mimosa trees.'

'That was different, and anyway I'm not sure Peggy knew about that. You gotta stop this always trying to prove a point. Peggy's happy with her life and her friends. You got no business puttin' her in awkward positions.'

'Like bringing her simple-minded uncle to her glorious party?'

She had called Peggy a few days before with the suggestion. Her aunt had collapsed into what Lou Venie called one of her 'screaming mimi' fits and it had taken Mert and Lou Venie most of the afternoon to calm her down again. Lou Venie took Canaan's arm and turned her away from the other guests.

'What are you trying to prove? That Luke ain't wanted? You think that's it? Before you start judging Peggy . . . and me . . . you better think about who you're doin' this for and why.'

'Luke has a right—'

'Do you think Luke would be happy here? Look around, Canaan. Do you?'

'He deserves to have a choice at least.'

'You may not like this, Canaan, or believe it, but this is his choice.'

Canaan pulled away.

'I'm going to get a coke.'

Lou Venie tried to call after her without the others hearing.

'Don't go agitating your aunt Peggy. Steer clear, you hear me?'

In the kitchen, Peggy was busy rinsing pasta for the beef stroganoff. She directed Canaan to the refrigerator for soft drinks.

'You'll have to move the Mississippi Mud out of the way, they're in the back. And Canaan, please don't drink out of the can. There's glasses on the middle shelf over there.'

Canaan opened the can and took a sip, then catching Peggy's disapproving eye, she obediently took a glass from the cupboard. Peggy piled the pasta onto a serving dish.

'You're lookin' a little plump lately, Canaan. I hope you haven't decided to let yourself go now that you're divorced.'

'Shit!'

The soft drink had fizzed over the side of the glass. Canaan reached for paper towels to wipe it up.

'I'm not divorced yet, Peggy.'

'Well, you know what I mean. You should be takin' a lot more care with the way you look. Decent men aren't easy to come by these days, 'specially at your age.'

'Maybe I'm not looking for decent men.'

Peggy laid a blanket of foil over the pasta, pinching it around the edges to seal in the steam.

'Obviously not, from what I hear. From what I hear, you're throwing yourself at men all over town. Spendin' the night with them and not even tryin' to hide the fact.'

She turned suddenly and faced Canaan.

'Is there somethin' you should be tellin' us?'

'Like what, Peggy?'

'Well, judging from your loose ways since you got back and from the loose clothes you've been wearin' lately, my guess is that you're pregnant. I tried to talk to Momma but she's stubborn as always. I can never get a straight answer out of her.'

Canaan smiled sweetly.

'Maybe she doesn't tell you things if they're none of your God-damn business.'

Peggy held up the pasta servers as if she intended to use the claws to torture the information out of her niece.

'I am family. It is my business. And I should know if there's somethin' goin' on that affects me.'

Canaan laughed out loud.

'Affects you?'

'I have worked very hard in this town to carve out a life I can be proud of. I didn't go runnin' off to New York tryin' to prove I was better than everybody else and I didn't take the coward's way out like your momma did.'

Canaan gulped the last of her drink and slammed it down on the counter. Peggy grabbed her arm before she could storm out.

'I've had a lot to overcome but I've got a good life now and I will not have you destroying it all by bringin' more shame on our family, you hear me?'

Canaan set her jaw.

'I've had about as much family togetherness as I can stomach. Tell Mert he'll have to take Lou Venie home.'

She took the bottle of wine with her when she left, then patrolled the streets of Lander wondering where the hell she could find a corkscrew on Christmas Eve. The nagging goody-two-shoes in the back of her head kept reminding her that she was pregnant but all she could think about at that moment was getting drunk. She ended up in the old abandoned gas station across the road from Zeke's apartment. Twice she got out of the car to knock on his door. The first time she'd decided to ask for a corkscrew. The second time she'd become so saturated in her misery that she'd passed the point of worrying about whether she had a plausible excuse. She watched as, one by one, porch lights along the street were switched off and Canaan imagined children trying desperately to go to sleep, hoping they'd been good enough to get that commando station or Space Stacy Mars-buggy. By eleven she decided it was time to go home. She was searching for her keys when

Zeke opened his front door to take Stonewall for a walk. She
sank into the seat out of sight. *Please God, don't let him look
over here.* She knew he'd recognize her car and if she had
trouble coming up with excuses before, there was without a
doubt nothing of value she could come up with now. The dog
followed him down the steps, slowly and one at a time. Zeke
waited patiently for him at the bottom before slipping the
collar and leash around his neck. To Canaan's relief they
turned the opposite way down the street and as soon as
they'd disappeared around the corner she drove off.

Luke

For more than twenty years there had been a whorehouse on the outskirts of town, owned and controlled by an ageing madam called Aunt Ivy who had gradually sunk into a bleary-eyed haze of moonshine and opium. Ever the shrewd businesswoman, Miss Nedra arranged a deal whereby she picked up the girls every Saturday evening and returned them to Ivy the next morning. Having lost the iron-fisted command of her youth, which had made her rich and dangerous to mess with, Aunt Ivy happily agreed to split half the takings with Miss Nedra, an arrangement that relieved her of the responsibilities she had begun to find tiresome and which allowed her an evening of solitary stupor.

Most of Miss Nedra's boarders worked on Saturdays and when they came home from the mill, hot and covered in sawdust, there were lavender-scented bubble baths waiting for them in preparation for the night's activities. The first few months Luke shied away from the raucous event, watching in fascination from the upper landing or a quiet corner as the girls seduced their way around the room.

One Saturday Miss Nedra called him down and he shyly squeezed past a couple of girls on the stairs who giggled and ran their hands down his arms, which were rigid with fear.

The brunette wrapped her arms around his torso and squealed.

'Ewww, Miss Nedra. I want this one if his cock is as hard as these arms.'

Luke stopped on the stairs, the look of terror shining brightly in his eyes. The other girl sank down on the steps.

'Can we take him upstairs, Miss Nedra? Might take both of us for this one.'

She ran her hand up his inner thigh then cupped his crotch and gave him a playful squeeze.

'Would you like that, darlin'? Would you like for Maggie to show you what to do with that thing?'

Luke looked desperately at Miss Nedra who was puffing patiently on her pipe near the piano.

'Leave that boy alone. I got other plans for him. Get on down here, Luke, that's a good boy.'

He pulled away from their grasp and stumbled down the remaining stairs, picking at his clothes as if they were covered in chiggers. He didn't know exactly what the girls had in mind, but he had enough of an idea to scare him half to death. He'd heard the stories around the campfires, and since he'd been at Miss Nedra's he'd seen plenty through half-closed doors or sometimes over the back porch railing. He knew enough to know that he preferred taking care of some chore for Miss Nedra if it kept him away from clutching, daring hands and the loud hoots and laughter of the other men.

Miss Nedra put a protective arm around him.

'Got something I need you to do.'

He nodded enthusiastically.

She led him towards the back kitchen and he followed gladly to the relative quiet of Miss Nedra's personal sanctuary. Once the supper dishes were done and the kitchen was cleared, it was off-limits to everyone else in the house. Her bedroom was just off the kitchen, connected by a small hallway lined with shelves that served as a pantry. It had once been the meat store, with thick stone walls and a hard-packed dirt floor. Some of the meat hooks were still there and she used them to hang the few clothes she still owned. The dirt floor was scattered with a few rag rugs she made from her old dresses and the single window was covered by an old wooden shutter. It was a sparse room – no knick-knacks, no frills, no mirrors. But the one beautiful thing was the ornate brass bed in the corner. It had been the best one in the house and she had moved it single-handedly downstairs. The boarders could make do with iron cot beds, but Miss Nedra had made up her mind that this would be her one luxury – a nice bed in a quiet, out-of-the-way room that was just hers.

Luke followed his landlady across the dark kitchen and down the hallway. He hesitated when she opened her bedroom door and took a few steps back towards the kitchen. No one had ever been in Miss Nedra's room before. She came back down the hall and took him by the arm.

'You're nineteen now, Luke. Time to find out for yourself what all this is about.'

He pulled away, but her strong arms pulled him back down the hall. She pushed him inside the room and he stood, rigid and anxious, with his eyes shut tight. He could hear her chuckle.

'Open your eyes, boy. Ain't gonna hurt you.'

Reluctantly he opened his eyes and looked at her. She nodded towards the bed.

'This here's Lilly. She's one of Aunt Ivy's new girls.'

He turned to see a small petite girl with a mass of dark curls that hung almost to her waist. Lilly sat on the edge of Miss Nedra's bed in a white linen nightdress that was tied demurely at the neck with a satin ribbon. The lamplight was low but it was enough to illuminate a sweet, but slightly exotic face. Her feet were bare and she played with the strands of the rag rug with her toes.

'Hey there, Luke. You wanna come sit by me?'

She patted the spot beside her but he shook his head. Miss Nedra shoved him forward.

'Get on over there. I paid good money for this.'

He stumbled and caught himself on the edge of the bed, sitting bolt upright two feet away from Lilly. He looked up at Miss Nedra with horror but she smiled encouragingly.

'Figured you were due a birthday present. Ain't often Ivy gets a pretty young thing in her stable and I'm givin' her to you before them other lugs get their dirty hands on her.'

Lilly moved closer to him, new to the game but experienced enough to know that she was the leader and that if she made any sudden moves he'd be out the door. Miss Nedra turned to go.

'You two take your time. But I want my bed back 'fore midnight.'

Lilly moved close enough for her leg to touch his and he shifted further along the bed, but she followed. Very gently, whispering softly in his ear the whole time, she started by lifting the clasp of his overalls and letting the bib fall to his lap, then unfastened the side buttons. He tried to protest when she knelt at his feet and slowly pulled down first one leg then the other, but she put her finger to her lips to shush him and he did as he was told. His hands were clenched and knotted around two great wads of bedspread as she kicked the overalls across the floor and took a step back.

'I want you to look at me, Luke. Can you look at me, Sugar?'

He continued to stare at the floor.

'Luke?'

Painfully he raised his eyes.

'That's a good boy.'

She pulled the satin bow at the neck of her nightdress and shimmied her shoulders through the opening until it dropped to the floor. She was just over five feet tall with a small waist and well-rounded hips and thighs. Her skin was a light olive color and he could smell the musky perfume she had dabbed on her shoulders and between her breasts. He tried to look away but seemed transfixed with fear and emotion, and physical stirrings he couldn't control. She tiptoed over to him as if he was a baby fawn about to bolt and whispered in his ear.

'You just be still now and let Lilly show you.'

She reached down between his legs, closing her hands around the bulge in his long johns and he reacted with a jolt, as if he'd been shot through with an electric current. She smoothed his hair to calm him down and made soothing noises while she untied the drawstring waistband and gently worked her way down to massage his soaring erection. She made soft appreciative noises before laying him back on the bed and straddling him.

The impact came fast and furious and was so powerful, he yelled out in fear because he thought it must surely mean he was close to dying. When his breathing returned to a more natural rhythm, she rolled over onto the bed and draped herself over him, but he scooted frantically to the side of the bed and grabbed his overalls. He could hear the other men still dancing and whooping with deep, drunken laughter in the sitting room, but all he could think about was getting back to his room. He clutched his overalls to his chest, making his way to the door to make his escape. Lilly was lying naked on the bed watching him. She turned on her side and smiled.

'You not hurryin' off to another woman already, are you?'

He shook his head firmly, staring at the floor, not able to look at her nudity. Without thinking he stumbled out the door, clutching his clothes in his arms and hurrying through the dark kitchen. He had one leg in his overalls and was trying his best to get the other one in when he came through the door into the light. An enormous wave of laughter and hollering rose up and nearly knocked him over.

'There he is!'

'Lookie here, fellas . . . the boy's finally had his first pussy!'

'Sure do look flushed, boy!'

'She tear the thing off? You look scared half to death!'

The taunts followed him up the stairs as he stumbled and fell, trying to get dressed along the way. He locked himself into his room and crawled under the covers, cupping his head with his pillow to block out the coarse jokes and laughter that continued on the other side of the door.

Every Saturday night after that, Luke left the house early and read in a secluded corner of the small town library until it closed. When it was near to closing time, he squeezed into a storage cupboard and waited until he heard the padlock clicked onto the front door chains before settling down to spend the night in the fiction section. He always woke up just before daybreak. His natural internal alarm clock never failed him. He sneaked out one of the back windows and made his way to the boarding house, and was still able to get a couple of hours' sleep before the men started emerging from their night of revelry.

It was at the library that he first saw Ollie Nicholson. She was not pretty in the usual way; her hair was too fine and wispy, her nose a tiny bit too pointed, and her chin a fraction too small, but her eyes were deep and intelligent and they softened sweetly at the corners when she smiled. He watched her from between the shelves, strained to hear her voice when she spoke to the librarian each night, but this admiration would have remained safely distant if he hadn't been reading *Robinson Crusoe*.

'Sounds good, doesn't it? An island paradise?'

He knew who it was. Knew she was talking directly to him, but he didn't look up, fearful that she might disappear, but hoping that she would.

'That's one of my favorites. It was top of my readin' list last year.'

He finally raised his eyes to hers, but was struck speechless by her nearness; she smiled, replacing a book on the shelves above his head, before returning to her seat. Every Saturday after that he hurried back to Miss Nedra's after work to be the first in line for a bath, skipping supper so that he could be in his usual seat when Ollie arrived at the library.

Much later he found out that she was training to be a teacher at Berry College and she was eagerly awaiting her first teaching appointment, but during those early tentative meetings their conversations consisted of little more than friendly greetings. It was several months before he gathered enough nerve to follow her to the front door when she rose to leave, and even then it was her suggestion that he walk her back to the Hollingsworth Hotel for Young Women.

A change came over him that he couldn't explain; a painful need to be near her, to hear her talk and to sacrifice whatever was necessary to make her life more perfect. He recognized the physical desires that gnawed away inside him, but he found there was something even more overpowering and that was a passion for companionship. From the beginning she had granted him an equality and shown a genuine interest in what he had to say. He read more than he ever had before, thirsty for more common ground. He started squirreling away small chunks of wood from the mill to whittle small gifts for her and they invented an intimate game of storytelling on the walk home from the library. She would begin a story and he would add a bit more, before passing it back to her. They took turns building the story until whoever had control, by the time they reached the front porch of her hotel, had to tie the story up with a suitable ending. They usually sat for another twenty minutes on the steps, talking about life or admiring the stars.

She was talkative and enthusiastic and free with details about her past, her home and the family she'd left behind. He had seen the flicker of hurt in her eyes each time he side-stepped her questions about his own personal life, but as far as he was concerned nothing that had happened before Ollie came into his life mattered. One night he let it slip that he had left Lander when he was thirteen and despite her gentle persuasion, he refused to say any more. Eventually, she stopped asking and seemed content just to share the here and now with him.

Canaan

'Hey, Harvard . . . get your ass out here. You cain't hide in there all day, we got a long night ahead and customers with parties to go to.'

Canaan flushed the toilet and popped some gum into her mouth to get rid of the bitter taste. She was four and a half months along now, but the changes in her body so far had been very slight so it was easy to hide. Nature had paid her back, however, by extending her sickness.

She checked her face in the mirror and readjusted the 'Happy New Year' headband Kyle had made them wear. She wondered if there was a company somewhere that specialized in producing headgear and rubber noses designed solely to humiliate employees. She joined the others behind the deli counter and Juanita gave her a small hug.

'Feelin' better?'

'Yeah, thanks.'

She took the order slip from the next woman in line. The woman gave her name as if Canaan couldn't read it herself.

'Wilson. I ordered the Festival platter.'

Dot sidled up beside Canaan and nudged her in the ribs.

'You're a delicate little thing, ain't you?'

'I just haven't been feeling very good lately.'

Dot winked at Juanita.

'We noticed.'

Juanita gave Canaan a 'don't pay her no mind' look.

'Are you gonna stay for the fireworks tonight?'

'I don't know.'

'You ought to. Kyle lets us go up on the roof. It's the best view in Lander.'

'Sure. I guess so. Next!'

As soon as the words were out of her mouth she realized too late that 'next' was Mim Simpson. Mim smiled sweetly.

'Well, my, don't you look like a droopy Miss Tinsel.'

Canaan took her order form.

'One Festival and two Celebration platters?'

'It's for the kids mainly. Nathan ordered lobster and prime rib from Ruby D's for the grown-ups. Oh, and give me a half-pound of the peppered pastrami. The mayor always likes my pastrami cheese ball.'

Mim tapped her long, hot-pink nails on the glass case for attention, as if she was preparing to make an important announcement.

'I haven't seen Zeke Forrest in a while. How's he doin'?'

Canaan dropped a handful of peppered pastrami on the floor. She picked it up and smiled back just as sweetly at Mim.

'I haven't seen him.'

'Oh? That's not what I heard. I heard you been seein' quite a lot of him.'

Dot let out an explosive giggle and Juanita elbowed her to be quiet. Canaan bent down to put the dropped pastrami into the garbage and put it instead in a take-out carton. Mim continued, appreciating the fact that Dot was taking in every word and smiling like a trained chimpanzee.

'Course, I guess you're not the type to care what other people are sayin'.'

Canaan put the take-out carton of pastrami on the counter for Mim.

'I'll check in the back for your platters.'

Dot called after her.

'You're not gonna be sick again, are you?'

Canaan ignored her and the stifled giggles she heard behind her. She was standing at her locker when Kyle came out of his office.

'Everything all right?'

'I'm just getting some aspirin.'

'You not feelin' good?'

'I'm fine. I've just got a headache.'

He moved closer to her, smiling what she called his slimy smile.

'Well, I might have just the remedy.'

He pulled a bottle of Southern Comfort from behind his back.

'Drove all the way to the state line for it.'

He held it out to her.

'Go on! I bought it for you.'

She hesitated before taking it.

'Thank you.'

'It's for the fireworks tonight.'

'That's real nice of you, Mr Bernard.'

'Kyle.'

'Kyle. But I thought we weren't allowed.'

'Oh, nobody else has to know about it. This is our special treat. Yours and mine.'

'I don't understand.'

He edged closer to her, whispering in her ear and pinning her to the locker.

'Well, when the fireworks start, you sneak on down here to my office and I'll show you exactly what I mean.'

He leaned over to kiss her and she pulled away.

'Kyle, I'm sorry if you got the wrong idea.'

'Shhh!'

He took a handful of her hair and inhaled.

'Stop it, Kyle.'

She shoved him away but he took her by the shoulders and continued to nuzzle her neck.

'You always acted like you were too good.'

'Please . . .'

'Livin' in that run-down place with that loony family you got and you still made me feel like I wasn't good enough for you.'

'I never meant . . .'

He smiled playfully at her.

'But now we know better, don't we?'

He lunged at her again.

'Stop it. Please, Kyle, don't.'

His face had turned a deep red and he shoved her against the locker, pinning her with one arm. Before she could call out he had reached up under her uniform and plunged his hand down her panties.

'Just let me have one little sniff to keep me goin' 'til the fireworks.'

In seconds she had overcome the shock, braced herself and kneed him in the groin as she pushed him to the middle of the storeroom floor. She screamed at him with a deep guttural voice that didn't seem to belong to her.

'No! No more! You are not going to hurt me.'

The doors flung open and Dot and Juanita stood dumb-founded as curious customers crowded around to get a better look. Kyle looked momentarily flustered but gained his composure enough to point an accusing finger.

'You . . . you're fired. Try and help you out, give you a job 'cause I felt sorry for you. Where does it get me?'

Dot knelt beside him.

'Are you all right, Mr Bernard?'

He let her help him up.

'Tried to bribe me. Said she'd have sex with me if I gave her a raise and when I turned her down she went crazy on me.'

Mim called over the counter.

'You want me to call the police?'

'No, I just want her out of my store.'

Canaan looked around at the faces. Even Juanita's usual sympathetic face had a certain edgy uncertainty to it. Something clicked inside her. They wanted trash, she'd give them trash. She reached up and unzipped her uniform, taking her time and for the first time enjoying the whispers. She let it drop to the floor and stood there in her slip while she kicked off her steel-toed shoes. Kyle ducked as one of them whizzed by his head. She reached into her locker and put on Lou Venie's old winter coat then grabbed her purse and winked at Kyle as she slipped the bottle of Southern Comfort inside. Then she walked barefoot through the store, head high, across the square and to her car. For the crowd who'd gathered outside to watch her go, she made a special effort to squeal her tires and rev the engine.

Lou Venie was waiting for her when she got home. A friend of Peggy's had been at the Piggly Wiggly picking up her cheese platter when Canaan had made her exit and Peggy had wasted no time in letting her mother know and warning her that something had to be done about Canaan's behavior. When Canaan walked in wearing nothing but a slip and a threadbare winter coat, she stood in the doorway to stop her.

'What in God's name were you thinkin'?'

Canaan squeezed past.

'Well, I see the Lander gossip factory has worked in record time.'

'Answer me, Canaan. What were you thinkin'?'

'Nothing much.'

Canaan slammed her bedroom door but Lou Venie pushed her way in.

'How could you do this? Things ain't bad enough as they are? What are you plannin' to do now?'

Canaan was opening drawers and rummaging through piles of clothes.

'I haven't thought that far.'

'I work sun-up to sun-down tryin' to keep this old heap from fallin' down around our ears.'

Canaan found an old pair of jeans and shimmied into them. They were a tighter fit now.

'I've heard this speech before.'

'Makin' sure we got enough food to get us through the winter. You think that garden just grows itself?'

'Saint Lou Venie.'

'All you had to do was climb down off that high horse of yours and work an ordinary job like plain decent ordinary people do.'

Canaan pulled her slip up over her head and replaced it with a sweater.

'Well, you've said it enough times, Lou Venie. I don't come from decent ordinary stock.'

She reached into the back of her drawer, feeling around under the scarves and T-shirts.

'You lookin' for these?'

Lou Venie took a bottle of pills from her sweater pocket and held them up.

'Still snooping I see, Lou Venie.'

'I didn't want to believe it.'

'I'm sorry I don't have a diary for you to rip up and burn.'

Canaan reached for the pills but Lou Venie pulled away.

'It's my house. I have a right to know what's going on in my own house.'

'It's always been your house. Not mine. Not Luke's. Yours.'

She reached for them again.

'Give them to me.'

'You're not takin' pills in my house.'

She lunged at her grandmother, grabbing her frail wrists.

'Give them to me.'

A veil of blue-black anger descended on Canaan and she wrestled with Lou Venie until the old woman was doubled over in a heap on the floor. She pried the pills from her fingers and shook the bottle triumphantly over her head.

'It must feel good to know you were right all along. I'm the town whore and a pill popper . . . just like my mother. Just like you said I'd be.'

She turned to leave and Lou Venie in a feeble attempt to stop her reached out for her ankle.

'Please, Canaan, don't leave . . .'

'Just do what you do with everybody else in your life who disappoints you, Lou Venie. Forget me. Like you forgot my mother. Pretend I don't exist. Like you pretend Luke doesn't exist.'

She turned back at the door and for the first time, there was a momentary shred of compassion as she realized how small and fragile Lou Venie looked on the floor. But the anger was still too hot, too close to the surface and the small moment of compassion soon evaporated.

'Don't bother waitin' up.'

Luke

Luke found Miss Nedra in the kitchen. He stood in the doorway, waiting for her to notice him. He was wearing a new shirt and the old work boots with new laces and a spit polish on the toes. She looked up from the pot roast she was basting and smiled.

'I'm tellin' you what . . . I always said there was a good-lookin' boy underneath all that dirt. Turn around, let me have a look.'

He gave an awkward turn and held up Cooter's old hair clippers.

'Could you give me a trim, Miss Nedra?'

'Take a chair out back. I'll be right there.'

She finished the basting and followed him outside, draping an old tablecloth around his shoulders. She took the clippers from him.

'They're a mite stiff. You sure you want to do this?'

He nodded.

'Well, I'll have to cut most of it off with the scissors first.'

He nodded again and closed his eyes.

'But then I want you to trim it with the clippers.'

Miss Nedra had arranged for the men to take her wagon out for a night of dancing, drinking and fighting in the next county. She told them it was because the spring sap was rising and she wanted them to get it out of their system somewhere else.

'Don't have hardly a chair that ain't been broke and mended. And I can't afford to replace any more china.'

They didn't argue with her and didn't ask questions when she said Luke was staying behind. He usually locked himself in his room on Saturday nights anyway or slunk off to the library.

Luke kept his eyes closed, glancing down once or twice to see long wisps of hair falling on the grass around him. He grabbed hold of the bottom of the chair with both hands when she used the clippers, steeling himself against the stinging pain. When she finished he rubbed his hands over the cold, vulnerable place on his neck where his hair used to be. She brushed his shoulders.

'There's some Brylcream on my dresser. You're welcome to it.'

He nodded his thanks and disappeared for another hour. She imagined he was in his room staring at his new reflection and experimenting with the hair cream. When he finally came back down he had that overprepared look of a man who isn't used to making an effort.

Miss Nedra whistled and made him blush.

'Everything's all set. You oughta answer the door when she gets here. Just bring her out to the back porch and I'll do the rest.'

He sat nervously in the front room and waited, wondering what Miss Nedra would do if he just went back upstairs and locked himself in his room. He was sure she probably had a spare key, but he figured she wouldn't bother with that, but would simply bust the door down and drag him out. He decided to stay put and suffer the unbearable fear that chewed away at his guts. Ollie had never seen him anywhere but at the library and it was only because Miss Nedra had insisted that it was time he moved things ahead, that he'd agreed to this night.

When the knock finally came he sat very still for a moment, hoping that maybe it was someone else.

'Luke!'

He could hear the determination in Miss Nedra's voice in the kitchen and he stood up immediately as if she'd slapped him on the back of his head. If he thought his nerves were shattered before, the minute he opened the door and saw Ollie Nicholson's sweet face, the feeling in his legs seemed to leave him and he stood rooted to the spot, afraid to move in case he fell over.

'My goodness, you look handsome, Luke.'

She smiled and he could feel his face turning a deep crimson. After an awkward gap, she stepped one foot over the threshold.

'Should I come in?'

He found his tongue at last and nodded.

'Miss Nedra says I'm supposed to . . .'

He fumbled for words and finally just headed towards the kitchen.

'We gotta go out here.'

He led her onto the back porch where Miss Nedra was waiting.

'How are you, Miss Nicholson? I'm the landlady here. Miss Nedra.'

Luke stood back and let them finish with the introductions, wondering what on earth he was supposed to do next. He needn't have worried. Miss Nedra was in control now.

'You two follow me out to the orchard. I've set up a special place for your dinner. Too nice an evening to waste it cooped up inside.'

She'd known that Luke would feel like a fish out of water if she'd set things up in the dining room. She led them down the path to a clearing at the back of the property that she called the orchard – a small gathering of apple trees that were in full bloom. The limbs were hung with lanterns, twinkling in the night sky. It reminded Luke of sorghum season at Squeaky's house years before. Beneath the trees she'd set one of her small work tables, draped in a white linen tablecloth with fresh spring flowers in the center.

Ollie hummed softly.

'This is beautiful, Miss Nedra. It's just . . . beautiful.'

'Got the good silver out. And the china. Don't get much chance to use it in this house. Not with the likes I got stayin' here.'

She waved them towards the table.

'You two sit down and have a talk. I'll be out directly with the first course.'

She scurried back up to the house and left them in secluded privacy. After a long, embarrassed silence, Ollie started the conversation and eventually, despite his terror, Luke joined in. Miss Nedra stayed away, except when she was serving another course, and although they never saw her, she came out onto the porch every so often to give the Victrola another crank. Luke was only slightly aware of the music lilting across the dark lawn. He'd kept his eyes down, afraid to look up, afraid of what he might see in Ollie's eyes, but after the first course he couldn't take his eyes off of her and he realized it was the first time he'd dared look directly into her face. She was the most beautiful creature he'd ever seen and he studied every little movement she made. The way she pushed her small wire glasses up by wrinkling her nose. The way she tucked the wispy strands of fine hair behind her ear, because they kept slipping from the pins that held her hair above her slender neck. He wished the night would go on for ever, but Miss Nedra came out to clear the coffee cups and the empty bowls of apple cobbler.

'The boys'll be back soon, Luke. Best walk Miss Nicholson home.'

He stood up obediently as Miss Nedra disappeared around the lilac tree, balancing the last of the dishes. Something in him realized there was something he should do, so he stumbled awkwardly around the table to pull Ollie's chair out for her. She stood and slipped her hand in his. He stood frozen for a moment, then gathered himself and led her towards the path, but she gently pulled him back. She stood on tiptoe and lifted her face to his. In the twinkling lantern light she kissed him – a long sweet kiss – and he stopped breathing, lost in the dizzying emotion of the night.

'Thank you, Luke.'

They walked slowly up to the house and then on to the hotel, hand in hand all the way. At her front door he agonized over what he should do, but before he had too much time to think it over, she reached up and kissed him on the cheek, whispering in his ear.

'I'm taking a walk tomorrow down by the mill path. Would you like to come with me?'

He nodded mutely and she smiled.

'Two o'clock. After church. I'll wait for you by the front gates.'

For the next two months, they were together four to five times a week. He saw her at the library every Saturday night and several times during the week. She was studying for final exams and he often sat quietly while she was buried in her notebooks, waiting for one of her frequent smiles when she'd reach over and squeeze his hand. He waited for her outside the church every Sunday and she often found him waiting for her outside the hotel when she arrived back from her classes. He was only allowed in the sitting room of the hotel during certain hours but he became a regular visitor and a willing help to the proprietor when she needed some repairs done or supplies carried in.

They had never talked about what would happen when

she finished her teaching classes. She had never brought it up and he was too frightened by what she might say if he asked.

In May he was waiting for her outside the hotel when she asked if they could sit on the front porch for a spell. He could tell by her smile that something had happened.

'It's wonderful news, Luke. I've had a letter from a school in Tuscaloosa.'

She took it out and showed it to him.

'They've asked me to start in September.'

He started counting in his head how many months he had left, trying to settle the deep aching in his gut. She seemed to know what he was thinking because she put her hand on his.

'I need to leave next week. I need time to find a place to live, to get settled in. And it's gonna take me awhile to get everything ready at the school for the new term.'

He sat in silence. Afraid to say anything. She slipped her arm through his.

'I'll write you as soon as I get there, Luke. We can write over the summer and soon as I get settled into the new school, you can come visit me in the fall.'

She looked away shyly.

'If you wanted me to, I could see if there's any mill work there. I mean . . . if you wanted . . .'

He turned to her and took both her hands in his.

'I could come work in Tuscaloosa? Be near you? You wouldn't mind?'

She laughed and squeezed his hands.

'Of course not, you silly thing. I'd be miserable without you. I'd tell you to come with me now, but I don't know what it will be like. It's my first job and I'm nervous. I think I need to get settled in on my own first. You do understand, don't you?'

He nodded, his heart racing wildly. *She wanted to be near*

him. She'd be miserable without him. He'd never been so completely and utterly happy in his life.

Over the next few days, he helped Ollie to pack up her things and the following Saturday he borrowed Miss Nedra's wagon to take her to the train station. The past week he'd been living off the euphoria of knowing that Ollie truly cared about him, but on the platform he stood awkwardly with his hat in his hand, battling feelings that made him weak with fear. When the porter hurried them along, she stood on tiptoe, kissing him with a sweetness that brought a choking lump to his throat. She handed him a package wrapped in perfumed paper.

'It's to remind you how we met.'

She touched his face one more time.

'I'll write as soon as I can. I'll write every week, I promise. And maybe you can come out sooner than we think.'

He was afraid to speak, so he just nodded and helped her up the steps of the train. He stood on the platform until her train disappeared then sat on the bench, clutching the package. He held it for twenty minutes, wanting to cling to the last thing she'd touched, unwilling to spoil the care she'd taken in wrapping it. When he finally opened it, it was a copy of *Robinson Crusoe*. Inside she'd left a card for him and he read it a dozen or more times before he went to bed that night.

The next day he started his daily vigil on the front porch, waiting for the mailman, even though he knew it would be several days before she reached Tuscaloosa. She'd said she had several stops to make along the way, but he couldn't wait. He didn't want to miss that first letter. He waited every day. He checked the main post office every week. For three months he waited, bursting into Miss Nedra's sitting room after work, hoping for some word, but getting instead sympathetic eyes and suggestions that maybe the letter would come the next day.

Eventually he stopped waiting and settled into his old routine, spending his evenings with Miss Nedra on the porch steps and letting his life drift back to the way things had been before. But his trips to the library were too painful to bear and he never went back.

Canaan

Canaan couldn't be sure how long she had been roaming the streets of Lander and she couldn't remember where she'd been, but she awoke as she pulled into Zeke's dirt drive. A half-empty bottle of Southern Comfort rested between her legs and she waved with drunken cheerfulness at Zeke who was standing over a Hitachi grill at the top of his steps. She slammed her car door with determined strength and wove a path through the weeds.

'You havin' a party?'

She climbed the stairs, taking ample swigs from the whiskey bottle. He put the tongs down on the grill in case he had to catch her.

'Just me and Stonewall. You want a hot dog? Or maybe a stomach pump?'

She sat heavily on the top step.

'I got fired today.'

'I know.'

She twisted around to look at him.

'Jesus – this must be some kind of record.'

He sat down next to her, on the open side of the steps to keep her from toppling off.

'I stopped by the deli for hot dogs. Saw the final grand finale. Gotta say, you've got style.'

He handed her a hot dog and she absently took a bite.

'I shouldn't have come back.'

'To Lander? Why did you?'

She shrugged and took another swig to wash down the bread that was stuck to the roof of her mouth.

'I made it out once, I figured I could do it again.'

'Is it that important to you . . . getting out?'

She snorted and nudged him a little too hard.

'That doesn't sound like the Zeke Forrest I used to know. *Out there*, you said, *out there. That's where life is. Not here in Lander-fucking-Alabama.*'

He wiped some mustard from the corner of her mouth with the cuff of his jacket.

'At least you did it.'

'You made it sound so easy. Like the world was this great big theme park and the tickets were free. Well, take it from me, the world ain't such a fun place.'

'So why are you in such a hurry to get back there?'

'You used to tell anybody who'd listen about that novel you were gonna write . . . how far you got with that – huh? What happened to that life you were going to lead? Where are you now, Zeke Forrest? Still teachin' high-school English to moony-eyed Southern belles.'

'I never planned on stayin'. The place just sort of grew on me.'

'Yeah, well, it's been better to you than it has to me.'

She waved her arms around to indicate the rambling apartment.

'If you choose to live like this – people call you eccentric. If I live like this I'm trash. And no amount of fancy education is gonna change that. You lied to me, Zeke Forrest.'

She struggled to stand and she reached for the front door.

'I've got to pee. You got a john in this place or is it out back?'

He led her inside and was waiting for her in the living room.

'Where's your car keys? I don't think you'd better drive anymore tonight. You want me to take you back?'

'No.'

'You can stay here if you want. It's not a sofa bed, and it's not what you'd call pretty but it's comfortable. It's also close to the bathroom.'

'Whatever you say, teach.'

'Keys.'

She dropped her car keys into the palm of his hand and curled up in the faded wing chair.

'So what was everybody saying about my big exit today?'

'I don't know. The usual, you know. I try not to listen.'

'Like the last time?'

She took another swig from the bottle.

'What last time? Oh, you mean . . . the gossip about you and me. They were just jealous of your success.'

'I was eighteen. You could have told them there was nothing going on.'

'You know how they are around here. It was better just to ignore it.'

'And get me out of the way.'

'Get you out of the way? I was trying to help! If I hadn't sent off all those forms, called all those colleges – I helped you get out.'

'Did she jump or was she pushed?'

'You couldn't wait to get on that bus out of Lander. It's all you talked about.'

'Because it was all *you* talked about, Zeke. I would've stayed if you'd asked me.'

She leaned forward to put the Southern Comfort on the

coffee table but missed and stumbled forward out of the chair. Zeke took the bottle from her.

'I think you could probably use some coffee. Black? White? Sugar?'

He headed into the kitchen.

'Black, no sugar.'

She stood up, carefully – steadying herself on the second-hand furniture – and wandered around the room she'd spied on from across the road so many times. She was finally inside Zeke's golden, lamp-lit, bohemian world. He was back before she'd made it to the back of the sofa. He headed towards the bedroom.

'Coffee's brewin'. I'll get the pillows and blankets for you.'

She continued her snooping, making her way around the room. His Christmas decorations were still up. If you could call them that. The Christmas tree was a large silver trash can set up in the corner of the room and filled with bare tree branches. Hundreds of Christmas cards were tied with kitchen string to every spare inch. She examined them and was not surprised to find that the vast majority of the cards began with *Dear Mr Forrest* and finished with curvaceous little Xs and signed with names that sounded as though their mothers had read too many romance novels . . . Tiffany, Amber, Melody. The Christmas card Canaan had bought for him during her senior year had been chosen with more care than her prom dress. She had finally found one she wanted at a craft fair, artistic and individual, and inside she had included a short poem she had written about admiration and friendship. She couldn't remember what the poem had said, but judging from the few insipid, angst-filled poems she had saved from that time in her life, she was grateful for the lapse of memory.

He came out of the bedroom loaded down with quilts and pillows.

'Thought I'd go ahead and make out the sofa. So you can crash as soon as you're ready.'

He tucked the quilt and blanket over the sofa and plumped up the pillow before ambling back to the kitchen.

'Coffee comin' up!'

He disappeared again and Canaan inspected a shelf in the corner that was laden with small plastic statuettes inscribed with variations of *World's Best Teacher* and a bushel basket overflowing with symbolic apples made from every conceivable material. She dug below the ones made from polished oak, painted pine, bronze, cork and calico fabric until she found the one she'd given him on her last day of high school. It was an apple-shaped candle in a tie-dyed pattern. *An apple for the teacher*. Even in her tipsy state she was embarrassed to realize that so many others had been blessed with the same 'inspiration'.

Zeke came in with the coffee and sat down in the wing chair. Canaan held up the tie-dyed apple.

'I gave you this one.'

He smiled.

'I know.'

'I thought I was so clever to think of an apple for the teacher.'

'Yours was the first. Everybody else followed your lead.'

She laughed, unconvinced, and crossed over to the chair. Sinking down to the floor and wedging herself between his knees, she held the apple up to him.

'But mine looks ordinary next to all the others now. It's not unique. I wanted to be different. Special.'

She stared into his eyes then slowly rose up to kiss him. His lips were warm, just as she'd always imagined, and she felt a deep ache between her legs just like she'd felt when she was too young to know what to do about it. She touched her cheek to his and whispered.

'I wanted you to think I was special.'

She continued to kiss him, more and more passionately as she crawled into his lap, straddling him, her breathing heavy and urgent.

Zeke too was caught up in the passion, but he had to at least try to be responsible.

'Canaan, are you sure?'

She stood up, pulling him with her and fumbled with his shirt before taking it off over his head. She kissed his chest, tenderly exploring its contours with her fingertips. She lifted her lips to his, rising up on her toes so that their hips matched and she could feel the unmistakable bulge through his jeans. He took her face into his hands and kissed her tenderly and softly and she led him to the sofa, lying him down and straddling him again. Lifting her sweater over her head she held his arms while she kissed his chest, his shoulders, the sweet hollow of his collarbone, then nuzzled up under his ear.

'I could love you, Zeke Forrest.'

She settled into his arms and he held her tight. He brushed her hair from her back, drawing circles on her skin with his fingers. He kissed the top of her head and took a deep breath, surprised by the emotion he was feeling that seemed even stronger than the passion.

'I could love you too.'

He held her for a few more minutes, letting his hands slide down the back of her jeans, feeling her heartbeat, breathing in the smell of her.

'Do you want to move to the bedroom?'

He ran his hand through her hair. *Hair you'd wanna run barefoot in.*

'Canaan?'

Her breathing had settled into a deep steady rhythm as she nuzzled against his chest. He laughed and rolled her gently onto the sofa, while he moved out from under her. She immediately curled up and he tucked the blanket around her and stared down at her for a few seconds, brushing her cheek with the back of his hand. He turned the lights off and headed for bed. Nearby, Stonewall was sprawled on the floor. He lifted his head as Zeke stepped over him.

'Don't look at me like that. You're as bad as Jim.'

Luke

A year later Luke had resigned himself to living the rest of his life at Miss Nedra's boarding house. He wasn't complaining. It was clean. The food was the best home cooking in the state of Georgia. And Miss Nedra was as good a friend and protector as anybody could ask for. In the time since he'd been there, he'd seen dozens of men come and go. He was the only one who seemed to be permanent, so he'd learned to accept the idea of staying put.

But that was before a part of his past walked into Miss Nedra's boarding house. Luke came home from the mill one afternoon, to find Major Clancy Maddux sitting on the front porch with his hand-stitched leather boots propped on the railing, picking his teeth with a matchstick. Luke stopped in his tracks like a rabbit with nowhere to run. The last time he'd seen the Major, Spoons and Cooter had run him off with a pitchfork and cost him a good haul of silver from the farmer's dining-room chest. He looked a lot older and if possible more sour than ever before. He squinted down at Luke.

'You stayin' here, boy?'

Luke nodded, afraid to move.

'Well, what time's the landlady get grub on the table?

I been eatin' shit on stale bread for the past three days and I'm ready for some hot home cookin'.'

Luke picked nervously at the seam in his trousers, looking down as he stuttered an answer.

'Five. Miss Nedra serves supper at five o'clock.'

The Major spit on the floor between his legs.

'Much obliged.'

For the next few days Luke avoided him, and it was another week before he realized that the Major didn't recognize him. Luke had only been fourteen when they'd traveled together and he'd changed a great deal since then. He relaxed once he realized that the Major wasn't there to settle old grudges, but he avoided him all the same. Miss Nedra took an instant dislike to her new boarder.

'Don't trust him no further than I could hurl him.'

She'd caught him examining her china figurines a little too closely, holding them up to the light and studying the imprint with a magnifying glass. She took to counting the good silverware every morning and every night and eventually stored it under her own bed for safekeeping. She didn't like the slimy way he tried to charm his way around her. Whether he was trying to get an extra pork chop or his fancy boots polished, his false flattery didn't work on Miss Nedra. She also didn't like the way he spent most of his time digging up little tidbits of information about the people around him. It wasn't long before he knew everyone's weakness, their strongest desires and their biggest fears, and he was an expert at playing them to his favor. Every evening he had a new selection of goods to sell that just happened to be exactly what one or two of them had sworn they'd always wanted. He knew when he could get away with outrageous prices and he knew who would buckle the quickest when he needed something done for himself. All he had to do was put a little pressure in the right place, and the Major had a knack for knowing the right amount of pressure and the right place to apply it. She'd seen him cheat at cards so she figured he cheated on damn near everything. She would have just thrown him out except that he always paid two weeks in advance and he kept his room cleaner than most. So, instead, she kept a close eye on him and was extra careful when she counted the money he gave her for rent. She also kept a close ear at his door on Saturday nights, because a few of the girls had complained about his nasty habit of punching or choking when he'd had too much to drink.

Saturday night at the boarding house was still whore night and although Luke still didn't join in with the popular event, he helped Miss Nedra with the preparations. One Saturday night he was helping as usual, collecting the filthy work clothes for washing, and giving out clean towels while Miss Nedra moved from tub to tub replenishing the bath-water from a hot cast-iron kettle. The boarding house had always had indoor plumbing, but Miss Nedra had never seen much reason for a fancy enameled bathtub when the men seemed perfectly happy with the three tin ones, lined up under the washing line in the back room.

The Major was taking longer in the bath than his allotted time, leaning back in luxurious bliss, blowing smoke circles from his cigar, the soggy stump clinging precariously from the corner of his mouth. He looked down at Luke as he knelt to collect a pile of work clothes.

'Boy, you got the God-awful-est feet I ever seen. No wonder that gal left you in such a hurry. You want me to get you some shoes? Cover them things up?'

Luke shrugged, his expression poker-faced, emotionless. He'd learned that it was best not to let the Major know if he got under your skin. He placed a towel over the rim of the tub and turned his back on him. The Major slid further into the gravy-colored bathwater and rested his head against the back of the tub.

'Yes-sir. I can get you any size shoes, any style you want.'

Luke began mopping up the puddles from the floor, while the Major settled in for one of his center-stage monologues.

'Course these days, I get 'em from a dealer over in Macon.'

He chuckled.

'I always had an eye for good shoes. I could spot a good pair in a minute, back when I was ridin' the lines. And once I fixed my mind to havin' 'em, I'd follow 'em to Kalamazoo if I had to.'

One of the boys waiting his turn for the bath chimed in.

'How'd you get 'em off 'em, Major?'

The boy was one of the few in the house who paid any attention to the Major anymore. He was an impressionable boy, eager for excitement, low on common sense. The Major smiled, pleased that he'd hooked a listener.

'Wait 'til they was asleep. I could take shoes off men in seconds and be on another train before they even felt a draft.'

He raked some of the melting bubbles onto his chest and closed his eyes.

'When I was a kid, there was this one ol' nigger . . . I followed him all the way from St Louis. Beautiful leather on them shoes, though, let me tell you. Perfect stitching across the toe, real high-falootin' shoes and I reckoned the old man who was wearin' 'em couldn't have put up much of a fight.'

He took the cigar out of his mouth and flicked the ash on the floor.

'Followed him all the way to some piss-ant little town . . . what was it? Lander. Lander, Alabama. I thought my luck had finally changed 'cause he crawled up under one of the boxcars and fell asleep. I'd been watchin' him on the train, drinkin' whiskey like there was no tomorrow.'

Luke stopped mopping and drew closer, his eyes never

leaving the Major's face. The Major became more animated, pleased that he had gained such interest in his story.

'I was watchin' him. Waitin' to make my move . . . Then, before I could do a damned thing, there were dogs and men from the town headin' our way and everybody in the rail yard was runnin' like hell. Everybody 'ceptin' my old boy with the shoes, that is. Well, I can tell you now, I wasn't 'bout to lose out on them shoes. I'd been followin' 'em for too long. I hunkered down, out of sight, where I could keep an eye on him and I'll be damned if them men didn't drag him out and beat him to a pulp before haulin' him off. He couldn't have been in town more'n fifteen minutes, poor bastard, and them people were on him like flies to cow shit. Thought he'd raped a little white girl. Left his body hanging on the square. Them shoes disappeared before they'd even strung him up. Ended up somewhere in a ditch, I reckon, after they'd dragged that boy over every back road in the county.'

He shook his head, sinking back down in the water with a sigh.

'Damn shame. Could've made a lot of money off them shoes.'

The next morning Miss Nedra was in the kitchen rolling out the biscuits for breakfast when Luke came in dressed for traveling and packed to go. She glanced up and tossed another handful of flour over the mound of dough.

'Thought I'd see you this morning. Seen it in your face soon as the Major mentioned your hometown. Figured you'd be leavin'.'

She nodded towards a pan on the stovetop.

'Got my first batch of coffee brewin' there if you want a cup 'fore you set off.'

He shuffled over and poured a cup.

'Miss Nedra, I want to thank you . . .'

She waved her flour-caked hand without turning around.

'You've been a good boarder. A fine companion.'

He drank the coffee while she finished the biscuits, enjoying the comforting silence they had both come to expect. She covered the biscuits with a tea towel, then pulled out a small flour sack from the bread bin. She handed it to him.

'Got about half a dozen corn pones I saved from last night. Don't know how long they'll last, but they'll be more use to you than to these rascals. They always complainin' 'bout leftovers anyhow.'

She followed him onto the porch but as he started down the steps, she stopped him. She reached into the large patch pocket of her shirt and handed him her pipe and a small pouch of tobacco.

'You got the kinda face built for a pipe, Feets.'

He took the gifts and nodded in gratitude, then hurried down the steps and into the dawn.

Canaan

Canaan woke up to the sound of cabinets slamming in the kitchen and felt a tremendous heaviness in her feet and in her head. The weight on her feet turned out to be Stonewall, his soulful eyes resting on his paws, watching her as she gingerly rotated her head to look around the room, blinking to clarify the jumbled signals in her brain. She pulled her legs from under the dog, drawing them close to her chest, too wary of the prickly sensations that pulsated across her scalp to risk sitting up just yet. Zeke popped his head around the kitchen door and smiled.

'Mornin', Glory. Got the coffee goin'.'

She gave a slight nod and closed her eyes, her memory suddenly betraying her by revealing selected images of the night before. She vaguely remembered climbing all over Zeke like a common whore and there were flashes of kneeling on the linoleum floor of his tiny bathroom, hugging the sides of the toilet. There was also an uncomfortable tightening in her chest as she remembered Zeke sitting on the side of the tub gently wiping her face with a washcloth as she rested her head on his knee. She remembered being aware of the mess she'd made and her inability to do anything but allow him to guide her back to the sofa and tuck her in.

She scrunched down under the quilt, hoping he would return to his kitchen duties and allow her time to make a cowardly exit, but he chased a grumpy Stonewall from his cozy corner of the sofa and sat down in the chair across from her.

'Right. I'm takin' orders for breakfast.'

She wrinkled her nose, attempting to shake her head without jarring the sharp-edged objects that seemed to be floating around inside.

'I can't.'

'Course you can. Now, the menu is a little bit limited, but fortunately I happen to be an expert in oatmeal makin'. So my real question is, do you eat salt or sugar with your oatmeal?'

She closed her eyes and tried to sound more firm.

'No, really. I don't think I can.'

He leaned forward with semi-sternness.

'Your head is full of cotton balls right now, so it's in no condition to make decisions, but your body is cryin' out for good solid food, whether you can hear it or not. So I'm not leavin' 'til I get an answer. Salt or sugar?'

She opened her eyes long enough to see his determined stare and sighed.

'Honey.'

He grinned, patting her foot as he stood.

'A woman after my own heart.'

As soon as he left she flung the covers back and heard him call from the kitchen.

'Your jeans are in the dryer downstairs. There's an old bathrobe of mine on the chair if you want to put it on.'

She stared down at her bare legs and shoved them quickly back under the covers. The sudden jolt made her eyes roll around in her head and when they finally settled into their rightful place she slowly inched her way down to the other end of the sofa. She reached for the robe and stood up to put it on. It was a plaid flannel that probably had matching slippers kicked under a bed somewhere and she pictured the elderly aunt who had given it to him, or maybe it had been a Christmas gift from his conservative ex-in-laws. At any rate, it was soft and comfortable and smelled of Zeke and she wrapped it tightly around her.

'Why are my jeans in the dryer?'

'You didn't quite make it to the bathroom last night. I put 'em in to wash. They should be dry in no time.'

She thought maybe pretending not to remember would be the best way forward.

'I was sick?'

'Yep. A real gusher. Finally figured it was better just to hold you over the bathtub. Don't worry about it, nothing a little Lysol spray couldn't take care of.'

He appeared with a bamboo tray.

'Afraid I don't have a table. I don't do much entertainin'. Think you can manage eatin' on your lap?'

She nodded, obediently sitting on the sofa. It had been difficult to get the first spoonful past her lips, but she had been surprised how good it tasted once the initial revulsion was conquered. Zeke rambled on about the most recent books he'd read, offering ample but unpressured opportunities for her to contribute to the conversation. Most of the time she simply nodded or shook her head between mouthfuls, but every once in a while he managed to get a more animated opinion out of her and she was grateful for his ability to ease the awkwardness she was feeling.

After breakfast she went into the bathroom to wash her face while Zeke went downstairs to the garage to get her jeans out of the dryer. A wet sponge, balancing on a can of cleanser, had been left in the corner of the tub and the air was thick with the smell of pine disinfectant. She tried to ignore it. She gave her face a quick splash and tried to erase the smudged remains of mascara from under her bottom lashes with her finger. He handed her jeans to her through the door and she hurriedly put them on. Hanging the robe on the back of the door, she pressed her face shamelessly into its folds and inhaled one last time.

She could hear him washing dishes in the kitchen and she thought if she was quiet and quick, she could probably sneak out without having to go through an awkward 'let's pretend nothing embarrassing happened last night' goodbye. She scribbled a note on the back of an old receipt, thanking him for the sofa and the oatmeal, and left it on the coffee table.

'Sneaking out?'

She was halfway out the door when he caught her. She stepped back in, not wanting to carry on a conversation on his front steps where anyone could see and hear.

'I thought it was better if I—'

'Canaan, you don't have to be embarrassed about last night.'

She frowned and rolled her eyes.

'Which particular episode are you talking about? Puking in your bathroom or throwing myself at you like a drunken slut?'

'Well, I have to admit I enjoyed the drunken-slut part better than the bucket-and-mop duty.'

She lowered her eyes and rubbed her forehead. He crossed over to her.

'I'm sorry, that wasn't—'

She dismissed it with a flick of her wrist.

'No, it's OK. Look, can we please just forget it?'

'What if I don't want to forget it?'

'I shouldn't have used you like that.'

'Is that what it was?'

'I was drunk and I was desperate.'

'Oh. That makes me feel a lot better.'

'No, that's not – I was feeling desperate.'

She wasn't doing a very good job with this. She wished he

would just let her walk out without trying to dig up her innermost feelings. She took a deep breath and finally looked him in the eye.

'I'm pregnant. Jonathon's final farewell. I was so stupid to think I could get away that easy.'

Zeke wrapped his arms around her and pulled her close. He kissed the top of her head.

'I'll put another pot of coffee on. We can talk.'

She wanted so desperately to stay. To curl up with him and talk all day and into the night and cry and shout and cry some more. But instead she pulled away.

'No – I can't. I've really—'

He finished her sentence for her.

'Got to go. I know. Story of our life.'

'Lou Venie will be worried sick. I let her think – it's just – I left her on really bad terms last night.'

He let go of her and opened the door. She tried again to apologize, but he stopped her.

'You've got a lot of sortin' to do.'

He touched her cheek with the back of his hand.

'Long as you remember – my door's always unlocked.'

'I know.'

As soon as the Mustang's tires touched the gravel drive, her grandmother was out of the house and standing on the front porch. As Canaan stepped onto the porch the two women stared at one another, each trying to gauge the other's mood. Lou Venie was the first to move, wrapping her arms around her and breaking down into heavy, emotional sobs of relief.

'I'm so sorry, baby girl. I thought I'd lost you. I thought I'd lost you.'

'I'm sorry I scared you, Nan.'

They stood clinging together, neither one of them wanting to let go. Canaan couldn't remember the last time her grandmother had made her feel so loved or safe. And now more than ever that was exactly what she needed.

She suddenly felt exhausted and Lou Venie suggested she take a nap before lunch. As she crawled into her bed, tired and emotionally drained, she ran her hand over the back of the headboard and made a wish, then fell into a deep, comforting sleep.

She'd been asleep for over an hour and was just beginning to stir when she heard a small knock on the door. Lou Venie usually just barged in, so she wasn't sure what she should do. She sat up.

'Come in?'

Lou Venie poked her head uneasily around the door.

'I brought you a cup of hot mint tea. Reckon we could have a talk?'

Canaan nodded and readjusted the pillows behind her back. Lou Venie carried a large shoebox under one arm and a steaming mug of tea in the other hand. She put the mug on the bedside table and sat down at the foot of the bed, the shoebox on her lap and her left hand grasping the bedpost. Canaan waited as she seemed to be gathering her strength to speak.

'I've been thinkin' for a long time now. When you came back I guess I hoped all the past hurts would blow over and we could go back to normal, but truth is I don't know that we ever had "normal". I was never very brave when I was growing up. I was scared to death of Momma's moods so I just used to work things around a little in my head, so I didn't notice so much. When Momma took to havin' one of her nasty fits, I pretended everything was all right. I made up things in my head that made me feel better. And after a while I believed it all, and all the nasty things were forgotten. The next day Momma was always sweet as pie and you'd never know nothin' had happened. So to me . . . it seemed to work just fine doin' things that way.'

She looked away and a sigh, heavy with dread, allowed her to catch her breath.

'I know that ignoring things don't make 'em go away, and I know that all the pretendin' in the world ain't gonna make things right for you, so I gotta try somethin' else.'

She lifted the lid on the shoebox.

'I want you to have these.'

She slid the box onto the bed.

'I spent all night huntin' for 'em. Lord knows why I kept 'em for so long, or why I kept 'em at all. I want you to know it's awful hard for me to do this, but if it'll make you . . . if it'll help . . .'

She took another deep breath and let it out slowly.

'I've buried too many people I love, Canaan, and I can't bear thinkin' of losin' you. I could've made a difference before, for other people, and I didn't. I just waited for it all to blow over. All them years when I took care of Momma – I let her bully me. I was so scared of her, I never once told her she was wrong, or said "that ain't right, Momma". I was a grown woman and knew better but I spent all them years acting like I was five years old again. I never tried to make it easier for Luke. I fed him all these years and I washed his sheets and I cleared out his rottin' vegetables, but I never talked to him. Never really loved him the way I should've. It was easier to pretend I was some kind of martyr for takin' care of him. It was easier to do that than rememberin' that I never took up for him, that I never took a beatin' for him the way he did for me. I didn't want to believe that I might've made a difference for him.'

Canaan leaned forward.

'You've made a much bigger difference than you realize, Nan.'

Lou Venie closed her eyes as if she was trying to focus. 'I need to finish . . .'

She pulled a bundle of letters out of the box and held them in her lap.

'These are letters my momma kept. I found 'em hid all over the house after she died. I figure she'd probably planned on gettin' rid of 'em some day, but I don't think she'd figured on her mind snappin' like it did. Those last few years, she didn't remember any of us. Didn't even remember losin' Gene Allen in Okinawa or John Curtis to polio, so I don't reckon she'd have remembered these.'

She worked her fingernails around the knotted parcel string.

'Most of 'em are signed Emma Scott, so I reckon she wasn't more than fourteen, fifteen when she wrote 'em. There's some more that are dated later and there's a few written to her.'

She finally loosened the knot and pulled the string loose, flipping through them like a deck of cards.

'I probably should have burned all these when I found 'em. Don't know what stopped me. But I'm glad now I didn't. Don't know if they'll help you understand me, or Luke, or the family we were born into . . . the family you were born into. But I guess maybe it's a start.'

She put them on the bed between them, then lifted another stack of letters in lavender envelopes. Her hands were shaking when she handed them to Canaan.

'I put these in together with Momma's letters years later. They're from your momma.'

Canaan looked into her grandmother's eyes, startled.

'You mean after she ran away?'

Lou Venie held them tightly to her chest and the tears she'd been fighting finally trickled down the bridge of her nose.

'She never ran away, Sugar. I know that's what I said, but . . . It was me. I threw her out and everything that reminded me of her. Threw it out on the front porch and told her I never wanted to see her again.'

'Why?'

'I was too ashamed, too stubborn, to see anything but the pain she'd brought me. The boy who'd got her pregnant wasn't even local, just some truck driver passin' through and I just couldn't stand the shame of it. I knew she ended up in Memphis, 'cause I started gettin' letters from her, but I never opened them. I just let 'em pile up and the longer I let 'em pile up the more determined I was to shut her out. It was my way of punishing her.'

She took a tissue from the sleeve of her sweater and wiped her eyes.

'The next time I saw her was when you got off that bus. I saw her same sweet face, the same frightened little eyes, and I thought it was God's way of givin' me another chance. But it looks like I got it all wrong again.'

Canaan put her arms around her grandmother, but Lou Venie pulled away and patted her granddaughter's knee.

'No. I didn't mean to get all teary-eyed about this. I just needed to explain some things.'

She stood and headed for the door.

'I don't know if there's anything here that's gonna help you, Canaan, 'cause I don't know what you're lookin' for.'

'Not sure I know myself, Nan.'

'Well, anyway, it's the only thing I got to offer and it's a chance I gotta take.'

She started to go.

'Lou Venie?'

She turned.

'Thank you.'

'Come on out when you're ready. I got black-eyed peas and turnip greens for New Year's luck.'

Canaan opened the first letter.

Dear Momma,
I named her Canaan . . .

Her first thought was to read all of them in one go. Like a starving man devouring a month's groceries in one sitting. But she could hear Lou Venie in the kitchen and was suddenly struck by the courage it had taken for her grandmother to do what she'd done. She carefully tied them up in their original bundles and stacked them on her bedside table.

'Don't want too much of the New Year to go by without our beans and greens, do we?'

Lou Venie looked surprised to see her.

'Beans for good luck and greens for prosperity.'

Lou Venie always said the same thing every New Year's Day as if Canaan would forget what it meant from one year to the next. Even when she lived in New York, her grandmother had called to make sure she hadn't forgotten.

'I figured you'd be readin' most of the day.'

'I've waited over thirty years. Thought you might like some company.'

Lou Venie turned to stir the pot, but not before Canaan saw a flicker of something in her face. Relief perhaps.

'They've been simmering all mornin'. They're ready if you are.'

'I'll set the table.'

Canaan turned to clear the table and saw that it was already done.

'You've laid three places.'

'Thought Luke might want to join us.'

Lou Venie seemed to find a flurry of things to do all of a sudden and Canaan could tell she didn't want her to make a fuss.

'I'll go down and get him.'

Feeling amazingly at peace, she left her grandmother buttering the cornbread. She expected to see Luke on the porch of the Little House, smoking his pipe, but the door was closed and the dish towels he used for curtains were pulled over the windows. Maybe he was working on his journals. Probably worked through the night and fell asleep at the table. She knocked quietly so she wouldn't startle him.

'Luke?'

She eased open the door and peeked in. He was in his bed, facing the wall. She started to leave him, but she felt the day's events were too important. He could always take a nap later. She tiptoed over and touched his shoulder.

'Luke, Lou Venie asked me to come get you. We've got beans and greens cooking. Wanted to know if you wanted to join us?'

He didn't move and her heart started pounding. She rolled him over and could hear short, shallow breaths. His skin was a dark gray color.

She raced back to the house, screaming the whole way for her grandmother to call an ambulance.

Luke

'Feets. Wake up, boy, you're here.'

Luke sat bolt upright, trying to make sense of the words he knew were important.

'C'mon, boy. Ain't gonna be a long stop. Didn't see no cotton to load.'

Luke scrambled up, grabbing the small bundle from beside him. The old hobo, who had been traveling with him since he'd left Georgia, grinned toothlessly and winked.

'Good ridin' with you, Feets. Maybe I'll see you 'round Chicago ways. Look fer my sign, if'n you get up that far.'

Luke nodded, and checking up and down the line, he waved over his shoulder as he hopped down and shimmied between two cars on the opposite track. He waited until the train pulled out, then reached into his pocket for the pipe and the pouch of tobacco Miss Nedra had given him. He propped himself on the hitch between the two rusting boxcars, and enjoyed the smoke as it billowed around the moustache he had nurtured along to adulthood. He could see Pete's store from where he rested, but he was in no hurry to go inside. He'd wait for a while, give himself time to brush off the travel weariness and clear his head. Except for an additional scattering of rotting boxcars, and an overall film of decay, the rail yard had not changed in the seven years since he'd left Lander. Beyond the carcass of an overturned flatbed, he could see a small community of vagrants gathering the collective contents for the evening's hobo stew. He knew they would make him welcome if he ventured over, but he stayed put, tilting his head back and shading his eyes from the afternoon sun with his hat. As he puffed, he listened for a familiar laugh or a name he knew. It was a habit he had developed over the years; always standing at a safe distance, assessing the group before joining them, and only then if he recognized someone he had traveled with before. He'd never had reason to be so cautious. With few exceptions, the men Luke met along the lines were generous and kind to him.

One of the hobos let out a piercing whoop of laughter, startling Luke from his rest and knocking his hat from his face as he jerked forward. He leaned down to pick it up, brushing the oily dirt from the felt rim. His clothes were caked with diesel oil and he knew the stink of bootleg whiskey and sweat from the strangled air inside the boxcar clung to his skin and hair. What he wouldn't give for one of Miss Nedra's sweet sudsy baths to soak in. He settled down again on the hitch and crossed his arms to balance himself. It had only been two days since he'd left the boarding house, but the thinking he'd had to do in those forty-eight hours had squeezed a lifetime from him; and coming back to Lander had certainly not been in his plans three days before.

Luke sucked on the last ember of tobacco in the pipe and tapped out the ashes against the side of the train before putting it back in his pocket. He'd eaten the last corn pone an hour before and a parched thirst at the back of his throat urged him towards Pete's store.

As he approached the door, Pete waddled out on his cane, carrying a lasso of barbed wire. He tossed it onto the warped flatbed of an old pick-up truck and made his way back up the ramp.

'If you want somethin' make it snappy. I'm closin' up for a while.'

Luke followed him into the store.

'What you want, boy?'

'RC.'

'That it?'

Luke nodded and Pete waved him over to the icebox.

As Luke paid for the bottle, Pete watched him closely.

'You from around here?'

Luke nodded and shrugged at the same time.

'Been gone a while.'

'Where you headin'?'

'Backside of White's Gap.'

'I can drop you, if you want. My old truck ain't the best there is but it's a damn sight quicker'n walkin'. I gotta ride out to Widow Patrick's, tend to her fencin'.'

He smiled wickedly.

'And maybe tend to more'n that, if I'm lucky.'

Luke hesitated before shaking his head. Pete used his cane to prod him out the door.

'C'mon, boy. You can help me load the rest of this lumber.'

Pete squatted on the running board of the truck, wiping the sweat from his forehead with a muddy gray handkerchief as Luke stacked the wood onto the back. When he was finished, Pete slapped the side of the door with the palm of his hand.

'Get on in, boy. Don't want no arguin'. I don't like drivin' this thing on my own.'

Luke got in, fidgeting uncomfortably on the tattered seat that bulged with broken springs. He stared out the window as Pete filled the air with squawking gears and angry flares of cursing. As they pulled onto the main road, Pete glanced over at him.

'You that Stewart boy, ain't you? Emma Stewart's oldest.'

Luke nodded slightly, wishing he'd been firmer in refusing

the ride. Automobiles made him feel uneasy and claustrophobic. At least on trains he could jump off when he didn't like the company. Pete smiled and stripped another gear.

'Comin' home to see your momma, huh? Cain't say I'd bother.'

The right tire slammed into the grassy mound that ran between the two tire ruts of the road, throwing Luke forward against the dashboard. Pete forced the steering wheel down to the right, manhandling the truck back onto the track.

'Now Thom, he was a fine man. Didn't know him all that much but you ask anybody and they'd tell you Thom was a fine man. I was sorry to hear of his passin'.'

From the corner of his eye, Luke could see Pete staring at him, searching for some reaction, but he held the grief inside, not allowing a single flicker of pain to creep out.

'Course, most people 'round here say it was a blessin'. Say Ol' Thom deserved better'n he got.'

The truck suddenly surged forward and Pete cursed as his head hit the top of the truck and knocked his hat into the floor-well. Luke picked it up and handed it back to him.

'Thank ye kindly. How old are you, boy?'

'Twenty, I think. Maybe twenty-one.'

Pete laughed.

'Well, I reckon you're old enough to hear this story. You like stories, boy? I got a bucket full of 'em, but this'n I'm gonna tell you, is one of my favorites. It happened about twenty years ago . . .'

He grinned at Luke and winked.

'Maybe twenty-one. See, I'd been havin' trouble with the damn hobos stealin' my feedbags. Decided I'd fill a few bastards with buckshot. I must've dozed off, 'cause a noise or somethin' woke me up. I sneaked over to the window to catch the thievin' sons of bitches, but hobos ain't what I seen. No-sir. Hobos ain't what I seen at all.'

*

Pete dropped him off at the mailbox. Luke watched as Pete's truck shuddered its way down a long stretch of tire-scarred road, the lumber rattling like loose teeth on the flatbed behind him. Pulling his hat firmly over his brow, Luke began to climb the narrow path. At the top of the ridge he could see the house, gray and dismal even in the bright afternoon sun and his pace quickened, the loose stones tumbling out of his way as he hurried down the hill. He took long careful steps across the yard, his eyes darting from side to side, then stopped at the porch. Swallowing the bitter fear inside his mouth he dropped his bundle of possessions by the door, eased it open and slipped inside. From the front room, he could hear the hum of a sewing machine and the steady pumping of the iron foot pedal. He moved clumsily around the kitchen table and towards the door, following the sound, his head dizzy with words.

'Lou Venie, that you? Come on in here. I want you to try this on.'

Luke stood at the door and watched as Emma worked, her head low, her face hidden beneath a heap of pale fabric.

'I know this is what you wanted but I don't think it's as nice as the one I made you last year. I don't know what's so all-fired important about a Halloween dance anyhow.'

She waited for a response then lifted her head above the machine. The color drained from her flushed cheeks and above the silver-rimmed half-moon glasses, her eyes flashed from fear to recognition and back to fear.

'What are you doin' here?'

He said nothing, but walked steadily towards her. She stood up, knocking the chair backwards and tearing the glasses from her face. She straightened her shoulders, a half-attempt to show her strength, but her voice betrayed her uneasiness.

'I had a feelin' you might show up. Thought you were dead. Thought it for years. Still would have if that girl hadn't showed up.'

In an instant the power that had built up inside him disintegrated and he could feel the words he'd prepared collapse around him.

'What girl?'

'Don't know what her name was. Some teacher. Said she was passin' through, asked about you in town. People sent her over here to see me, and you can bet I set her straight on a few things. I told her exactly what you was.'

Luke slumped onto the edge of the sofa and put his head in his hands.

'She's gone?'

'Course she is. Won't be back neither, I made sure of that.' She laughed, her voice regaining the sarcastic flair he'd known so well.

'A teacher and you. The very idea.'

With painful slowness Luke raised his head, his eyes burning with anger and grief, but his voice soft and impotent.

'What have you done?'

She moved towards him, empowered by his weakness.

'Nothin' any decent person wouldn't do. I couldn't let some innocent girl believe whatever lies you told her. Like father like son, I said. I told her she was lucky to get away when she did.'

The fury erupting from Luke's lungs as he leapt forward forced her backwards with its power.

'WHAT HAVE YOU DONE?'

She shrank away from him, cowering against the sewing machine, which blocked her path of escape. A rage he had never known, never imagined was inside him, swamped him, pulling a dark drape of hatred over his eyes. He moved even closer to her.

'I know, Momma. I know what really happened.'

'What are you goin' on about?'

'I know about your lies and what really happened that night.'

He could see the fear in her eyes, feel the heat of it. She looked away.

'I don't know what you're talkin' about.'

'You let me live my whole life believin' I was no better than a dog. The filthy son of a rapist.'

His voice had rarely ever been raised above a mumble and the scream scraped against his throat. He could feel a throbbing pain bulging from the side of his head as he moved within inches of her.

'I want you to tell me what happened. I want to hear the truth from your lips.'

Lifting her chin with a mocking glare, she made one final attempt to defy him.

'Who do you think you are?'

'I know I'm not who you say I am.'

He felt as though he had floated above his body, separated from all he had ever been, and he watched in uncontrolled horror as his hands slipped around her neck, forcing her backwards against the sewing machine.

'So tell me, Momma. Tell me who I am.'

Canaan

Canaan pulled another box of books from under the bed and started going through them, checking the spine of each before discarding it in one of several piles that littered the floor of the Little House. Luke's bed was neatly made and the corncob dog he'd carved for her was propped on the pillow. She stopped just for a moment when she heard the taxi pull up, then her search became more frantic.

'Canaan, honey . . .'

Lou Venie came in quietly and sat on the bed. Canaan didn't look up, but just kept working.

'How is he?'

'The same. They was hopin' the pneumonia might take him last night.'

'They said that last week. And the week before that, they said it was any day now. And the week before that and the week before that.'

For the past eight weeks, Luke had been in a nursing home and although he'd been lucid from time to time, Canaan had watched him steadily go downhill. Two days before, he'd slipped into a coma and they transferred him to the hospital. She and her grandmother were taking turns sitting up with him. Lou Venie rested her hand on Canaan's shoulder.

'It would be the best thing.'

Canaan stood up and pulled a stack off the shelves.

'Why is everybody in such a hurry for him to go?'

'He's already gone, sugar.'

'Well, I think he's still in there. And I'm not leaving him by himself.'

'What are you lookin' for?'

'His *Robinson Crusoe* book. It's his favorite.'

'He won't be able to hear you.'

'You don't know that.'

She suddenly had a burst of inspiration and went to the table where he'd been working on his book ledgers. The book she wanted was on top. She flipped through the pages as if that would verify that it was the right book, and noticed a card inside. It was faded and brown but she could still make out a handpainted watercolor of an apple tree in bloom. On the back of the card was a beautifully written note.

> *My dearest Luke*
> *You are my island. The paradise*
> *I always search for.*
> *Yours always*
> *Ollie*

She tucked the card back between the pages and shoved the book into her handbag.

'I'll stay with him today, and then I'll take the night shift.'

'Just don't go wearin' yourself out.'

Lou Venie stood and Canaan saw how tired she looked herself. She stifled a yawn.

'You want me to fix you some food to take with you?'

Canaan shook her head.

'I'll grab something in the canteen.'

Lou Venie looked doubtful.

'I'll eat. I promise, Nan.'

The dimness of the room and the flashing lights of the moni-
tors and machines made reading more difficult than usual.
Canaan tried her best to read with the feeling and enthusiasm
she knew Luke loved.

> *My raft was now strong enough to bear any reasonable*
> *weight. My next care was what to load it with, and how*
> *to preserve what I laid upon it from the surf of the sea;*
> *but I was not long in considering this . . .*

Canaan stopped and closed the book, rubbing the fog from
her eyes with the heel of her hand.

'I'm gonna rest for a while, OK, Luke?'

The only answer was the steady 'kush-kush' sound of the
machine that forced him to breath. She leaned forward and
rested her hand on Luke's arm.

'You need to hang on, Luke . . . just for a little while
longer.'

Carefully avoiding the drips and IV, she clasped her hand
around two of his fingers and squeezed gently, watching for
some change in his empty face. She thought she saw his eye
twitch, a movement so slight she couldn't be sure if she'd seen
or imagined it. She sat back in the chair and massaged her
forehead.

A nurse stuck her head around the door.

'Miss Phillips, they've called from the front desk. There's
a visitor for Mr Stewart.'

Canaan nodded, giving her a less than enthusiastic smile
of thanks. Word must have already reached Peggy's hospital-
visitation group from church. In the nursing home, there had
been a constant trickle of strangers, sent in the name of sympathy and compassion, bearing gifts of salvation. Canaan
couldn't bear the thought of filling them in on Luke's prog-

nosis, as if it mattered to them. And she wasn't in the mood to discuss her own state of salvation. She'd hardly eaten anything since breakfast and for the first time she noticed the hollow emptiness in her stomach. It was better to head down to the canteen for a slot-machine sandwich before the earnest smiles and Bible-clutching hands appeared at the door. She had just slung her purse over her shoulder when the door opened, almost knocking her sideways. It was Zeke.

'Oh hey, sorry, Canaan. Hope you don't mind, but I went to see him at the nursing home and they told me he was here. I've got a surprise for him.'

He pulled a small barrel lid, warped and curved, from behind his back and smiled.

'I found it at Hincey's Hardware. Manager there was using the barrel to store penny nails. Said I could have the lid.'

He proudly held it up for her to see. On the outer edge, she could just make out the faded carved image of a small foot. She felt her eyes fill up.

'He'll be real tickled. Thanks, Zeke.'

He looked over at Luke.

'Is he . . .'

'He's in a coma, but they said he's stable.'

Zeke walked over to the bed and touched Luke's hand.

'Hey, Feets. Got a little present for you. I'll put it over here and you can take a good look at it later on.'

He propped the lid on the bedside table and turned to Canaan.

'Were you leavin'?'

'Just going down to the canteen for a sandwich.'

'Can I join you?'

She nodded, secretly glad for the company. They walked together to the canteen, its walls and tables awash in fluorescent white. Zeke chose two sandwiches and paid for two anemic cups of hot chocolate. She was surprised to find comfort in the fact that he made the choices for her. Lately it was the small, insignificant decisions that seemed to overwhelm her.

'Why don't we take these out into the courtyard.'

'I didn't bring my sweater.'

It was the first week of March and, while the ice and snow seemed to have left for good, there was still a pretty strong nip in the air. Zeke took off his jean jacket and handed it to her.

'Here. You look like you could use some fresh air. And it's too much like the high-school lunch room in here.'

He led the way through the tables, winking over his shoulder.

'It'll be like old times with the brown-baggers.'

She followed him outside to a concrete bench tucked inside an alcove. A tall brick wall enclosed the courtyard and with two of the ground lights burned out, the corner where they sat was dark and secluded, safe from the bright brashness of the canteen. She took a bite from her sandwich, but found herself filling up again and the bite seemed to expand in her mouth. She struggled to swallow and washed it down with hot chocolate.

'He's not going to wake up again, is he, Zeke?'

She didn't have to look up for an answer. Her voice sounded small and vulnerable.

'I don't think I can face losing him right now.'

Zeke cupped her face tenderly with his hands and turned her towards him. His touch was warm and gentle and the kindness in his face shimmered beyond the tears that filled her eyes.

'I'm scared, Zeke, and I'm so tired.'

She looked wearily into his face as his fingers softly smoothed the creases from her forehead. He leaned forward and, with lips as warm as his hands, covered her mouth and face with tiny intricate kisses. An initial feeling of panic gave way to exhilaration. As she leaned closer, he wrapped his arms around her and she felt as if she was being towed into a quiet harbor. She lifted her fingers to his face, tentatively caressing the curling wisps of his hair. He lowered his head, kissing the small hollows of her neck, then pulled her closer to him. The closeness of their bodies brought her sharply back to earth and she shrank back, suddenly self-conscious of the huge physical barrier of her pregnancy. She pushed him away.

'Stop. Stop it. I don't want this.'

'I'm sorry, I thought . . .'

'What? That a little kissing and groping in the dark would take care of everything?'

'Canaan, look . . .'

'I don't need you to save me, Zeke. So you can just climb down off the white horse.'

His voice was soft.

'I wasn't offerin'.'

'Then what were you doing?'

'I thought it was obvious, but then I never was very good at timing.'

'Oh, I think you are. You're just better at it with high-school girls. Stick with what you know, Zeke. You've had years of experience.'

She knew her words were unfair, could see how deeply her cruelty wounded him, but she didn't waver.

'I have enough going on in my life. I don't need you confusing things more.'

'Why does it have to be confusing? Canaan, maybe this is the one thing in both our lives that isn't complicated. The one thing that is right and natural?'

'I want you to leave now, Zeke.'

She handed him his jacket.

'And I don't want you popping into my life when you start getting bored with the choices you've made.'

She turned away into the shadows, trying to swallow the choking feelings in her throat. He stood and looked down at her.

'Does it matter that I love you?'

'Not now. Now it just sounds lonely.'

She watched as he made his way across the canteen. Through the iron railings she could see the hospital parking lot and she waited until his van had driven safely out of sight before sinking down on the bench and letting her feelings wash over her.

She remained at Luke's bedside for two days straight, living off soggy sandwiches from the canteen and a few thermoses of soup that Lou Venie forced on her. Visitors had drifted in and out, voices had whispered from behind curtained partitions and the good-natured banter of orderlies had floated in from the corridor, reminding her that other people were leading normal lives. Canaan ignored them all, reading until her eyes ached and her voice cracked. At four a.m. on Tuesday morning, the hospital was still and she was asleep with her cheek resting on the side of his bed. A sudden sense of awareness, a sound or a thought, had lifted her sleepy face to his and his mother-of-pearl eyes stared back at her. One corner of his mouth tried to curl into a smile. She stood over him, thrilled by his presence, but panicked by its suddenness and what it might mean.

'You want anything? More morphine? I can ring the nurse . . .'

They were not the first words she had been waiting to say if he regained consciousness, but her mind seemed stupidly void of anything beyond his comfort. The shake of his head was more of a tremor and she moved closer, holding his hand to her face. Carefully he pulled his hand free, bringing it to rest on the curving bulge of her stomach. He worked hard to get the words out. Taking his time.

'Don't be afraid, Candy-Cane.'

She grappled with last-minute words she'd rehearsed – goodbye, thank you, I'm sorry – but nothing came out. He gave her hand a weak squeeze.

'Ain't we lucky?'

She dared not blink, her eyes locked with his, willing him to stay, but determined not to miss that final flicker that would signal his departure.

After all the weeks of tears and emotional storms, and clinging, when the moment finally came she couldn't cry.

Luke: The Beginning

October 1904

The feedbags had scrubbed the skin from his knees but he was only faintly aware of the stinging pain as cold air sucked at the raw graze. He rested his head on her stomach, his breathing slowing to a steady, less desperate rhythm. It had not been his first time but he had been just as nervous and the pain in his belly had been just as fierce. The first time had also been a hurried affair, but driven more by the fear of getting it wrong and by the revolting body odor of the whore who'd bedded him. Tonight had been different. The passions of the night had been planned and played over in his mind, time and time again, like the song his mother listened to, in endless repetition on the gramophone. And it didn't matter to him that he had not actually planned on tonight being the night. She had been the one to lead him down to the railroad yard; said it was more private and more comfortable than the woods outside the school and he had followed meekly, too sick with anticipation to worry about the unexpectedness of it. And he had to admit she had been right. The back porch of Pete's rambling shack of a store was tucked away, offering three sides of protection from the cool night air and the corner where they lay was cushioned with a pile of feedbags and half-empty cotton bales.

'David-Wayne? You love me?'

He lay perfectly still, mulling over his answer. He had known Emma most of his life, had tormented her when they were younger, at a time when a three-year age difference had made him think of her as no more than a childish nuisance. But newly developed curves and long flirtatious eyelashes had changed all that. In the few months since he'd first noticed how pretty she was and how much he liked it when she accidentally brushed against him as he walked her home from Sunday school each week, he had guiltily allowed the fantasy to take over both his waking and sleeping hours.

'Well, do you?'

Her soft gurgling voice was now edged with aggravation and he forced himself from a delicious doziness, rolling over to button his trousers.

'Why you askin' me that, Emma?'

''Cause Reba Wilson says only people in love can do this.'

He lay back with his hands behind his head.

'I guess so.'

Emma straightened her skirt and petticoats and snuggled into a warm nest under his shoulder. He put his arm around her protectively as she rested her head on his chest. Her hair smelled sweet, like corn, and felt silky to his cheek.

'David-Wayne?'

'Yeah?'

'Are you gonna marry me?'

'Good Lord, Emma. You're only fourteen. What are you thinkin'? Your momma wouldn't let you get married.'

'Oh, I don't mean now. When I'm older.'

He grunted, hoping she would accept it as a suitable answer. She tugged on his shirt.

'Well, are you? Gonna marry me?'

'Never thought about it.'

'You said you loved me, though.'

'I do, I guess.'

'I don't believe you. You're lyin' and I only let you get on me 'cause I thought you loved me.'

She rolled over, turning her back to him and he was dismayed to hear soft, pitiful sobs.

'Oh now, Emma. Stop. Don't cry. Course I love you. Here . . .'

He dug into his pocket, wriggling as his hand plunged deeper.

'I was gonna give you this tomorrow, after church, but you can have it now.'

He held up a tiny gold locket, no bigger than a raindrop, and she snatched it from him, her tears immediately dry.

'It's beautiful. Put it on me.'

She sat up and he fumbled with the latch while she admired it in the moonlight.

'I ain't ever gonna take it off. It's like a promise, ain't it, David-Wayne? A promise that you're gonna marry me and nobody else.'

The relief David-Wayne had felt seconds before sank into his chest.

'Well now, I don't know . . .'

He looked down at her upturned face, her eyes teetering on the fine line between tears and elation.

'Oh, all right. I guess it could mean that . . . but some day, Emma, not any time soon.'

She nestled back down against him and he stared at the sky, trying to come to terms with the gnawing feeling in his stomach. He hadn't been untruthful with her; sitting in the pew behind her each Sunday, he had often daydreamed of spending a lifetime buried in the milky sweetness of her neck.

'Can we move away from Lander when we get married?'

'If you want to.'

'I hate it here. I want to live somewhere nice like Atlanta. And I want a piano in the front room, and velvet curtains and tapestry cushions on the chairs . . .'

She stopped her list and looked happily into his face.

'You're always gonna take care of me, ain't you, David-Wayne?'

'Course I will.'

'Always . . . you promise?'

'Yes, Emma. I promise I'll always take care of you.'

He sat up, gently moving her with him.

'And I'd better start now. I gotta get you back to the school.'

He stood up and checked his father's pocket watch.

'Hell, Emma, it's after nine-thirty. The dance finished at nine.'

She jumped up, brushing the cotton twigs and fluff from her skirt.

'It always takes time for Mr Hammond to get everybody out. We'll be all right.'

'But it's a ten-minute walk, Emma, they'll be lookin' for you.'

He hopped off the back porch and around the corner of the store and Emma followed him.

'Wait up, David-Wayne. I ain't fixed yet.'

He turned to see her stretching the wool socks to just above her knee, fussing over the wrinkles that had twisted around her ankle.

'Leave that, Emma. We're gonna get in a heap of trouble.'

'We're gonna get in a heap of trouble if I go back lookin' like this.'

He sighed in exasperation and continued to weave between the boxcars, leaping the rails like a runner over hurdles. He was almost to the path that led through the woods when he heard her scream. He held his breath as he ran back, retracing his steps. He found her behind a boxcar, sprawled at the base of a junk pile; an old bicycle frame, a mangled mesh of bedsprings, engine parts and railroad spikes. She was examining a gash that peeked beneath her torn sock. Blood had already begun to soak in around the edges making it look like black tar in the moonlight. As she looked up at him the flesh above her left eye had begun to swell around a small cut.

'Good Lord, Emma. What happened?'

He squatted beside her, taking a closer look at her leg.

'You went too dern fast, David-Wayne . . . fell right on top of it. Couldn't get out . . . ever'thing kept catchin' at me.'

'Can you stand up?'

She nodded and he helped her up. The sash of her dress had been ripped from its seam, hanging limply to the ground and the skirt was streaked with diesel oil.

'What am I gonna do now? My momma's gonna kill me.'

He took her by the arm, guiding her to the edge of the yard.

'I'll take you back to the school.'

She pulled away from him.

'I can't go back like this.'

'Then I'll take you home. Tell your momma it happened on the way from the dance.'

'You ain't supposed to be at the dance, David-Wayne. You're too old. Only reason Momma lets you walk me home on Sundays is 'cause it's church and she can watch me. She'd whip me senseless if I showed up with you, lookin' like this.'

'Well, what do you wanna do then?'

She limped a little further.

'You go on home, David-Wayne.'

'You crazy? I can't just leave you.'

'I'm goin' straight home. It ain't far from here. Better than goin' back to the school.'

'But Emma . . .'

She shoved him away.

'Don't argue with me, David-Wayne. I know what's best. I'm gonna take care of it. You go on home and I'll talk to you tomorrow.'

He hesitated but finally agreed as long as he could watch until she had made it safely to the road. When she turned back to wave him on, he reluctantly hurried home through the woods.

The sound of pounding woke David-Wayne from a deep sleep that had not been easy in coming. At first he thought someone was beating on his own bedroom door but as he sat up, swinging his feet to the floor, he realized it was somewhere else in the house. He crept to the door, trying not to wake his younger brothers and saw his father stumble from the back room in his long johns and dragging an old pair of work pants. David-Wayne joined him, still groggy, but his heart beating out of control up near his Adam's apple. His father opened the door and David-Wayne peered around his shoulder to see three men carrying guns and lanterns.

'Sorry to bother you, Gordie, but Travis Scott needs some help.'

Gordie pulled the door open and nodded for them to come in.

'What's the problem, boys? It's awful late.'

One of the men stepped forward to serve as spokesman.

'It's Travis's little girl . . . Emma. Nigger hobo got hold of her, beat her real bad.'

The fuzzy sleepiness evaporated from David-Wayne's head and he was suddenly alert and wide awake.

'She was in an awful state, Gordie. Raped her down by the railroad yard.'

'What the blue blazes was she doin' down there?'

David-Wayne was holding onto the back of a chair. He squeezed until his knuckles turned white and he was sure that the others must hear the thundering noise his heart was making. The man nodded to Gordie as if he had asked the same question himself.

'Says she was at the Halloween dance. Says he caught her

outside the school, held a knife to her throat, dragged her down to the yard where nobody could see.'

One of the other men took over.

'Travis is gettin' a group together down his end, we're takin' care of the west side of town. Gonna meet down the railroad yard.'

Gordie struggled into his trousers.

'Well, you can count me in. And my boy. David-Wayne, go get some britches on and bring your gun with you. Try not to wake up your brothers.'

David-Wayne stared at him, unable to move or speak. His father grabbed a gun from beside the door and rummaged in the basket for cartridges.

'You boys walked over here?'

They nodded.

'We can use my wagon. Come on out to the barn with me and help me get the horses hitched.'

He turned to his son.

'Go on, boy. Get goin'.'

David-Wayne walked to his room in a daze and fumbled in the dark for his clothes, trying to hold onto thoughts that bashed around in his head. He sat on the edge of his bed, slowly buttoning his shirt, and began panting like a dog in high summer heat. A knock on the door and his father's coarse whisper jolted him back to reality.

'C'mon, boy, get a move on. They're waitin' on us.'

David-Wayne took one more breath then grabbed the gun from the corner and followed his father out to the barn. He tossed his gun into the back of the wagon where the other men sat in a solemn horseshoe, lanterns at their feet, the upward light creating grotesque shadows of their noses and chins. They spoke quietly, but their voices were tinged with an almost boyish excitement.

'I been sayin' we gotta do somethin' 'bout these God-damn vagrants.'

'My brother-in-law over in Watobie County, he says if they find anybody loiterin' in town after dark, they just hang 'em right off. Don't even wait for 'em to try nothin'.'

''Bout time we started settin' some examples. Make them niggers think twice 'fore settin' foot in this county.'

David-Wayne helped his father close the barn door then noticed with growing panic that his father was holding a rope as he walked back to the wagon. He hurried alongside him.

'Pop . . . you ain't gonna . . . you ain't . . .'

His father patted his shoulder.

'You're old enough to understand this now, boy. I don't usually go along with these things, but in a case like this . . . justice has gotta be quick. It's kinder on ever'body. 'Specially that little girl.'

His father climbed into the wagon, shoving the rope under the seat.

'C'mon, boy, we're wastin' time.'

David-Wayne stared at him, then looked at the three men beyond, their eyes glazed over with a stupidly enthusiastic anger. He turned and started running across the field, away from the barn.

'David-Wayne! Get back here!'

He kept running and heard one of the men's voices squeak with impatience.

'Leave him be, Gordie. We gotta get goin' or we're gonna miss it all.'

Canaan

For ten weeks Peggy had stayed away from Luke's sickbed, content to let her church friends do the visiting on her behalf. But when the time came to make decisions for his burial, she suddenly appeared, full of her own ideas about how things should be done. She showed up at the funeral home waving a pair of shiny black patent-leather shoes, a brand new Brooks Brothers suit, navy with a pale gray stripe and a red silk tie with a matching handkerchief for the pocket.

'He may have embarrassed us his whole life but I'm making sure he does us proud at his funeral.'

Canaan exploded and would have physically thrown Peggy down the steps of the Chapel of Rest if her grandmother had not intervened. In spite of the grief that had driven Lou Venie into a quiet depression, she had served as peacemaker, taking each of them aside until a compromise had been agreed. Peggy, she decided, should choose the casket and the family flowers, but Canaan should decide how he was buried.

Later, Canaan felt foolish that she had kicked up such a fuss, behaving like all the other families she had ridiculed for bickering over the dead. But she had also felt relieved satisfaction that Luke would be laid to rest as she'd known him all her life, barefoot and in overalls. With that small victory won, she was willing to let Peggy have her way on the venue.

'We have a brand new fellowship hall at Lander Methodist. Much nicer than that basement room you've got at White's Gap.'

She'd joined the Methodists when she married Mert and its high percentage of upper-middle class had suited her much better than the farmers and, in her opinion, common folk of White's Gap Baptist. The day of the funeral the church was packed. Mainly with curiosity-seekers, Canaan thought. She and Lou Venie sat behind Mert and Peggy who was dressed in a tailored black suit with bouclé cuffs and collar. The minister cleared his throat and took his place as the hushed conversation ceased.

'Most of us didn't know Luke Stewart to speak to, although I doubt there's a one of us who didn't recognize him on sight when we saw him around town. We do, however, know of his family, including our own Sister Peggy Swan, and it is for her and her family that we're gathered here today to pay our last respects.'

Canaan imagined the photocopied sermon, typed years before by the minister's wife, scattered with underlined blank spaces to fill in the appropriate names. There was very little in his words that pertained to Luke, and Canaan found it easy to contain any emotions that might have overcome her otherwise. If he had spoken of Luke's gentle ways and love of knowledge, or if he had told them about the people he had loved and the hardships he had known, then perhaps she would have found it difficult to remain so dry-eyed and indifferent.

After the burial everyone gathered on the front lawn of the church. Lou Venie and Peggy worked their way around, thanking people for coming and inviting them to the fellowship hall for some food. Canaan stood on the steps searching the crowd for Zeke. From the corner of her eye, she saw someone waving and she turned to be greeted by Juanita who engulfed her in a hug.

'Hey, hon. We sure do miss you at the deli.'

Canaan raised her eyebrows and Juanita shrugged.

'OK! *I* sure do miss you at the deli.'

'What are you doin' here, Juanita?'

'I came to see you. Tell you how sorry I am.'

'You could've just sent a card.'

'Yeah – well, I kept meanin' to come see you after the – you know. I reckon things ain't been too easy for you these past few months.'

'No, things have been pretty damn shitty actually.'

'Well, I just wanted to tell you . . .'

She leaned closer.

'You ain't on your own.'

'What?'

'That Mim Simpson person? There's always plenty of her type around, but there's also plenty of us around who think she's full of shit and don't pay a bit of attention to her and her gang of bullies. Just thought you ought to know that. I know you probably felt like you were out there all by yourself, but when it's aimed at you it's easy to pay more attention to what those kind of people are sayin' and doin' 'cause they're sayin' and doin' it a lot louder than the rest of us.'

It was the most Juanita had ever said to her in all the months she'd worked with her, and she wasn't sure if she completely understood what she was trying to say. She decided just to take it with the kindness she obviously intended. Juanita looked around the crowd again, then took Canaan's arm, leading her around the side of the building.

'And just so you know . . . I know that story Kyle tried to pass off was a pile of cow dung.'

She glanced around, looking for eavesdroppers.

'He made a pass at you, didn't he?'

'How'd you know?'

'He tried a couple of times with me. Kyle has a thing about pregnant women. He's a pervert, pure and simple. Guess he thinks we'll be more'n happy to lower our standards, bein' in the state we're in. And Lord knows, I've been in that state a lot over the years.'

'What did you do?'

'Reminded him I had a husband who worked in the slaughterhouse. Didn't stop him from trying to have a grope now and then, though. Anyway, I'm sure he'd heard all the rumors goin' round about you, thought he'd get in early. I just wanted you to know that a lot more people know the truth about things than you think.'

Canaan thanked her, not sure if that was really the right response or not and Juanita hurried back to the Piggly Wiggly for the afternoon shift.

Canaan still hadn't seen Zeke. She couldn't believe he wouldn't come. Lou Venie and Peggy had already walked over to the fellowship hall and the crowds were beginning to make their way over as well. She was about to join them when she glanced across the road to the cemetery. Squeaky was standing at Luke's grave, under the green awning. He was wearing a bright blue Golden Eagles baseball cap and a dirty lightweight raincoat that swallowed his tiny frame and fell almost to his ankles. She crossed the road to see him. She had left a message with Treva but she hadn't expected him to show up.

'Hey, Squeaky. I'm glad you came.'

She took his hand in both of hers and he looked down, nodding uncomfortably.

'Treva said I was bein' pig-headed. Said I shoulda gone to see him 'fore now. All these years livin' in the same town.'

He shifted his weight from one foot to the other.

'Didn't think he'd wanna see me. Not after the way I treated him. He was like family, Miss Canaan, and I should have put things right a long time ago.'

She invited him to join her at the fellowship hall but he shook his head.

'I'd rather say my goodbyes on my own, Miss Canaan. Thanks all the same. I only came by to tell you I was sorry 'bout your loss and for bein' so blunt with you before and to say if you still want to talk to me 'bout my days with Luke . . . well, I'm willin'.'

He smiled shyly.

'Might even get Treva to rustle up some supper. That girl of mine got a real gift with the fryin' pan.'

'That'd be nice. I'd like that.'

He nodded and gave a small wave then walked briskly towards an old Chevy where Treva was waiting for him.

The fellowship hall was built to look like a ski chalet – all soaring wood ceilings and large plate-glass windows. It was a beautiful building but it looked as though it should be filled with tanned, good-looking people in ski suits, drinking hot mulled wine. The main hall was filled with tables that were overloaded with fried chicken and gelatin desserts. A large contingency from White's Gap Baptist fought for equal space on the tables, clucking around the food to make sure there was a spoon in every dish. Nearby, her grandmother stood in a circle of friends who were talking quietly to her. The weather had warmed up considerably that week, so everyone had used the opportunity to bring out the first hints of their spring wardrobes. Canaan had decided to forget the camouflage habit and to go for comfort. She was seven months along now and there was no way she could pretend anymore. She'd bought a navy blue summer maternity dress for the funeral and had made up her mind to flaunt her new shape.

Her grandmother joined her at the table.

'Please have somethin' to eat.'

'I don't want anything.'

'Well, can you at least thank the ladies who did all this work?'

'They didn't know him. They're only here because they're curious old buzzards who want to swap stories about him and pick over his bones.'

'I know you're hurtin', Canaan, so I'm gonna try to be gentle. These women have been my friends most of my life. You're right – they didn't know Luke. That's my fault. But what they did here today . . . this . . . they did for me . . . and for you. 'Cause they're good people.'

Canaan crossed her arms.

'I doubt that.'

'They got flaws like anybody else, but it ain't right for you to judge 'em anymore than it's right for them to judge you.'

Across the room, Kyle Bernard stood with a small group of friends. He made eye contact then quickly looked away, saying something low to the others who one by one tried not to look like they were looking her way.

'I'm leavin', Lou Venie. Get one of your good friends to take you home.'

As she crossed the parking lot, digging into her purse for her keys, she stopped when she saw Zeke leaning against a tree. He straightened up as she joined him, and gave her an awkward kiss on the cheek.

'I'm so sorry, Canaan.'

'I didn't see you at the service.'

'I sat in the back.'

'You could have sat with us. You were Luke's friend, Zeke. Practically family.'

'I didn't want to make things worse for you.'

She laughed and turned sideways, showing her bulge.

'Did you say worse?'

He smiled.

'How are you? I mean, physically?'

'Why don't you ask the rest of the town?'

'I heard I'm the odds-on favorite – for the daddy, I mean.'

Canaan frowned.

'So that's why you didn't sit with us.'

She walked briskly to her car.

'Well, I wouldn't want to sully your good reputation, Zeke.'

He followed quickly behind her.

'Whoa. Hang on.'

'Can't have the heart-throb hero of Lander mixed up with the likes of me.'

'Damn it, Canaan! Why do you make this so hard?'

'I don't remember inviting you into my life, Zeke.'

'I know that. But I was hoping maybe you'd eventually take pity on me and let me in just a little bit.'

She unhooked the canvas top of the car and Zeke helped her fold it down.

'Well, I'm leaving soon so you'd better find somebody else's party to crash.'

'Leaving? When?'

'Soon as the baby's born. I'm going to Atlanta. A friend from college has agreed to put us up until I can find a job and a place of my own.'

'When did you decide this?'

'A few days ago. What have I got to look forward to here, Zeke? Waiting around until Lou Venie dies? Going through all this again? I've got to get on with my life.'

'This car won't make it to Atlanta.'

'I'm selling it. It was silly for me to hold on to it so long. I was just being sentimental. It'll give me enough money to keep me going for a few months.'

She opened the door to get in and Zeke touched her arm.

'Canaan, please stay.'

'It's too late.'

'You said once you would've stayed if I'd asked you. I'm saying it now. Stay.'

'Leave it alone, Zeke.'

'I can't!'

'Why not?'

'Because I know that nobody else will ever love you the way I do.'

She carefully maneuvered herself behind the steering wheel.

'You're always so sure of yourself, aren't you?'

'No. But I'm sure about you. That's why I pushed you to leave the first time. I was a coward. I didn't have the guts to do it myself and I thought I was being noble by not standing in your way.'

He brushed a strand of hair from her face.

'How could I not have loved you? You were intelligent and brave – the brightest, most perfect thing in my world.'

Canaan started the engine.

'That perfect girl was a lie – you made her up. You can't love a lie, Zeke.'

She couldn't look back. She drove straight out, her wheels churning up the chalky white dust, and she didn't look in her rear-view mirror until she was on the old Patterson road. The car made a grinding noise and she tried to shove it into a lower gear, but the noise it made was even worse.

'Damn it!'

She tried to use both hands to get the gear in the right slot, but it wouldn't budge. The car veered to the right and she jerked the steering wheel to get it back on the road. She pushed the gearstick with one strong heave and hit the gas. When she looked up the car had left the road and as she tried to regain control the front wheels slammed into a large rock sending her plummeting, out of control, down the steep embankment.

The convertible started to sink fast. She gasped as the cold water gushed over the windshield. She took a deep breath as the water closed quickly over her head. As the car sank below the surface, Canaan stopped struggling and was suddenly filled with a deep feeling of calm.

Luke: The Beginning

October 1904

The quickest way to Emma's house was across the back fields
of the Pig Wilson farm, then through the middle of Lander.
The town square was deserted, except for a mongrel dog who
trotted along the sidewalk, scavenging with his nose down
and ears back. It passed David-Wayne without so much as a
sniff in his direction. On the other side of the square, David-
Wayne left the road again and cut through the Cypress Creek
Woods to Emma's house, ignoring the twigs and pine cones
that tortured his bare feet. When he reached the clearing that
marked the boundary of Travis Scott's land, David-Wayne
could see a lantern floating through the dark house, and he
leaned against a tree to catch his breath. He watched as Myra
Scott bolted the front door, then drifted down the hall to
check on her daughter who was hidden beneath a mound
of quilts. She stood there for a moment, listening for signs
of sleep, then satisfied, closed the door and disappeared to
the other side of the house. David-Wayne crouched low as he
crossed the moonlit yard and quietly but urgently tapped on
Emma's window. There was a slight stirring from the bed,
then suddenly she sat up, her puzzled frown turning to a
broad smile. She hurried over and opened the window.

'What you doin' here? I told you I'd talk to you tomorrow.'

He heaved himself up through the window and she scurried back to the bed, modestly tugging the quilt up to her chin. As David-Wayne sat on the windowsill, trying to control the nervous panting that had erupted again in his chest, she leaned over and lit the bedside candle.

'You're crazy comin' here, David-Wayne. If Momma hears you, there's no tellin' what she'll do.'

'Emma, what happened after I left you?'

'Nothin'. I came home like I told you.'

'Nothin' else happened?'

'No, course not.'

'And what did you tell your momma happened?'

She smiled with coquettish pride.

'I told you I'd take care of it. Don't you trust me?'

'Did you tell her that a nigger hobo raped you?'

His voice was snappy, agitated. She frowned.

'Yes . . . well, not exactly. Momma said it, and I told her yeah, that was what happened.'

David-Wayne crossed the room and sat on the edge of her bed, taking her hands in his.

'Emma, you gotta come with me right now.'

She pulled away from him.

'Have you lost your senses?'

'You lied, Emma . . . you told 'em some hobo forced his way on top of you, now you gotta set it straight.'

In the candlelight he could see a dark flush creep over her face.

'Forced his way . . . got on top of me?'

'Yes, Emma, that's what rape means.'

She looked confused.

'I thought it just meant . . . to hurt somebody.'

'It means more'n that so you're gonna have to come with me and set everybody right.'

She shook her head, her eyes dark with disbelief.

'I cain't do that.'

'Emma, they're gonna catch some poor old hobo and hang him. I saw the rope. They're out there now . . . lookin'.'

'Maybe they won't find nobody.'

'The eleven o'clock from Chattanooga just came through. There's bound to be somebody down there.'

She sank back against the headboard.

'Well, I ain't goin' and you cain't make me.'

'You got to.'

She stubbornly turned her head to the wall.

'Just some nigger hobo. Don't know why you're gettin' so worked up.'

He stood up, slowly backing towards the window.

'If you don't do it . . . I will. We done wrong, Emma, but it ain't as wrong as lettin' a innocent man get killed over it.'

As he crawled through the window Emma flung off the covers and ran to him.

'David-Wayne, you cain't. I'll get in trouble.'

'It's the only way, Emma. I gotta go. I already heard a gunshot on the way over. Means they got somebody.'

He couldn't be sure but he thought he saw a flicker of relief on her face. He leapt down to the ground and she leaned out the window.

'You still gonna sit with me on Sunday?'

He looked up at her, his guts knotted together.

'No, Emma. And I ain't gonna be speakin' to you neither. You ain't the kind of girl I thought you was.'

'You made a promise.'

'I was wrong.'

He turned and started across the yard. Emma whispered after him, as loudly as she dared.

'You cain't tell, David-Wayne. I'll call you a liar to your face. I'll tell 'em it was you who hurt me. Held me down and hurt me – that's what I'll tell 'em. I swear! You hear me?'

He didn't look back but entered through the curtain of trees and into the eerie stillness of the woods, running faster and faster, pushing himself to take longer strides. All the air in his lungs seemed to have escaped and was having difficulty finding its way in again. The pain in his chest made him dizzy and he doubled over with the stitch in his side. When he reached the road that led into town, he continued to run, holding his side, the rolling gait of each step deformed by the pain. From a distance he could see lanterns on the town square, gently bobbing like fireflies clustered around a camp-ground. As he drew closer he could see the men, assembled in small clans around the square, smoking and leaning pleas-antly on their shotguns. Something in their staccato chatter and easy laughter told him that he was too late, but he picked up his pace, determined not to give up. Gradually, like the stiff, clumsy brake of a steam engine, he stuttered to a halt, as the dark, limp shadow of a man came into view. He was hanging in the center of the square, from a lamppost that proudly illuminated the Civil War cannon, a memorial to the Lander boys who had died in the battle of Chickamauga. Against the physical feelings of sickness, and ignoring the warning voices in his head, David-Wayne forced himself closer, made himself look.

The man must have been in his sixties, his limbs frail and spindly. His right arm was broken, held in a crooked arc beside his body as if it had been twisted from its socket and replaced the wrong way around. One eye was battered to a pulp, the lids swollen up like a bright red plum in a vain attempt to protect the eyeball beneath. A black trickle of blood oozed from a gaping split of flesh above it. The other eye was untouched but it was open, bulging from a blood-gorged head, his lips strangely puckered into a hideous ver-sion of a kiss. The man's good eye, although glassy and life-less, still bore evidence of his final mortal terror, and it peered accusingly at him.

A soft whimper escaped from the boy's exhausted lungs and he sank into the grass beside the cannon, leaning his head against the cold, black iron shaft. The mongrel dog he'd seen earlier zigzagged in an excited state nearby and across the square the sound of his father's voice rose above the others. David-Wayne stood up, gouging his fist into the pain that still burned in his side, and slowly made his way back home.

By the time the sun came up, David-Wayne had left town. He didn't leave a note and only packed what he could get into a small potato sack. Over the next year he worked his way across the state line and ended up logging for a company in Georgia. On his first day he was sent up to the north quadrant and was partnered with a boy from Lander. Bear Dempsey was a big barrel-chested boy, whose kind-hearted ways did not match his fearsome appearance and freakish strength. He'd left home to make money for his family and his family was all he talked about. David-Wayne made it clear that he wasn't interested in conversations about his own family or his life back in Lander, but he had to admit he enjoyed Bear's stories and letters from home. There was a sweetness in Bear's excitement over the smallest detail of his family's life and David-Wayne looked forward to hearing the details over supper every night. Dovie Dempsey, Bear's little sister, started writing to David-Wayne, addressing him as 'Bear's Loggin' Friend'. Her letters were very simple and child-like, but they showed the same sweetness that David-Wayne had come to love and appreciate in Bear. Before long they were writing three or four letters a week to each other. Dovie had no idea that she was writing to David-Wayne, a boy she'd known since she was seven years old.

He occasionally thought of Emma, but the sick feeling in his gut prevented him from dwelling on her. He'd heard through Dovie's letters to Bear that she was married and had a baby now. Bear continued his campaign to reconcile his friend with his family but it wasn't so much his family that he couldn't face, as Emma. He'd seen a darkness in her soul that he'd never seen before and he didn't know if he could ever look her in the face again. Bear's only concern was David-Wayne's family.

'I know they're worried sick. Ain't right them not knowing you're all right. Just send 'em a note. Let 'em know.'

But David-Wayne said he wasn't ready. He might never have felt ready if Bear hadn't been killed in the spring, crushed by a logging crane. In his grief, David-Wayne wondered if his friend had planned it this way, because after all of Bear's nagging, David-Wayne would finally be going home. He accompanied Bear's body on the train and revealed himself to Dovie on the station platform. He filled in every detail about Bear's death that the Dempsey family needed, no matter how many times they asked, no matter how many times he'd told them before. Over the next few days he grieved with them and they embraced him into their circle as the last connection to their son and brother. He spent most of his time with Dovie. There was a connection that he didn't feel with anyone else. She wasn't an attractive girl, but there was so much of Bear in her face and her nature, David-Wayne felt a safe familiarity.

In the afternoon after the funeral David-Wayne and Dovie took a walk, to get away from the crowds and the macabre questions about Bear's accident, and ended up in the old corn mill. In the midst of grief, and fear, and loneliness – on top of a cool, dark millstone – they fumbled and cried and clung to each other and let the soothing distraction of sex bind them together.

Two weeks later, they eloped and came back to Lander to start again.

Canaan

The rays of sun lit up the water like those postcard pictures of heaven she'd seen as a little girl. She was struck by how quiet everything was, considering the painful roar of noise that had filled her head as the car hit the surface and water poured in around her. She lay her head on the back of the seat and looked up at the blue sky and clouds shimmering like a dream through the water. This was so much easier. She didn't have to be afraid anymore and Lou Venie didn't have to be embarrassed by another suicide in the family. The water no longer felt cold and she was ready to surrender.

At first she thought she imagined it. It was so weak. Then she felt it again and realized it was a fist. A tiny fist. Or maybe a foot. She opened her eyes and as she looked up, she saw the silhouette of a turtle swimming across the top of the water. The baby moved again inside her and she suddenly remembered that she wasn't alone. She wrestled with the seat belt but it was wrapped under her belly and she couldn't see what she was doing. Her lungs were beginning to burn and she knew she only had seconds. She worked frantically with the lock.

She wasn't aware of how it happened. She just knew that suddenly she was swimming, fighting to get to the surface,

TERRI WILTSHIRE

leaving the car at the bottom of the lake and reaching for a life that she knew with crystal clarity that she needed and wanted more than anything.

The sun was setting when Zeke pulled up. Canaan was sitting at the top of his apartment steps waiting for him. There was a puddle of water where she'd been sitting and her hair was still full of twigs and leaves. He jumped out of the van and took the steps two at a time. Emotion rushed from deep inside her and the tears spilled over without warning.

'Can I stay?'

As soon as he took her in his arms a torrent of pain and grief and love engulfed her, and her body shuddered as it poured out from her. She didn't care that they were sitting out in the open, that neighbors could look out at any moment, that people walking by might hear her. All that mattered, at that moment, was feeling safe. And she knew that Zeke was the only one who made her feel that way, the only one who had ever made her feel that way. He held her until her sobs had settled to quiet whimpers then led her inside.

She sat on the edge of the bathtub as Zeke poured bubble bath under the running water. He hadn't said a word since he'd arrived. He sat beside her and slowly, gently began to pick the twigs and leaves from her hair. She was so grateful for his silence. No questions. Just quiet acceptance – and overwhelming care and tenderness. He dipped a cloth in the bathwater and washed her face, then took her hands and gently pulled her to a standing position. He undressed her one sleeve at a time then unhooked her bra and, taking his time, began to peel the wet clothes from her body. She flinched as her dress reached the top of her belly and he stopped until she looked into his eyes and let him know she was ready.

He helped her into the bath and she sank down below the warm suds as he quietly washed the lake water from her neck and arms and back. He scooped up a cup of water and poured it over her tilted head. She lay back and closed her eyes as he massaged the shampoo into her scalp, letting him wash away her sins.

He dried her off with a large towel that smelled like honeysuckle and helped her slip into his bathrobe before picking her up and carrying her to the bedroom.

In bed she curled up in his arms, her head resting on his chest, and listened to his heartbeat. It seemed like hours that he held her, kissing the top of her head, the deep hollow of her neck. Holding her safe. When she was ready she lifted her face to his and kissed him, opening the robe and putting his hand on her breast. It wasn't the body she'd imagined unveiling to him in all the years she'd daydreamed about Zeke, but his reaction was exactly as she'd always imagined. His eyes, his smile and his hands told her everything she needed to know. She felt beautiful and desirable and loved beyond anything she had ever hoped for. When he made love to her, it felt like the only right thing she'd ever done in her life and she cried softly again, but this time it was triggered by pure joy. She was home.

Luke

October 1925

Lou Venie heard the dishes before she reached the porch –
the grating and clashing of china stacked with force, one
upon another. She had come home early, hoping her mother
would help her wind the more difficult sections of her hair
into the tight curls she wanted for the dance that night. In
spite of Emma's scathing disapproval over her daughter's
choice of fabric and design, she had promised that the dress
would be ready on time and Lou Venie was eager to see it.
Dropping her book satchel on the porch swing she hurried
towards the screen door but stopped abruptly as a low moan
floated from the dark kitchen beyond. A shabby bundle of
rags, rolled snugly and tied with various lengths of abandoned
string, had been cast carelessly outside the door and she
nudged it nervously with her toe as another moan crawled
from the darkness.

'Momma . . . you all right?'

She eased open the screen door and stepped inside, trying
to focus through the gloom of the fading afternoon light. As
her eyes adjusted, she was relieved to see her mother shuffling
from the pantry shelves to the kitchen table, but a different
uneasiness soon took its place. Emma held tightly to a single
dinner plate, slamming it onto a pile of newspapers and aggres-

sively wrapping it up before adding it to a nearby stack. The familiar anger of her movements made the muscles in Lou Venie's throat tighten but she took a tentative step forward, praying that the rage had not emerged over one of her own transgressions and hoping to God that what she said would be the right thing.

'I woulda been home sooner, Momma, but Mizz Cooper needed to talk to me 'bout graduation.'

Emma ignored her as she retrieved another plate from the shelves. Lou Venie heard a sob and moved closer.

'Momma? You ain't hurt, are you?'

'Ain't never gonna get this done on time. He shoulda been here 'fore now.'

Lou Venie reached out and touched her mother's shoulder, but Emma jerked away, letting the plate slip from her fingers and crash to the floor.

'Now look what you've done.'

Emma's eyes were dark and hateful but strangely veiled and Lou Venie sensed there was no real recognition in her mother's glare. In an instant Emma's face changed and she swiveled her hips playfully from side to side as she crossed the room to get another plate.

'Don't matter, though. I can have as many as I want. David-Wayne said so. Any kind I want.'

Emma began to hum to herself, then as she picked up a coffee cup from the side, the anger returned and she flung it at the wall. Lou Venie flinched at the sound of shattering china but straightened up as she heard another shuddering sob that melted into a soft moan. She moved carefully around the table and peered into the dark corner beside the stove. Luke was hunched as far back in the shadows as his gangling frame would allow, his long legs drawn up close to his chest. His forehead rested on his knees and his hands were locked behind his neck as he rocked in steady rhythm. Another moan erupted from deep within his chest, forcing his head back against the wall and revealing a face streaked with dirty tears. He looked up through glassy, empty eyes. Behind her, Emma continued to pack, banging things around in frustration and mumbling to herself.

'Told him I'd need more time. But David-Wayne got no sense of what's gotta be done.'

Lou Venie turned around.

'Where you goin', Momma?'

Emma stopped what she was doing and put her hands on her hips, shaking her head as if Lou Venie had lost her senses.

'Atlanta, of course. David-Wayne's been gettin' it all set. Got me and him a house. Just for us.'

She winked at Lou Venie and whispered, leaning closer.

'Been a secret up 'til now, but ain't no more. Gonna have a piano. David-Wayne promised.'

She pointed to Luke, her face stern.

'And he ain't gonna stop me. He ruined everything before, but not no more. He cain't do nothin' now. Me and David-Wayne's meant to be together and he ain't gonna stop me again.'

She snapped her fingers at her daughter.

'You one of my momma's new girls, ain't you? Get me my trunk down from the barn. My daddy'll show you where it is.'

She swept out of the kitchen and Lou Venie watched as Luke slowly fumbled his way up the wall to a standing position. He picked up his hat from the floor and without so much as a glance at his sister, he stumbled outside and down the steps. Lou Venie could hear her mother singing in the front room, the clinking of ornaments being gathered and the scraping of picture frames from the walls. With increasing dread she watched from the kitchen door as Emma collected and discarded her belongings, throwing offending items at the walls or floor in flares of sporadic temper. The dress her mother had been sewing was still draped over the sewing machine and Lou Venie's earlier elation dissolved into a weary melancholy.

'Momma, you look tired. Why don't you take a nap? I'll get supper.'

'Don't have time for that. I'll miss the train.'

Lou Venie took the china ornament from Emma's hands and hoped her mother's state of mind would embrace the appeasing words that were forming at random in her own head.

'The train's been cancelled tonight, Momma. Won't be leavin' 'til mornin'.'

Emma's face crumpled.

'Canceled? Them hobos causin' trouble again?'

Lou Venie nodded and Emma shook her head in disgust.

'No-good low-lifes, all of 'em.'

'Why don't you lie down? Have a rest?'

She gently took her mother's arm but Emma pulled away.

'David-Wayne's comin'. He promised.'

She looked around, panic-stricken.

'And I ain't ready.'

'Well, I'll help you. You come on back to your room and I'll help you freshen up.'

Emma obediently allowed her daughter to guide her through the broken china. Lou Venie glanced again at the forgotten pink dress and wondered if there would ever be another time to wear it. From Emma's room she could see Luke outside, sitting in the doorway of the empty corncrib with his head in his hands. As she started brushing her mother's gray hair, she saw him go inside the dark shell and shut the door behind him.

www.panmacmillan.com